# ALL YOU HAVE TO DO

## Autumn Allen

ISBN: 978-0-593-61904-9

Trim: 5 ½ x 8 ¼

On Sale: August 2023

Ages: 12 up | Grades: 7 up

432 pages

$19.99 USA | $26.99 CAN

Kokila

# ALL YOU HAVE TO DO

**Autumn Allen**

*With lyrics by Kahlil AkNahlej Allen*

Kokila

KOKILA

An imprint of Penguin Random House LLC, New York

First published in the United States of America by Kokila, an imprint of Penguin Random House LLC, 2023

Text copyright © 2023 by Autumn Allen
Illustrations copyright © 2023 by Salaam Muhammad

Kokila & colophon are registered trademarks of Penguin Random House LLC.
The Penguin colophon is a registered trademark of Penguin Books Limited.

Visit us online at PenguinRandomHouse.com.

Library of Congress Cataloging-in-Publication Data is available.

Printed in the United States of America

ISBN 9780593619049
1 3 5 7 9 10 8 6 4 2
[vendor indicator code]

This book was edited by Zareen Jaffery, copyedited by Kaitlyn San Miguel, proofread by [TK], and designed by Asiya Ahmed. The production was supervised by Tabitha Dulla, Nicole Kiser, Ariela Rudy Zaltzman, and Caitlin Taylor.
Text set in TT Tricks

Sources:

Excerpt(s) from INVISIBLE MAN by Ralph Ellison, copyright 1947, 1948, 1952 by Ralph Ellison. Copyright © renewed 1975, 1976, 1980 by Ralph Ellison. Used by permission of Random House, an imprint and division of Penguin Random House LLC. All rights reserved.

Phoenix and Michael Graves, "Speak Out: Graves Assails Apathy, Laments End of Activism," Black Liberation 1969 Archive, accessed January 6, 2023, https://blacklib1969.swarthmore.edu/items/show/308

Excerpt(s) from BLACK POWER by Stokely Carmichael and Charles V. Hamilton, copyright © 1967 by Stokely Carmichael and Charles Hamilton. Used by permission of Random House, an imprint and division of Penguin Random House LLC. All rights reserved.

Excerpt from The Miseducation of the Negro by Carter G. Woodson. Copyright © 2005 by the Association for the Study of African American Life and History. Originally printed in 1933. Reprinted by permission of the Association for the Study of African American Life and History.

"our living, Black manhood" – "A Eulogy for Malcolm X," Ossie Davis, February 27, 1965

John Lewis, "Speech at the March on Washington," 28 August, 1963 https://voicesofdemocracy.umd.edu/lewis-speech-at-the-march-on-washington-speech-text/

"A Black Woman Speaks to Black Manhood" from A BRAVE AND STARTLING TRUTH by Maya Angelou, copyright 1995 by Maya Angelou. Used by permission of Random House, an imprint and division of Penguin Random House LLC. All rights reserved.

"And still we rise" Maya Angelou. Used with permission by Caged Bird Legacy, LLC

*In the Name of God,*
*the Most Gracious, the Most Merciful*


*I dedicate this work to my brother,*
*to our mother,*
*to Black youth everywhere and always,*
*and to the child inside all of us.*

Or again, you often doubt if you really exist. You wonder whether you aren't simply a phantom in other people's minds. Say, a figure in a nightmare which the sleeper tries with all his strength to destroy. It's when you feel like this that, out of resentment, you begin to bump people back. And, let me confess, you feel that way most of the time. You ache with the need to convince yourself that you do exist in the real world, that you're a part of all the sound and anguish, and you strike out with your fists, you curse and you swear to make them recognize you. And, alas, it's seldom successful.

—Ralph Ellison, *Invisible Man*

We can't always wait for all the facts to be in, for all the facts are never in. Succinctly, stop being so rational and move. Awaken your soul.

—Michael A. Graves, "Speak Out"

# 1

## GIBRAN
*Massachusetts | September 1995*

The bass is thumping. I can feel it in my bones. It's begging me to bob my head, laugh, and shout. In another place, I would get up, my boys in step with me, rush the stage, dance. But in Thatcher Hall, at Lakeside Academy, I freeze.

Three white boys—two seniors and a junior—bounce onto the stage, smirking. The bass becomes a warped noise as my eyes take in every inch of their costumes.

Six pairs of sneakers, all mixed up on three pairs of feet. Yellow and red. Red and black. Black and green.

They're high-top sneakers—good ones. Expensive ones. And they're brand-new. No doubt bought on their parents' credit cards, just for this one stunt.

They march back and forth, pretending to warm up to the music, acting like they're going to rhyme. I watch those sneakers, obsessed with the fact that they'll never wear them again.

They wear baggy jeans so new, they're creased and saturated with dye.

Crisp white T-shirts, extra extra large.

The jeans, the shirts—they won't wear those again either.

They got the brands right mostly, but their ignorance shows in the details.

Their Red Sox caps betray them. Faded all over and frayed at the edges. If they knew anything about us, they'd know you can't perform in that. The contrast is almost funny.

But those mismatched shoes. And the walk. An exaggerated pimp walk. Dip, hop, dip, hop. Arms swinging, greedy grins on their faces, swaying to a rhythm that doesn't match the beat still rattling my bones. Mics held to their thin lips, their mouths move, but I can't hear the words they're lip-synching. I can barely hear the muffled laughter of the other white students who watch.

I tear my eyes away from the stage and scan the audience. The boys' friends crack up and cheer them on. Other white students cover their smiles with one hand, wide-eyed, not sure if they should find this funny.

The boys onstage are laughing. Their blue, green, hazel eyes gleam with something that feels sinister. They wear a confidence that was never taken from them. I want to steal it now.

What can I do? Stop the show? Bash the speakers? Slap the microphones out of their hands? I savor the fantasy, but there are too many witnesses. To be the aggressor in front of the whole school—that would guarantee my expulsion. I wouldn't mind; it could be worth it. If only it weren't for my mother's tears. My family's pleas. *You're almost there, Gibran. Just graduate. Finish your last year.*

Like it's easy. No. The longer I'm here, the harder it gets.

On my right, James's dark eyes are narrowed, following the boys across the stage, trying to figure out if this is for real.

On my left, David glares at the wall behind them, expressionless, holding himself together.

The three of us make eye contact and exchange thoughts silently.

*Here we go.*

*These dudes.*

*Are they serious right now?*

I check for the other Black students. The new ones are surprised and confused. The student-of-color orientation ended today—that blissful week of brown and Black faces making this place our own. Now, this "talent show," the first all-school event of the year, reveals what Lakeside is really like.

The rest of the Black students stare—at the stage, at the floor, some at the wall—determined not to be provoked. Not to put their emotions on display. They wear their discomfort, disbelief, and disgust as lightly as possible, trying not to offend. They wait. Wait for it to be over.

None of these white people, students or faculty, can see what I see. The boys onstage commit the offense, but we're the ones being careful.

I can't do it anymore.

I get up. I'm thinking I'll go outside, get some air, wait til this insult is over, and come back. It's not much—barely a protest—but it's something. At least I can liberate myself. I walk toward the auditorium door. But I slow down as something catches my eye.

The speaker is plugged into an extension cord that runs by the door to the hallway. It's an old building in an old boarding school—several hundred years old. Its prestige comes from age and pedigree. My eyes travel the length of the wire.

People accuse me of acting without thinking. The thing is, though, I'm *always* thinking. I just calculate differently. I think one thing: Right or wrong?

Is it right for me to let everyone else sit here, subjected to this nonsense, while I go get some air? No.

Is it right for me to stop this show if I can do it without damaging any property or injuring any bodies? Hell yeah.

So I continue out the door. And as I go, I bend down and yank the cord out of the wall. The music stops. The roaring in my ears stops. My back feels lighter, and my chest opens up. I can breathe.

There is a sweet moment of silence.

Then the reactions begin.

Gasps. Murmurs. A boy calls from the low stage, "Hey, what the—"

A voice from the Black students: "Ohhh snap!"

I let the door swing behind me.

I cut swiftly through the hallway, where the old stuffy white guys on the walls stare down at me. I resist the urge to give them the finger: *How ya like me now?* I act casual, just in case. I could maybe pretend it was an accident.

I reach the door to outside and shove the brass bar to open it. It creaks and falls closed behind me with a clang. The night is warm, and the stone steps glow silver gray. I take a deep breath and smile.

4

I'm slurping instant oatmeal and bobbing my head to Mobb Deep when Mom rushes into the kitchen. Her soft suede jacket and boots meet at her knees, layered over jeans and a blouse. She caresses my head as she passes me. She opens the fridge, scans its contents, checks her watch, and closes the fridge. She never eats breakfast. I don't know why she pretends to consider it every morning.

I finish scraping the bottom of my bowl and then find Mom looking at me. I reach to pull off my headphones, but she beats me to it. She shakes them at me, her silver bracelets jingling, and then drops them in my lap.

"These things are the death of the family unit."

"Sorry," I say, suppressing a smirk. I only wear headphones at home when I'm playing music with "explicit lyrics." Which is most of my music. But that's not why she calls them "the death of the family." She thinks I don't listen to her. But it's not the headphones. "What's up?" I ask.

"I *said*, are you going to make your bus?"

"Oh yeah. I got plenty of time."

"Famous last words."

I stand up. "I'm heading out right now. Don't worry."

She exhales. "Okay." She squares her hips and points her finger. This is her lecturing stance.

"Be careful," I recite for her. "Follow the rules." I get up and rinse my bowl in the sink.

She pulls me around to face her with surprising strength for her petite frame. The concern in her eyes makes me shift my gaze to her freckled nose, her soft curls, her beaded earrings.

"Listen," she says. "You are there for one reason and one reason only."

"I know—"

"I said listen. It doesn't matter what anyone else does or says. Don't let it bother you. You have to work—"

"Twice as hard to get half as far," I chime in.

She raises her face to the ceiling. "I tried, God."

I wonder if she thinks she failed. But then she gazes at my face, puts her arms around my middle, and squeezes. "I hate being at separate schools," she says into my chest.

Until high school, I went to White Oak School, where she teaches. In my earliest memories, the four of us rode to school together after a mad rush to get everyone out the door, backpacks in one hand and egg sandwiches in the other. Now the house is quiet. Ava at college and Ashanta married. We usually have someone who's down on their luck staying in one of our extra rooms for however long they need, but right now it's just me and Mom.

At first I was excited to go to a bigger school with more Black kids, but it didn't take long to realize Lakeside is just another prep school full of rich white kids. The few students of color are supposed to try to blend in. Without Mom as a buffer between me and the faculty, it's even harder to stay out of trouble. I don't miss her chasing me down the hallways. I do miss knowing she was in the building—that someone who believed in me had my back.

Mom finally releases me. "My baby," she says. Her eyes crease with worry. "Almost a man. I can't believe you're

6

about to be eighteen." Another sigh, then she pokes my chest with each command. "Be good. Be careful. Take those off your head the moment you step onto campus."

"Yes, ma'am," I joke.

When I started at Lakeside, Mom dropped me off and picked me up every day. I decided getting myself there and back could give her one less thing to stress about, so now I take two buses. She was relieved in a way, but now that she doesn't have the car ride to lecture me, she has to check me before we're out the door.

She inspects me from my hairline to my shoes.

"Yeah, you know I'm lookin fly." I grin and flip up the collar of my sports shirt.

She's finally smiling. "Okay. I'm late." As she backs out of the kitchen, she calls out, "One more year. Nine months."

"Yup." I send my voice out behind her. "I got this."

Maybe.

*What I don't say*

Every year on the first day of classes, I remember our very first day in private school: you as new faculty, us as new students. The memory isn't real, but it's real to me. Like something alive, it changes and grows. Instead of fading with time, it brightens. A black-and-white photograph developing slowly, and then touched up in color. It's a created memory. An origin story, a myth, a legend of you, my mother.

You were baby-faced, and your summer glow was fading. Petite and slender, you wore your typical uniform: tall leather boots, soft suede jacket, and dangling earrings made of beads. You held my hand and Ava's in your strong artist's hands. Ashanta ambled alongside, lost in her own thoughts, her backpack stuffed for third grade. You walked us from the faculty parking lot through the sprawling, impeccably landscaped grounds. We felt free in the expanse, and we longed to run, but your firm grip kept us close.

A blond woman with aggressively tanned skin came out of the building and started to hold the door for us, but you slowed down and stopped far from the entrance. The woman let it close and walked past us with a cheerful, "Good morning!" You shaped your face into a performative smile, trembling with the effort.

Other children skipped past us. Parents shrieked at each other, "OhmyGod, hiiiii, look at you!" They hugged and chatted about their summers and their families before returning to their shiny cars with a wave.

You knelt in front of us and fiddled with us for the thousandth time that morning. You smoothed Ava's bangs, creased my collar, folded Ava's lace socks, and tugged on my plain ones. You straightened the straps of Ashanta's backpack. You looked at the building with its sparkling glass doors.

"Listen," you said, your voice low, almost conspiratorial. "You are not here to make friends." You glanced at the families going in and out, laughing together. "I mean . . . they don't have to like you. They may not like you. But it doesn't matter. You're only here to learn. Don't worry about what anyone else thinks. Okay? Do you understand?" You looked at each of our faces.

We said nothing. We did not understand. It would take

years for us to understand. For a long time, we would think there was something wrong with you.

You pulled us close for a hug and breathed us in: our hair grease and our new, off-brand clothes. I squeezed you back, hoping somehow to restore the mom I knew from home. The mom who taught us to draw and paint. The magical mom who took us to Brigham's for ice cream and had all of our friends over at the same time and treated every child like her own and gave until there was nothing left.

Before you let us go, you whispered something, so softly that I'm not sure you really said it.

"Don't trust them."

A warning to us, a reminder for yourself, or both? It echoed in my ears, knocking at the back of my mind until the days became years and the years dragged on and the long, long years finally taught me what it meant.

First day of classes, senior year. Mr. Wheatley, my advisor, looks pained to see me. The feeling is mutual, but I might be better at hiding it than he is. In his office, sunlight streams in through the old, wooden window, highlighting his sparse hair, peeling sunburn, and the dust on his elbow-patched tweed jacket. He closes a folder and rests it on his lap, crosses his legs, and adjusts his brown-framed glasses.

"Welcome back," he says without a hint of warmth in his voice. "I hope you had a nice summer."

I don't have a chance to respond before he continues.

"We've got a few important notes to discuss. You are

aware that your disruption at the talent show last week goes into your permanent disciplinary record?"

I let that sink in. "Now I am."

"Now you are. So you are also aware that one more appearance before the discipline committee will earn you not suspension but expulsion from school?"

My mouth goes dry. "Okay."

"Two more small strikes like the talent show or one big strike such as inappropriate conduct with another student, and your final year will be cut short. Is that understood?"

I attempt to smile. "Got it."

"Good." He folds his hands together like he's about to say grace. "Gibran, I would hate to see you waste this wonderful opportunity—"

Blah, blah, blah. I tune him out. I can recite this speech from memory. I've heard it so many times from so many people with different intentions. As if he personally knows my family and what sacrifices were made to get me here. Please.

The funny part is when people like Mr. Wheatley say I can talk to them about anything. Yeah, right.

What if I tried to explain why I pulled the plug at the talent show? What if I told him I did it for all the Black kids? I can predict how that would go.

*Everything isn't always about race, Gibran.*

*They didn't mean to offend anyone.*

I don't want to hear all that.

And they don't want to hear me either. If they did, they would have asked me why I did it before they went and put it in my record.

When he takes a breath, I interject. "Are we all set here, Mr. Wheatley?"

He sinks in his chair and looks deflated. Maybe he thought I'd have some big moment of enlightenment. "Well . . . I suppose we are. Unless you have any questions about your schedule or college counseling or—"

"I don't." He's already told me everything I need to know.

He rubs the arm of his chair, annoyed. "All right, then." He pulls out a sheet of paper and an envelope. "This is your schedule, and this letter goes to your parents. I presume I can trust you to deliver it."

"Of course."

I fold the envelope and put it in the back pocket of my jeans before throwing my backpack over my shoulder and leaving his office.

The hallway is lined with students holding recommendation forms and other papers in their hands. Their meetings will go differently. Mr. Wheatley will smile when they walk in, genuinely happy to see them. He'll ask how their summer vacations were—what internships they completed and where they traveled overseas—before discussing their schedules with them, making sure they're happy with their courses. He'll encourage them to keep up their strong academics and extracurriculars. He'll want details about their college visits and application plans.

I don't know if he knows that I'm already going to Howard. With my test scores, I only had to write a few essays to qualify for early admission with a nice scholarship for their business administration program. I'm not sure I'll like business, but I figure it could help me be more in control of making my music.

I'm not even sure I want to spend four more years in school after this, but it's what my mom and her parents expect, so it's the path of least resistance.

My admission and scholarship depend on my successful high school graduation, of course. For anyone else, that should be easy. But for me, with one strike left? It's like they're holding the door open, waiting for me to walk right out.

My schedule is filled with the usual—honors calculus, physics, AP English, Spanish—but I do have one class to look forward to.

Lakeside is proud of its elective seminars, and the teachers love them. They offer topics they're passionate about, going deep into niche subjects like social persuasion or *Hamlet* with juniors and seniors. I've heard about Mr. Adrian's African American history seminar since freshman year. Older Black students hyped it up, so most of us take it when we can.

My mom's generation fought to have Black studies in colleges. She used to tell me the stories of the Black students taking over the administration building at Boston University to get the school's attention to their demands. She would laugh when she remembered how they answered the main phone line during their occupation: "Black BU!" She stopped telling me those stories when she saw that I had a rebellious streak in me too.

I bet they thought by now Black studies would be included

in the required curriculum. Instead, we're still supposed to feel grateful to have this one elective class about ourselves while "Western civilization" gets twelve years.

By the time I enter the classroom, I'm almost resentful. I can't help it—whenever I sense that gratitude is expected and not deserved, I go hard in the opposite direction. But Mr. Adrian's open smile disarms me. I am the last to arrive, and instead of checking the clock, he looks at me, excited, like I'm the person he's been waiting for.

"Gibran! Welcome."

He seems sincere. I have to give it to him; he's the only teacher who doesn't shrink when he sees me or avert his eyes. He's a full head shorter than me too. His bright blond hair wisps around his balding head.

The large oval oak table is lined with students sitting in heavy wooden armchairs, crisp notebooks open in front of them. I take a seat next to James, who wears his favorite Champion sweatshirt and baggy jeans. I lift my chin to nod whassup to David, who sits across from us, next to another soccer player. There are more brown faces in here than I've seen in any of my classes ever. It's nice. Comfortable. Though it'd also be nice if more than five white kids cared enough to be here.

Mr. Adrian leans on the tabletop, his fingers spread like a runner's getting ready to race.

"Welcome, everyone." His voice sounds like tires on gravel but in a warm, relaxed way. "Let's discuss what we expect from a course on African American history. What is the relationship between African American history and American history in general?"

Does he want my real answer? African American history is what you learn at home, when Moms drops names over dinner or when you go through your parents' and grandparents' bookshelves. So-called American history is the white his-story you learn at school for twelve years until, if you're lucky, you get one "special seminar" to throw some color in there. Black history messes up the hero narrative of white history, so for the most part, Black history is left out.

James is the first to raise his hand. Let's see how diplomatic he'll be. "I mean, they're supposed to be one and the same, right?" he says. "Like, without African Americans, there would be no America. And without America, there would be no African Americans. So they shouldn't really be divided."

"Yeah," Lisa says, pushing her glasses up her nose. Her tight curls are pulled back in a puffy ponytail, and her dimples dig deep into her cheeks as she talks. "They're totally interdependent. But people treat African American history like it's . . . supplemental."

"Okay." Mr. Adrian turns to the blackboard and writes *interdependent*. Then he leans on the table again. "Other thoughts?"

A white boy named Eric cocks his head. "I guess I thought of American history as including African American history," he says. "American history is general. Then when you focus on African American history, it's more . . . specialized? Or exclusive, I guess?"

"Pfff." I can't help myself.

Mr. Adrian and the other students turn my way.

"I'm sorry," I say to Mr. Adrian.

"Please," he says, "respond."

I clear my throat. "I mean, when you say it's exclusive, that's kind of funny to me, because really, it's American history that's exclusive. Black people and Native Americans are like a footnote or a sidebar in most American history books. The fact that there's a separate class for African American history kind of proves that the general curriculum focuses on white people. Everything that was skipped over gets squeezed into these special seminars that aren't even required."

Some of the Black kids nod. Eric frowns and fiddles with his pen.

"So you're saying," Mr. Adrian responds slowly, "that African American history is not separate or exclusive, but separated and excluded. In curricula. In classrooms."

"Yeah, even in the culture overall. Schools just reflect society and reproduce the same old systems."

He writes *separated* and *excluded* on the blackboard and turns back to the class, one hand in the pocket of his khakis and the other twirling the piece of chalk. White dust covers his fingers.

Kate, a white girl wearing a faded Dartmouth T-shirt, speaks next. "I don't think of them as separate. Or separated or whatever." She pulls at the ends of her auburn hair. "We have learned about, like, African Americans before. We read *The Bluest Eye* in English last year."

I take a deep breath.

Mr. Adrian blinks. He opens his mouth and then shuts it.

David says, "Yeah, we also read *Huckleberry Finn* in eighth grade."

"Exactly!" Kate says as if he's proving her point.

David, James, and I glance at each other and then back at Kate.

"Did y'all read *Uncle Tom's Cabin* too?" I ask, keeping a straight face.

"What?" Kate asks, confused.

The other Black kids stifle laughter. Lisa tries to hide it, but her dimples give her away.

Kate turns red and frowns at me.

"Well," Mr. Adrian says, scratching his neck. "We can at least agree that there's more to learn about African American history than what's been included in the general history curriculum. That's why we're here today, right?"

Kate trains her eyes on him.

Mr. Adrian lets a silence stretch for almost a minute. Eric looks like he wants to say something, but he just twists his mouth. Finally, Mr. Adrian continues. "Well, we won't have time to dive deep into every era this semester. Your research project will give you a chance to go deeper into a topic of interest to you."

He straightens a stack of papers and hands it to the student on his left, who takes a sheet and passes on the stack.

"I want you to really bring your creativity to this project. You can work alone or in pairs. You can meet with me any time to talk about your ideas. Your project should pose a big question about African American history: the presence, contributions, and/or struggles of Black people in this country. It's entirely possible you won't find an answer or resolution. I'd like you to focus on presenting your questions and your research in a way that is thought-provoking and engaging."

Mr. Adrian fields questions about the project and about the syllabus. For the last fifteen minutes, he gives a mini lecture about the arrival of the first enslaved Africans in the colonies. When class ends, notebooks slap shut and chairs scrape the floor. Students shuffle out of the room.

I walk with David and James toward the dining hall. It felt good to talk about our history in class for once. It feels easier to speak up when more of us are in the room too. I wonder how much further we'd get if we didn't have to wait for the white kids to catch up.

At home, I leave the letter from the school on Mom's dresser. Between her overflowing jewelry boxes and her art supplies, there's a chance it'll go unnoticed for a few days.

Wrong. She hasn't been home for ten minutes when she bursts into my bedroom, pulling the letter out of the envelope.

"What's this?" She lowers herself onto my bed. Worry lines form all over her face. "What . . . what did you do?"

"Nothing."

She glares at me.

I shrug. "I guess I kinda, like, tripped over the extension cord in the middle of the talent show? The cord came out of the wall and—"

"Boy. You can't even get that lie out your mouth with a straight face. Tell me what happened."

I drop my head. "Aight, I didn't trip. I kinda did it on purpose. But Ma, it was ridiculous. They deserved it. These white boys—"

"Of course they deserved it," she snaps. "That is not the question. The question is, do you deserve the punishment *you're* going to get for giving them what they deserve?"

I suck my teeth.

"Don't suck your teeth at me."

"I'm not."

She holds the letter so tight she might rip it. "Jesus," she whispers. She shoves the letter back into its envelope and stares at the floor. "This is not good. You know what this means, don't you?"

"Yeah."

She grinds her teeth. "Don't give them another excuse, Gibran."

On Thursday, we have our Brother Bonding meeting. After school, I wait for James outside of Thatcher Hall, pacing across the wide stone steps from one oversized Roman column to the other. I practice some new lyrics while I wait.

*I wake up in the morning, I give thanks for living,*
*Then leave the house wit my mind focused on banking riches*
*I handle business*
*and still I witness*
*my people dying*
*The sun keep shining*

Other students push open the heavy doors and bounce outside. I laugh to myself as they make a wide arc around me, parting for me like the sea for Moses. They cross the street to the library or to the snack bar, or race to the campus green. As the flood of students slows to a trickle, I stop pacing and rhyming and watch the door. Maybe James forgot we were walking over together and went out a different way. I scratch my scalp with my cap and start missing my locks again. Mom made me cut them off for high school, but I don't even need my dreads to scare white people anymore.

I'm about to start strolling toward the meeting when the door flies open and James jogs out.

"Sup, G?" We clasp hands and pull away with a snap.

"What's up with you? Had a brother standin out here all day."

"Pshh. Five minutes. My bad. I had to ask Mr. Murphy for a recommendation. You don't know about that life though."

"Nope."

It's a good thing I don't. I can't think of a single faculty member here who would write me an enthusiastic recommendation. Maybe Mr. Adrian, but this is my first class with him. Moms was more relieved than I was when I got admitted to Howard. For her, it seemed like the light at the end of a long, dark tunnel. A weight lifted. Until she saw that letter from my advisor.

We follow a concrete path through the grass toward Carroll House, a two-story brick building built in the early days of the school. In the grass, boys throw Frisbees and girls tuck up their sleeves, hoping the sun burns strong enough to give them one last tan.

"So you wrote some new lyrics?" James says. "Lemme hear what you got."

"You sure you're ready for this?"

"Oh, you got jokes? Aight, bet, let's go." He gives me a beat, and I flow.

> We do the knowledge, speak the wisdom so you see
> the science
> The power structure full of demons so we be defiant
> Mental warfare ain't for the likes of the feeble-minded
> The truth is all around you just have to seek and find it
> I hear your silence
> That's how we move cause the mind a weapon
> And find our blessings
> In the weed cause we high as heaven
> I'm a teacher
> I give my shorties a private lesson

"Oooooh!!!" James laughs, then cups his hands around his mouth and plays the crowd of astonished fans. "Word, you got that, you got that."

It's my turn to make a beat, and he freestyles. We take turns spitting rhymes and egging each other on.

"Aight," I say as we reach the path to the dorm where the Brother Bonding meeting has started. "Those lyrics were nice, but you gotta admit defeat."

"What? You buggin."

"I mean, we can take it to a third party to judge if you really wanna embarrass yourself. . . ."

"Whatever!"

We open the door to Carroll House and pause for a second to let our vision adjust to the dim indoor light. In the common room, ten brown boys sit on couches and chairs, chatting. My shoulders relax as soon as I walk in.

"Whaddup, y'all," I say, nice and loud to everybody. I make the rounds, dapping everybody up.

David's wearing his soccer shorts and shin guards so he can run over to practice from the meeting.

"What's up?" he says. "Nice of y'all to join us."

"His fault," I say, pointing at James.

"Anyway," James says. "We miss anything?"

"Not really. We're introducing ourselves to the freshmen and assigning mentors for the new boarding students." David picks up a piece of paper from a table by the door and runs his finger down a list. "Gibran, you have Chris, who is . . ." He scans the room. "Right over there." He points at a scrawny, wide-eyed boy in a striped polo shirt. He's sitting in the corner with his hands folded in his lap, listening to the other boys.

"Aight, cool."

"And James, you have Zeke." David points out a tall boy with dark skin and thick glasses. "You know the drill. Check in with them, let 'em know how to get in touch with you and all that."

"No doubt," James says.

I pull up a chair across from Chris. "Chris! My man!"

"Hi!" he says. "Nice to meet you." He looks like I'm the

21

latest in a series of surprises that have come at him since he arrived at Lakeside.

"I'm Gibran."

"I know."

"Oh, word? I hope you've only heard good things."

His eyes go wide as golf balls.

"I'm just messing with you, man. Relax. I know if it was white kids talking, you probably thought I was the boogeyman. Anyway, the good news is, I'm your senior mentor. That means nobody should be messing with you, 'cause they know I'll handle it, nahmsayin?"

Chris blinks.

"I'm not trying to scare you," I say. "I'm just sayin, white kids have a habit of stepping out of line. So you gotta nip it in the bud from jump. Let 'em know you're not the one."

Chris shifts in his seat and sits on his hands, looking down at his knees. He's so open and vulnerable. That makes him an easy target. I can protect him this year, but next year I won't be around. I have nine months to teach him how to hold his own. Operation Man Up begins right here and now.

"Where you from?" I ask.

"Chicago."

"Dang, that's far! I think you're the only student I've met who's from outside the Northeast. Well, I live twenty minutes from campus, right in Boston. Definitely let me know if there's anything you need anytime. I got you."

"Okay. Thanks. They also gave me a . . . host family? Like, a day student who can host me when I want to get off campus or something?"

"Right, right," I say. "They white?"

"Well . . . yeah."

"Mm. They like to adopt us. Like pets, nahmsayin. It makes 'em feel good. They may smile in your face, but that don't mean they have your back. Remember that."

Chris kicks the legs of his chair.

"You know what though," I say, "don't worry 'bout all that yet. Be cool, be comfortable. Just lemme know if anybody bothers you."

"'Kay." I can barely hear him over the voices around us.

"You play any sports?"

We chat for a few minutes, and I learn that Chris is not an athlete either, but that he's into science and math and is thinking of joining the debate club. Soon David calls for everyone's attention.

"Aight, listen up. Some of us have to get to sports practice, so before people leave, anyone want to put stuff on the agenda for this year?"

I raise my hand. "The Million Man March."

Sounds of surprise, interest, and trepidation break out around the room. I wait for the voices to die down.

"We should do something," I say.

"That'd be tight," David says. "Like what?" He twists his torso, then bends his knees to get warmed up before his jog down to the field.

"I mean, ideally, we should go."

"What?" Trey squints at me. He's a junior who's been here since middle school. He's built like a footballer but acts like a little kid.

"Yeah, in our dreams," James says. He pulls his cap off his head and puts it on his knee.

"Hold up," I say. "They got a French trip, a Spanish trip, a freakin national debate competition in a different state every year. Why's it so crazy to think we could go to DC? Anything for a Black man is outta the question?"

Silence.

"I mean, I feel you," James says. "I'm just sayin. It's not the kind of event the school would support. So we'd be on our own."

"Plus, it's coming up soon, right?" Trey asks.

"Yeah, it is," David says. "Middle of October."

"That might be enough time to propose an off-campus trip," I say.

James and David look skeptical.

"Well, let's find out," I say. "Show of hands, how many of us would be interested if we could actually go?"

David and James raise their hands high. Everyone else looks around like it's a trick question.

"Yo, it's not a promise! Damn," I say. "Aight, raise your hand if you would potentially, maybe, possibly be interested."

One at a time, five more boys raise their hands, two of them twisting their hands in the universal "maybe" signal. The freshmen, including Chris, are still too surprised to consider the question.

I chuckle. "Aight, cool. We'll look into it, find out what kinda rules we'd be up against."

"Sounds good," David says. "We could also think about hosting something on that day. Like, take the day off and do something together. Maybe with Black students from other schools or something."

"Yeah," James says, "aren't they saying that people who can't go are doing a Day of Absence-type thing? Like, don't go to work or school?"

"Okay, now I'm listening," Trey says, rubbing his hands together.

Everyone laughs.

"That could definitely work," I say.

"Cool," David says. "Let's talk more about it before next meeting and come up with a plan." He checks the clock above the fireplace. "All right, we'll see everyone here next week, same time, same place. And we'll see you around campus too." He heaves his gym bag onto his shoulder and gives his mentee daps before turning to me and James.

"What y'all doing this weekend?" James asks. He's a boarder and usually spends at least one night at my place or David's each weekend, just to get off campus.

"Colin's having a party on Saturday," David says.

"That's right," James says.

"Oh, word?" I feign shock. "Someone's having a party and didn't invite moi?"

"Yeah—actually," David says, "he specifically asked me not to bring you."

"Me too!" James says.

"For real?"

We crack up.

I do my best nasal voice: "'Oh yeah, and, um, your friend, the troublemaker, please don't bring him, he's a little too Black for us?'"

"Yup," James says. "They scared of you, nigga."

25

"Bet," I say, "I can't wait to go check out Colin and his lil party now. It's on!"

On Friday during a free period, I go to the library to ask Mrs. Johnson what she thinks about us proposing a trip to the march. Other than the principal, Mr. Clarke, one staff member, and the dining hall and maintenance crew, Mrs. Johnson is the only Black adult on campus. You might think having a Black principal would be great for us, but not really. It's like he has something to prove, so it ends up being almost worse than having a white principal and knowing what we're up against from jump. We've gotten over the disappointment by now, but we still get caught off guard from time to time. Mrs. Johnson is cool though. She's typically the go-to person for stuff we need.

Mrs. Johnson is helping a student with the card catalog when I come in, so I stand by the desk. The other two librarians look up, smile skittishly, and go back to sorting books. Fine with me.

"Hello, Gibran," Mrs. Johnson says as she walks around to the other side of the desk. She adjusts her tortoiseshell glasses and pushes her thick bangs to the side.

"Hi, Mrs. Johnson, how you doing?"

"I'm all right, thanks. How's your senior year going so far?"

"Not too bad," I say. I'm guessing she knows about my disciplinary status, but even though I'm relieved that I stayed out of "trouble" all week, I don't bring it up. I put my backpack at my feet. "I have a question for you."

"Sure, what is it?" She leans her forearms on the desk.

"If a group of students wanted to take a short trip out of state—like either a day trip or overnight—how would we get approval for that?"

"Ooh," she says. "Out of state, huh? This would be on a weekend, right?"

"Well, actually, we might need one day off school."

"Oh, I see. That might be tough—but it's been done before. The Office of Extracurricular Activities has the application forms for trips. Of course, you'd need a faculty sponsor as a chaperone, and that person has to sign the application."

"Okay." I drum my fingers on the desk, considering.

She tilts her head. "Can I ask what the trip is about?"

"Yeah," I say. "Actually, maybe you can tell me if you think we should bother proposing it. We were talking about trying to go to the Million Man March next month."

She straightens her shoulders and raises her eyebrows. "Oh! Hmm."

"You think we have a chance of getting approved?"

"Well," she says. "I haven't served on the committee before, but . . . I suppose it would be a hard sell."

"Yeah, that's what we figured. But it's a historic event. I mean, didn't people skip work and school to go to, like, the March on Washington and stuff like that?"

"Well, yes, they did. But that wasn't exactly mainstream either. They were actually seen as pretty radical at the time."

"For real?"

"Oh yes. Now they teach it as if everyone loved Dr. King and what he stood for. But it was quite divisive. Some people

27

thought it was too much, too pushy. And that was a pretty tame event. Whereas the Million Man March . . ." She smiles. "Actually, it's funny, part of what offended some people about the March on Washington was that it was integrated, and now we have the opposite. The Million Man March is controversial in part because it's specifically for Black men."

"See, that's the thing. People always want to tell us how to protest. If those same people were helping correct society, we wouldn't have to protest in the first place." The march isn't even a protest, really, and that's part of why I want to go. It's not for other people to hear our message. It's for us to come together. Something I never get to do.

She looks sympathetic. She must be used to these barriers. Maybe she doesn't even think about it much.

She glances behind me. Another student is waiting. One of the other librarians who didn't offer to help me bounces over to help him.

"Well, I really want to try and go. But we can't think of a sponsor who would take us there."

"I wish I could help you with that," she says, "but I don't do long-distance trips with students."

"No, I understand. We wouldn't ask that of you." I bite my lip. "Our other idea was, if we can't go, maybe we could plan our own Day of Absence. Organize an event for Black students on that day or attend something in Boston."

"That might be easier to get approved," she says. "Although you'd still have to make a strong argument for why it's important. How it enhances your education."

"Right. I can do that." I'm not thrilled with this compromise, but it's probably the easiest way to participate. "Well,

I appreciate your help, Mrs. Johnson. We'll let you know what happens."

"Any time, Gibran. Good luck."

I pick up an application at the Office of Extracurricular Activities. Five pages full of red tape. I spend the rest of my free period thinking about our options for getting to the March.

My uncle Kevin lives in DC. He's invited me down a few times when I've seen him at my grandparents' house for holidays. But whenever I've asked my mom about going down to see him, she would shake her head like he wasn't serious or it wasn't a good idea. She never explained, and after a while, I stopped asking. He never visits us either. It seems like Mom's always making some excuse not to invite him up.

I'm sure Uncle Kevin will be going to the march. Anything having to do with Black people, he's all about it. I'm old enough to get to DC by myself. The school may not approve, but if I could convince Mom to let me go and stay with Uncle Kevin, maybe some friends could come with me. Instead of a school-sponsored trip, we could sign them out to my house and go from there.

It's a long shot, but it's worth a try. The Day of Absence is a decent plan B, but I want to be at the march.

# 2

## KEVIN
*New York City | Thursday, April 4, 1968*

At five thirty, the other Columbia undergrads close their books and ask their tutees if they're all set, in that tone that leaves them no room to say anything but *yes* and *thank you for spending your precious time with me.* Assured that they've done their good deed for the week, they pick up their own books and shuffle off to their other activities or to their dorm rooms, to the library or to the dining hall for an early dinner.

Valerie and I stay in our seats.

Mike, my assigned tutee, is working so much faster than he was in the fall. I wait until he finishes the last problem on his math homework, and then I stand and applaud.

"Mike finished math *before* leaving today!" I shout.

He ducks his head and twists his mouth to hide a grin as other students join in the applause.

"Seriously—this is cause for celebration, man," I say, punching his shoulder lightly. "Good job."

"Thanks." He shuts his notebook and joins the other

students who are joking, laughing, and debating.

Jerome sits across from me. "Kevin, could you help me with this essay question?"

"Of course," I say. "Let's see."

After another half hour, the homework is done, and we've moved on to talking about the students' families, their neighborhoods, their schools. Their love for Harlem and the work they're doing to hold on to it. Their hopes for the future. I wish I had their focus when I was in high school.

When it's too dark inside to see by the light of the windows, we straighten up the room instead of turning the lights on, a rule Valerie and I came up with after some parents got upset about their kids coming home late. We leave as a group and walk each student home, covering half of Harlem. The students talk about an upcoming rally for tenants' rights and compete over who's invited more people.

"You're coming, right?" Sandra asks me and Valerie.

"If you want us, we're there," Valerie says.

"Definitely," I agree.

Sandra lists the community groups that are organizing the rally and the people in power who they hope will pay attention. The second list includes the entire administration at our university.

By the time we've said goodbye to the last student, the streetlights have flickered on, illuminating the city streets. Valerie and I walk back up toward our sparkling campus on the hill. We pass by Morningside Park, one of Harlem's only green spaces. Behind a chain-link fence, the construction site of Columbia's new gym threatens to swallow the park whole.

The neighborhood protested to save the park from being taken over by Columbia. Almost everyone objects to the construction of the gym—militants to conservatives. Only the white athletes and the administration are for it. The administration says it will benefit Harlem residents, but only the bottom two floors of seven would be accessible to community members unaffiliated with Columbia—and they would use a separate entrance at the bottom of the hill. The racist, elitist design is how it earned the nickname Gym Crow. Despite the continued protests, they broke ground in February. My jaw tightens as I survey the darkness beyond the fence.

"This is the part of the walk that I hate," I tell Valerie.

"Am I too boring for you?" I can hear her smiling without seeing it.

"Please," I say. "You make it tolerable. It's the dread of getting back to campus. If it weren't for you, I might not come back."

"You have somewhere else to go? I can walk you there." She stops midstride, calling my bluff.

"I wish."

We continue on, her boots echoing on the concrete.

"How'd that exam go?" she asks. "Western Civ?"

I groan. "I haven't gotten it back yet. But I can guess how he'll react to my answers about our so-called democracy."

"Hm."

"What?" I ask.

"What what?" she says.

"You have an opinion," I say. "Spill it." When I see the golden crown on the campus gate, I pick up a stone and throw it. It pings off the crown without leaving a mark.

"Eh. I'm not gonna waste my breath." She zips her lips with her hand and throws away the invisible key.

I lower my eyelids. "Fine. Where are you studying tonight?"

"I can't tell you that."

"Why not?"

"Remember last time you came to 'study' with us? No one could concentrate. All your debating. We almost got kicked out of the library."

"Oh, come on. You were into it too."

"I know," she says. "That's how I learned my lesson. Kevin and studying do not mix."

"I see. So that's how it is."

"That's exactly how it is."

"Well, I have something with me that might make you change your mind," I say.

We stop at the entrance to Barnard's courtyard. I pull out a brand-new, first edition copy of *Black Power*.

Her jaw drops. "Ohhh—where did you—Micheaux's?"

"Of course."

She reaches for the book. I hand it to her, and she opens it reverently, holding it up to the dim light to pore over the table of contents. She smiles so eagerly I have to smile too. "Right on," she says.

I let her enjoy it for a minute, and then I ask, "Now can I study with you?"

She laughs. "No. But you can lend this to me when you're done."

"Using a brother for his books."

"You know that's right."

"Well, if that's all I'm good for," I say, reaching into my bag, "you can keep that copy."

She looks up at me, and I show her the other copy I bought.

"Really?" she asks.

"Yeah. I need my partner to stay on her toes. My debate partner, that is."

It sounds corny, but her eyes truly sparkle. I love that she's as excited as I am about the book. She'll probably finish reading it tonight too. I put my copy back in my bag and shove my hands in my jacket pockets. "I can't believe it's already April."

"Yeah," she says, hugging her new book. "It'll be finals and then summer before we know it."

"You know," I say, "I keep thinking about the mentorship we've been talking about."

"Me too," she says.

"I think we should tell the students about it before the end of the school year. We can test it out now and roll it out in the fall. What do you think?"

"I guess so," she says. "I'm excited to start, only . . . I still wonder if we should run it by the other Black tutors."

"You know what they'll say. They're so proud of giving their time as tutors. They don't have the vision."

"True." But still she hesitates.

"I say we go for it. Full speed ahead. The other tutors can join if they want to once they see how to really make a difference. Besides, it's a separate thing, if anyone asks. We may have met most of the kids through Columbia's tutoring program, but our mentoring program is separate."

"Right." She nods. "Okay. Let's meet on Saturday to finish up our proposal."

"All right, sistah. That's what I'm talkin' about."

She laughs.

"And our proposal is for information, not asking permission."

"Oh Lord," she says. "You're a mess."

"Part of my charm, right?" I offer my handsome-movie-star smile.

"Fool. We're gonna miss dinner."

"Right. Better hustle. Hey, if there's nothing good left, come throw a rock at my window. I'll be happy to run back to Harlem to get us some real food."

"You would, too."

"Of course I would!"

"Don't tempt me. Bye, Kevin."

"Be cool, sister."

She heads to the women's dining hall at Barnard, and I break into a light jog to make it to John Jay Dining Hall.

For the hundredth time, I think how nice it would be for my sister to meet Valerie. And for the hundredth time, I remember that my sister isn't interested in anything I'm doing now.

Charles rushes into the dining hall just before dinner service ends, probably coming from an intense study session at the library. He spots me and heads my way. When he sees my nearly empty plate, he keeps his book bag on his shoulder.

"Go ahead and put your stuff down, brother," I say, marking my page in my book.

"Aren't you getting ready to leave?"

"I'm not in a rush."

"Don't you have finals to study for? Papers to write?"

I wave those thoughts away. "We have a month until finals. I'd rather be reading this." I hold up my copy of *Black Power* proudly.

His shoulders sag dramatically. "For your sake," he says, dropping his bag in the seat opposite mine, "I hope you do get your Black studies courses created before you graduate. You need to get credit for all this extracurricular reading."

Leave it to Charles to not be excited about a first edition hardcover of Stokely Carmichael's and Charles Hamilton's brand-new book.

"Why do you say 'your,'" I ask him, "as if you're not one of us? It doesn't make a difference to you that this entire university doesn't have a single class about our people?"

"I'm a science major," he says as if that answers my question.

"And? Do they talk about the work of George Washington Carver in your science classes?"

"I studied Black folks for twelve years before I got here," he says. "Probably the one benefit of going to a segregated, one-room school. I bet I know more about Black history than all of your political science professors combined."

He pops a leftover meatball from my plate into his mouth

and maneuvers his way through rows of tables and chairs to get food.

"You don't act like it," I call after him, sulking a little as I turn back to my book.

When he returns, I flip back to the preface and read aloud to him.

"'This book is about why, where and in what manner Black people in America must get themselves together. It is about Black people taking care of business—the business of and for Black people. The stakes are really very simple: if we fail to do this, we face continued subjection to a white society that has no intention of giving up willingly or easily its position of priority and authority. If we succeed, we will exercise control over our lives, politically, economically and psychically.'"

"Mm," Charles mumbles, glancing around at other tables between bites.

"Oh—am I making you nervous?" I joke, raising my voice. "What's wrong? You don't want to be seen listening to radical militant propaganda?"

"Nope." He keeps eating.

"Man, you're ridiculous."

He chuckles. "And you're funny. I still think you should have gone to a Black college."

"Ha. No thanks. My parents went to Howard. It's no better than Columbia or Harvard or anywhere else. Maybe worse. They're trying so hard to imitate these places. I bet they're still using the paper bag test."

"Hm." He chews and swallows, then points at me with his fork. "You'd pass it though. They'd love you there."

Charles is probably the only person who can get away with saying something like that to me. He knows I don't like being so light-skinned. I know in some ways my life would have been even harder if I had Charles's dark brown complexion. But you couldn't tell me that when I was eight years old hearing kids count "eenie, meenie, minie, moe, catch a nigger by the toe."

"Anyway," I say. "You know anyone who graduated from a Black college with a Black studies major?"

He leans back in his seat, looking at me.

Of course he hasn't. He's the first person from his small town to go to college.

"Well," I mumble, "they don't exist. So-called Black colleges are about preparing Negroes for the white man's world. That's where they train up the Black bourgeoisie. We need to change the white man's world, not just join it."

"Right," Charles says. "That's why you're here at Columbia. To change it. And if you don't pass your classes, you won't be changing much. So maybe you should study . . . a little bit?"

"You sound like my parents."

"I like your parents."

I throw a balled-up napkin at him. "Man, get outta here."

He laughs, dodging it, and gets up, saying, "I do have to go. *I* have studying to do."

"Mm-hm."

He stacks my tray underneath his.

"Thanks, man," I say. "I'll finish reading this to you later."

"I'm sure you will." He sounds less than thrilled.

Hours later, in my dorm room, I resist the urge to finish my new book. I save the last two chapters for later and open an old favorite, *The Mis-Education of the Negro*.

*When a Negro has finished his education in our schools, then, he has been equipped to begin the life of an Americanized or Europeanized white man, but before he steps from the threshold of his alma mater he is told by his teachers that he must go back to his own people from whom he has been estranged by a vision of ideals which in his disillusionment he will realize that he cannot attain.*

Voices in the hallway startle me, and I lose my place on the page. People are yelling. Shrieking? What the hell is going on? Are people drinking already? It sounds like everyone on our floor. I stay still and listen.

The voices build and gather, like a flock of geese approaching.

I put my book face down and listen for a moment from behind my closed door.

"This can't be happening...."

Is someone crying?

"It's because he spoke out against the war, man...."

"...that radical talk..."

I crack my door open and peek out. A crowd of students fills the hallway, and more come to join them. Their faces are pale or red and blotchy, streaked with tears. They pace or stand still. They rake fingers through their hair or lean their hands against the wall. Eyes are bloodshot or staring in shock. They are all white.

When I enter the hallway, they see me and go silent. They look from me to one another, and the air between us fills with what they won't say. A chill runs through me.

I walk in the opposite direction, toward Charles's room, and knock on his door. Waiting for a response almost brings me to a panic. Then I remember I never knock on Charles's door. Charles doesn't want to be distracted. He knows I'll walk in whether he answers or not.

Inside, Charles sits at his desk, hunched over books and notebooks, a lamp shining on his papers. The sight of him studying is a momentary relief. I look back at the crowd in the hallway. They talk in low voices now. I shut the door firmly behind me.

"Hey," I say, my voice almost a whisper.

He holds a finger up in the air while he writes. Finally, he puts his pencil down. "What's happening? You want to go to the library?"

"No—there's something going on out there. Didn't you hear those voices in the hallway?"

He looks at the door, listening.

"People were yelling and stuff."

His face is blank.

"I went out there, but they didn't talk to me. . . ."

"No surprise there."

"I'm serious. It's something big."

A knock on the door makes me jump. My heart thumps hard in my chest.

Charles eyes me like I brought trouble. I'm just glad we're together.

He gets up slowly and pauses with his hand on the knob before opening it.

Richard, an upperclassman, stands there in his collared

shirt and sweater-vest, with two other brothers behind him. Sweat gathers at Richard's temples, and his wingmen look up and down the hall like bodyguards.

"We're checking on people," Richard says. "You two all right?"

Dread fills my belly. We stare at him, and his face changes.

"You haven't heard?"

Neither Charles nor I can speak.

"It's Dr. King. He's been shot."

Charles stumbles backward as if he's been shoved. I gulp for air.

"No."

"In the neck," Richard adds.

"Is he—".

"We don't know yet. He's in the hospital." He reaches out and grabs each of us by the shoulder. It steadies me. I feel the solid ground beneath my feet.

"There'll be an emergency meeting tomorrow morning to talk about what to do. Some brothers are gathering in Melvin's room tonight."

A shout moves through the crowd of people down the hall. Someone turns a radio up full blast.

*Again, this just in. Dr. Martin Luther King Jr., who was being treated for a bullet wound at St. Joseph's Hospital after being shot on the balcony of the Lorraine Motel, has been pronounced dead. . . .*

In Melvin's room, fifteen brothers sit together in shock. We seek comfort in each other's presence. Someone's brought a radio, and we listen to newscasters' announcements, politicians' damage control, and crowds of people in distress. We think of our families and our hometowns. Our new reality settles over us. Shock gives way to anger. Pain gives way to rage. Despair lurks at the edges, and we try to fend it off.

We part before midnight, agreeing to try to get some rest before the SAS meeting in the morning. I gave up on the Society of Afro-American Students early in my first year here, but everything feels different now.

Charles and I cross the cool campus lined with towering buildings of brick and limestone. The names of ancient European philosophers haunt us from the carved walls. Will King's name ever join theirs? The Alma Mater gazes out from her perch on the steps of Low Library. Below the wreath on her head, stains run down the green patina on her face, giving her the look of a bleeding Jesus stuck with thorns.

In the dorm, Charles follows me into my room and sits on my bed, staring into space and worrying his hands. I open my window and lean out, gazing at the chaos the night has brought forth.

Harlem is on fire. Orange flames reach out of broken store windows and lick the sidewalks. Black smoke escapes through iron bars, rising to reach the sky. I can almost smell the smoke, almost hear the tinkling of shattered glass. It brings me calm, relieves my tension, as if I'm out there throwing things and screaming at the world too.

"You think the riots will reach campus?" Charles breaks me out of my reverie.

I imagine Columbia students fleeing a burning campus, facing the devastation of an oppressed people instead of tsking from afar. "I almost wish they would," I say.

Charles joins me at the window. He watches the clouds of smoke, and he trembles. "No," he says quietly. "No, you don't. You think you do, but you don't."

We stand in silence for a minute.

"Remember when we burned those newspapers?" I ask him. "So close to the student center, people thought we were gonna burn this mother to the ground." We had asked the campus newspaper to apologize for its "joke" about the new Black fraternity on campus, but we were met with claims of free speech and humor. So we broke into the newsroom, collected the newspapers, and made a bonfire outside, right in the middle of campus.

Charles gazes out the window. He wasn't with the group of brothers who burned the newspapers, but he heard about it, like everyone else did.

"Violence is the only language some people understand," I say.

Years of peaceful protests. Change is coming, but how slowly? How many lives have been lost chasing integration? Because they're disposable lives. Let a threat come anywhere near a place like this, then we'll start to see some change.

Charles turns away from the window, and I think he's going to storm out of my room. Instead, he turns again and paces back and forth. "Violent revolution is not an option," he says. "We can't win."

"That's what Dr. King said."

Charles stops pacing and wipes his face with his hands.

I can't tear my eyes away from the smoke. A distress signal. A warning. If we can take the rest of the country down with us, self-destruction feels better than doing nothing.

Charles is anxious about his future. His college degree. If the riots reach Columbia, how long will school shut down? Will we have to repeat the semester? Will graduation be delayed? Charles's plan to become a successful doctor and take care of a long list of family members has been in place since he was little.

He has everything to gain here. If this chance slips through his fingers, his everything is lost. That's the burden his family sent him with.

For me, the expectation is casual. Of course I'll get my degree. Just like my father did, and his father and mother before him. I'm not allowed to call my family's pressure a burden. I'm supposed to be grateful for the leg up.

Tonight Charles can't study. He stays in my room until the uprising ends. It stops far short of Columbia's gates and not long after midnight.

Harlem is our neighbor, but it is a separate world. Not even the murder of the King of Peace can bridge that divide.

Thin rays of light stream through my dirty window. I barely remember Charles leaving, and I don't remember falling asleep. I stare into space for a minute and relive last night.

The shouting in the hallway. The radio. Richard. Melvin's room. The fires. The fires. Harlem.

Mike.

I sit up quickly.

How could I not think of him last night?

The flashing lights were red, not blue, so I let myself hope the police were standing down. No billy clubs, snarling dogs, or bullets. I hope.

I have to go see him. If I know his mother, she had him locked inside, and I'm glad. Mike, tall and broad-shouldered but baby-faced, is a boy often mistaken for a man. There will be a day soon when his mama can't hold him back anymore. I know this because I see myself in him, I see my cousin Robbie in him, I see the desire to know, to make a place for himself in the world, and I see the world saying no, just like it said no to us. But he hasn't given up yet, and I hope he won't.

I change clothes quickly and put on my watch, a gift from my dad. Its elegant face reminds me I'll have to call home soon. I push the thought away and calculate how much time I have to get to Harlem and back for the ten a.m. SAS meeting. Ninety minutes. I can do it if I hurry.

I jog down the stairs and through the common room. Small groups of students sit and stand together, speaking in hushed tones. A bulletin on both sides of the front door announces, *Morning classes canceled due to national mourning.* So they expect us in class this afternoon. I shouldn't be surprised.

I make my way toward the gate on Amsterdam Avenue, scanning the campus green for Black folks. A few brothers

45

stand close together, talking intensely. Lots of white students sit around looking stunned. Some coeds from Barnard huddle together and comfort one another openly. I pass through the black, cast-iron gate topped with golden crowns, and turn north toward Harlem. Block by block, the landscape changes. The buildings, the streets. Even the color of the sky.

Alone in Harlem, I think of Robbie, my cousin who first brought me here, sneaking me out when I was barely a teenager to make me listen to Malcolm X on the crowded corner of 125th and Adam Clayton Powell, back when it was 7th Avenue. I was terrified and thrilled and forever changed. If I am perfectly still, I can hear the echoes of the microphone and the crowd on that hot day in late summer. Especially when I go to Micheaux's bookstore, Malcolm's ghost welcomes me.

After ten minutes of walking, I reach the damaged parts of town. Broken glass shines in the sunlight like diamonds and crunches under my shoes. Iron bars that used to protect store windows have been pulled down so their tops touch the ground. Shelves sit emptied of overpriced milk and diapers.

When I reach Mike's apartment building, I'm relieved that homes are not damaged. I ring his bell and stand back on the sidewalk, where he can see me from his window. His face appears four floors above me, and I wave. Thirty seconds later, he bursts out the front door, still putting his arms through his jacket sleeves, laces undone on his worn shoes. I make a mental note to find out his shoe size.

We clasp hands, and I can't help myself—I bring his head

to my shoulder in a protective embrace. He groans and I let go.

"All right, all right. I was worried. How are you holding up?"

He shrugs his shoulders and sits on the stoop. "Ain't nothing new. Was only a matter of time before they killed him too." His jaw is tense, and his brown eyes hold a hardness that I haven't seen before.

I sit beside him on the stoop.

We have seen so much death. I was ten when the violence became visible, broadcast on national and international news. He would have been six. Police watched racists drag activists from lunch counters and attack freedom riders as they escaped burning buses. I picture Mike at nine years old seeing photos of Black girls a few years older than himself who'd been killed in a church bombing. Watching President Kennedy crumple in his convertible, bleeding out in the First Lady's lap. Mike would have been twelve when Malcolm X was killed just a few blocks away from here.

Mike and I are closer than some of the other pairs in the tutoring program, the university's attempt to show some investment in the local population. Giving with one hand while it steals—land, buildings, and hopes—with the other. Like ambassadors or spokespeople, we are supposed to show them that Columbia, and the world, can and should be theirs too. But this offering, this road map out of the ghetto, becomes meaningless when the world keeps showing you that no matter how educated you are, no matter how well-spoken or religious, respectable or middle class, you will always be Black, and that is all that will matter.

An elderly woman in a blue housedress arrives at the stoop and holds on to the railing, catching her breath. Mike and I stand to let her pass.

"Good morning, Mrs. Washington," Mike says in his talking-to-grown-folks voice.

"Mikey. How are you today? And how's your mama?"

"We're fine, thank you. You need any help getting upstairs?"

"Aren't you precious. No thank you, sweetheart. You enjoy your visitor. Who is this fine young gentleman?" She looks me up and down as if she could gobble me up.

"This is Kevin, my tutor from Columbia."

I hate being introduced as "from Columbia" when I'm in Harlem, but there's no explaining that, so I keep letting it happen.

"Oooooh, my my my!" Mrs. Washington puts her hand to her chest. "Handsome *and* smart?" She beckons me closer and mock-whispers, "I have a granddaughter, you know." She giggles like this is the funniest thing in the world. Then she actually pinches my cheek, which is already hot.

Mike laughs at me. As she climbs the stairs, I recover enough to say, "Nice to meet you, ma'am."

"You too, darling," she calls. "See you later, Mikey."

"Yes, ma'am."

We sit on the stoop again. I'm grateful for the spring breeze.

"Mom won't let me go anywhere," Mike says, "even though the riot's over. And it wasn't nearly as bad here as it was in other cities. She still thinks I might get in trouble. Does it look like trouble out here to you?"

"Maybe not. But you know parents. She's scared."

Mike glares down the street. "I bet my friends were out last night. Getting stuff their families need. I heard nobody got hurt and there was hardly any arrests."

I nod. "It definitely could have been worse. That doesn't mean it was safe though." I feel selfish, worried more about Mike's safety than about his integrity as a young man. I know that living every moment safely is hardly living at all. I know that being forced to stay calm rots the soul. I admit, "I wanted to be out here last night too."

He pauses. "You did?"

"Yeah. The rage is real. There's no denying it. We can't get used to it. It keeps building. You don't want to feel helpless. You don't want to accept what's happening. I feel that. We all feel it. I bet your mom feels it too."

He scoffs. "Not her. 'Patience and the Lord.'"

"That's where some people get their strength. Faith can protect a person so the rage doesn't destroy them. It doesn't always mean they have to stop fighting. Sometimes it can help them to keep fighting." I'm thinking of my cousin, but I don't mention him.

"Well, if she's gonna keep me in like this, I'm gonna have to sneak out or something. She knows about the student coalition. She supported it before. But now she's talking about lying low and letting things quiet down."

A window opens above us, and his mother calls out.

"Mikey?"

He stands up and faces her. "Yes, ma'am."

"Bring that boy up here for something to eat."

"Oh!" I stand too. "Thank you, Mrs. Hammond, but I can't stay—"

She puts her hand up to shush me. "While it's hot!" The curtains fall closed.

I check my watch and tell Mike, "I have a meeting soon."

"Too late now," he says. "Eat quickly."

He opens the door, lets me in, and looks down the street both ways before following me inside. The hallways are dark, even in the daytime, and reek of mildew. On the walls are flyers for the upcoming rally.

"Hey, did you put these up?" I ask him.

He puts his finger to his lips, grinning. "Don't tell."

I follow him up four flights of stairs and wonder how older ladies like Mrs. Hammond and Mrs. Washington make this climb every day. Mike knocks on his own apartment door, letting his mother know we're entering. His manners always impress me.

His mother stands in the tiny kitchen, serving up a plate of food that reminds me of my nana's house. "Come on in." She sets the plate on the table along with a fresh cup of coffee. "What's this nonsense about not having time to come upstairs?"

My stomach rumbles as I gaze at the plate and savor the aromas. Grits and gravy and fried eggs with buttered toast vie for my attention. "This is incredible," I say. "You really shouldn't have—"

She holds up her hand again, and I shut my mouth. Like my nana, Mrs. Hammond doesn't want praise and thanks. She wants to watch me eat. So I do.

"I appreciate it," I tell her, picking up my fork. "I just came by to check on Mike and make sure you were doing okay."

"That's very thoughtful of you," she says.

Mike stands at the window in the living room, watching the street. I wonder if he held vigil there all night like I did from my room.

"Michael," Mrs. Hammond says. "Aren't you going to sit with our guest?"

He joins us at the table as I'm stuffing my mouth.

"There's more," she tells him.

"No thank you," he says, confirming my fear that she cooked this spread just for me.

"They're saying Harlem was nothing compared to some other cities," she says, folding over the newspaper. "Chicago. DC."

"Is that right?"

"Mm-hm. They've got the National Guard out in several cities. The army in DC."

"The army?" I repeat, dumbfounded.

"The army, Kevin." She puts the paper down and sighs. "I should let you eat. No use ruining your appetite. How are you students doing on campus?"

"Well," I say, between bites, "mostly it's a lot of shock. I stayed in last night."

Her eyes send I-told-you-so darts at Mike, who looks away.

"But this morning . . . It feels different somehow. Like, maybe there's going to be a deeper divide?"

Mrs. Hammond fans herself. "That's how it goes," she says. "One step forward, ten steps back. People who haven't been paying attention have no idea how we got here. This one really struck me though. I know some people thought he went too far supporting the sanitation workers' strike. And criticizing the war. Still . . ." She shakes her head. "I can't hardly believe they would shoot down that man. For his principles. Mm."

My throat tightens. It was a shock. At the same time, it is not only believable but inevitable. I trace a circle around my plate, sopping up the gravy and egg yolk with my last bite of toast. I chew slowly and fight the urge to lick my fingers.

Mrs. Hammond watches me approvingly and reaches for my empty plate. "I'm going to serve you some more."

"Oh no, please," I say quickly. "Thank you so much—this was delicious. I haven't eaten like that since—since I was last home, I guess! But I really do have to get going. We have a meeting, the Black students, in . . ." I check my watch. "Oh, twenty minutes. I have to get back. I will come by again though." I nod at Mike.

Mrs. Hammond eyes me skeptically, one fist on her hip, the other hand holding the plate.

I pat my stomach, offer my best I'm-so-satisfied smile and push out my chair. "Do you mind if I take a look at the paper before I go?"

She hands me the newspaper and refills my half-finished coffee mug.

Mike drums his fingers on the tabletop. He looks like a bird trapped in a cage. I unfold the newspaper and scan the lede lines and photographs. Other cities are still burning. There are places that resemble war zones. The riots advanced to only blocks from the White House. I check for Boston, thinking of my sister. There were riots but no casualties. That's a relief.

The president, mayors, and other men with loud voices chastise the people who display their anger in the city streets. Dr. King lived and died for nonviolence, they say. Let us honor his memory and be peaceful in our grief.

They do not quote King directly. They do not promise to heed his advice to eradicate these displays of grief by eradicating the causes of the anger, despair, and discontent. They do not talk about equality and jobs and justice. They haven't even caught the killer. All those policemen surrounding the Lorraine Motel and not one saw a suspect running from the crime scene.

As I refold the paper, an envelope falls out and drops to the floor. I bend to pick it up, but Mrs. Hammond says, "I'll get that," and scrambles to grab it. In the second before she takes it, I catch a glimpse of block letters stamped on the outside of the envelope: EVICTION NOTICE.

Mrs. Hammond tucks the envelope into the pocket of her apron and folds her hands over it protectively. She glances at Mike and then back at me with a small, tight smile.

My mind races. Is she hiding this from Mike? She's trying to keep home, and this would fuel his fire even more. But how long can she pretend?

I place the newspaper gently on the table, as if to prevent more devastation from tumbling out. I have so many questions, and I can't ask any of them. I take a final sip of coffee, which I can no longer taste, and place the mug gingerly on the table.

"Well," I whisper, standing.

Mrs. Hammond pats my arm and beams at me with the confident eyes of the faithful. I bend down and give her a hug. Maybe I hold on for a second too long.

"You come by anytime, Kevin," Mrs. Hammond says. "We'll be right here."

*How long?* I wonder.

Mike walks me back downstairs.

I consider walking the long way to pass by Robbie's office, but I don't want to be late for the meeting. I hurry toward campus with that envelope on my mind. Is a notice a warning? Does it mean eviction is imminent? How can I talk to Mrs. Hammond in private to find out what's going on? Not that she wants me in her business. She sees me as a kid too. But maybe I can help. Maybe if she's behind on rent, Dad could help out. But what if it's not about overdue rent? What if Columbia is pushing them out to get control of their building?

Every time the university expands, people get displaced. The university has been trying for years to "clean up" surrounding neighborhoods to make them more desirable and offer them to the families they want to teach and work here. I've heard horror stories of people getting pushed out by the university. Evictions of the most vulnerable. Increasing rent while being worse than slumlords—releasing rats into buildings to make it impossible to stay. What if it's not about overdue rent? And what if it's not only their family?

But I've heard success stories too. Tenant organizations

that fought the university, using all sorts of tactics to stay in their homes. We've supported some of those groups in the past. We need to make this a top priority now. I decide I'll bring it up at the SAS meeting.

I'm lost in my thoughts when I rush past the statues, through the tall iron gates and into campus. I edge my way around a mass of students who are moving slowly.

Behind me, someone calls out, "Excuse me! Hey!"

Then a hand grips my shoulder. I throw it off as I turn around and put my fists up, ready to fight. A group of brothers got into it with some athletes a few weeks ago, and I'm always on guard. This isn't a student though. A campus security officer in a crisp, beige uniform holds his hands up.

"Easy," he says. "Sorry to startle you. I just need to see some ID."

He thinks this will calm me down. As if I won't notice I'm the only person he's stopped.

This is not the first time this has happened, and it won't be the last. But I can't help it. Every single time. A part of me is angry, and a part of me is incredibly sad.

Looking into his dark brown face, I want to see a brother. I want *him* to see a brother when he looks at me. Instead, I see an agent of the system, using his uniform for authority against his own.

And what does he see? A bougie young Black man he can take down a notch by humiliating me? By reminding me this is not my territory? Does he see that by stopping me, he's stopping himself? Does he think I can't belong here because he never could? I crave the proud smiles of

Mrs. Hammond and Mrs. Washington now.

I put my hands on my hips, considering my options. Refuse on principle and escalate the situation, or give in and be angry all day.

I try not to sound as defensive as I feel. "I'm a student. I left through this gate an hour ago."

"Okay," he says amicably. "I just need to see your ID."

I watch some white students pass by unbothered. I grind my teeth.

I want to be calm. This man is older—not old enough to be my father but close enough. No hint of malice shows on his face. Maybe I can wake him up.

"Tell me," I say, "were you instructed to stop only Afro-Americans? Or did you make that decision yourself?"

He looks me up and down.

"What about that large group of white people who came in at the same time I did?" I point after them. "You didn't ask for their IDs."

Something crosses his face. He's forming a new opinion of me. His voice becomes gruff. "Look, I have a job to do, and I'm doing it. I have to make sure everyone's affiliated—"

"What exactly makes you think I'm not affiliated with Columbia?" My voice is too loud, but I can't bring it down.

He blinks at me with steady eyes. The black visor on his cap shines in the sunlight. He smirks and looks to the side, like he's decided who he's dealing with. He fingers his walkie-talkie.

That's when I decide I would rather miss the SAS meeting than pull out my ID.

I look pointedly at his hip. "Need to call for backup?" I fold my arms and broaden my stance.

From the corner of my eye, I see another guard pacing at the gate, watching us. The other guard is Puerto Rican, and he looks younger than this one. He looks like he's considering coming over. Would he defend his colleague or me?

A familiar voice at my side jars me, and our standoff is interrupted.

"How's it going, officer?" Charles. He holds up his ID for the guard. "He's with me. Always leaving his ID in the dorm. Right, Kev?"

I can't even look at him.

"Everyone's kind of tense today," he says to the officer apologetically. "You understand."

The officer looks between us for a few moments. Then he nods once at Charles. He adjusts his cap, turns slowly, and strolls back to his post at the gate. He hooks his thumbs in his belt loops and pretends to monitor who's entering campus, but he's still watching me.

The guards are trained to look for outsiders. I am always an outsider.

Charles puts a hand on my shoulder and starts walking. "Let's go. We're already late."

I shrug his hand off me.

"Were you gonna stand there all day arguing with him and his supervisor and the head of security?"

I might have, but I don't respond. The clean walkways, the manicured lawns, the memorials, and tall Roman columns make me want to break things.

"We have to get to the meeting," he says. "It's important."

I scoff. "It's always important. Doesn't mean anything gets done."

Charles says nothing. We walk across the plaza, past students standing on steps and sitting cross-legged on squares of grass.

I let out a forceful breath. "You Negroes love to think that just being here is doing something," I say. "If we don't even stick up for ourselves, we're not changing this place, so what does it matter that we're here?" My hands are clenched, and my whole body is tense. "Defending this place is even worse," I mumble, mostly to myself.

Charles puts his hands in his pockets. "I know it's not right, the way they stop us, but . . . I think you're a little hard on them. From their perspective, they think they're just doing their job. They need these jobs. Just like the cafeteria workers and everyone else. They don't have this opportunity we have." He sighs. "I try to be patient with them."

I do not understand Charles sometimes. Patience? Where has that gotten us?

"By the way," he says, probably eager to change the subject before I can wax political again, "I saw Rich and Wesley at breakfast. They say we're taking our grievances straight to the president today."

I say nothing, but I pick up my pace, eager to see what that will look like.

A year ago, Charles came home with me for spring break. Ever since he visited our suburban home, I think he's been less tolerant of my politics. Maybe he decided I have nothing to complain about. To change his mind, I'd have to go way back. And still, I don't know if he'd understand.

Charles didn't have money for a ride home for spring break, so he planned to stay in the dorm. I wanted to pay for his ticket home, but I knew he wouldn't accept it, and I feared he'd be offended if I offered. So instead, I asked if he wanted to come visit my home in Finchburg. A bus ticket as my guest wasn't too big a deal. He smiled so wide, I was immediately glad I had thought of it.

He was like the son Mom and Dad never had. He sat quietly with Dad, appreciating his jazz records. I showed Dad some of my new books from the bookshop in Harlem, maybe hoping to provoke an argument for old times' sake. Mom glanced over nervously. Dad simply peered over his glasses at the titles and said, "Uh-huh!" Like I was a six-year-old showing off my crayon drawings.

Charles complimented Mom on her cooking at every single meal and made polite small talk too. He asked her about the art displayed throughout the house and listened, truly fascinated, as she told him about the cultures from which they hailed. He refilled the bird feeder for God's sake and sat outside watching the sparrows and robins land, peck, and fly away, his face radiating delight. He made it seem easy to get along with my parents.

He called home once, and he described our little brick house to his sister like it was a small palace.

"He has his own room, with an extra bed!" he said. "And

they have two bathrooms, both inside the house. One up-stairs, one downstairs!"

On the bus back to the City at the end of the week, I claimed a pair of seats near the front. Charles glanced nervously at the bus driver before stowing his bag and sitting next to me. I faced the window as more passengers got on, but I could feel his gaze on me, so I turned to him.

"What?" I asked.

He chuckled. "You really have no idea how lucky you are, do you?"

I turned back to the window. There were things I couldn't explain to him without sounding like the ungrateful son our parents already thought I was. Even if I could explain, he would have gladly traded my struggles for his. So I didn't try. I trained my eyes out the window and said, "Yeah. Of course I do."

On the bus, I pretended to sleep, but really, I let myself remember the first time we saw that house.

### August 1956

Mom and Dad had been house hunting for weeks. Dad's new job in Albany wanted him to start as soon as possible, and Mom and Dad wanted us settled before the new school year began. Normally Dawn and I stayed in Brooklyn with Nana while Mom and Dad went upstate for the day, hunting for homes to rent or buy in the suburbs of Albany. They would return in the evening tired, frustrated, not quite defeated, but more discouraged with each passing week.

This time, they were confident. So confident they brought us with them.

It was August. Hot in the City but not unbearable. Dad drove with the windows down, and he and Mom smiled at each other every now and then, sharing thoughts without speaking. I felt my shoulders relax in the back seat—I hadn't noticed how much I had been worrying. I started to imagine our new town. What would our school be like? What parks would be nearby? What sports would the neighborhood kids play?

Dawn was unusually quiet in the car. She gazed out the window and stared up at the sky. I would glance at her, and sometimes she would catch my eye and giggle like we had a secret.

This was the beginning. This car ride. The four of us— quiet, in our own thoughts, but together too. Expecting.

The drive was long, about three hours, and as we pulled off the highway, we sat forward in anticipation. We were ready to see the place, to turn the idea of it, the promise, into our reality. As we entered the suburbs, the houses flattened and spread out. Concrete gave way to grass and trees, yards and gardens, cars and bicycles parked outside. We practically leaned out the windows, inhaling that fresh air, adoring the sunlit green. Dawn scanned the yards for people, gasped slightly when she saw a child her age. Neighbors chatted, leaning over fences, and I wondered what they thought when they watched our car pass slowly by.

Dad referenced the directions, scribbled in his illegible doctor's script, as he drove carefully through the calm streets. Finally, Mom said, "That's it!" And Dad turned onto

Melon Street. I read the street sign, thinking I would need to memorize our new address.

We pulled up to a brick house with white shutters and flowerpots out front. Number eighteen on the white mailbox. He parked the car and shut off the engine. We sat looking at the house for a few moments, holding a collective breath, sensing, perhaps, that we were saying goodbye to Before and crossing a threshold into After. Our Happily Ever After at last.

"Well," Dad said. A man of few words.

Mom turned to him, broken from her reverie. They both looked back at us and smiled. Mom appraised our faces and hair and double-checked our clothes. Were my shoes still shiny, my slacks clean and pressed, my collar straight? Was the bow of Dawn's dress tied, her curled bangs in place, her Mary Janes still unscuffed? Mom nodded her approval, then smoothed her own short black hair and the pleated skirt of her summer dress.

Finally, Dad opened his door, then the three of us opened ours. Dawn squinted against the sunlight as I rounded the car to stand next to her. Dad put his arm gently on Mom's back, and we followed them up the slate path toward the porch.

I wonder at what moment they regretted bringing us along.

When the front curtains rustled and then closed? When the owner stepped out onto the porch and closed the door behind him instead of stepping aside to let us in?

"Hello!" he said, a bit too loudly. His brown hair was hastily combed away from his face. His short-sleeved, button-up shirt was tucked into his creased slacks.

"Mr. Adams." Dad stuck out his hand.

Mr. Adams took his hand and shook vigorously. "Great to meet you. So, you're, uh, you're Dr. Wilson?"

"I am," Dad said. "And this is my wife, Mrs. Wilson. And these are our children, Kevin and Dawn."

We were lined up on the side of the porch, gazing at the yard, and we plastered polite smiles on our faces at the sound of our names.

"Lovely," he said. "Beautiful family." He stood in the shade of the covered porch. The air was much cooler than in the City, but Mr. Adams had begun to sweat. He dabbed his temples with a handkerchief and placed it back in his breast pocket.

"It's a very nice street, as you mentioned." Dad reached for something to say.

"Oh yes, absolutely. Best neighbors a person could want. Nice families in every direction, I tell you. Very open and accepting." He looked off down the street. Cleared his throat.

"I'm glad to hear that," Dad said. "I was pleased that we came to an agreement over the phone. It's a relief to have found a place in time for the children to enroll in school. We would love to see inside before signing the papers." He gestured toward the door. "Shall we?"

Mr. Adams shrank. He scanned the street again, as if there might be spies. It was eerily still. "You see, the thing is . . ."

Mom's feet shifted in her low heels. Her eyes widened and flew to Dad's face, and Dad's face dropped. Her Beside me, Dawn started to fidget.

63

"I, uh, I don't know...," the man said. "I don't know if this will work after all. I mean, I wasn't aware... You see... Well, this is the kind of neighborhood where everyone knows each other, see? Everyone knows that Grace and I are leaving. So they're counting on us to sell to a family that will be... the right fit for the place." He looked everywhere but at our faces. "I hope you understand."

Dad put his hands in his pockets and cocked his head. He was no longer smiling, but he didn't look angry either. To a stranger, his face looked blank, but I watched a shadow draw the warmth from his eyes.

Mr. Adams kept talking to cover Dad's silence. "If it were me, I'd have no problem with it, see. I treat everybody the same. I believe in equality, I really do. How are we going to learn to get along if we can't live together, right?" He smiled. A heartless, broken smile. He peeked, finally, at Dad's face. He glanced at the window behind him. "Well," he said, "I would show you the place, but it's, uh, it's not a good time, and I... I just don't think it's going to work after all. I am sorry."

"I'm not sure I understand, Mr. Adams," Dad said. "We spoke on the phone a few hours ago, and you assured me we were agreed—"

"Right, right. I truly am sorry about the misunderstanding. Someone called—a bit after we spoke... a friend... and they're considering buying, and—well, there was no way to reach you to tell you not to come, so..." He sniffed, looked down at his shoes and then at me and Dawn with a pitying frown.

Mom folded her arms and drew her eyebrows together.

She opened and closed her mouth as if gasping for air, for words, for sense.

Dad took in the house, as if appraising it from the outside, imagining its interior. Finally, he said, "I see." He extended his hand again. "Mr. Adams." They shook, and Dad wished him a good afternoon before turning us toward the sidewalk.

Mr. Adams stood on the porch, watching us walk away. Dawn looked back at him, at the house, at the window, where the curtains parted slightly again. I didn't want him to think we were longing for what he was denying us, so I put my arm around her and said, "Come on." Knowing somehow that our dignity was on the line.

We piled back into the car, closed and locked the doors. As Dad started the car and drove back the way we had come, we all stared straight ahead.

### Friday, April 5, 1968

Charles and I slow down as we approach the lounge where SAS is meeting. The room is packed with Black undergraduate and graduate students. Fatigue shapes every face. The sisters from Barnard sit on one side of the lounge. Some have red, swollen eyes and cheeks raw from wiping away tears.

I think of Dawn again. How hard is she taking this day? When we were younger, I would have been the first person she'd want to talk to at a time like this. Now I'm not even sure if I should call her.

Valerie sits with the Barnard sisters. Her soft, brown

afro is fluffed cloudlike around her head. Her normally vibrant face is drained and somber. Her intense dark eyes are focused on Wesley.

"This is a moment of reckoning," Wesley says. "It's a time to reassert our demands and priorities. We need to push this institution to change. It's our duty and our obligation."

"That's right," other voices add on.

The strong language and forceful tones take me by surprise. I haven't been to an SAS meeting in over a year. I had expected the group to be an activist space, but when I got here, the conservative members were in control, so the radical members couldn't get very far. Instead of sitting around arguing with bougie Black folks, I took my energy to the tutoring program, where the need was real.

It's not that I couldn't have done both. I didn't want to. Something about the differences between Black students on campus made me feel like a third wheel. I wasn't integrationist like the other middle-class Black students, but I wasn't down like the radicals, most of whom were working-class or poor. Or maybe that was all in my head.

Maybe I shouldn't have stayed away for so long. It looks like I've missed a big change. The leaders now are more radical, and almost all the Black students are here today. From the nods and murmurs around the room, it sounds like everyone wants some action.

*Good*, I think as I pull up a chair. *It's about time.*

# 3

## GIBRAN
*Massachusetts | September 1995*

When I get home from school on Friday, my friend Supreme from around the way is sitting on my steps. I glance at the driveway and am relieved to see it's empty.

"Peace to the god, how you be?" I say as I approach the house.

"I'm maintaining, sun." He extends his hand, and we dap each other up.

I drop my backpack on the porch and sit next to him.

"You coming from school?" he asks.

"Yeah," I say. "It's my last year."

"That's good, that's good," he says. "Keep doing your thing. That's righteous."

I want to say I don't have much choice. I don't know how much school Supreme finished, but he doesn't clown me for going to prep school, even though we build on other kinds of knowledge together. The way he sees it, any kind of knowledge can be helpful if you use it right. But he doesn't know firsthand what it costs to get some of it.

"We're having a little house party tomorrow night over at Rakim's house," he says. "You should come through."

"Aight, no doubt, I'll be there."

He's been drinking already. I hope Mom won't notice if he's still here when she gets home. She doesn't like the friends I've found in the hood. Or the fact that I've found friends in the hood. She took us from the streets when we were little, and I keep trying to get back. She thinks they're a bad influence, the streets and the friends I find. But I don't want to separate myself from any of my people.

A blue hatchback chugs up and stops in front of the house. Ashanta's in the passenger seat. She waves at me and glances at Supreme. She talks to her husband for a minute, then opens her door and steps out of the car. Her long-sleeved dress ripples to her feet as she stands.

"Hey," she says to me. "Mom's not home?"

"Nah," I say. "She should be home soon."

"Okay." She shuts her door, and Kareem leans over to roll down the passenger-side window and wave at me.

"How are you?" he calls. He nods at Supreme.

"Aight," I say, throwing him a peace sign.

Ashanta opens the back door of the car and throws the edge of her hijab over her shoulder before reaching in to unstrap her baby from the car seat. She sits baby Zakiyyah on one hip and pulls a diaper bag onto the other shoulder.

"Salaam alaykum," Ashanta says to Kareem as she shuts the door.

"Walaykum assalam." Kareem pulls off carefully from the curb, his old car sputtering with the effort.

Ashanta stands, waiting. There's enough space for her to

pass, but I guess she wants more. I get up and stand behind Supreme.

"Thanks," she says, climbing the stairs.

"Assalaam alaykum," Supreme says to her, slurring only slightly.

Ashanta barely looks at him. "Walaykum." She tries the doorknob, but the door is locked. I dig my key out of my pocket and unlock it for her. "Thanks," she says again. She lets out a breath as she enters the house.

"Aight, man," I say, picking up my backpack. "I'ma go catch up with my sister."

"Oh, okay, no doubt, do your family thing. I'll see you tomorrow then." He stands and then, as if it's an afterthought, says, "Oh hey, you got anything for me, just a little something? I don't have much on me though. . . ."

"No problem, I got you," I say. "I'll be right back."

I run up to my room and take a small bag of weed out of my drawer. I jog back down the stairs and hand it to Supreme as my mom pulls up.

"Thank you, I appreciate that, sun. I'll hit you back, I promise." He stuffs it in his pocket before Mom gets out of the car.

"It's all good," I say. It's putting me out a little bit, and he's probably not good for it, but Supreme's my boy, so I take care of him.

He waves to Mom, ecstatic to see her. "How you doing, Mom?"

She hates when he calls her that, but I don't have the heart to tell him to stop. He needs a mom, and he needs brothers.

"Hi, Supreme," Mom says, barely containing an eye roll as she pulls her shoulder bag out of her Volvo sedan.

She glares at me as she approaches the steps.

"Peace!" I hold up my hand to wave to Supreme, and Mom takes the opportunity to sniff me. I back up, nearly stumbling on the steps.

"Dag, Ma!"

She pats me, satisfied that I don't smell of any substances, and pushes open the door to the house. "My baby!" she cries when she sees Zakiyyah.

I follow her inside.

Mom kneels on the floor, still in her jacket, and hugs the baby. "Nana," she says, pointing at herself. "Nana." And then squeezes her some more before setting her down to crawl on the rug.

I sit on the couch, put one leg up, and stretch the other out in front of me. Baby Zakiyyah crawls over to me and pulls at my shoelace. She looks up at me to see what I'll do. I untie my shoelace and wave it at her like a nunchuck, making karate sound effects. She laughs. When I stop, she pulls my laces and watches to see if I'll do it again. I pick her up and throw her in the air until she screams and loses her breath giggling.

"Don't you drop my baby!" Ashanta and Mom say at the same time.

"Aw, see? They a bunch a scaredy-cats. Come on," I tell Zakiyyah. "Let's go have fun without them." I pick up her rattle and bring her to my room.

We play peekaboo, and she screams every single time. I teach her to shake the rattle to the time of my beatboxing.

"I need that baby!" Mom calls after just a few minutes.

"What I tell you, Z? They don't want us having too much fun. They just jealous." I carry her back downstairs and hand her to Mom.

I sink onto the couch, throw my arm over the back of it, and say to Ashanta, "So what's up with you? You can't talk to nobody?"

"Hm?" she asks. Her eyes go wide. "What do you mean?"

"My boy."

She frowns. "I responded to him."

"Yeah, like it was gonna kill you to speak."

"Gibran," Mom says, "you know those friends you pick up off the street aren't exactly compatible with—"

"Whoa—really? Are they stray cats or something?"

Ashanta and Mom look at each other as if to say, *If the shoe fits* . . .

"Wow. Okay. I mean, you can have your opinions. You don't have to like my friends. But you could not be rude to them. I'm not rude to Kareem."

"Kareem is a perfectly respectable person."

"So you're saying my friends aren't respectable."

She wrinkles her nose. "I mean . . . what kind of person names himself *Supreme*? I'm not calling a person by that name!"

"Okay," Mom says, cutting us both off. "I just got home from work. I'm trying to enjoy my baby."

Zakiyyah's wide eyes are flying from face to face.

Mom kisses Z's face. "Nobody meant to offend you or disrespect your friend, Gibran. Though I wouldn't mind seeing less of him."

Ashanta smiles, managing to look smug and conciliatory at the same time.

Ashanta became Muslim when she was younger than I am now. She was in college when she got married, and she insisted she'd finish school, but when she had the baby, she took a semester off, and no one's pushing her to go back. She's the first in generations to not finish college right away, but I'm the one getting hassled for having the wrong kinds of friends.

"I'm just saying, it wouldn't kill you to be polite," I say, not letting it go.

"Ashanta," Mom says, "clearly you hurt your brother's feelings."

I scoff, and Ashanta makes an impressive effort not to roll her eyes.

Mom stares both of us down.

Ashanta makes a face like she's tasting something nasty. "I'm sorry, Gibran," she mumbles.

"For?" Mom prompts her while tugging on the baby's frilly skirt.

Ashanta, deadpan: "Being rude to your friend?"

Mom turns to me.

"Aight," I say.

I swear, Mom's still gonna be making us kiss and make up when we're fifty and she's on her deathbed.

Mom holds Zakiyyah under her arms as the baby bounces on her tiny feet. "We do have a right to be concerned, Gibran," Mom says. "You'll have plenty of time to hang out with men who smell like alcohol *after* you graduate high school. Preferably after you graduate college since the legal drinking age is twenty-one. In case you've forgotten."

And just like that, the tiny, good feeling from the forced apology is gone.

*What I don't say*

It's funny that you want me off the streets now. Our earliest days, the ones we spent on the streets, were the happiest of our lives.

Growing up in Mattapan, our street was a world of its own. Everyone knew each other. Everyone was some shade of brown. There was no danger—not that I knew of—just fun, going from house to house collecting friends for games of hide-and-seek and tag, using the whole block as our playground until dusk. Our babysitter lived at one end of the street, and the corner store stood at the other end, beckoning our little fingers with all the penny candy a kid could want, although we rarely had pocket money to spend there.

I know you had every intention of keeping us in the city, among our people. It was the Boston public schools that spoiled your plans. You were teaching middle school, and your students adored you. But one day you came home with a black eye. You had tried to break up a fight, and one of your favorite students accidentally sent a fist into your face instead of the other kid's.

"I'm so sorry! I'm so sorry, Miss Wilson! Are you okay? Why'd you get in the way?"

At twelve, the kid was a head taller than you. You loved those kids, but you loved us more, and you couldn't see it, putting us in those schools. As soon as the bruise faded, you went to interview at White Oak School. The next week, after confirming the three of us would get scholarships, you brought us in for interviews too. You weren't planning to give over our entire lives. But it was inevitable.

We still lived in the city, but our days moved to the suburbs, and the days became so long that all we saw of our street anymore was the tired waves of families going inside at dinnertime.

By the end of our first year at White Oak School, our school friends had stopped laughing at our slang. We had transformed. Our tongues had absorbed the speech patterns we heard all day. When we rejoined our friends on the block for summer games, they were the ones asking, "Why you talking like that?"

A few years later, we moved. You hadn't admitted to your parents how much we were struggling, but when you needed help to get us into a "better" neighborhood, you swallowed your pride and let Gramps buy us a house. Still in the city, but in an enclave tucked away from the rest of Dorchester. The street is lined with stately Victorian homes so valuable that white flight never happened. One of few integrated neighborhoods, the streets are quiet and well-kept. It's a bubble, though from our end of the street, we can hear groups of loud, defiant teenagers passing by the bubble's edge.

We found friends in our new neighborhood. Approved friends. Kids who were in METCO, bussed out to suburban public schools each day. Kids whose parents valued education, "opportunities," and middle-class aspirations but didn't want to live divorced from their people. Kids who were

Black but spoke "proper" English with slang intentionally thrown in.

The older I got, the more I poked at the bubble. I was always the one to stray beyond the "good kids." Our new house was just close enough to the real world that I didn't have to stray very far.

Saturday, at last.

Colin's house is a modest mansion with expansive grounds hidden behind it. The boy who opens the door looks familiar, from school, but I don't know his name.

"Dude!" he says to David. Most of the white kids know David, either from sports or from coming up through Lakeside together in elementary and middle school.

"What's up?" David says.

"Come in, come—" He stops short when he sees me. He cuts his eyes at David. *You traitor*, he's probably thinking.

David steps inside. "Brought my boys."

"Whassup, man?" I give the kid a playful handshake and man-hug. "You glad to see me or what? Where's my man Colin at? Tell him G's in tha house!"

James shuts the door behind us, turning his face away to hide his laughter. David has mastered the straight face.

The boy who let us in decides to get away from us before Colin appears. "Coats upstairs. I dunno where Colin is. Probably in the kitchen. Maybe outside." He glares at David again before stalking off to a room where "Player's Anthem" blasts from some nice-sounding speakers. David gives him the finger as he walks away.

A double stairwell curves around the enormous entryway. Upstairs, we find the room with a pile of coats on the bed and toss ours on top.

Downstairs, we get drinks—no alcohol for me since I don't trust these people. I dig into a bowl of chips. Sliding doors from the kitchen lead out to a deck and a lawn that disappears into darkness. Someone going out the door asks, "You coming out?"

"Nah." We shake our heads.

He shuts the door behind him.

"White people love them some outdoors," I say.

James squints through the glass. "Is that a lake back there?"

"Dayum," David says. "How much you wanna bet they'll be skinny-dipping by the end of the night."

I gag. "We better be gone by then. Don't nobody need to see that shit."

A loud voice takes over the room. "Heeeey! My homies! What's up!" Colin, grinning and drunk, puts his arms around David and James. His plaid shirt hangs open over khaki shorts, and his bare feet are pale against the tile.

"Dude!" I yell.

Colin blinks at me. His eyebrows come together. "Wait—"

"Thanks so much for the invitation, man!" I clap my hand on his shoulder. "Oh wait . . . maybe it was your girl who invited me. What's her name again?"

Colin swallows. "Emily?"

"Yeah, that's right. Emily asked me to come. Yup, we're cool, me and Emily."

"What?" Colin says.

"Yeah, we go way back! She didn't tell you?" I laugh. "Anyway, this party is totally rad."

"Uh . . ." I can practically see a wave of nausea rise from his stomach to his face. He grips the sliding door in slow motion and struggles with the handle as if he's forgotten how it works. I reach in front of him and pull the door open real fast so he stumbles out.

"You're welcome! Anytime, dude!"

David and James laugh. "You're so foul."

"You don't even know who Emily is, do you?"

"'Course not."

We find the room the music is coming from. "Gangsta's Paradise" is playing now. The bass sends vibrations through the floor.

"Man," I grumble, "I actually liked this song for a minute."

"I'm sayin'," James agrees.

"Why they gotta steal everything?" My voice is drowned out by a chorus of white kids singing along with Coolio.

We sit on the arms of the biggest couch until its occupants get up in pairs and disappear. Then we take over the couch. We entertain ourselves by freestyling over the music.

*I could plant a seed in your mind and watch you make it grow*
*All my people fighting the power in high ratio*
*You could never humble me down I let my greatness show*
*Just don't let your lady know she just might want my baby yo*

"Oh snap!" James and David egg me on.

*I don't like to leave it to chance nah I'ma take control*
*If it's problems I'ma lay low until the case is closed*
*You can't fake the code cause the real do the knowledge*
*and wisdom*
*Ain't no competition not possible you stopping my vision*

After we run out of steam with our real lyrics, we make each other laugh with stupid rhymes over TLC's "Waterfalls." That's when I notice we have an audience. Kate, Christy, and Melissa are watching us and whispering behind their big red cups. When I stop laughing, I hear them saying, "Ohmygod, they're so good!"

I eye David and James. Our bubble has burst. We've become part of the entertainment, and I can't have that.

We stop rhyming and chill for a minute.

"Yo, you know if any of the girls are coming out?"

"Nah, I don't think so," David says. "I asked Malika. When I said Colin's name, she made a face like *ew*."

The Black girls don't usually make it out to these parties, which makes sense to me.

I find a clock. "Y'all wanna go check out that other spot?"

"Yeah," James says.

"Let's bounce."

As we're putting on our jackets in the bedroom upstairs, I notice two shoeboxes stacked on top of each other in the corner of the room. They're in perfect condition.

"Hold up a second," I say.

I peek inside the top box. Gleaming red high-tops with

78

no sign of wear. I've seen these before. I know what's in the other box, but I lift the lid to confirm. Another pair of the same sneakers, identical except in color. These ones are black.

"Yo, y'all remember these?" I ask. "This dude Colin was in that garbage talent show act?"

"Oh snap," James says.

I check the size of the sneakers. Size ten. "What size you wear?" I ask them.

David's an eleven and James wears a nine and a half.

I could fit a ten if I want to.

I pick up both boxes and tuck them under my arm.

"What you doin?" James asks.

"I need a bag." I scan the room. "Lemme check the kitchen." I bring the sneakers downstairs and open cabinets, looking for leftover shopping bags. A tall cabinet holds a broom, a mop, and . . . bingo. I shake open a bag and put in the sneaker boxes side by side. "Ta-da."

We leave Colin's house and head to Roxbury.

The bus ride is long. We spend it analyzing rich white kids' love of hip hop and gangsta rap. When I imitate their singing "Gangsta's Paradise," the bus driver glares at us in his wide rearview mirror, willing me to shut up. So I sing louder.

The party in Roxbury is filled with people I don't know, but I find Supreme quickly. He introduces us to his people. Judging by their names, most of them are Five Percenters like Supreme. Before I sit down, I give Supreme the box with the red sneakers.

"What's this?"

"A gift. Somebody was giving 'em away."

He opens the box. "Oh snap, these are nice! Who didn't want these?"

"Some kid at my school," I say. "You'd be surprised how much stuff they use for a day and then throw away."

We build with the guys, who are mostly older than us, and talk to some girls. We stay until we have to run to catch the last bus from Dudley Station.

Walking from the train station to my house, we're loud, but as soon as we turn the corner onto my street, we start whispering. Inside, I shut the door softly, and we tiptoe up the stairs.

The TV in Mom's bedroom plays her recorded soap operas at medium volume, which doesn't mean she's awake. I hope it'll cover the sound of our steps, but the floor creaks under our feet in the hallway. Dangit. This old house.

"Gibran?" Her voice is thick with sleep. If it wasn't the floor, it would be her psychic mom-sense. She probably woke up when we turned onto our street.

"Yeah, Ma," I say softly to her closed door. "We're home. It's me, James, and David."

"Okay." She yawns. "Goodnight. You boys better not be drunk or high. You know I'll know, and I won't feed you in the morning."

"Never!" I say as they creep past me into the safety of my room. "'Night, Ma."

Monday comes too quickly. After a morning full of classes, I have the busiest lunch period. The line for hot food snakes out of the kitchen area through the dining hall, almost to the double wooden doors at the entrance. Students sit at long, gleaming solid-wood tables talking, laughing, whispering, and flirting in between bites of their food. I swerve around tables, aiming for the front of the line, but when I see Chris standing alone near the end of the line, I change direction.

"Chris! Whassup?"

"Hey!"

"What you doing back here?"

"Waiting for food."

"Nobody told you we don't wait in the back of the line?"

He giggles as if I'm joking.

"Come on." I put my arm around his shoulder and steer him to the front of the line. "Pay attention. Stay with me."

His eyes dart everywhere.

"Don't worry," I tell him. "Nobody's gonna step to you. First of all, you're with me. Second of all, our people been waiting too damn long at the back." I lower my voice. "This is lesson number two. You remember lesson number one, right?"

He blinks.

"Lesson number one was, don't make the mistake of thinking these white kids have your back. Here's lesson number two. Embrace the fact that they're scared of us. Use it to your advantage. Watch."

At the serving area, I reach in front of some other kids to grab two trays. I hand one to Chris, who looks apologetically at the boy I reached in front of, a white boy wearing ripped jeans, chewing gum, and looking us up and down. I stare him down with a straight face. He rolls his eyes and turns away. *That's what I thought.*

When the kids getting their food move forward, I step right in with my tray, practically dragging Chris with me.

"D-Nice!" I call out to my man Derek, who's serving sandwiches. "What's up!"

"How you doing, young man?"

"I'm good." I push Chris in front of me. "This is Chris. He's new. Chris, that's Derek. You late for lunch, you need anything, just find Derek. He's the man."

Derek laughs.

Chris whispers, "Hi."

"Good to meet you, Chris. How's Lakeside treating you?"

"Fine." This boy's timidness does nothing for his tiny stature.

I pat him on the back. "He's a lil shy. He's learning. So what we got today?"

"Your favorite. Chicken sandwiches. Two, right?"

"You know that. Thank you, my man. You have a good day."

"All right now, you too, Gibran."

Chris thanks Derek for his chicken sandwich and follows me as I slide my tray down the railing to the next server. The boy we cut in line holds his plate toward Derek without looking at him, still talking to his friend. Derek's smile fades.

"Cheryl!" Steam from the food trays makes her brown cheeks shine like apples as she smiles warmly at us.

"How are you today, Gibran?"

"I'm great now that I've seen some friendly faces. We got fries today?" I rub my hands together. "Word. I'll take a big pile of those, please."

"And broccoli, right?" she teases.

I groan. "Okay, I guess. Just one piece. Thank you. Cheryl, this is Chris. Chris, that's Cheryl."

"Hello." She waves at him.

"Hi."

"See y'all later," I call over the shielded trays of food.

"Take care now," Derek says.

I throw a peace sign to Angel, who's working in the back, and he waves.

We fill glasses with juice, and I grab some brownies from the dessert counter and then lead Chris to the far table at the end of the dining hall. It's already lined with Black students. I slide between chairs and take a seat across from James and David. Chris surveys the dining hall before squeezing past me to sit down.

"Whassup, people."

"Nice kicks," James says.

"Thank you," I say.

We laugh. Chris waits for the joke to be explained.

"They just jealous of my style," I tell him. I don't want to give the poor kid a heart attack or make him an accomplice. It was pretty bold of me to wear dude's sneakers to school, but I couldn't help it. Part of me wants to see if he'll ever notice.

"We were talking about O. J.," David says.

"O. J. Simpson?" I stuff fries into my sandwich and pour ketchup on top. "Please. Y'all need to leave that nigga alone.

He got enough white people ready to lynch his Black ass." I take a big bite of my oversized sandwich.

"That's what I'm saying," James says. He leans in and lowers his voice. "The way they talk about him in my dorm? Man, you'd think he killed their mama."

"Of course," I say, still chewing. "They wish they could handle him like they did Emmett Till. They're pissed they have to go through the courts. Then they don't even bother to prove the case against him."

"They probably won't have to," David says. "It looks bad enough. A big Black guy and a dead white wife?"

"Yeah," I say. "That's why I don't mess with white girls. Well, that's not the only reason." I raise my voice and grin at Malika and Tanya. "They can't hold a candle to my Black queens, nahmsayin?"

They roll their eyes.

"Whatever," Malika says.

But they're smiling.

"For real though," I say, turning back to my boys. "You can't mess with white chicks. You're guilty as soon as you talk to 'em."

"Yeah, I know," James says. "But they swear they want his head for the sake of justice, like it has nothing to do with race."

"Yeah, right." I practically cough up my fries. I take a sip of juice. "If it was some white dude on trial, a football hero they adored, they'd be calling for 'justice'? I don't think so. They'd be shaking their heads saying, 'Damn, that team lost a good player. If only she hadn't cheated on him. They should let him keep playing.' "

"That's messed up," David says, "but it's true."

"They're hypocrites, and they don't even know it," I say. "Don't let it be some Black woman who's the victim. We wouldn't even hear about it."

I finish my chicken sandwich and pick up the second one.

"Chris," David says, "what's up?"

"Not much."

"Gibran's not getting you into any trouble, is he?" James asks.

Chris pauses.

"That was a joke," James says. "Gibran, what'd you do? The kid looks traumatized already."

"Me? Nothin! I'm helpin him get acclimated and shit. I introduced him to the kitchen crew today. Showed him the express VIP line for food. I'm takin care of him."

"Aight."

Chris still looks tense. I need to spend more time with this kid.

"You get to talk to your moms about the march yet?" David asks me.

"Nah, not yet. I had to show her the letter from my advisor, so I didn't wanna push my luck."

"Wait," Malika says. She leans toward us. "Are you guys talking about the Million Man March?"

"Yeah," James says.

"Are you trying to go?"

"Why you say it like that?" I ask.

"So you are?"

"I mean, we want to."

"Wow." Her eyes are wide beneath her curled bangs.

"Wow what?" James asks.

She turns back to Tanya and Lisa, one eyebrow raised, and tucks her chin-length hair behind one ear. "Nothing," she says.

We look at each other.

"Anybody know what that's about?" James asks.

We don't.

"Anyway," I say. "Our biggest problem is not having a chaperone from the school."

"Oh!" David says, holding back a laugh. "How 'bout Mr. Clarke?"

"Yeah, right," James says.

"That's perfect," I say. "We'd just have to drug and blindfold him to get him there."

It's kind of a fun thought. I'd love to see his face when he wakes up at the Million Man March.

I munch on my fries. "I was thinking," I say, "maybe a few of us could go down and stay with my uncle. Like not an official school trip. Take a Greyhound or something. That wouldn't work for the whole group though."

"That sounds dope," David says. "But yeah, I'd feel kinda bad leaving when we could do something here all together, including the younger kids and maybe other schools and stuff."

"Yeah," James says.

The sounds around us fade from students laughing and talking to the clatter of dirty silverware being dumped into bins and the clack of trays being stacked on the cafeteria's kitchen conveyor belt.

"Well, we have a few days before the next Brother

86

Bonding meeting," David says. "Let's try to bring a plan to the meeting."

"Word."

The girls push by us. "Excuse me," Malika says with fake attitude.

"My bad." David stops balancing his chair on two legs and scoots closer to the table so they can get by.

"By the way," Malika says, "are y'all coming to the BSU meeting?"

"Oh yeah," David says. "That's today, right?"

"Yeah."

"Bet. I'll be there"

She looks at me and James.

"No doubt," I say. "You should come too," I tell Chris. Then I turn back to Malika. "You can help us with our plan to go to the march."

"Yeah, right," she says, pursing her lips. "If you don't need us at the march, you don't need our help to get there."

"Oooooh," James and David say in sync.

"That's foul, Malika. I'ma remember that when the Million Woman March comes around. You know I'd help you."

She arches an eyebrow at me and saunters over to bus her tray.

The BSU meets in a classroom in the center of the main campus. The tall windows let in bright afternoon sunlight that highlights dust in the air and the grains in the old wooden table and chairs. There are way more kids here than at the Brother Bonding meeting, since there are more Black girls at the school than boys. Plus, it's more of an official school club, with elections for leaders and a faculty sponsor and everything. Chris sits with another ninth grader, who's wearing a leotard and sweatshirt with jeans, her curly hair in a neat bun. After five minutes of loud chatter, Malika calls us to order.

"Okay, everyone, let's get started. Hopefully most of us have met the new students, but let's go around and introduce ourselves anyway. Say your name, your class, your dorm if you're a boarder, and . . . uh . . . favorite cereal."

Everyone laughs.

"I'll start. I'm Malika, I'm coleader of the BSU this year. I'm a senior; I live in Jefferson. My favorite cereal is Cap'n Crunch."

When everyone's answered, including Mrs. Johnson, the faculty sponsor, Malika takes back the floor.

"Today we want to check in with the new students, take any questions, and then talk about some of the activities we do throughout the year. People can add ideas today or anytime, and join existing committees."

I'm tempted to bring up the march, but judging by the way the girls responded at lunch, now is probably not the best time. They announce events with other schools—some parties coming up this fall and the student-of-color conference in the spring—and talk about how to sign up and catch the school vans to the events.

After the meeting, Mrs. Johnson leaves for the library and students pack up. David gives us pounds and jogs over to the fields for soccer practice. James sticks around. Auditions for the fall play are tomorrow, so he's not that busy yet. When most of the lowerclassmen are gone, I turn to Malika, who's pushing in chairs around the table along with Lisa and Tanya.

"Lemme ask you something," I say.

Malika glances at me.

"How come you're against the Million Man March?"

"Oh my God," Malika says. "Are you for real?"

"Hell yeah," I say. "Why wouldn't you support it? Y'all complain enough about Black guys. I thought you'd want us to get our act together."

Lisa grins, showing her dimples. "Nobody's saying y'all don't have issues."

"Okay, then," I say.

"No," Malika says. "Not *okay, then.* You think you're gonna solve your problems by yourselves? Go off and affirm your place as the man, come back to the women and kids, and everything's gonna be fine?"

"I mean, it's not like everything's gonna be all good afterward. It's just a step. It's a commitment to man up. What's wrong with that?"

"Um, Farrakhan?" Tanya says, pulling her thick braids over one shoulder. "What more is there to say?"

"Come on," I say. "That's weak. You're gonna throw out a whole initiative of a million people 'cause you don't like everything the organizer ever said?"

"Well, yeah, kind of," Tanya says. "Leaders can't lead if they're not okay."

"Plus," Lisa adds, "it's not as if he made some mistakes in the past and regrets them now. The stuff he says wrong is ongoing. It's who he is, and he stands by it."

I suck my teeth. "The media nitpicks at Farrakhan 'cause he speaks the truth about racism in this country. They wanna discredit him so no one'll listen to anything he has to say. So many other Black leaders are endorsing the march. Socially acceptable people who wouldn't agree with half of Farrakhan's beliefs. They know how important this one point is, so they support it. You can't deny that."

Lisa sighs like I'm dense. "The whole concept is patronizing though. Men have to go off and make a show of being strong and responsible so they can come back and 'protect' the family?" She puffs out her chest in a show of mock-masculinity.

That is not how I see it. To me, it's a lot like our Brother Bonding meetings. The girls haven't objected to that, so why is it wrong on a bigger scale? We need this.

"Okay," James admits, "maybe it sounds kind of old-fashioned or whatever. But tell me this. Why is it so ridiculous to think the Black woman needs the Black man? Think about it. White women get put on a pedestal. Why can't we put our women on a pedestal too? Why is it insulting all of a sudden when it's us trying to be caretakers and Black women being queens?"

"'*Our* women,'" Tanya repeats.

"You know what I mean."

I throw up my hands. "Yo, if the white man hadn't convinced the Black woman that she didn't need us, we wouldn't even be having this conversation. Y'all would be telling your man to go do his thing and come home stronger and ready to protect you."

The girls shoot daggers at me with their eyes.

Malika shakes her head. "You should study our history more. Yes, of course we need our men. Our men also need us. That's all we're trying to say."

"I don't think anyone's disagreeing with that," James says.

I don't know what we're disagreeing about or if we're disagreeing at all. Of course we need Black women. As far as I'm concerned, we've relied on them too much. I don't have to study to see that. My mom's always worked harder than my father. I don't want to get into that here though.

There's a tense moment of silence while the girls sling their backpacks over their shoulders and straighten up some chairs.

"I'm hungry," Malika says to the girls. "Snack bar?"

"Okay," Tanya and Lisa agree. They file out the door.

"Later," Tanya says over her shoulder.

"Later."

The door swings closed behind them.

"Well, that went well," James says.

Neither of us has the energy to laugh.

It can't get much worse as far as support for the march, so I decide I might as well talk to Mom too. I get home before she does and cook dinner. I thaw some salmon and season it real good. I let it marinate while I chop potatoes and cook them on the stovetop, covering the pan when the oil pops. When the potatoes are almost done, I sauté some broccoli with garlic.

When she walks in at six, everything is ready. She pulls off her boots at the front door. "Ooh, you've been cooking? Smells good!"

"Yup! Dinner is served!"

She peeks in the kitchen. Her jacket is still on, and her big bag hangs from her shoulder. "Mmmm!" She grabs my chin and pulls me down to her level to kiss my cheek. "Thank you, baby. I'll be right back."

Two minutes later, she plops down in front of the gray Formica table, wearing a fluffy knit cardigan and slippers. She's left her earrings and necklace upstairs, but her rings and bracelets still shine on both hands.

I pour melted butter on the broccoli so she'll eat it, and arrange the food on her plate with a sprig of parsley and a wedge of lemon for fun. I place it on the table in front of her with a flourish. "Water? Juice?"

"Is there any mango juice left?"

"Yup." I pour her some and then make my own plate and sit down.

"Boy, you can cook!" Mom says with her mouth full.

"Glad you like it." I almost lick my fingers but then grab a paper towel before she smacks my hand.

Mom eats the good stuff first. She starts with the salmon, then the potatoes, then the broccoli, eating more slowly as she goes.

"So I'm in the art room today," she says between bites. "And this white boy comes up to me and says, 'Yo! Miss Wilson!' I looked at him and said, 'Excuse me?'" She makes her are-you-talking-to-me face. "You know he opened his mouth to repeat himself? I said, 'Young man.'" She crooks

92

her finger the way she does at her students when they're in trouble. "'Step into my office.' Now that was nice of me. I could have cussed him out in front of his friends. But did I? No. I brought him into my office and shut the door. I told him, 'I am your teacher. Do you address Miss Pearson this way? Do you address Mr. Reynolds this way? Or did you think because I look like this that you can talk to me like that?' Goodness gracious."

I laugh.

"Then he had the nerve to get all anxious. 'Oh! I'm so sorry, Miss Wilson! I didn't mean to offend you!'" She shakes her head. She gives up on her broccoli and pushes her plate away. "Well, this was the best meal I've had in quite a while."

"Good!" I finish my plate and wipe my mouth. "Can I ask you a question?"

"Uh-oh," she says. "What's up?"

"Nah, it's not bad. I don't think." I let my eyes roam over the faded yellow paint on the wall as I ask, "What you think about the Million Man March?"

"Oh. Wait, why? You want to go, don't you." She folds her arms and stares at me hard.

I squirm a little bit. "Um . . ."

She moans. "I should have seen this coming." She puts her hands on her face, and I can't tell if she's about to cry or pray or cuss me out.

I wait. Then I ask, "So . . . you're against it too?"

She pulls her hands down like I woke her up. "The march? Oh, no. Not at all. I am one-hundred-percent for the march. Black men stepping up and taking responsibility? Squashing beef and healing the community? Yes, please. I haven't seen enough of that since my father's generation. You know I've had a bad run with men."

"Yeah."

"I know plenty of men who need to go pull themselves together." She rests her cheek on a fist. "At some point, it became about ego. Profiling. Being right. Men in my daddy's generation? They were men of service. They were all about family. Community."

"That's what I'm saying. The girls at school don't get it. The Black girls—they're against it. They don't see why it should be only men."

She frowns, considering. "I can see that. When you're young and you have the energy to be on the front lines, you don't want to be excluded. We were like that too." She leans back and gazes out the window. "I changed when I had you kids. Once you have a family and you're trying to build a life with someone, there's a big difference between being with a man who takes responsibility for his family and one who doesn't. I didn't think about it that way when I was younger."

"Yeah," I say. "That makes sense." I've already vowed to be there for my family and treat them right. I've seen the toll it took on my mom not having that support. Maybe if my father were around, I'd feel differently about the march.

"Well," Mom says, "they're not wrong. If the men had tried to make a movement by themselves back in the sixties?" She whistles. "They would have self-destructed. Faster than they did, I should say. Y'all do have a tendency to need our energy. You men can burn yourselves out pretty quickly. Look at my generation. But I'm tired. At this point, I say, 'Good for y'all.' Go get yourselves together and then come back and talk to me. Shoot."

"Exactly," I say. "We're not going off to work on our own forever. We're in crisis right now. We need to get stronger so we can come back and work together."

"Mm-hm," she says, like it's the truest thing she's heard all year. She takes a toothpick from the paper cup on the table and picks at her teeth. "So. You actually want to go down to DC for the march?"

"Yeah, I mean, if we could figure it out. We were thinking of proposing a school-sponsored trip."

She raises her eyebrows.

"I know. It's a long shot. There's no Black faculty who would chaperone, so that probably won't work."

"Hm. It's a shame there are no Black men on the faculty. I mean, other than Mr. Clarke." She snorts. "After all that fighting we did in the sixties to change education. We got Black studies and Black people onto college campuses, but I guess it didn't trickle down to prep schools."

"Yeah, definitely not." I pick up her plate and stack it on mine. "I was brainstorming how we could still go. Maybe James and David and me could take a bus—"

She shoots me a look like I've lost my mind. "The three of you? By yourselves?"

"Just for the ride down—"

The same look.

"—then we could stay with Uncle Kevin—"

Her eyebrows meet, and her voice rises. "Did you talk to him? Did he come up with this?"

"No, no—I haven't talked to him since, what, Christmas! I'm just saying, he's always said his door is open—"

"Ha."

"What's that about, Ma? Why are you always so negative about him?"

She throws her toothpick on the empty plates I've collected and starts to chew her cuticles. "It's not a good idea. You boys are too young. I wouldn't send you down there by yourselves. Besides."

I wait. "What?"

"It's risky, Gibran, and you don't consider risk. You have to think about consequences. You're assuming nothing could go wrong."

"What could go wrong?"

She scoffs. "Should I make a list?"

"I mean, I can't make my life choices based on what might go wrong. That's not living. That's definitely not being a man."

She kind of glares at me.

"Now what?"

She shakes her head. Not in a disappointed or surprised way. In a sad way. Or scared.

I push my chair back. "All right. Fine. Forget it," I say, louder than I mean to. I stand up, stack the dishes, and dump her scraps into the trash. "I'm sick of this," I mumble as I put our dishes in the sink and turn on the faucet. "We're trying to do something responsible. Something meaningful, to show the world who we really are as Black men. But no one wants to hear it. Everyone has a problem with it. White people can't stand to see us come together. Even Black women won't support us. No matter what we do or how we do it, there's something wrong with it. And then everyone wonders why we don't care anymore."

She sits still in her chair.

"You are so much like my brother," she says. She takes a big breath and blows it out slowly.

I turn off the water and lean on the edge of the sink. "Is that a bad thing?" I ask.

She's quiet for a long moment. Then she says, "It doesn't have to be."

I don't know what that means, and she's not in the mood to elaborate. She's rubbing her temples, which means a headache is coming on. I don't want to trigger a migraine and ruin her whole week, so I decide to leave it alone.

We obviously don't have enough support to make the trip to DC. We'll have to settle for the Day of Absence. I can live with that. What I can't figure out is why Mom's so cold about Uncle Kevin. I always thought he was cool. His bookstore is more for love of the people than for making big money, but I've always wanted to go and check it out. The books he gives me for Christmas are always on point. I love hearing his stories about traveling in Africa. Is he a disappointment to the family, a bad example, because he didn't do one better than Grandpa? Was he supposed to get more degrees, earn more money, and buy more property? Was he supposed to grow up and forget about the revolution like everyone else did? If that's what their problem is, then I'm glad he's not following the family.

Next year, I'll be close enough to visit him on my own. I'll let Mom calm down about the idea of me going to the march before I ask about my uncle again. If she still won't tell me what the deal is, I'll have to ask him myself.

# 4

## KEVIN
*New York City | Friday, April 5, 1968*

The Society of Afro-American Students, SAS, is almost four years old. Richard and Wesley are outgoing leaders. Claudius, a junior and a newly elected leader, brings more of the military spirit that might shake things up if the conservative members don't hold him back. The three of them sit together by one wall, the rest of us in a messy semi-circle on couches and chairs around the windowless room.

"We have about six weeks left of the school year," Richard says, "and we want to make it count." He adjusts his large, black-framed glasses. The gap between his front teeth flashes when he talks. "We're preparing a statement about Dr. King. We see this as a chance to bring up some ongoing campus issues and demands."

Years of diplomatic discussions and well-written petitions to the university president and the board of trustees achieved nothing. I remember the long meetings we held to draft those letters and petitions. The requests for hearings that always ended in disappointment. And yet, SAS couldn't agree on more aggressive tactics, which is why I haven't been to a meeting in months.

Wesley, a light-skinned brother with wavy hair and a smooth but intense voice, adds, "We want to be sensitive and thoughtful about the moment we're in, with the loss of Dr. King. At the same time, it's important to name our anger and frustration, and channel it into making change. If they don't learn the importance of being part of change right now, I don't know if they ever will."

Claudius is small and thin, with thick glasses and an occasionally unruly afro. With his trademark seriousness of purpose, he reads from his notepad, listing the issues we've discussed and brought to the administration over the past year. "On-campus issues: including Black studies in the curriculum, recruiting Black faculty and more Black students, scholarships for Black students. Community issues we've had on the agenda: stopping the university from seizing public lands, especially green space like Morningside Park, stopping the eviction of Black and Puerto Rican residents in Harlem for campus expansion, and the new gym construction." He flips a page. "And then there are the global issues, like the war."

I raise my hand. "I think we should move those community issues to the top of our agenda."

I'm not sure yet that Columbia is directly responsible for Mike's situation, but as the City's largest landowner, the university's land grabs have been ongoing for years, pushing poor residents out directly or indirectly. The community pushes back in a never-ending tug-of-war. Maybe if we get loud and active, we can add strength to Harlem's side.

"They want a stable city surrounding their precious campus, right?" I say. "We can cite the Kerner Commission. Connect the university's pressure on the community to the riots that just happened last night."

The Kerner Commission report came out last month. White folks spent year after year scratching their heads, wondering why people in the ghettoes kept rising up in "violent" displays of frustration. The government finally did a formal study of the situation. It confirmed what Black folks already knew: there are two Americas, one Black and one white, and segregation and unequal treatment are the causes of urban uprisings. Even with the facts, people still act surprised. They don't want to admit that segregation and unequal living conditions are a form of violence too.

"That could be a good strategy," Claudius agrees. "They claim to mourn Dr. King and his ideals of equality, but they're still stealing land from Black folk for their own gain. Let them walk the walk."

"Right. We need to expose their hypocrisy." My voice burns with desperation.

"Community coalitions in Harlem have tried to block the takeover of Morningside Park for years," Wesley says. "Now that Columbia broke ground on the new gym site, I don't know how much we can do. But maybe adding pressure from inside campus could help."

Valerie twirls a silver ring around her finger as she considers her words. "I agree this is one of the most important issues. It's also one of the hardest. If we can partner with the people on these demands, we can send a strong message to the establishment. People are thinking about the 'race issue' right now. Let's seize the moment."

"That's right," someone says.

"The hypocrisy has to end."

People nod and murmur.

"What about the war?" Chester asks. He's a sophomore from Connecticut, wearing a sweater-vest and corduroys. "Dr. King had just started to criticize it. More and more people are realizing how unjust and senseless the war is. We could build solidarity around the anti-war movement."

"It affects Black people and poor people more than anyone," another undergraduate adds.

Most young people are against the war and the draft, but poor people are more likely to get shipped off since they don't have the exemptions of college students or the connections to get some doctor to declare them unfit for service, like some of the rich do to avoid the draft. And Black folks have taken up Muhammad Ali's quote, "No Viet Cong ever called me nigger."

"The anti-war faction on campus is definitely growing," Wesley muses. "The student demonstrations have really heated up, especially around the IDA issue."

Columbia's membership in the IDA—The Institute for Defense Analyses—aligns them with government agencies that fund military research. Earlier this month, a group of students delivered their petition to the president, calling on the university to sever its ties with the IDA. The petition had over one thousand student signatures, but the president didn't even look at it. He identified the most prominent students and declared them in violation of the edict against "indoor protests." Those students became the IDA Six.

Wesley moves to put the community issues and the anti-war movement at the top of our agenda for the rest of the academic year. The vote is unanimously in support. I feel a surge of hope for Mike. We only have a month of school left, but with this momentum, maybe we can make a difference.

Valerie pulls out a flyer for the rally that she got from our students. We all list our contacts at the organizations that are planning it and decide who will communicate with them to coordinate our support.

Voices float in from the hallway. Everyone turns to see three seniors walking in, loose-limbed and giddy.

Wesley stands. "Success?"

These must be the brothers who went to confront the president.

"Man, you should have seen him!"

"We went right to his door. Knocked loud but polite. I don't know who he expected, but when he saw the three of us, his face went white as a ghost!"

"Looked like he wanted to call the cops."

They slap hands and laugh so hard at the memory they can hardly continue. The rest of us are on the edges of our seats.

"Then what?" Claudius prods.

"We said our piece." He makes a serious face and recites the statement. "'We represent the Black students of Columbia and all students of conscience on this campus. A national hero has been gunned down, and a symbol of racial equality died with him. If this institution has any respect for his memory and what he stood for, no less than a full day of mourning is in order. We demand that you cancel classes for the entire day, and we will protest any classes that are held.'"

Everyone is grinning now.

"He said, 'I-I-I suppose that's reasonable. . . . How did you find me? . . . Yes, we can do that. We can cancel classes. Is that all?'"

They get weak with laughter again.

"So that's that. Classes are canceled for the rest of the day."

"That was easier than I thought it would be."

"Yeah," the third brother jokes, "he's not so tough when you catch him in his pajamas."

They slap hands, and Richard and Wesley pull them in for congratulatory hugs.

I wish I had been there to witness the moment.

A graduate student starts to clap, and the rest of us join in. We get up and give them a standing ovation. We hoot and holler and raise our fists.

In the midst of the noise, I look over at Valerie. Her smile radiates the thrill of the moment as she claps hard, her earrings shaking with the effort. It's been a devastating twenty-four hours, but I cling to the hope that we can do something to make a difference.

Since classes are canceled, Valerie and I arrange to meet after lunch. Until then, I obsess over Mike, the security guard, Charles, and my parents. And I can't think of my parents without thinking about Dawn.

I last saw her at home over Christmas break. It's her first year in college, and I knew she'd have lots of stories to share. I hoped she would share them with me. My last year at home was strained, and we didn't spend much time together during my trips home my freshman year. By last summer, I couldn't deny it any longer. She wasn't just too busy for me; she was actively avoiding me. We used to stay up late talking in my room after Mom and Dad turned in. How long ago was that? When I talk to her now, it's polite. Her drama, her gushing, her emotions, and now her stories about college are for Mom and Dad. I'm in the background, listening in.

By the time I meet with Valerie, the good feeling I had at the end of the SAS meeting is only a memory.

We find a spot by a window in the library. Valerie opens a notebook, runs her hand over a clean sheet of paper and grips her pencil. She taps her foot on the floor, a nervous habit.

"Okay," she says. "We want to be firm but polite."

I nod.

"Did you draft anything for the letters to the schools?"

"No." I pull out my papers and hand them to her. "This is what I have. Ideas for field trips and stuff with the mentees. You can handle the bureaucracy."

She eyes me warily. "I did not agree to that division of labor." She picks up my papers and flips through them. "Nice drawings."

"They're sketches," I say.

"Oh, excuse me. I'm not an artist. They look like drawings to me." She gasps. "Is that Mike?"

"Yeah."

"Wow. You're really good."

"Thanks."

BLACK & WHITE
DRAWINGS
TO COME

Valerie puts the papers down and asks, "What's going on?"

I stare at the table. "What do you mean?"

She folds her arms. "You've been talking about starting this mentorship program all year long. You have solid ideas." She gestures at the papers. "It's the perfect time. To help channel our anger and the kids' anger into something that matters. And now . . . you're acting like you can't be bothered."

My leg bounces up and down. I want to get up and run.

Valerie pokes her pencil into her hair and leaves it there. I take a mental picture of her just like that. "Talk to me, Kevin," she says.

I take a breath but can't find words. I don't know if I can share what I learned about Mike. Mrs. Hammond is proud. If she didn't want me to mention it in front of him, I'm sure she wouldn't want Columbia students knowing her business. But this is Valerie.

She points at my papers with her chin. "Why are these wrinkled?"

"I . . . crumpled them up."

"Why?"

I shrug. "I was feeling . . . hopeless, I guess."

"Hopeless?" she says, as if the word itself is absurd. "Oh boy. Kevin, we can't start something we're not prepared to finish. We can't disappoint these kids. We can't afford to feel excited one day and hopeless the next."

"I know that," I say. "It's just . . . a lot happened."

"Yeah, I know. I know." She twirls the pencil through her afro, pulls it out, and pushes it back in. "It's a hard time to act, but … it's the most important time too. We have to show the kids and the world that we don't give up, even when progress seems impossible. You hear what I'm saying?"

I look through her. "Mike's got an eviction notice."

"What?"

"Yeah."

"He told you that?"

"No. I went to check on him. His mom invited me up to eat, and . . . it was tucked inside her newspaper. Like it was … just a piece of mail."

"Oh. Oh God."

"We can't say anything. She didn't want it mentioned in front of Mike."

"Of course." Valerie slumps down in her seat. Worry lines crease her face.

I mutter, almost to myself, "Soon Harlem will be faculty housing and new student centers and—"

"No," she says harshly. "It won't. They'll try, but we won't let them. The people won't let them. The kids are already fighting this. We have to fight it too."

The idea of trying to fight a university that has ties to all the power holders in the City makes me want to vomit. I'm prepared to fight, but right now I don't believe we can win. Columbia keeps growing. Harlem is in the way. It doesn't matter about community, history, or justice.

"Here I was planning trips to hear speakers and study groups on Pan-Africanism." I lean forward. "Who knows how many of them are living with this threat over their heads? Two other kids from the program live in that same building."

"Yeah," she says, thinking. Then the fire returns to her eyes. "All the more reason to fight."

"But Valerie, we're part of the system. It's Columbia that's pushing people out. That means *we're* pushing them out. We're giving poison with one hand and medicine with the other."

"It's not that simple, and you know it, Kevin. If we all stay outside the system, we have no chance against it."

"Yeah, well. See how that's working out."

She stares at me. "So that's it? You're just gonna roll over and play dead?"

I glare at the papers between us.

She flips her notebook closed and stands. "Okay, then." She puts her notebook in her bag. She stacks my papers together and hands them back to me. When I don't reach for them, she places them on the table and lifts her bag onto her shoulder.

"Valerie, wait," I say.

"For what? I'm not here to sit around watching you mope. There's work to do." She turns to go.

"Valerie."

"What."

I pick up my papers. The kids' faces, etched in pencil, demand action. "We already told them we'd go to the rally next week," I say.

"Yeah, we did." She watches me.

"When I went to visit Mike, he said his mom is trying to keep him inside. . . . She doesn't want him out in the streets right now."

"So what do you want to do?"

I take a deep breath. "I don't know. His mom likes me. Maybe . . . maybe if I tell her we'll chaperone the group . . . that we'll get them home safely, before dark . . . maybe she'll let him go. I think he'd appreciate that."

She crosses her arms. "That's a start. And what about your ideas? What about the proposal? Seeking funding? Everything we've talked about?"

I rub my forehead. "I think it's better to take it one step at a time right now."

She taps her fingers on her forearms. Looks away and then back at me. "Well," she says. "We have to go to the rally anyway. It would be cool to go together with the students." She thinks for a minute. "All right. If I draft a note to the parents, will you copy it and bring it around to the families? Talk to anyone who's nervous?"

"Yeah," I say. "I'll do that."

"Okay. Kevin, this is your last chance. If you go all hopeless on me again, this is not going to work. My energy is for action, not for pep talks."

"Understood."

She sits and pulls the pencil back out of her hair. I take a fresh sheet of paper from my bag and start to sketch her. I glance at her a few times, but mostly I work from memory. From the mental picture I took earlier, while she was still smiling.

Back in the dorm, the phone is in constant use, as it has been since the news broke about Dr. King's assassination. I get a book from my room and take a place in the line trailing down the hallway to use the phone. I start to read, but I keep stopping at the end of the same page. My mind drifts to my parents and then to Dawn.

We were always together at home in times of national crisis, the whole family. I hated where our home was, but being together made me feel secure. Secure enough to challenge them to think more deeply about what the murders and the uprisings said about our country. Secure enough to argue. To push the limits at the most sensitive times.

"Are you making a call?" The person in line behind me asks.

Pulled back into the moment, I pick up the earpiece and wait for the operator to connect me to home.

"Hello?" Mom is breathless, as if she ran to pick up the phone.

"Hi, Mom."

"Oh," she sighs. "Kevin! What a relief. Where are you calling from?"

"The dorm," I say. "Where else?"

"Good. Okay. Good."

Mom's voice brings on an unexpected longing. Nostalgia pulls me back toward childhood, my youngest days, a time when I felt safe and cared for. My voice cracks when I speak again. "I'm just calling to check in. Are you and Dad okay?"

"Yes. Yes, we're okay. We're shocked of course. Upset. Devastated. This is the danger of doing the work. When you speak out and stand on principle. He knew it could happen. We all knew it could happen. But it's still a shock."

"Yeah."

"How are you doing? How are things on campus? We saw that there was some looting in Harlem. Has everything calmed down? Is campus safe?"

"Of course campus is safe. It's always safe here. Harlem is broken. But what's new?"

Mom knows better than I do about the poverty in the ghettoes of New York City. It's why she and Dad left.

She shuffles around the kitchen. She's thinking. Being careful. Trying not to start an argument.

"Well," I say, "I should go."

"Wait a minute," she says. "Why so fast?"

"I'm tired, Ma. I was up all night."

"Were you out?" Her voice becomes urgent. "Tell me you weren't out in Harlem last night."

"Are you serious?"

"I'm just asking. Well, it doesn't matter anyway. You're safe; that's what matters. How are classes?"

"Classes? Ma. They're canceled. For today, at least."

"Okay," she says. "Well, you're so close to the end of the school year. It's important to see it through."

"Wow."

"What's that?"

I roll my eyes to the ceiling.

"Kevin?"

"I'm here."

"Did you hear me about staying focused?"

"I don't know what to tell you, Mom. I'm not exactly focused on classes right now, and I can't promise that I will be. Jesus." I think that last word is under my breath.

111

"Watch your mouth, Kevin."

I guess not. I'm grateful she can't see my face.

Mom sighs again. "Take some time to mourn. But remember what Dr. King stood for. What he died for. So that you young people would have the opportunities you have right now."

"Mom. I can't make the choices you and Dad made and just hope everyone else can figure out their own way."

She is silent for a moment. Then she says, calm and steady, "That's not fair. We have done more than hope. We spoke up. With our actions and our words. We made the choices we made so that you and Dawn would have more choices than we did. And you do. We have nothing to apologize for or to feel guilty about. And neither do you. You have your whole life ahead of you. All you have to do is take advantage of the opportunities that are right in front of you."

"Right. All I have to do."

I close my eyes and lean my head against the wall. I consider telling Mom about what's happening with Mike. I've told her about him and the tutoring program before. Maybe if I tell her how Columbia ruins lives, remind her that the riots are more about exploitation of poor Black communities than they are about Dr. King, maybe she'll understand. Maybe she'll see that I have a bigger job here than being a student.

But no. I can't trust her to understand. Instead, I say, "I'd better free up the line. Other people need to call home too. Have you heard from Dawn?"

"Yes, this morning. She called us. She was inside the

dorm and safe. I wish you both could be home til everything calms down."

"We'll be okay."

"Before you go, say hello to your father."

She hands over the telephone. "Hello!"

"Hi, Dad."

"Kevin! How are you?"

"I'm . . . all right."

"Are you staying on campus, staying safe?"

"Mostly."

"Good. Glad to hear it. Classes are going fine?"

"Yes." No more complications.

"Very good." I expect him to say goodbye right away, but he surprises me with some words of advice. "You know," he says, "in times of shock and grief, people do unusual things. They lash out. They take risks. They behave in ways they normally wouldn't. We have to be smarter than that, son. We must stay focused. This is a major blow. But it will pass. All right?"

This is the psychiatrist talking. His cool, dispassionate detachment makes me want to scream.

"Dad, I hear you. But maybe we shouldn't let it pass. Maybe it's good to do unusual things. It's an unusual time. I mean, we need to call attention to what got us here. Sometimes you have to take risks to get anything to change."

"Son," he says. His voice is so gentle it makes me want to throw the phone. "I know you're angry. We are all taking this very hard. I'm cautioning you. Acting on anger does not end well."

I don't want to believe that. Our anger fuels our action, and I don't think that's wrong.

"Dad, I've got to go. People are waiting to use the phone."

"Sure. Call again soon. Your mother worries."

"I will."

I've never seen Mom or Dad express anger. They've suffered more indignities than I have, but it doesn't seem to affect them. Maybe that should make me admire them, but it doesn't.

When I was little, it confused me. It made me think the storms inside me were wrong and somehow my fault.

Like the house. How could they love that house? For them a symbol of victory. For me a symbol of rejection.

I loved it too at first. We finally moved out of our grandparents' apartment and spread out in our own home. We enjoyed more grass than concrete. We started school and got to know our neighborhood. Then, barely a month into the school year, I discovered what our new neighbors already knew.


### October 1959

We were playing ball at recess. I tagged out a boy named Steve, but he refused to step out of the game. He had a temper. Some boys tried to calm him down, but he accused them of taking my side. Then he called me a liar.

"That figures," he sneered. "Your daddy's a liar too. A liar and a thief."

"What?" I didn't understand. What did our ball game have to do with my parents? Dad couldn't lie if he tried. And anyway, Steve had never even seen my dad, as far as I knew.

"I said you're a liar," he yelled. "And your daddy is too. Everyone knows it. My daddy told me so." He threw the ball at me hard and ran off.

The other boys stared at the ground, not speaking. None of them seemed the least bit confused. What did they know that I didn't?

When school let out, I ran home and went straight to Dad. He sat in his office, reading scientific journals.

"Dad," I said, still panting from the run.

He peered at me over his glasses. "Hello, son."

"Dad, Steve Sackler called me a liar today, and he said you're one too." I waited for him to explain.

Mom wandered over, wiping her hands on a dish towel, and leaned against the doorjamb.

"Did he now," Dad said, pursing his lips to suppress his amusement. "And are you?"

"Am I? A liar? No!"

"Well, then. I don't suppose it matters what Steve Sackler says. As long as you're not really a liar. And neither am I."

"But why did he say that? About you? Did you—do something?" How could I explain that I was the only one shocked by his accusation?

Dad put his journal down on his desk, folded his hands over it, and examined my face. "Can you tell me why he called you a liar?" he asked.

I shrugged.

"What's that?" He cupped his ear with his hand.

"I don't know. He was mad at me. We had a disagreement in a game. He was mad because I tagged him out."

"I see."

I wrung my hands and stared at Dad, then at the window behind him, then at Dad again.

"Well," Dad said at last. "I suppose he must have said it for that reason. What do you think?"

I shrugged again.

"I can't hear you."

"I don't know," I said. "Maybe."

He pushed up his glasses and picked up his journal. "I believe Mama has some treats baked for you and Dawn."

That was my signal to leave his office. I wasn't satisfied, but I would have to find out more later.

"Cookies are on the table," Mom said to me. When I left, she stepped inside his office and shut the door behind her.

At dinner, after our silent moment of gratitude and filling our plates with roast chicken and vegetables, Mom cleared her throat. "Children," she said, "your father and I have something to tell you."

Dawn and I put our forks down.

Mom said, "It's about the house." Her eyes stayed on Dad.

Dad chewed vigorously while we all waited. Finally, he swallowed his food.

"Yes," he said. "Well. Your mother feels you should know how we were able to purchase this home."

Mom nodded encouragingly, and he spoke more words than I had heard from him in one sitting.

"You remember how difficult it was to find a house to rent or buy upstate. So difficult that we almost declined my job opportunity in Albany and stayed in the City." He clicked some food out of his back teeth. "We found this house. We knew it would work for us. When the owners were reluctant to sell to us, we decided to buy it anyway. We couldn't do it directly. So we had our friend, Mr. Reid, a white man, buy it from the owner with money we gave him. He then sold it to us for one dollar. As you can imagine, some of the folks in the neighborhood were not happy when they found out that we were moving in and not Mr. Reid. It may have been the talk of the town for a while. It is a small town, after all." He took a sip of water. "I suppose it will die down soon enough, if it hasn't already."

Dad went back to his plate. I turned to Mom, hoping she could tell me why I felt queasy.

"It was a difficult decision for us," she explained. "But in the end, we felt it simply wasn't right to let ignorant people determine our lives. We have a right to live where we want to live. You deserve a yard to play in and good schools. Your father works very hard, and there is no reason to accept such limitations."

She watched us digest this news. My mind buzzed. We were there, in our little home with its little yard and its shutters and its flowerpots, in spite of all that rejection— almost to spite it. We had infiltrated enemy lines. Of course everyone resented us.

More details came out over time, and I became amazed at what they had kept from us. When word spread about us buying the house, some families pooled their money and tried to buy the house for a higher price to prevent us from moving in. Those were the angry ones who felt they had been fooled. I imagined Steve's father leading that crusade, warning his family at the dinner table about the lying Negroes who had snuck into their pristine town.

They were ignorant. But we were unwanted. I wanted to move back to Brooklyn, where apparently we belonged.

Instead, Dawn and I set out to prove to everyone that they were wrong about us. We took on the burden of representing The Race.

### Friday, April 5, 1968

When I hang up with Dad, I start to walk back to my room, but something pulls at me. I pass the end of the line for the phone and pause. Then I step back in line to wait again. I know Dawn's number at school, but I haven't used it yet. If there's ever an excuse to call her, it should be now.

The line inches forward. My muscles twitch. My stomach feels heavy at the thought of getting her on the phone. When's the last time we had a conversation, just the two of us? The last time we were both home, even when we were in the same room, she never really looked at me directly. What if she has nothing to say?

Finally, it's my turn again.

"Hello?" A young woman's voice on the other end of the line.

"Dawn?"

"No, this isn't Dawn—hold the line." Shuffling. "Dawn!" she yells.

How did I think a stranger was my sister?

"Hello?" This voice is familiar. I cling to the sound of her voice directed at me.

"Hey," I say. "How's it going?"

A pause. Then, "Kevin?" Like it's impossible that it's my voice on the line.

"Yeah!" I try to sound upbeat. "It's me."

"What . . . did something happen?"

"Well . . . the assassination. Riots are sweeping some cities. . . ."

"But Mom and Dad . . . I just talked to them this morning—"

"No, they're fine. Everyone's okay. I'm just . . . calling to check on my little sister."

She doesn't respond.

"You there?"

"Yes. I'm here."

"How are you holding up?" I ask.

"I'm all right." She sounds tired.

"No real danger near you?"

"No."

"Good. I'm glad to hear that." I pause for a moment, wishing she'd fill in the silences like she used to. "Well. You have my number, right? I'm here if you need me."

After a pause, she says, "That's really why you called?"

"Yes. Why?"

"You didn't call to . . . gloat or something?"

"What? Why would I do that?"

"Well . . . You're probably not mourning. . . ."

I wipe my face with my hand. When I speak again, my voice is low. "Dawn. I wouldn't gloat at a time like this."

Her jewelry clicks against the earpiece. "It wouldn't be the first time," she says.

"What . . . oh geez, Dawn. I'm trying—"

"I've gotta go, Kevin. Someone's waiting for the phone."

"Yeah." I sigh. "All right."

I tap the phone against my forehead and then place it in the receiver. How far would I have to go back to start over with her?

# 5

## GIBRAN
*Massachusetts / September 1995*

Sometimes Mom realizes she was trippin for no reason and changes her mind. This isn't one of those times. When I meet with James and David after school to come up with a plan for the march, I have to break the bad news.

In the snack bar, James pushes his steaming fries to the center of the table to share. "What'd your moms say?" he asks, stuffing his mouth.

"Basically," I say, dipping fries in ketchup, "she's for the march, but she's scared to let me go."

"Mm," James grunts. "Sounds like a mom. Maybe I should have asked her."

"Yeah, probably. She thinks you're such a good kid."

"She's not wrong." He runs a hand over his waves.

"Please."

"Did you ask about staying with your uncle?" David asks.

"She wasn't feeling that either. When I mentioned that part, she shut it down real quick."

"Man," David says. "That sucks."

"Yeah. I guess we should focus on doing something local. Did you find out what's goin on in Boston?"

"Well," David says. "There's an event in Roxbury that might be cool. We could maybe organize for Black students from local private schools to meet up there. We'd need to get the day off school."

"So we write a petition or something?" James asks.

"Yeah," David says. "We can argue that it's like a holiday for us. Something important to our identity. So we shouldn't be marked absent."

"Word."

"Wanna draft it right now?" I say, pulling out some paper. "If we get signatures at the meeting tomorrow, we can submit it on Friday and then start planning with other schools. Maybe even help organize the event."

We spend the next half hour crafting a petition. I write our words down on a sheet of paper, and we each take turns scribbling on top of it and adding to it. Finally, we end up with this:

*We, the Black men of Lakeside Academy, hereby petition to be released from classes and school activities on October 16. Since we cannot attend the Million Man March in Washington, DC, on that day, we will participate in the Day of Absence. The purpose of the Day of Absence is to stand in solidarity with the event and to reflect on the role of Black people in America. This purpose is vital to our lives and has been overlooked by our education at this school. For this one day, we ask that any consequences of missing classes and activities be withheld for the Black students at Lakeside who wish to focus on the improvement of ourselves and our community.*

David nods. "That's dope."

James takes the paper with him to the dorm, where he can type it up on a computer and print it out for the meeting.

We may have compromised, but at least we have a plan.

Mr. Adrian opens class with a discussion about the Transatlantic Slave Trade and its lasting effects on the Americas.

"This is a sort of preassessment, if you will," Mr. Adrian says. "I wonder if your views will change by the end of the course. From what you know now, how do you see slavery affecting modern society?"

A white boy named Hunter raises his hand. "I guess maybe because it was so brutal, people are more committed to making things right? Like, desegregation and then anti-discrimination laws. We have rules in place to make sure we don't go backwards."

Lisa sits up and kind of squirms in her chair. "I don't know about that. It's not like society as a whole is determined to progress. Certain people—people of color mostly—fought for those laws to be approved. And they're hard to enforce. I think it's more like . . . two currents fighting each other."

"And whenever progress is made, there's always backlash," James adds.

Mr. Adrian nods.

"Mm, I dunno." Kate sounds as if she's not convinced. "I mean, there may be a few racists out there who don't like it, but as a whole, as a society, we've clearly moved on.

Nobody's against antidiscrimination laws."

Maya tucks her jet-black hair behind one ear and says softly, "Affirmative action is an antidiscrimination law."

Kate tosses her head. "Well, that's different. That's controversial."

"Why is it controversial though?" Lisa pushes. "If nobody's against antidiscrimination laws?"

Kate tsks. "I mean, having a quota system is kind of going overboard. Now that everything's equal, people can compete based on merit. It's not fair to just favor a different group."

Lisa's lips form a tight line.

Mr. Adrian stands up and steps over to the board. "Kate contends that everything is equal now. We're going to study present-day statistics a bit later. For now..." He draws a horizontal line across the blackboard. "Two hundred fifty years of chattel slavery, which, as we've discussed, differs from other forms of slavery." He draws a shorter line. "Segregation enforced by law for another ninety years." He draws a very short line. "And then thirty years since discrimination has been outlawed." He stands back and considers this time line, then turns to us. "And yet, as a society, we can't seem to agree when enough is enough. When will the ill effects of those centuries of mistreatment really be behind us?" He looks around the room, twirling the chalk in his hand.

I raise my hand. "I think the real question is, *will* the effects ever be behind us? Especially if people can't see what's right in front of them. I mean, it's obvious to anyone who's not white that we're still living with the effects of slavery every day."

Several white students press their eyebrows together in confusion.

"This is the whole reason for the Million Man March." I know it's touchy, but if anyone can handle it, it's Mr. Adrian, I think. "The slave mentality hasn't gone away—in white people and in Black people. We still have to actively fight against it. Everything about the way our society is set up today is a result of slavery. Everything people think and feel about race is a result of slavery."

"Isn't that a little extreme?" Hunter asks.

"No, it's not," I say. "We could go through every single stereotype about Black people and trace it back to slavery." I list stereotypes on my fingers. "Black men are dangerous and scary. Black people are lazy. Black women are loose or seductive. Everything white people had to say about us to justify how they treated us."

"Yeah," James says. "And breaking Black families apart. That's still happening today. Instead of sending people farther south, selling them down the river, they send people to jail."

"Black men weren't allowed to be head of household," I say. "They couldn't *have* a household. You do that for generations, you break people." I point at the board. "Thirty years of so-called equality can't fix that. That's wishful thinking. So now we try to reclaim what was taken. Redefine ourselves on our own terms. And people call *that* extreme. When really, everything before this was extreme."

"The Million Man March isn't the answer though," Eric says.

I cut my eyes at him. Who is he to say what the answer should be?

"Yeah," Hunter says. "Farrakhan is a racist. Don't he and his followers believe that white people are the actual devil or something? And I heard he's an anti-Semite too. I don't see how someone who's racist can solve racism."

"Yeah, if the goal is unity," Eric says, "why have a big, divisive event?"

"Who said the goal was unity?" I ask.

The white students look at me like I have three heads.

I shrug. "You may want the illusion of unity so you can pat yourselves on the back and say racism is behind us. What we actually *need* is respect. And that's the last thing white people want to give us. Letting us into your schools and your neighborhoods and your clubs—that's not equality. And it's definitely not respect."

Students tap their pens and stare at me or at the board.

I look back at each of them. "You have no idea what we have to give up to be here. People think they're doing us favors by letting us into their little clubs." I shake my head. "A Black man with an opinion is still the scariest thing in this country. The more accurate he is about racism, the quicker everyone jumps to tear down his character so people won't listen to him. For us? Hearing that truth aired out in the open is refreshing. It hardly matters where it's coming from."

I've never had a chance to say these things in class, and you can tell some of them have never heard this before. The quiet that falls over the room rings with objections. Someone clicks a pen real slow, and some students steal glances at each other out of the corners of their eyes. Mr. Adrian watches and waits.

David speaks next. "I also wanna say, the Million Man March is not a Nation of Islam event. People get freaked out about the Nation's beliefs, but that's not the point of the march. Not everyone agrees with everything they preach. The march is still supported by all kinds of people and groups. They have pastors and preachers, actors, musicians . . . women too." He looks at Lisa, whose eyebrow is arched. "It's just a chance to cut through the noise about what everyone thinks Black men are and just . . . be who we are. For one day, with no drama. I don't think people realize how rare that is. Or maybe they do, and that's why they're against it."

Mr. Adrian leans in, concentrating on our words. Students fidget and avoid our eyes, visibly disengaging.

After a minute, James adds, "Back to the original question though, the whole structure of society is shaped by slavery. White people still have everything they stole back then. The wealth people have now is built on all that stolen land and stolen labor. People say they worked for it and other people need to pull themselves up by their bootstraps. They conveniently forget how they got theirs. We built this country. But what do we get from it?"

I answer his question. "Ghettoes, poverty, and mass incarceration."

The room is so still, we can hear the clock ticking. Outside the tall windows, the tree branches sway in the wind. Ten seconds pass. Hunter folds his arms over his chest. Eric clears his throat. I know what they're thinking. *Melodrama.* Whatever.

Mr. Adrian asks if anyone has reactions or thoughts. No one wants to speak. When he can't get conversation going again, Mr. Adrian decides to end class a few minutes early. He thanks us all for sharing and for listening. People may have been listening, but I don't think anyone's trying to hear me.

When I get home, I pull down some of the books I've borrowed from Mom's shelves over the years. A lot of them are from her college collection, her Black Power days. Some of the newer ones have a stamp from Kevin's bookstore in DC inside the covers. I wonder if he sent them to her as gifts or if she ordered them herself, supporting his business. The older ones are marked-up and dog-eared. The newer editions are pristine.

I'm still thinking about this idea of the past influencing the present. Maybe it could help me frame my research project. I flip through a beat-up copy of *The Autobiography of Malcolm X*. I remember watching the Spike Lee movie *X* with Mom and my sisters a few years back. Mom loves Denzel Washington, but she was disappointed with the movie because it gave the white women in Malcolm's life so much airtime. I loved the movie, but when I read the book, I had to agree with her. Malcolm had multiple phases. I could do a whole project on him and what his example and reception show about America and its treatment of Black people. How his public perception changed over time and keeps changing. He's an icon to us now, but in his time, he was hated and feared. He still would be too, if he were alive.

I check the copyright dates of the books in front of me and line them up in chronological order.

*David Walker's Appeal to the Coloured Citizens of the World*

*The Souls of Black Folk*

*The Mis-Education of the Negro*

*Black Bourgeoisie*

*A Raisin in the Sun*

*The Wretched of the Earth*

*The Fire Next Time*

*The Autobiography of Malcolm X*

Does this tell a story?

I could take one of the oldest books and apply it to today.

I could use *The Mis-Education of the Negro* to make a case for a second semester of African American history at Lakeside.

I hear the front door open and Mom's strong voice singing "Love Me In a Special Way" by DeBarge. I laugh to myself, remembering how she would always play that tape in the car and sing louder than the music. She locks the front door, trudges up the stairs, and goes into her bedroom, still humming. I give her a few minutes to get settled, and then I go stand in her doorway and lean on the frame.

"Hey, Ma."

"Hi, honey." She's sitting on the edge of her bed, massaging her feet. "How was school?"

"Okay. I have this project I gotta do for African American history."

"Oooh. What are you thinking about?"

"That's the thing, I can't decide. I've been looking through some of your books. Trying to think of something that could connect to the present. Maybe to the march."

"Hmm."

"Today in class we were talking about the legacy of slavery, and the white kids were like, 'What do you mean? That's all in the past.' As if everything's been fixed."

"Ha. Right."

"I know." I bite my lip. "Maybe something about Malcolm X? Like, what he's meant in different times. Or Black manhood in general? How it's been perceived over time. How this idea of the scary Black man comes straight from slavery times. I dunno, I have too many ideas."

"Hm. Who was it—Ossie Davis, I think, who read the obituary for Malcolm, and he called him 'our living, Black manhood.' So beautiful." She takes off her dangling earrings and hangs them on her jewelry stand next to her bed, then pulls the scrunchie out of her hair and tosses it on her dresser. She runs her fingers through her loose curls. "The hardest part will be narrowing it down. Once you get going, it'll get easier. I have more books in the attic. And we could always make a trip to my parents' house to look through theirs. Your grandpa has a whole library in his office. I always used his books for my school projects. He has some unique ones, really old ones."

"Cool. That must be where Uncle Kevin got it from?"

She raises her eyebrows. "Got what?"

"That obsession with books."

"Oh." She makes a face. "Don't let him hear you say that."

"What do you mean?"

"Kevin thinks he's the opposite of Dad. And he's pretty proud of it."

"Really? Why?"

She sighs. "I don't know." She wraps her fuzzy bathrobe

around her and ties it at the waist. "Let's see about dinner."

I follow her downstairs, still thinking about Uncle Kevin and Grandpa.

She pulls a pack of ground beef out of the fridge and asks if I feel like cooking. I know that means she doesn't want to, so I say, "Sure." I find a packet of chili seasoning, canned beans, and tomatoes. I chop onions and garlic and turn on the fire under the pot. While the chili simmers, I chop a quick salad. Everything's ready in twenty minutes.

Over dinner, I try to get her talking about her Black Power days. I like hearing the stories. And maybe it'll give me ideas for my project.

"Did you read all those books when you were in college?"

"Heck yeah. You had to. To be down with the revolution, baby. Especially if you were 'high yellow' like me. And don't let people know your daddy's a doctor. Shoot."

I chuckle. "What was your favorite book?"

"Oh, I don't know. I was more into art than intellectual stuff. People got so passionate about politics, you know, the debates would get personal. If you didn't see it their way, you weren't Black enough. That really turned me off. People you knew and loved would change on you." She takes another bite of chili and chews slowly, staring into space.

I wait for her to say more, but she doesn't.

After a minute, she snaps back to the present. "What was I saying?"

"Your favorite book? Debates?"

"Right. I read the treatises and the nonfiction stuff so I could be hip. But really? My favorites were novels and plays. Have you read *Things Fall Apart*?"

"No, I don't think so."

"Oh." She scrapes the bottom of her bowl and licks her spoon. "That one. That's one of my favorites."

"Were a lot of people reading that?"

"Oh yeah. Especially when we got into Pan-Africanism."

"I'll have to find it. You think it's upstairs in the attic?"

"Probably."

By the time we finish eating, it's too dark to search the attic. I decide I'll explore the boxes over the weekend.

I ask Mom one last question before she goes to bed. "What's something you thought would be different by now?"

"For Black people?"

"Yeah. Or just, I dunno, race relations and stuff."

She bites her cuticles. "Hm. I guess . . . I didn't think people would get so scared to talk about race. I mean, we were so out with it, you know? 'I'm Black and I'm proud.' That was our anthem. All we did was talk about race. I guess we thought we were making a permanent change, bringing it out in your face like that. It's strange now how people tiptoe around it and hope if they don't mention it, it'll go away."

*What I don't say*

I can remember a time when race didn't matter to me. I can remember a time when you didn't have to talk about race because we were comfortable in our skin. You had carefully engineered our lives to expose us to Black people everywhere. You took us to Black doctors, Black dentists, Black teachers and coaches for music and sports. When we got older, you told us you did this on purpose. You knew that in order to make it that far, those Black professionals had to be the best at what they did. You also knew that the more we saw Black folks around us, the more we'd feel normal. You wanted us to know we could be and do whatever we wanted.

When we entered White Oak School, though, we discovered this other, separate world, a world of whiteness.

In this new world, Ava and I decided that I was white and she was Black. I was light-skinned, nearly your color, and she was brown, almost as dark as our father, so we placed ourselves in categories by color. When we told you this, you laughed like it was the most ridiculous thing you'd ever heard.

"I don't know where you got that idea," you said. "We are all Black. And proud of it."

We were driving. You turned up the music. That was the end of it.

Ashanta giggled. Apparently she knew what it meant, this Black-and-white thing. Ava and I looked at each other, confused. We compared our arms again, as we had done when we were figuring it out. My arm the color of hay, hers the color of a cinnamon stick. It didn't make sense.

We learned quickly though. Being Black wasn't a visual category. It was a matter of where you belonged.

In the white world, at school, I was a curiosity. The teachers watched me. They weren't unkind, but they seemed to be searching for something, and I wasn't sure what it was. I showed that I could play nice, and I showed that I could answer questions. And still they watched me. Maybe they were watching to see if I would fit in. Maybe they were waiting to see if this experiment would work. If, by starting early, they could make me become something other than society's nightmare. Did you know that was how they would look at me? Did you know that I wouldn't be able to explain it to you? Is that why you warned me not to need friends?

The other kids were fascinated, sometimes amused, by what was so ordinary to us that we'd never even thought about it.

"Why are you ... all brown?"

"How come your palms aren't brown?"

They were just questions.

The kids were friendly. We played together. They didn't make fun of me or put me down.

But their curiosity, their questions, taught me how different I was to them, how strange. The more time I spent in their world, the more strange I became to myself.

You had engineered an illusion, and the illusion was fading fast.

I couldn't tell you that people were rejecting me. I couldn't tell you that you were right about us not fitting in. We were welcomed—enthusiastically. When they peeked at my hands after I washed them, to see if the brown had come off, their curiosity became my shame. I was different. There must be something wrong with me.

Luke was the one who didn't whisper. He didn't look away when I caught him staring at the coils on my head. He reached out and touched them, smiling his crooked smile. There was relief in this somehow. His wide, open face displayed everything. He hid nothing in his wild blue eyes. He was dangerous, but in this context, where so much went unsaid, I needed him, the one who let it all hang out. I needed him for clues to what lay beneath the neat surface everyone else presented.

Luke's house was a five-minute walk from the school. By the third grade, I was going to his house every day after school while you cleaned up your classroom, attended faculty meetings, or created and led the school's first multicultural club for middle schoolers. The first time I went home with him, I thought his house was an apartment building. Luke pushed open the unlocked door, and we walked into a huge foyer that swallowed me whole. The hanging lights and expanse of mirrors gave the feel of a hotel lobby. Across the marble floor, a wall of glass displayed a yard with plush grass, thick and bright like the playing fields at school. I followed Luke through a massive living room into a spotless white kitchen, where he dropped his school bag and grabbed a glass of cold milk and a handful of warm cookies from a plate on the counter. A woman carrying a laundry basket appeared from somewhere beyond the kitchen. She didn't look anything like Luke. Her skin was my color, and her thick, straight, jet-black hair was pulled into a tight ponytail.

"Hello, boys," she said, picking up Luke's bag off the floor.

Luke had half a cookie in his mouth. He mumbled, "Mmm," while walking away toward the stairs. I knew I could get lost in this house, so I said, "Hi," and then trailed after him before he vanished from sight.

In Luke's room, we played video games for an hour. I said I had to go back to meet you, and he said, "Okay, see ya tomorrow," and started a new game. I waited for a minute, not sure what to do. Finally, I stood up and found the stairs and then the front door.

I knew where the school was. A straight shot up the street. I had walked down my own street alone hundreds of times. This wasn't our home though, and I was terrified. My heart beat fast, and I tried not to run. Every time a car passed by, I worried that they would think I was lost because I didn't belong. It was a primal fear, that being out here alone was one step away from disappearing.

When I reached the school, I wanted to cry with relief. I wanted to run to you, hold you tight and never let go. Instead, I slipped my hand in yours as you finished chatting with the school secretary, the janitors, the landscapers. You knew everyone's name, and everyone was always happy to see you.

We followed you to the faculty parking lot and piled into our old beige Toyota. You played The Jackson 5 and sang at the top of your voice. Only when we crossed the bridge at Forest Hills did the faces change and the buildings change, and I started to feel like myself again.

Too soon, though, the two worlds switched places. The world at school and Luke's house became the norm, and our home became foreign and strange. When that happened, there was nowhere where I could feel myself.

When I was little, I thought you went overboard talking about race all the time. Everyone else said it didn't matter. What was wrong with you? It took me years to realize how brave you were. How real. You didn't bring it up because you enjoyed having debates. You did it because it mattered. You did it because you wanted to protect us.

On Thursday, we bring the Day of Absence proposal to the Brother Bonding meeting. Some of the juniors joke that they'll do anything for the day off and ask if they really have to attend the event. Some sign without reading it. Chris reads the proposal carefully and looks a little worried, but he takes a deep breath and adds his signature. When the paper comes back around to me, everyone has signed.

After the meeting, James and I drop off the proposal at the principal's office and then go to the snack bar to get some food. The sweet scent of warm chocolate chip cookies reaches down the hallway. We toss our backpacks on the floor and go to the counter to order fries and cookies. As we claim a table near the door, a wave of students comes in. Clubs and activities are letting out, and this hour before the dining hall opens for dinner is one of the busiest times of day in the snack bar.

Malika, Tanya, and Lisa come in together. They wave at us before they get their food, then they come sit at a table next to ours.

"Aww, that's cute," I tell them. "You drink milk with your cookies."

"Shut up," Malika says. "You're just jealous."

"Yeah, I am," I say, "'cause I already finished mine. Lemme get yours."

"Boy, don't even think about it." Malika picks up her warm cookie, holds it up in both hands, and pulls it apart in slow motion, showing off the gooey chocolate chips and soft inside. She takes a dainty bite. "Mmmmm."

"That's foul. You're cold."

She laughs. She and Lisa take turns dunking their cookies

into the same carton of milk while Tanya pulls out a note-book and starts some homework.

"You can actually study in here?" James asks her.

"I have four younger siblings at home," she says. "I can study anywhere."

Malika wipes her mouth with a napkin. "So," she says to us. "Y'all still trying to go to the march? Lisa said you brought it up in class."

I look at Lisa. She looks back.

"I mean, it was relevant, right?" I ask her.

"Relevant? I guess. Necessary? Not really."

"Are you really going or what?" Malika presses.

"Nah," I say. "We couldn't get Mr. Clarke to come with us."

The three of them crack up, and so does James.

"You're so stupid," Malika says.

"What?" I say. "He'd be the perfect chaperone. He wanted to, but I guess he was too busy. Kissing white people's—"

"Stop," Lisa says. "You're so wrong."

"Just sayin."

"You don't always have to say what's on your mind, you know," Tanya says without looking up from her books. "There's this thing called a filter. It's pretty useful sometimes."

"I don't know nothin 'bout that," I say.

A loud group of white boys wearing intentionally tattered blue jeans and faded T-shirts passes through the double doors, joking and shoving each other. Malika stops laughing, and her smile fades to a frown. She looks from the boys to Tanya, who scans the group, stiffens, and ducks her head. The boys order food at the counter and claim a booth.

Malika says to Tanya in a low voice, "Do you want to go?"

Tanya covers her forehead with one hand and says, "It's fine." She taps her notebook with her pen. She's lost her focus.

"What's going on?" James asks.

Malika looks at the group of boys again and then back at Tanya. She asks permission with her eyes. Tanya lifts one shoulder. Malika scoots her chair closer to us and lowers her voice. We lean in to hear her.

"You know Colin?"

We automatically look over at the group.

"Don't!" she whisper-yells, exasperated. "Don't look." She takes a breath and huffs. "Okay. He was asking Tanya how she does her braids and how long it takes and everything, right? Normal, annoying conversation. Then he picks one up and flicks it! Then he said she looks like a Black Medusa."

My jaw drops. "What?"

"That's mad ignorant," James says.

"I know!" Malika says. "He tried to play it off like a joke or a compliment or something." She sucks her teeth. "He's such a jerk!"

I stand up.

"What are you doing?"

"I'm sick of this dude." I bounce on the balls of my toes. "He needs to get checked."

I stroll over to Colin and his friends, putting my hard face on.

"Hey, yo, Colin," I say.

He looks at me.

"Lemme talk to you for a minute."

"I'm right here," he says, turning away.

"I need you to come here for a second," I say.

He eyes me as if I must be joking. That arrogance I love to destroy.

I widen my stance and fold my arms. "I'll wait."

He talks to his friends, probably hoping I'll leave if he ignores me. I stand there and watch his face grow red.

The worker at the counter calls an order, and Colin looks over. Perfect. He has to get up. He stands reluctantly. I meet him at the end of the table, walk a few steps with him, and then block his path, backing him up against the wall.

"Dude, what the hell?"

"I got a message for you," I say.

He tries to step around me. I grab him by the shirt and push him back against the wall in one move. With my forearm at his collar, I keep my back to the room to block their view. I know if it's my word against his, he'll win, but I don't think he's the type to go crying to a teacher 'cause I set him straight. He knows he was wrong to say what he said; now he needs to know there are consequences.

"What are you doing?"

"I heard you had something to say about Tanya's hair. I heard you called her a Black Medusa. You think that's funny?"

Colin sputters. "What? I don't know what you're talking about."

"Oh, you don't remember? That's interesting. 'Cause she remembers very well. She was pretty upset about it. What, you just insult people and go on about your day like it was nothin? You think if it's a Black girl, it doesn't matter?"

140

"That's not true! What the hell? I don't know what she told you, but—"

"I don't wanna hear it." I let go of his shirt, but I stay in his face. "I'm telling you right now, and don't forget this. If you ever insult a Black girl again, you will be dealing with me. You understand what I'm saying?"

He tries to stay defiant. We're so close I can see the specks of green in his hazel eyes. I'm prepared to wait until the snack bar closes and night falls. I want him to say it. I want him to give in.

Then a hand grabs my arm from behind. I throw it off with all my strength and spin around, ready to attack. But it's not one of his boys.

Tanya flinches and jumps back, shocked by the force of my movement and the venom on my face, which wasn't meant for her.

She whispers as if she doesn't want Colin to hear her. "Why are you doing this?"

I drop my hands and swing my arms, shaking off the adrenaline.

"Why do you do this?" she says again. She's not whispering anymore, but her voice shakes. She looks away and then fixes her eyes on Colin's Rolling Stones T-shirt. "I didn't ask him to do this."

Colin straightens out his wrinkled shirt. He opens his mouth as if to say something to Tanya. His eyes roam the length of her thick braids.

"That's true," I say. "She didn't ask me to do nothing. That doesn't change what I said."

Tanya glares at me and storms back to our tables.

Colin shakes his head and sidesteps me to get to the counter, where his food waits for him.

I follow Tanya and sit down across from James.

Tanya is packing her bag furiously. When she's finished, she frowns at me again.

"You're seriously mad at *me*?" I ask her.

She throws up her hands. "Really, Gibran?"

"Oh, my bad—did you *like* that little nickname he gave you?"

She turns to an invisible audience to witness her struggle. Then she looks back at me and folds her arms. "We have to live with these people, Gibran. We have classes with them, and activities, and lunch, and dinner. Maybe you don't mind them hating you, but not everyone wants to be in a war all the time!"

"I didn't choose the war," I say. "I just choose to fight back. If you'd rather they look down on you, I guess that's you. But you're not doing any favors to the next Black kids that come through here. You let 'em know what's up, they think twice before they do that to someone else." I take a last sip of my soda, letting the ice hit my teeth and fall back into the cup. "Sorry if I embarrassed you. I don't know why you'd tell us that and not expect me to do something about it."

Tanya scoffs. "Believe me, I'll never do that again."

"Aight, then. But if you change your mind, I still got your back."

The girls throw out their trash and say a muted "later" to us as they walk out, surrounding Tanya like she's been through another ordeal.

I crush my paper cup with one hand and throw it at the garbage can. I miss. The top comes off, and the ice falls onto the floor with a clatter and skids across the tile. I get up and kick the ice into a pile.

That's when I remember I have Colin's brand-new shoes on my feet. At least there's that.

On Saturday, I open the door to the attic and duck my head to see inside. There's a layer of dust over everything, and I sneeze before I even enter. I don't want to provoke my asthma, so I go downstairs and find a bandanna to tie around my nose and mouth. I climb the stairs again and take a deep breath before going in.

Paintings and framed drawings of different sizes lean against one wall. A pink half sun—Mom's artistic signature, representing her name, Dawn—peeks from the corner of each piece. I pick up one of her self-portraits. Her head is turned to one side, and her afro surrounds the soft lines of her face.

My eyes start to water and my throat itches. I remind myself what I'm here for. The cardboard boxes aren't labeled, so I take off the lids. I get distracted by some photographs. In a black-and-white photo, Mom wears bell-bottoms, a wide afro, large hoop earrings, and shades. Mixed in with the photos are a few more pieces of art. I pull one out. It's a half-face drawing, the kind Mom teaches her students at school. One side is a reproduced photograph of a face, cut down the middle. The other side is a drawing that completes the face. The drawn side is less polished than Mom's college work. She must have done this at home when she was younger.

I wonder who the woman in the picture is. Her pale face has deep wrinkles. She wears bright lipstick and wire-rimmed glasses. Her mischievous smile shows off a straight row of small teeth. I bet it's Mom's nana, who I never met.

I open more boxes. One is filled with journals. Another is filled with books.

I pull the box of books closer and rummage through them. What was the title she mentioned? I can't remember, and these all sound interesting. I bring the whole box downstairs. In my room, I pick up a book that catches my eye. *Black Power* by Stokely Carmichael and Charles Hamilton. I haven't heard of Hamilton, but I know who Stokely Carmichael is. He has a new name now though, something African-inspired. On the title page, in faded black pen, is cursive handwriting. *For Dawn. With love, Kevin. May 1968.* Most of her other old books are battered, marked-up, stained, and falling apart, but the binding is still tight on this one, the pages clean, except for the dedication.

Mom told me she read all the nonfiction to keep up with everybody. Why wouldn't she have read this? The back of the book bulges with a thick envelope. *Dawn* is written on the envelope in the same handwriting as the dedication in the book. I pull at the seal a little, wondering if being pressed in the pages of the book over so many years made it stick back together. The flap doesn't give. There are no tears in the envelope.

It's hard to resist opening it and reading it right away. I doubt it holds the answers to my mom's attitude toward

Uncle Kevin, but it might hold some clues. I'm tempted to try the steam trick to open the envelope, but if I did that, then she'd be too mad to talk to me about the letter. I'll have to catch Mom in a real good mood to get permission to open this. I tuck it back into the book and leave it there for now.

# 6

## KEVIN
*New York City | Tuesday, April 9, 1968*

The air is charged, and the time is ripe for action. Daily strategic meetings and impromptu gatherings revolve around an effective response to Dr. King's assassination. We meet to plan action, to direct our outrage. But we also meet to find solidarity, comfort, to be together.

After five days, the university holds a memorial service. We decide almost unanimously not to go. Just the thought of it makes us sick. Watching President Kirk and the trustees and the provost and whoever else speak of their sadness over King's death while they ignore Black leaders, Black history, and Black cultures in the curriculum? While they displace local poor Black and Puerto Rican communities? While they continue to support imperialism overseas by working with the IDA war machine? Enough hypocrisy. Showing up feels like supporting them, and we won't do that.

Some brothers share news of a local event planned for the same day. A freedom school for children in Harlem. I'm all in. I spend the weekend preparing coloring pages of Black leaders past and present. Most of them I can draw from memory, but for those before my time—Frederick Douglass, Marcus Garvey, Toussaint L'Ouverture, Jean-Jacques Dessalines—I find pictures to use as models. I lose myself in the line drawings, first with pencil, then with thick black marker, outlining their noble features, stoic expressions, and formal outfits. At the bottom of each page, I add the leader's name and a quote.

On the day of the event, I hurry out the door with a stack of pages and see Charles in the hallway. He's dressed in his only suit, and he looks down when he sees me.

"Hey, brother," I say. "You ready?"

He rubs the top of his head. "Actually, I was going to stop by the chapel first."

"What? Why?"

"I know you won't understand. I just ... skipping it doesn't feel right to me. I want to pay my respects." He nods, as if assuring himself he's thought this through.

"We are respecting Dr. King. More than Kirk and his clowns, that's for sure. They don't care about him. They're disrespecting his memory. We're trying to make things better for our people. They're not."

"Yeah," he says. "It's not really about them." He watches other students shuffle down the stairs in their jackets and ties. "For me ... there's something important in the ritual."

I don't know what to say. "Okay, then ... I guess I'll see you later?"

"Yes. I've got the address. I'll meet you there."

We leave the dorm together, him to follow the crowd across campus to the chapel, me to walk out the campus gates and find the community center in Harlem.

I reach the modest brick building quickly and follow the handmade signs for the freedom school. Inside a wide room with a linoleum floor and caged windows, volunteers are setting up tables. I offer the coloring pages I brought, and a brother smiles when he takes them from me.

"Right on!" he says, and sets them up with other activities and crayons on a main table.

I help line the tables with chairs. It feels good to get out of my head and do something physical.

More Columbia students trickle in. Community members enter carrying trays of food that smell divine, and some bring fruit in bags. Leaders confer with one another. Eventually, families arrive and settle in, and the program gets started.

A brother wearing a dashiki gives the children a lesson about self-determination. Many of the kids are young, between four and ten, but they seem to be paying attention. They're either well-trained and well-behaved or really interested in the lesson. Next, some volunteers spread boxes of crayons throughout the room and pass out coloring pages and plain paper.

"You can choose a Black hero to color in," the brother says, "or you can draw a Black hero in your life."

I sit with some of the children and tell them about the people they're coloring in. I add spare paper under their pages so their strokes are smooth. Not for the first time, I wish there were more shades of brown in the crayon box. But I doubt Malcolm X would mind seeing himself colored in the shade of chestnut. "Indian red," Crayola calls it.

BLACK & WHITE
DRAWINGS
TO COME

Lunch is plated and served. We Columbia students hang back until all the families have food. Then we eagerly devour what's left, savoring every bite of the baked chicken, macaroni and cheese, and greens. There's nothing like a plate of homemade food to make you forget your woes.

After lunch, some sisters lead freedom songs. They clap a rhythm and teach the children the call-and-response. Once the rhythm is established, brothers add baritone notes. The angelic chorus of children's voices promises a new tomorrow. The harmonies vibrate in my chest, and my heart feels so full it might explode.

A memory of Dawn singing loud and strong makes me close my eyes and imagine. What if that moment never ended, and this one never ends, and we could always exist in a moment of beauty, together, just like this?

The sisters applaud, and the children join in. A few children who didn't finish coloring pick up crayons and bend their heads over their papers, lips pursed in concentration. A sister who's been running things behind the scenes comes to the front of the room. She tells the children how smart and beautiful they are and how blessed we are to have this community. Amen.

Some of the volunteers begin to clean up around the edges of the room. I won't join them yet because I don't want this to end.

Charles arrives in time to chat with some of the families and help clean up. When most of the children have gone off to show their drawings to their grown-ups or siblings, I finally stand too. I pile chairs slowly and drag my feet folding tables.

No one is ready to return to campus. Jack, a graduate student who lives in an apartment in Harlem, invites us all to his place. We walk together, talking and joking as loud as we please, as if the streets belong to us.

Once we've settled in Jack's place, lounging on the floor of his tiny living room, Charles asks if we heard what happened at the chapel.

"Yeah," Jack says from the galley kitchen, where he's pouring drinks, "a bunch of honkies in suits put on a show. Clowns and hypocrites."

We slap hands.

"Did you hear about the protest?" Charles persists.

"Protest?"

"Yeah," he says. "The service got interrupted by a student."

We quiet down and pay attention.

"A white guy," Charles continues. "He walked right up to the microphone and started making a speech. He called the service an obscenity. Said, 'King fought for human dignity, and this administration degrades human beings.'"

"Whoooo!" Richard claps.

"He ran down a list of Columbia's crimes. Taking over public parks, preventing the Black and Puerto Rican cafeteria workers from forming a union, being slum landlords in the City . . ."

"Okay!" Wesley says, nodding.

"What happened next?" Jack asks. "Did they stop the service?"

"No." Charles shakes his head. "They turned off the microphone, but he raised his voice. We could still hear him.

151

They tried to get him offstage. He said they were gonna walk out. Some twenty or so students stood up and followed him out."

"What did everyone else do?" Wesley asks.

"A few heckled him, told him to shut up. Most were shocked and silent."

"Interesting," Jack says, handing us cups of soda.

"I'll hand it to him," Richard says, "that took guts."

"It's easier to take risks when you've got white skin to protect you," Wesley says.

"I know that's right," Jack says.

"The timing was brilliant though," I say. "Right in front of the whole university? Who was he?"

"Alan Russell? From SDS?" Charles clearly hadn't heard of him before today, but Richard and Wesley nod their heads.

"Ah," Richard says.

Students for a Democratic Society has a reputation on and off campuses nationwide for their radical politics. Their membership is growing, along with their notoriety.

"He traveled to Cuba recently," Wesley adds. "Rumor is he came back on a mission."

Claudius looks intrigued but skeptical. "You think he's really committed? Or is this a phase?"

Richard and Wesley look at each other as if they haven't made up their minds about him yet.

"Alan approached us about working together," Richard says. "We're considering teaming up with SDS on the gym issue."

I'm skeptical of partnering with white groups. SNCC,

the Student Nonviolent Coordinating Committee, was criticized for asking white organizers to work in their own sphere, because they hurt a lot of white people's feelings. But I thought it was brilliant. They didn't tell them to quit. They simply said, if you're so committed, don't come into our communities and try to fix us. Go into your own communities and try to fix racism at its source. How powerful would that be?

"We'd have to support some of their priorities," Wesley adds.

There's the catch.

"Like what?" I ask.

"They're trying to get the ban against indoor protest dropped, along with the charges against their members who violated it."

I'm reluctant to admit that makes sense.

Claudius adjusts his glasses. "It would benefit everyone to get rid of that edict," he says. "It's obviously a way for the school to shut down dissent. But SDS? I'm not sure we have enough common ground with them to work together."

Richard and Wesley wear neutral expressions.

"People hear the way they talk about overthrowing the government," Claudius says, "and they walk the other way. We can't afford distraction from our issues."

Claudius is right. If we agree to putting all the issues together in one pot, their voices might eclipse ours. If we are going to team up with anyone on campus though, this Russell guy at least has the guts to stand up to the administration. At this point, I'm willing to try almost anything to pressure Columbia to back off of Harlem.

"Well," Wesley says, noncommittal, "we've agreed to support their rally for the IDA Six in a few weeks. The gym will be on the agenda too. I guess we can see how things go from there. We'll see how useful they can be."

### Thursday, April 11, 1968

A week has passed since King's assassination. I sit in class, hunched over my desk, drawing Valerie. Her afro fills the space around her head. Her dark eyes burn through the page until I have to close the sketch pad. I slip it under my books and uncap my note-taking pen. I lean my head on my fist and try to focus on the professor, who's droning on about the achievements of the Greeks in the classical age and the uniqueness of American democracy. I slouch in my seat, stretch my legs out into the aisle, and cross my ankles.

"American democracy is an experiment," he says, pacing in front of the blackboard. His wiry white hair reaches past his ears, and his glasses keep slipping down his nose. "It is unlike any other nation. Therefore, how we handle our freedom is an example for the rest of the world."

"Hm," I say under my breath. Some students glance at me.

"Constitutions. Taxes. Armies. The city-state, or polis. And a deity protecting each polis. Many similarities with American nation-building. Before we move on to review the unit, does anyone have any questions?"

People scribble notes or fiddle with their pens.

I raise my hand.

"Yes!" He's way too enthused about someone having a question. I almost hate to disappoint him.

"Can you explain why the United States is considered unique when it acts precisely like any other colonizing European nation?"

He stops pacing. He keeps his hands together behind his back.

"If you look at US actions abroad," I say, "it's classic imperialism. And if you look at the government's actions on its own people, it's colonization. They colonized the Indians, and they continue to colonize the Africans they kidnapped. From the perspective of the nonwhite peoples of the earth, practically speaking, the US isn't unique. It's just like its European brothers."

The lecture hall, filled with no less than eighty students, is dead silent. No papers rustle. No one moves. The professor stares at me for so long I start to wonder if he's going to respond.

"Well." He takes a few steps, as if moving gets his brain working. "That's an interesting perspective. No doubt taken from some of the popular pseudointellectuals writing books nowadays. However, what I'm presenting is the established view, which is not really up for debate."

"I'm not debating," I say evenly. "I'm simply pointing out some facts that have been neglected. I did pose it as a question, which you haven't answered."

Now some students are giving me the evil eye, as if I'm the one wasting their time.

The professor strokes his sparse beard. "Well. As to your question, why is the United States of America considered unique, I believe we've been building up this argument throughout the semester, and it's a bit late to question it.

However, in a nutshell, I'll reiterate that American democracy, the Constitution and the rights it grants to its citizens—"

"Hm."

"Did you have something further you wanted to say, Mr. . . . ?"

"Wilson." I briefly contemplate whether it's worth pointing out that not all citizens are treated as citizens. Everyone remembers when the Civil Rights Act was signed only four years ago to encourage the idea that Blacks have equal rights.

"Mr. Wilson. If you're quite done, let's continue with the lecture. You can find me in my office hours if you'd like to continue the lively discussion. Now then. Where was I?" He continues his lecture, painting a lily-white picture of our nation.

After class, a white student brushes past me, practically shoving me with his shoulder. My books fall to the floor and skid to a stop at the wall. He turns around.

"Oops," he says. He's got the build of a football player, thick and dense.

I pick up my sketch pad and dust it off. He stands there, watching me as I gather the rest of my books.

"Can I help you?" I ask.

"Yeah," he says. "You can. You can stop interrupting class to complain about our country. You should feel lucky you're here."

"Oh really?" I draw myself up as tall as I can. He still towers over me.

"Yeah, really," he says, taking a step toward me. I don't move.

The crowd of students has thinned to only a few. The professor comes ambling out, holding his briefcase in one hand and a mug in the other. "Gentlemen," he says. He senses the energy between us and stands there until we both move.

The jock doesn't take his eyes off me as he slowly turns around to leave.

Nice to know I can still make more enemies this late in the year.

## Saturday, April 20, 1968

It takes me all day Friday to get copies of our letter to each student's family. To my relief, every parent I talk to says yes to letting their kid go to the rally. They're familiar with the community groups that are running it, including the high school students' coalition. The tension in the City is less palpable than it was a week ago, though the outrage and energy are still in the air. I think parents know it's better to direct that energy than to let it fester. The fact that Valerie and I will chaperone is simply a nice touch.

Saturday afternoon, Valerie and I wait for the students at the corner of Amsterdam and 110th Street. Stacey runs up to us and hugs Valerie and talks a mile a minute about everything that's happened since the last time she saw her. Valerie isn't Stacey's tutor, but Stacey flocks to her every chance she gets.

I watch Mike messing around with his friends, and I feel myself relax. After a few minutes, Valerie does a head count.

"Think this is everyone?" she asks.

"No," Stacey says. "Ricardo and Jerome are coming. They said to wait up for them."

"Cool, no problem," Valerie says.

Soon Ricky and Jerome arrive, racing each other, carrying big signs.

"Let's see," Stacey says.

They hold up their signs proudly.

Jerome's says: COLUMBIA, GET THE HELL OUT OF HARLEM.

Ricky's says: AND STAY OUT.

The kids clap and cheer. Valerie and I look at each other, eyebrows raised.

"That's effective communication," she says.

I know I shouldn't take their statements personally, but I get that feeling again that I don't know what I'm doing here. I'm split in ten different pieces, and I don't know how to find the real me.

The kids lead the way through the streets to the rally while Valerie and I follow behind. Stacey falls back to link arms with Valerie. I tune out their conversation, still processing those signs.

When the sound of a voice on a megaphone reaches us, the kids pick up their pace.

"The time for change is yesterday," the speaker says.

The people respond, "That's right!"

"Columbia uses its power, its wealth, its connections, and its resources to steal from the community, to push us out. And we say, no more!"

"No more!"

"We are joined today by brothers and sisters from Columbia and Barnard."

BLACK & WHITE
DRAWINGS
TO COME

Wesley, Richard, and Claudius step forward. I scan the crowd for other Black students. We are spread out in small groups and pairs, but we're here. Richard accepts the megaphone and expresses our support for the community.

A hand pats my shoulder.

"Kevin? I thought that was you!" It's my cousin Robbie. He wears an army green jacket on top of a black T-shirt, and his afro is perfectly round. I can't understand how he gets it to stand so obediently. We have such similar genes, but my curls can barely be called an afro.

"Hey!" I say with forced enthusiasm. "What's happening, man?"

He pulls me in for a hug.

I remember that I never stopped by his office after the riots. The heat rising in my cheeks tells me I've been avoiding him again. "How have you been?" I ask. "How's the office? No damage, I hope?"

"Oh no," he says, dismissing the thought with a frown. "The people know who we are! Ain't that right?" He grins at the boys, who have drawn closer.

"You work at the SNCC office, right?" Mike asks.

"That's right," Robbie says. He takes off his sunglasses and rests them on his hairline.

"Yeah," Jerome says, "I've seen you before. With H. Rap Brown and Stokely and them."

"Guilty as charged," Robbie says, grinning. "Love those signs," he adds.

The boys form a circle around him, and the girls edge closer too.

"You all are welcome to come by our offices anytime, for

any reason. We always welcome young people to join our cause. And sisters too." He nods at Valerie.

"You've met Valerie before, right?" I ask. "Valerie, my cousin Robbie. Robbie, Valerie."

"Nice to see you, Robbie."

"The pleasure is mine, sister," he says, a little too smoothly.

My forced smile slips. Valerie eyes me questioningly, and I try to fix my face. I turn back to the speakers on the make-shift platform, but my mind wanders to every other time Robbie has appeared to make my efforts feel inadequate.

### *August 1963*

When we were younger, Robbie relished being a know-it-all. My family would support the movement from our part of the world. We would hold little fundraisers for the NAACP or picket at the Woolworth's in downtown Albany to support the young people integrating Woolworth's lunch counters down south. Robbie always had a smirk and something snide to say about how begging and plead-ing the white man did nothing but get Black folks busted in the head. I learned not to tell him about our efforts.

I was sure that the March on Washington for Jobs and Freedom would be different. It was historic. It was huge. The whole country was watching.

Dawn was the one who convinced our family to go to the march. From the moment she saw the announcement in Dad's newspaper, she was determined. Mom and Dad had considered leaving us with Nana and going without us, but Dawn wouldn't have it. She found out there were seats available on the chartered bus from Albany, and she begged and pleaded until Mom and Dad gave in and bought four tickets. Dawn could talk about nothing else all summer.

The day of the march, we stumbled into the bus before the sun appeared on the horizon. We put our picnic basket at our feet. Our pillows rested on our laps; we were too excited to sleep.

As the sun rose and the day began, the passengers on the bus emerged from their own worlds and started talking. By the time we were halfway to DC, one of the college students had pulled out his guitar and was strumming tunes everyone could sing along to. Mom and Dawn sang loud and strong, harmonizing, while others hummed. They made friends while Dad and I listened and smiled. I can still hear them singing Mom's favorite, *This land is your land, this land is my land* ... as the trees whizzed past the window and our bus captain tapped her feet.

When we got off the highway close to Washington, DC, the neighborhoods were filled with children out on the sidewalks, most of them Black. They waved at our bus as we passed through. Dawn had given me the window seat so she could socialize on the bus, but now she made me swap seats again so she could see outside. The children cheered and waved tiny American flags on sticks. Dawn waved back wildly like they were cheering for her.

We passed the White House and finally arrived at the National Mall.

There were buses from all over the country. Some had hand-painted signs representing churches, schools, youth groups, towns, or sponsor organizations. A hostess, another white woman with tidy, dark brown hair, climbed into our bus, gripping a clipboard. She welcomed us and congratulated us for arriving. She spoke with our bus captain, who then turned to us and announced that we would meet back here at seven o'clock sharp to depart. We stretched our bodies and filed off the bus.

There were people everywhere, as far as the eye could see. Youth groups and choirs sang and danced. A group of young men in maroon jackets was stepping, clapping and singing while a ring of people watched.

*This may be the last time you march for freedom*
*This may be the last time, but I don't know*

To the side, a group of young men shared cigarettes and compared their bus rides from California, Florida, and Boston. One man motioned with his cigarette as he talked. The agitation in his voice caught my attention.

"I got off the bus in Maryland to buy cigarettes," he said. "They wouldn't serve me. When I got back on the bus, my bus captain gave *me* hell for having gone in the store! You believe that? 'We have to be organized.'" He imitated a high-pitched voice. "'This isn't about making a statement. If you're going to act on your own, you should take off your button, because you're not representing the march when you do that.'" He sucked his teeth. "Shiiiiit. I had half a mind to get off the bus and go home. White lady had some nerve. 'Making a statement.' Expecting to be served like a human being is making a statement?" He took a deep drag of his cigarette and blew the smoke out with a grimace. His new friends shook their heads and made sounds of disapproval.

Mom and Dad flanked us and steered us onto the grass around the Washington Monument, where volunteers handed out signs, flags, and programs with maps on the back. Dad chose a sign that said, *We demand equal rights NOW.* He told Mom they would take turns carrying it so her arms wouldn't get tired.

People lined up and began to march. Row after row joined in singing "We Shall Overcome" until the harmonies surrounded us. Dawn linked arms with me and Mom and sang her little heart out.

The late August sun shone down steady. We waited below the stairs of the Lincoln Memorial while the speakers caught up with the crowd and ascended to their places near the podium. People exclaimed when they saw Diahann Carroll, Sidney Poitier, Harry Belafonte, and other stars. Dawn stood on tiptoe, grabbing my arm.

"It is!" she squealed. "It's them!"

They were every bit as classy in real life as they were in the movies.

All went still as Marian Anderson filled the air with her operatic voice.

Everyone remembers Dr. King's speech from that day, and that's the one they quote. But I remember a young man who spoke. John Lewis from SNCC. I had read about him in the papers, but I hadn't realized how young he was. Suddenly, SNCC was something I could soon join. I listened hungrily to his words.

He invoked the hundreds and thousands of brothers who could not be there with us. People who were paid so little they could hardly afford to eat. Students who were jailed.

He criticized the civil rights bill. He criticized the Dixiecrats and the federal government, the party of Kennedy, for doing nothing to protect the people working for change. Unsatisfied with their inaction, he asked for a political party that would make it unnecessary to march on Washington.

We were tired, he said, and he named what had worn us out. Being beaten by policemen. Seeing our people locked up. Being told to "Be patient." "We want our freedom," he said, "and we want it now."

He told us to get involved in the great revolution, to get out and stay in the streets until true freedom came, until the revolution of 1776 was complete.

I would remember his words more than any of the others. His was a demand, not a plea. He threw down a challenge to us all.

Back on the bus, Dawn and I slept almost immediately. We woke up when the bus stopped in New York City. Uncle Robert and Aunt Ruth were waiting for us in their Lincoln Continental. We dropped our overnight bags into the trunk and piled into the back seat.

When we got to their brownstone, Robbie let us in. Susie was sitting in front of the television, and she sprang up to hug Dawn. After Uncle Robert took our bags to the guest room, the grown-ups settled in the kitchen for coffee and tea while we sat on the couch. Footage from the march played on the evening news. Dawn told Susie every detail of our day, focusing on the movie stars and the college-age friends she had made on the bus.

Robbie smirked at me sideways. "How was the 'revolution'?" he asked.

On the television, Dr. King recited his beautiful words again. I studied the crowd, looking for the four of us.

"The biggest march in history," Robbie said. He glanced at his parents and lowered his voice. "More like the biggest farce."

I frowned and shrank in my seat.

He patted my knee. "I'm sorry. I know you're proud of yourselves. But this whole thing"—he waved dismissively at the television—"this was all a part of the man's plan. You know that, right?"

I took the bait. "What are you talking about?"

Robbie leaned toward me and talked with his hands. "Minister Malcolm explained everything. See, it was supposed to be a revolution. A real march on Washington. Poor people from the ghettoes. People who were fed up and tired of being beaten and refused our rights."

Robbie always talked as if he were part of the working poor. I wanted to point out that he was middle class like us, but I also felt that he was closer to the people than I was.

"People were going to sit on the roads and sleep in front of the White House. They were going to shut down Washington and not leave until change was made. *That* was gonna be a revolution. Then President Kennedy heard about it, see? They couldn't have all those colored people showing up and making them look bad in their own capitol city. So the president met with those so-called Negro leaders. King, Abernathy, you know. He said, 'You've got to stop this.' They told him, 'We're not running it, and we can't stop it. The people are fed up. It's out of our hands.'" Robbie laughed and clapped his hands and rubbed them together like this was the good part. "So Kennedy said, 'Look, let's make a deal. We'll support the march if you organize it. Reign it in.' They gave the Negro leaders money and told them to keep the people in line. No more revolution. They turned it into something they could control."

My head ached. "Well . . . they didn't cancel it."

"Of course they didn't!" he said gleefully. "They have to act like they're friends of the Negro. But they have to make sure we don't take things too far." He watched, satisfied, as my expression changed from confusion to a vague sense of betrayal. "Yeah, they talked about passing a civil rights bill. But did Kennedy come to the march? No. They did just enough to pacify the people."

My eyes burned. I wiped my sweaty palms on my slacks.

"Chartered buses," Robbie continued. "Official printed signs. Approved songs. They controlled the whole thing and made got everyone out of town by sundown. Then, back to business as usual."

I thought back to our bus captain's warning about making it back to the bus on time. We had been told it was for our protection that we be on the road before nightfall.

Robbie had a habit of making me question everything I thought I knew. But on the heels of our glorious day, it stung more than ever. I decided to keep John Lewis to myself. He wasn't shown on television, and Robbie didn't mention him, and I didn't want to learn anything that would take away the glow of his challenge. Not while I was still turning over how to meet it.

Robbie whispered to me that he was going to bring me to Harlem to hear Minister Malcolm speak. I knew Robbie went often, lying to his parents about visiting nearby friends. But me? Harlem might as well have been Mars. If they had egged Dr. King's car when he visited Harlem, what would they do to me?

I went to bed that night plotting how to get out of it. Should I tell Mom and Dad? Could I betray my cousin? That would only prove his point, that I was on the wrong side of the revolution. I had to go.

It didn't take long for my curiosity to overpower my fear. My hurt feelings faded. I wanted to know the truth.

### Saturday, April 20, 1968

Robbie doesn't stay with us long at the rally—he has plenty of other people to greet, and he also has to speak. The students talk about how cool it was seeing him, and they ask if we can go together to visit him at his office.

"Sure," I say. I should be happy to do it—I should have suggested it myself—but I'm already hoping they'll forget about it.

After the rally, Valerie and I walk the students home, one by one. They ask me if I've worked with Stokely and H. Rap Brown. Now that they know Robbie's my cousin, they expect more of me. I try to pretend it doesn't bother me, but by the time we say goodbye to the last student, I'm exhausted from the effort.

"I'm not ready to go back to campus," I tell Valerie as we approach an intersection.

"No?" she asks, checking her watch. "It's been a long day. I'm ready to eat and crash."

I look around the wide streets. The daytime scene is turning to evening. Families disappear into apartment buildings. Well-dressed couples step out, arm in arm, laughing. Apparently the nightlife hasn't suffered from the riots.

"I guess I'll see you back on campus tomorrow?" The cars stop, and Valerie steps off the curb to cross the street.

"No," I say, taking her hand and pulling her back onto the sidewalk. "Stay with me."

Valerie looks down at our hands.

"Sorry," I say, letting go. "You're hungry, I'm hungry. Let's go get some food. My treat."

"Um . . ."

"Please," I say. "Don't make me beg. I will embarrass you right here in front of all these people."

"Oh Lord." She laughs. "You'll embarrass yourself. I don't embarrass easily."

"When's the last time you ate off-campus?" I ask.

"Last time I was home," she says.

"Exactly. There's a Caribbean place not far from here." Before she can protest again, I add, "If you pass up Caribbean food for dining hall food, I'll . . . I'll tell your parents on you."

"Oh, will you now?"

"I will. They'll probably disown you, right?"

"Ha. If I tell them I was trying to get back to campus before dark, they'll be thrilled."

I hold an arm out toward the hill. "Look at that long walk. Your stomach is rumbling, I can hear it. And you wanna go back to campus to fill it with some tasteless chicken and potatoes? When you could be right here eating curry goat, rice and peas...."

"Okay! Goodness! Stop talking. Let's go eat."

"All right now!" I steer us in the direction of the hole-in-the-wall restaurant.

"This place better be good," Valerie warns me.

"Or what?"

"Or else."

"Yes, ma'am."

The place has no sign, and we almost pass right by it. I hold the door open for her. As she enters, she assesses the servers and cooks, the patrons, and finally the menu. West Indian accents sing out in the tiny kitchen and at the tables. She smiles at me. She orders stewed chicken, and I order curry goat.

When the steaming plates are ready, we sit at a tiny table and devour our food. The meat slides right off the bone, and the spices play on my tongue. We barely talk, only grunting our approval, until we're stuffed. My plate is empty, and hers is clean except for a neat pile of plantains on the side.

"You don't eat plantains?" I ask her.

She twists her mouth. "I hear enough about it at home, okay?"

"Oh, I'm not complaining. I'll help you out." I stab her plantains one by one and savor these last bites. I wipe my mouth with a napkin and pat my stomach with both hands. "Now I know the meaning of 'fat and happy.'"

She laughs. "Yeah. This was really good. We don't eat out at home. I didn't even know you could get this kind of food in a restaurant."

It surprises me that she's never eaten in a restaurant, but I try not to show it. Our class at Columbia and Barnard was the first to have more Black students from working-class backgrounds than from the middle class. That's caused some of the tension in SAS between conservatives who want to blend in—mostly middle-class students who've spent their lives trying to blend in with white folks—versus those from ghettoes who want to change society.

"Now you know," I say. "Maybe we can make it a habit."

"I don't know about that," she says. "Who has money to be eating out all the time?"

"It's not that much," I say. "I mean, I don't mind. It's a taste of home."

"We know we're not at home. Might as well face it," she says. "Thank you though. I appreciate your introducing me to the City's hidden charms. I feel like the rich white folks who come into Harlem to get some culture." She giggles.

"Wait, what? How is that? I'm not rich or white."

Her smile is patronizing. "Rich is relative," she says.

"But I'm—" I can feel myself getting defensive, so I bite my tongue. My good mood fades quickly. Does she really think I'm that far removed?

She changes the subject, and I hope it's out of mercy and not indifference. "So," she says. "You ready to talk about today and next steps? I've got more energy now that I've eaten."

I don't want to think about the rally or the kids or Robbie. I stack her plate on top of mine and make a show of checking my watch. "Maybe we should head back to campus," I say.

Outside, it's getting cooler as darkness settles on the City. Valerie zips up her jacket.

"What you know about curry goat anyway?" she asks.

"Are you serious? I never told you my mom's from Barbados?"

Her jaw drops. "No! You did not!" She looks at me sideways. "You are full of surprises. A cousin working for SNCC in Harlem. Mom from Barbados. Huh." After a moment, she says, "Well, that's a missing piece of the puzzle."

"What puzzle?"

"You say how unfair it was for your parents to raise you in the suburbs as the only Black family. People didn't struggle to get to the US so they could raise their kids in the ghetto. They could do that back home."

"Well, my mom didn't choose to come here. She was a kid when her parents brought her."

"The principle still applies," Valerie says. "I'm sure her parents raised her with that mentality. Each generation has to do better than the last. Trust me, I know."

Valerie's parents are from Trinidad. I know they're fiercely proud of her, and she doesn't complain, but I can tell their pride comes with pressure too.

I don't argue with her, even though I hate when people try to explain my parents to me.

Valerie breathes in the night air and lets it out with a contented sigh. "So the rally went well."

First my parents, now my cousin.

"What did you think?" Valerie presses.

"It was . . . all right."

"Just all right? Did you see how into it the kids were?

Those signs they made! I was not expecting that. And they were really digging your cousin."

"Yeah."

"So . . . ?"

"So what?"

The columns of Barnard grow taller as we approach the women's campus.

"So . . . are you inspired? Don't you think we got a good start today?"

I shrug. "I guess. I just don't see where it goes next. What can we actually do?"

She holds her hands out to her sides. "Exactly what we're doing. Partnering with the community. Supporting the youth. Uniting for the cause."

"And then what?" I say. "When they're forced out of their homes and we're moving on with our degrees? What's more important than everyone having a home?"

"That's why we support the tenants' organizations! They were there today."

"But we're part of the reason they have this fight. Columbia couldn't run without its students." And its security guards. And the politicians in the trustees' pockets. And everyone else who helps the system run, plays along, doesn't rock the boat.

"This again?" Valerie slows down as we approach the flowering courtyard surrounded by brick buildings. She comes to a stop and folds her arms, facing me. "I still stand with Baldwin. When he came to campus and he sat with us and he told us how important it is that we're here."

173

I look away. "Baldwin is an intellectual. He's not an activist."

"So?"

"So of course he thinks it's more important to sit around reading the white man's books. While he sits at his desk writing books, the people on the ground are trying to survive."

"Are his books hurting the cause? No. They're helping. We need activists *and* intellectuals. We need artists too. Like you."

I scoff at that. "My sketches are not part of the revolution. The people who are organizing are doing the real work."

"Okay," she says. "If that's how you feel, if it's really that black and white to you, why don't you drop out of school?"

I wish I could. This life that's expected of me feels like a moving train. I can stand at the edge, but it takes more courage to jump off and walk than to ride it out.

"I'm serious," she says. "You could work with your cousin at SNCC. Hell, join the Panthers. Take a year off. Whatever it's going to take to get you unstuck. Because right now . . ." She shakes her head. "I can't work with you like this."

My chest freezes. "What do you mean? Just because we see things differently . . ."

"That not it." She shakes her head again. "You're not . . . you're not focused, Kevin. You're so busy pointing out the faults in everyone and everything, you can't focus on doing the work. You hear what I'm saying?"

"That's not fair," I say. "Everyone does this. Thinking about our role in the struggle . . . that's part of participating in the struggle."

174

"Yeah, it's *part* of it. I'm saying . . . it's as if you're thinking and criticizing *instead* of getting to work. You're so self-conscious. It's like—I don't know—like you're too scared to put your whole self in because it's not going to be perfect or easy or fast. So instead you just blame everyone else for why you can't do anything. Your parents. Columbia. The world." She throws her hands up.

I glare at the ground, clenching and unclenching my jaw.

After a minute, she says gently, "Thank you again for dinner, Kevin. Please call me when you're ready to do the work."

She turns, jogs up the stairs, and slips inside the door, a few minutes before curfew. I'm left standing by myself again, watching another best friend walk away from me.

# 7

## GIBRAN
*Massachusetts | September 1995*

It's been less than a week since we submitted the proposal for the Day of Absence, and Mr. Clarke has the school's official response. He told David he'd come to the Brother Bonding meeting to deliver it, so I'm here early to make sure I don't miss anything. I'm sure it's been approved—otherwise, I think he'd be ashamed to show his face. They'll probably put conditions on our plans though.

While we're waiting for the meeting to start, I check in with Chris.

"You straight? Everybody treating you good?"

"Yeah," he nods. "And I got on the debate team."

"Cool, cool," I say. "Let me know when you're having an event. I'll come out."

"Oh! Wow. Thanks!" he says.

"Of course. Gotta support my peoples."

Mr. Clarke walks in wearing his usual gray striped suit, red tie, and glasses. The thinning hair above his round, brown face lies flat in shiny waves. He pulls a handkerchief—an actual cloth handkerchief—out of his suit jacket pocket and dabs at his damp forehead.

"Good afternoon, boys," he says, sounding nasal and strained.

I wonder if he has ever been in a room full of Black people besides his own family. He looks so uncomfortable it's almost funny.

David offers him a chair, and Mr. Clarke perches himself on its edge.

"I'll make this brief," he says. "I received your proposal to be excused from classes for the, uh, the Million Man March. I wanted to deliver the school's response in person so as to convey that your concerns have been heard and considered. Unfortunately, we have to deny your request."

Looks of confusion fly across the room.

"Hold up," I say, but he continues. He's prepared.

"I expect this will come as a disappointment to you. However, as you know, there are fairly stringent rules about missing classes. I'm afraid this event does not meet the school's standard of a holiday or a cause the school can endorse by sanctioning time off to honor it."

James jumps on this. "Can you say more about that? I mean, how does the school decide what's worthy of time off and what's not?"

"Yeah," David says. "It sounds like we're being dismissed because we're a minority. If the school doesn't care about what's important to us, that's not fair."

Mr. Clarke scrunches his nose to push his glasses up. "Well, the march is advertised as an exclusive event, by race and gender. As such, it's simply not appropriate for the school to endorse it. It would be divisive and unfair to the rest of the student body."

"But we're allowed to go to the Student of Color Conference," I say. "Is that 'divisive and unfair'?" I make air quotes with my fingers and practically singsong his words back at him.

"The conference is different," he says, avoiding my eyes. "It is specifically for students from independent schools. While it was created for students of color, it is not explicitly exclusive or antiwhite."

"Seriously?" I can't with this man. "This is ... Okay. Wow. I mean, I don't know why I'm surprised."

David tries one more time. "Mr. Clarke, we were hoping that you'd understand our interest in this event, at least on some level, and be able to stick up for us, just this once. . . ."

Mr. Clarke makes a pained expression and says, "I do not support the Million Man March myself. And even if I did, I am the principal of the entire school, not of one small group."

"Well, if the school was doing its job for this small group," I say, "we probably wouldn't need this event. We'd be happy like everybody else. We're left out of things here at school every day. And you're concerned about them feeling left out for one day of their lives? I'm sorry, but that's ridiculous."

Mr. Clarke clears his throat. "I understand you're passionate about this," he says in a let's-wrap-this-up tone. "I'm not discouraging your passion. That said, politics can get ugly pretty quickly. We want to keep campus a neutral place where everyone can feel comfortable."

I lean forward. "You're not hearing me. You say you're

here for everyone, but you're clearly not here for us. You say 'everyone,' but you really mean 'white people.' That's who you're working for."

His face draws closed.

We stare at each other for a few beats. No one speaks. The sounds of other students coming in and out of the building float toward the closed door. Mr. Clarke averts his eyes again. "Well. If there are no further questions. I'll let you get on with your meeting. For your records." He hands David a folder and wishes us a good afternoon.

As he steps out the door, I say, just loud enough for my words to follow him out, "Sellout."

He pauses. The others cringe, gaping wide-eyed between me and the door. I stare at his back, daring him to turn around and face us. He doesn't. The door clicks shut. His footsteps recede.

David opens the folder, and I peer over his shoulder. A single page is inside. Our proposal, typed and signed by all of us, with a dated stamp at the top. Rejected.

We don't discuss next steps. People munch on snacks and sit around for a while before getting up to leave. David has soccer, James has the play and applications to work on. I decide to stop at the snack bar before heading home.

As I trudge across the grass, I daydream about cussing out Mr. Clarke or confronting the board or hijacking a school van and driving a group to DC. I'm annoyed with myself for being surprised. Since when has the school ever supported us? But we were asking for so little this time.

When I cross the street to the north side of campus, I hear a voice calling, "Hey! Hey!"

The voice carries aggression and contempt, and that's how I know, without looking, that it's directed at me. I have never heard a white person addressed this way: with this mixture of spite and glee, disguised as disappointment, when an adult finds me behaving like the delinquent they expect me to be.

"Hey!" Again.

Against my better judgment, I turn toward the voice. It's a campus security officer, pointing a finger at me. "Don't cross the street that way," he says. His voice is unnecessarily loud.

I look back at the street. "Excuse me?"

"I said, don't cross the street like that." He points out the path I supposedly took.

This must be a joke. "Like what?" I ask.

"Diagonally."

"Diagonally?" I repeat.

"Yeah. Walk straight across the street. It's shorter. Don't make the cars wait for you. You're not the center of the world, you know."

I make a show of looking up and down the street. No cars in sight. Other students cross the street in both directions, some on crosswalks, most not. Some zip straight across, some zigzag. They change their minds in the middle of the street. They stop to laugh or flirt, slowing down as if on purpose for drama.

"Are they the center of the world?" I ask, gesturing with my head at a group of friends shouting, shoving, and tripping each other as they cross the street in a long diagonal. A car has appeared, driving the obligatory fifteen miles per hour. The driver waits for the last of the students to step onto the sidewalk before proceeding.

The officer barely looks at them. "Just pay attention, okay?" he says to me. "It makes the school look bad."

I grit my teeth. "Do me a favor," I say.

He chews his gum with his mouth open and adjusts his pants.

I walk up to him. When he realizes how close I'm getting, he steps backward and bumps into his white patrol car painted with the school colors.

I point my finger in his face. "Don't. Ever. Talk to me. Again."

He looks at me with wide eyes. His chewing slows.

"Ever!" I shout.

He flinches like I shouted *Boo!*

I'm fantasizing about smashing his face into the top of his little white car, so I walk away before he can recover enough to speak again. Continuing toward the snack bar, I check my watch. The snack bar closes in two minutes. I fling open the door of the building and jog down the stairs. Just in time to see the doors clang shut.

I want to kick down the doors. I want to scream until my throat is sore.

I could cry right now. I can't even get a fucking cookie.

After Mr. Clarke, the guard, and the closed snack bar, I can't leave campus fast enough. I walk down the long street to the bus stop, leaving the bright green grass and the old brick buildings and the stone library and the glass arts center and the fields full of athletes and the dining hall full of workers preparing to feed hundreds of rich kids. I leave the toy cop behind me, but I hope he drives by as I zigzag across this street in the longest diagonals I can manage. I wish some cars would appear so I can make them wait and dare them to say something to me.

On the bus, I stare out the window. Shaded, tree-lined streets with tall fences hiding spacious yards give way to city blocks of concrete. Then the city streets become neighborhoods lined with triple-decker apartment buildings ten feet apart.

I walk home from the station, kick off my shoes, climb the stairs to my room, and throw my bag on the floor. I open a window, thinking I have time to smoke before Mom gets home. I open my drawer. My notebook lies on top. I pull it out. It's covered with tags and filled with months' worth of rhymes. I flip to a fresh page.

I pick up a pen and start writing.

Not rhymes. Not lyrics. I write a letter. A letter to the school.

*What I don't write*

I used to wonder why it scared you so much, letting us join their world. Now I think it's because you couldn't save us from it once we'd entered.

By the time I realized Luke and the other kids at school couldn't replace my friends from home, they already had. I went to Luke's house every day after school until your workday ended. Ava and Ashanta made friends who lived near the school, and they did the same. We got used to spending hours at friends' houses during the week, and then there were sleepovers on weekends. You would drive us out to Brookline, Wellesley, Needham, and Newton.

182

It was so different outside of the city. In the city, the streets were shared spaces. Brown people strolled, lingered, people-watched, hung out, lived out loud. In the suburbs, the streets were too clean, like a house that's staged and unused, and there were no people on the streets. There were fences and sometimes dads or landscapers doing yard work, but no one on the sidewalks. We learned that there was so much space inside those houses, people could hide from their own families too. And there were backyards where they could enjoy the outdoors in private.

Sometimes you got lost driving us out to friends' houses, and your fear made us hold our breath. You would drive slowly, gripping the steering wheel tight, getting more panicked with each block we passed, as if something bad would happen if the house didn't appear soon.

Then you would pull the car to the side of the road and burst into tears.

We would be quiet, not sure what to do. What had broken our brave, strong mom? When your sobbing got lighter, one of us would quietly suggest you ask someone for directions. You would wipe your eyes and look around like a small animal caught in a net.

"I hate coming out here," you would say. The bitter fear in your voice shocked us.

When we'd finally find the house, we'd be late for the party. You would pull yourself together to walk us to the door, and we'd feel guilty saying goodbye to you.

In middle school, things started changing. I was old enough to go to events for students of color from the area's private schools. And Kris Kross came out.

Everyone said I looked like Chris "Daddy Mack" Smith. We really only had light skin in common, but I embraced the comparison. They were popular, so I could be too. It didn't take me long to decide to complete the look: braids on top of my fade, baggy clothes—worn backward when I could get away with it, which wasn't often. You weren't having it.

The braids didn't last long. The combing required to get those straight parts was torture. Ava and Ashanta couldn't believe how tender-headed I was. Ava hated my whimpering and holding on to my hair, so she helped me switch to twists, which could be redone without all the combing and brushing.

By eighth grade, I had a handful of Black friends from other schools who I'd met at parties and events. One night, we were getting ready for a party at Brookline High School. That place had more students of color than any of the private schools, I guess because it was the closest METCO school to Boston.

Everyone came to Alex's house already dressed for the party. His mom ordered pizza, and we ate like we might never see food again. We went to Alex's room and played the music we expected to hear at the party. Kris Kross, Arrested Development, House of Pain. I started redoing my twists, trying to act casual about it and not get in the mirror too much. I had already learned that you couldn't be light-skinned *and* vain, or you were a pretty boy. You had to destroy that notion by being hard-core.

Alex had no shame about being in the mirror though. His skin was a medium brown, and he brushed his hair real slow and intentional, trying to make waves.

"Man, stop tryna smooth out them nigga naps," Trevor said. "Tryna make people think you got good hair."

The other boys laughed.

Alex didn't blink. "Shut up. You just mad 'cause you black as tar. Asking girls to dance and they can't even see you in the dark."

"Oooooo!" Matt called, like he was watching an unbelievable game of ball.

Trevor turned on Matt. "Don't get me started on *your* nigga naps. Why didn't you get a haircut, man? Nobody wants to see that. Somebody give him a hat."

I laughed with them, knowing I would be dragged into it eventually. I worked quickly to smooth my kinks into fresh twists.

Here came Trevor again. "And check out Gibran's big-ass naps," he started.

That's when Harold snapped.

Soft-spoken, easygoing Harold.

He shouted, "Man, what the hell are we *supposed* to have growing out of our heads?"

Everyone stopped, startled, as if he'd thrown a glass against the wall. I didn't even know Harold could yell.

"We're Black, right?" he said. "What the hell is wrong with that?"

No one spoke. We had no idea what to say.

Until loudmouth Trevor cracked another joke. "I don't know about y'*all*," he said. "*I'm* half Indian."

Someone pushed him, and we laughed again. But the echo of Harold's indignation lingered. We didn't talk about it. But I thought about it all the time.

I thought about it at the party, watching who got asked to dance and who was considered "fine."

I thought about it at school, noticing every glance that came my way when anyone—or anything—Black was mentioned, and feeling my body heat rise.

I thought about it at home in the mirror, watching my twists grow fuzzy, knotting and curling into themselves.

I stopped having Ava do my hair.

She warned me it would lock. I didn't know anyone who had locks, but I felt daring and dangerous the more untidy my hair got. Maybe I shouldn't care. Maybe I didn't.

People started to look at me differently, and I started to enjoy it. The waiting, searching for something, which I had never understood, was replaced by recognition. I was becoming what they expected, and it scared them. This felt like power. And it felt brand-new.

The more wary they became, the more outlandish I wanted to be. They saw something unpredictable, with a threat of danger close beneath the surface. I explored how I could use it.

You saw me growing cocky, and you worried. But if I had to choose between this power and the cowering I was used to, there was no contest. I could be untouchable. Why wouldn't I be?

By the time I left White Oak School, this was my way to survive.

James and David know something's up when I ask them to

meet me in the library after school. They show up right on time. We sit around a table and I hand my notebook over, open to the letter I started. I need their help to finish it. It needs to come from all of us.

James takes the notebook, and David scoots closer to him to read over his shoulder. I lean on the table and watch their faces while they read. When the words run out, James flips the page.

"Oh man! That's it?"

"That's where I ran out of steam."

"Damn. You were on a roll," David says. "So you're picturing this going out to the whole school?"

"Yeah. I don't know how though. They wouldn't put this in the school newsletter."

"We could stuff mailboxes," James says. "But that's a lot of paper. And if they caught us, they'd probably stop us."

We think for a minute.

"What about if we post it up in all the buildings?" I say. "On bulletin boards and stuff."

They nod. "That should work," James says. "We could put them up on doors and walls too. Make sure people can't miss it."

"Cool," I say. "What else should we add?"

I click open my pen.

We read over it again and add bullet points. I show them the copy of *Black Power* that I found in the attic. While they take turns flipping through the book and adding to the letter, my mind turns to the envelope I found in the book. It's stashed in my drawer at home, waiting for me to find the right time to ask Mom about it.

We meet every day for five days. We add, cross out, tweak, and revise until we can't say it any better.

On Wednesday, I stay late. In the computer lab, while other students write papers and lab reports, we type up our letter to the school.

# 8

## KEVIN
*New York City | Tuesday, April 23, 1968*

A few days after the rally in Harlem, SAS supports a rally with SDS in the middle of campus. I'm one of hundreds of students leaving class at noon, just as they're getting started. It's a sunny day, and people who would normally walk by, huddled over with their heads down, avoiding the eyes of the radical students, slow down to hear what they're saying. I join the growing crowd gathered around the sundial.

Alan Russell, the student who disturbed the school's memorial service, yells into the megaphone. "They say, 'Don't worry about the war, don't worry about the draft—you're young, you're in college.' I say, how can we not worry about an unjust, immoral war being fought in our name? The government has canceled military enlistment deferrals for graduate students. Do you know what that means? Any senior standing here today could be weeks away from getting drafted."

I run through the Black students I know who are seniors and graduate students. Richard, Wesley, Jack, and more.

We all know people who have been drafted, but the thought of fellow students with plans for law school and medical school being called to fight makes me sick.

For me, the draft is two years away. I hope the war is over by then. My dad could probably get a colleague to declare me psychologically unfit. But using that kind of privilege only alienates me more from the majority.

"This school takes our money to educate us, only to send us out to fight and die? How can we sit here at this institution and not speak up? Without us, this place falls apart. And they don't care about us. Enough is enough. We are not disposable! We will not be part of a capitalist war machine!"

The crowd cheers and claps.

Richard climbs up onto the base of the sundial and Alan hands him the megaphone.

"The Society of Afro-American Students is here," Richard begins.

We make some noise, and white students clap. It is unusual for us to officially collaborate with another group on campus, and the excitement on the white students' faces is visible.

"We are here supporting SDS and the IDA Six. And we are here because we want a just society. SAS opposes oppression in all its forms. SAS stands against racism, whether it's across the world in Asia, here in the United States, or right here on campus."

We clap and holler. "That's right!"

"The university takes land from the community. The university invites Black students to campus and does nothing to help us succeed. The university controls how students express their dissent. We stand together to say that our opinions count. We stand together to make the university listen to us. And this is for the school's own good."

"Yes!" the crowd yells.

Richard wipes his forehead with a handkerchief and continues. "We saw an uprising in the streets of Harlem a few weeks back. The community is tired. The community is fed up. And we students are on the community's side. We will not sit down and let our school bulldoze the people who live around us. The university must change, or the university will come to regret its immoral actions."

"Yes!"

"That's right!"

We cheer and shout.

The crowd continues to grow, and momentum is building. Anticipation. Readiness. For what? Some sort of action. People seem ready to charge.

The leaders put their heads together.

While they confer, someone from the crowd calls out, "Let's take Low Library!"

Low Library houses the administrative center of the entire university. Inside are the president's offices, where the IDA Six were delivering their petition when they were declared in violation of the indoor protest ban.

The message to seize Low Library spreads quickly, and the crowd rushes across the green toward the building. I wonder if the president is inside, and what will happen if he is. They can discipline six students, but can they discipline hundreds of us?

I move with the crowd. The surge, this movement, feels good. We're part of some action at last, and perhaps something will come of it.

Someone pushes against the flow of the crowd toward me. It's Charles. When he sees me, he angles over.

"What's going on, Kev?" He's panting slightly.

"We're about to take Low Library." I grab his arm and try to turn him around. "Come on."

"Whoa—hold it." He eyes the folks rushing the stairs.

"It's okay," I tell him. "Look around you, man. They can't arrest everyone here, can they?"

Charles was wary when the SAS leaders told us to come out and support SDS. He was concerned about their reputation as an extreme, borderline fringe group. Now he looks even more worried, like this frenzy is a case of his fears coming true.

"I don't know about this." He runs his hand over his short hair.

A commotion on the steps of Low Library makes the crowd flow back.

"It's locked!" someone cries. "They shut the building! They locked us out!"

"Damn. That was fast." I turn back to Charles. "See? They're afraid of us!"

The crowd's energy sways and throbs, waiting for the next great idea or direction from the leaders.

After less than a minute, a woman's voice calls out, "To the gym site!"

Alan repeats into the megaphone, "To the gym!"

People behind him repeat, "To the gym!"

And people take off.

To the gym site. Where protestors were arrested in February.

The symbol of Columbia's disrespect for Harlem.

A perfect place to display our discontent.

The crowd gets louder, and people run. Charles bites his lip.

"It's cool, Charles," I say. "They can't arrest hundreds of students. And they can't kick us all out of school either."

He huffs, skeptical. "Is there even a plan?"

"It's a protest, baby! Make our voices heard. Maybe burn some shit down."

He doesn't laugh.

"You know I'm joking. These crackers wouldn't go that far."

"You probably would."

"Consider it training, my brother. When the revolution comes, you can't hide in your room studying for exams."

He frowns. "You know what, I'm gonna come to keep an eye on you. Keep you from getting your head busted in. I couldn't look your parents in the face if I let you do something stupid."

"Okay, then—let's go!" I jog along with the crowd. I don't know what it'll take to make a difference, but I feel ready to try anything.

We're near the back of the group when the construction site comes into view. We rush down the concrete steps, leaving the sounds of Manhattan streets behind us as we enter the clearing in the park.

"All right," Charles says irritably. "We're here. Now what?"

A twelve-foot chain-link fence protects the construction

site. Students spread along its length. Inside the fence, a wide, shallow hole in the ground gapes up at the sky. Trees bordering the site loom over us, watching. A handful of folks from the neighborhood who saw us marching have followed us and now stand back to see what we'll do. We have no protest signs. No megaphone. No plan. Only our bodies, our voices, our pent-up rage.

What now?

At a community meeting in December, SNCC leader H. Rap Brown told the people that if Columbia built the first story of the gym, blow it up. If they sneak back and build three stories, he said, burn it down. And if they get nine stories built, "it's yours. Take it over, and maybe we'll let them in on weekends."

Shouts in the crowd grow louder, and someone near the front starts a rallying cry.

"Strike a blow at Gym Crow, you strike a blow at the war!"

I feel the eyes of Harlem on us. A handful of Black college students in a sea of white. I belong to neither group. But I want to. I want Harlem to claim me.

I push through bodies toward the fence. I hook my fingers into the chain links and pull, testing the strength of the fence. Before I know it, the fence bends. Dozens of students now have hands on the fence, yanking at the metal loops. The sound of metal clanging against metal grows louder and louder. The crowd chants, "Pull it down! Pull it down!" I think of Mike as I pull with all my strength.

The chanting fades into sounds of scuffling feet. Two blue hats and gleaming badges on uniforms have entered the fray.

A white protestor climbs up the chain links, trying to use his weight to collapse the fence to the ground. He only needs a minute to make it happen. Before he can do it, a cop yanks him by the shirt and he falls, landing on his feet, knees bent. Richard puts himself between the boy and the cop. Richard, a leader of SAS. Richard, a Black brother. The sweat on my skin chills, and I am frozen, watching Richard grapple with the officer. The cop reaches for a weapon, but Richard stays his hand.

Then Charles is beside me, grabbing my arm. "Come on," he says urgently, "we have to go."

I don't want to let Richard out of my sight. Whatever happens, I have to witness. I am still breathing hard from pulling on the fence. I strain to see Richard through the frantically moving crowd, but Charles shakes me. There are at least five policemen now, trying to back us off the property and threatening to make arrests. Some students yell at the cops. A few keep trying to grab at the fence and get pushed back. Some are jogging back toward campus. Not everyone is prepared to confront the police. Most stand out of reach of the officers and jump backward when they swing their billy clubs at their legs.

More white students run away. More Black students stand their ground, determined to be treated like people.

"Come on," Charles says again. "Back to campus, now!"

"We can't leave," I say.

"Kev! Do you see the cops over there?" His eyes are wide, urgent. "Kids are fighting them! Do I have to explain what happens next?"

I know what can happen next. We've spent our lives

watching police side with violent racists, allow vigilante "justice" and enact extrajudicial violence themselves. Police dogs biting youth protestors in Birmingham, police beating marchers in Selma. All of it is etched in our minds.

"We have to fight them." I say this even though my legs won't bring me closer to them. I'm stuck in place. I can't go back to campus, and I can't fight the pigs. "It's our school doing this, Charles." I gesture at the construction site. "The pigs are here to protect them. They'll beat people to protect this—this stolen property. We have to stop them, or else we're no better than President Kirk and the board of trustees."

Charles stares at me. He looks around at the chaos. "Okay. Fine. I can't stop you. I don't know why I try. If this is your scene, if you have to do this, you do it. I know I am nothing like them, and I don't have to prove that to anyone. I'm at Columbia for one reason. I can't get shot. I can't get arrested. And I can't go home empty-handed." He backs up. "Be careful, Kevin. Please. Don't forget Orangeburg."

He walks away as quickly as he can without breaking into a run.

I consider Charles's words. Orangeburg. Three Black college students murdered by police. It sobered us back in February. It might have kept some of us away from protesting, thinking we had to stay out of harm's way. Then King was killed too, right in front of his police escort. Even his nonviolent program was too radical.

There are so many reasons to leave with Charles. To run from trouble. To keep my head down and stay safe. This is the long game. Acquiring the white man's education and tools and then using them to chip away at his rules. But it's taking too long, and people are dying. People are getting pushed aside. How can anyone focus on building a middle-class life for themselves and hope for equality later? It's never worked. We need to demand equality now.

The police have dragged a few protestors over to their cars, one of them in handcuffs.

"Why are you taking him?" students yell.

"Let him go!"

But they don't. A supervising officer has arrived and called off his men, but they still push the handcuffed student into the police car.

"You have one of ours, we'll get one of yours!" someone shouts.

"Back to campus!"

"We need a teach-in!"

"Let's go!"

The crowd moves together again, and I make myself move with it.

Back on campus, the number of protestors has swelled to hundreds. We flood the green in the middle of campus and spill into Hamilton Hall, the undergraduate academic and administrative center.

Inside, students fill the lobby, sitting on the floor, standing against the walls, and leaning out of windows. In the hallway, people are setting up instruments—drums, a bass, a microphone—a band. I step around people to cross the lobby and get to the wall lined with open oversized windows. I take off my jacket and sling it over my shoulder. I lean back and rest on the column behind me, briefly closing my eyes and allowing the sweat on my face and neck to dry. My arms ache and my feet are sore. I've been running on adrenaline since we left campus. Above the many animated conversations filling the air, the band starts to play funk. Odors of cut grass and sweat hang in the air. My stomach rumbles, and I realize I never made it to lunch.

Someone jostles me on their way toward a window.

"Sorry," he says, patting my shoulder and continuing on.

There are hundreds of white kids in here, and I recognize hardly any of them. As more classes let out, more students join. You can't move without bumping into someone. The megaphone goes around the room, and people give spontaneous speeches or lead songs. Even a few faculty members stop by and give mini-lessons on democracy and philosophy of revolution.

Scanning the crowd, I see some afros. Students sitting in a ring on the floor. Valerie is among them, nodding as another sister speaks, her sharp eyebrows drawn in concentration. When Valerie looks up, our eyes meet, and I realize I've been staring. I look away quickly and drum my fingers to the music.

A hush falls over the space, and I look to see what's happening. A man in a suit jacket with sand-colored hair enters the lobby.

Most of the Black undergraduates at Columbia know Dean Coleman, and he knows us, because he recruited most of us. He was tasked with diversifying the student body, and he did it. He convinced us that Columbia wanted us here. But when we got here, it was another story.

Dean Coleman takes in the crowd with dismay. He

studies the large clock on the wall opposite the entrance. He straightens his spine and starts across the room. The crowd parts for him and watches him open the door to his office.

"Wait," a student tells him, "we need to speak with you."

He looks at the student and again at the crowd. "Is this a demonstration?" he asks.

No one answers. He knows he can't take down the names of everyone in the building.

"The police arrested a student," someone tells him. "We need to get him released."

"Yeah," another says, "we could use a hostage."

"Am I to conclude that you will prevent me from leaving?" Dean Coleman asks.

"Yes!" a few students blurt.

"No," others say.

"We want to talk to you."

"I suggest that those of you who don't want to hold me hostage ought to leave," Dean Coleman says. He enters his office and closes the door behind him. The crowd swallows up the path it made for him. Students argue over holding the dean hostage.

"How would we stop him from leaving?"

"No one's gonna touch him."

"It's just a symbol. We need some leverage. How else will we force their hand?"

I don't mind getting in trouble. But I don't want to do anything to delegitimize our cause. Taking a hostage sounds extreme and foolish. Even if we don't plan to hurt him, the people outside don't know that.

The leaders from the rally make their way into the center of the room, carrying a megaphone and speaker.

"Friends and comrades," an SDS leader says, "can we have your attention?" He waits as people nudge one another and quiet down.

"We have some updates. We've formed a joint steering committee with leaders from SDS and SAS. We've worked together to finalize our demands to the university. We have six demands." He hands the microphone to Richard, who reads from a sheet of lined paper.

"Our six demands are as follows.

"One: All disciplinary probation against the six students originally charged must be lifted with no reprisals.

"Two: President Kirk's edict on indoor demonstrations must be dropped.

"Three: All judicial decisions should be made at an open hearing.

"Four: All relations with the IDA must be severed.

"Five: Construction of the Columbia gym must stop.

"Six: The university must see that all charges against persons arrested for participating in demonstrations at the gym site must be dropped." He adjusts his glasses. "We will stay in this building until our demands are met. There's no telling how long that will be, but it helps that there are so many of us and that we're in the administrative headquarters of the college. Get comfortable. Enjoy the music. We'll prepare for next steps."

After the committee leaves the lobby, the bands resumes its song.

Running through the demands in my head, I wonder how

long this will take, how likely we are to succeed, and whether we'll be in time to make a difference for families like Mike's.

The lobby overflows as students continue to stream in from classes letting out upstairs and from other campus buildings. Word has spread about the sit-in, and people come in solidarity, in curiosity, or just to get in on some action. From the windows, protestors call out to other students passing by the building.

"Come inside! Join the sit-in in Hamilton Hall!"

SDS students have put up posters of Che Guevara and Mao Zedong. When I see Eddie, a senior, carrying posters, I edge my way through the room to meet him.

"Need some help with that?" I ask.

"Sure, thanks, brother," he says, handing me a poster and some tape.

We decide to put them up on either side of the dean's office door. We reach above our heads to place them as high as we can so they can be seen from across the room. When we finish, we stand back to check their alignment. On one side, Malcolm speaks, wearing his iconic suit and tie, one finger in the air, light reflecting off his glasses. On the other side, a hooded Stokely Carmichael holds up a hand between himself and the camera.

"This is good," Eddie says.

As we back away from the door, a handful of white jocks elbow their way over and post themselves outside the dean's door. They give us a cold stare. Do they think the dean is in danger?

"You think the dean will leave soon?" I ask Eddie. "The workday's over."

Eddie checks the clock. "Honestly? I hope he does leave. We haven't done anything illegal yet. But if anyone tries to stop him from leaving, a case could be made for kidnapping. We don't need that."

Ed's father is a lawyer. I've judged everyone else's families just like I judged mine—bourgeois and disconnected. Now I feel grateful that so many of the Black students' parents are professionals. We'll need their help if the situation gets intense.

Ed collects the tape and other supplies he brought. "Some people are working on signs to hang out on the balcony. You want to help with that?"

"Sure," I say. Before I follow him, I admire the posters again. Malcolm speaks into the future.

## August 1963

Robbie kept his word that weekend back in 1963. He took me to hear Malcolm in Harlem. I never told a soul.

I wanted to tell Dawn so many times. Maybe if I did, the changes I was going through could have made sense to her. Maybe we wouldn't have grown apart. But the experience was mine. It was too precious to me. I could have trusted Dawn to keep the secret. But I was afraid that, not having been there, she wouldn't understand what it meant to me. How could I put it into words?

Dad dismissed Malcolm out of hand when we first saw him on television, four years before I saw him in Harlem.

"This man has suffered greatly," he said. "He needs to assign blame."

As if that explained the whole phenomenon of Malcolm X.

We kept the television on though. We needed to know what our neighbors were seeing when Mike Wallace narrated *The Hate That Hate Produced*, introducing the Nation of Islam to an appalled audience.

It was my first time seeing a Black man telling white people how we really felt and thought, and fearing no consequences for saying it—indeed, demanding that something be done about it. Dawn watched, unblinking, resting her chin on her fists. Did she feel the same awe, this strange mixture of relief and dread? I felt in my gut that he could change the world, that he *was* changing our world, by lifting a veil. Even if the ideas of having our own economy and land for Black people sounded far-fetched. He was so assured, his certainty was contagious.

But nothing could compare to seeing him in person.

On television, he was a spectacle. He was separate from us, as we sat in our suburban living room. He was formal. He sat across from white interviewers and gave voice to our pain, holding it up to the light—that innermost part of ourselves which we barely acknowledged privately. He revealed to a shocked white audience that they were its source.

Live, in Harlem, he was talking to us.

I had never been among so many Black people in one place. Mostly men. There was a platform set up with speakers and a row of chairs. Flags I didn't recognize stood at each corner of the stage.

The street was wide, and people came from every direction until the area around the stage was packed. Many of them wore the suits, white shirts, and ties favored by members of the Nation of Islam. I felt nervous, as if they would see through me, know that I lived among the "white devils," and kick me out.

Robbie scanned the empty stage and said, "Good, there's time to show you the bookstore. Come on!"

I tried to object. "We could just wait out here. There's no space in there."

"No way," he said. "You have to see it. You'll never see half this stuff up in Finchburg."

I looked around, hoping no one had heard him mention where I was from. Of course no one was paying attention to us. Still, I worried I would be exposed any minute as an outsider. Robbie moved through the crowd, and I rushed to follow before bodies closed the gap between us.

It's funny to remember. Micheaux's bookstore in Harlem is now one of my favorite places. That summer, just fourteen, being dragged along by Robbie, I felt I might faint.

The bright sign above the door read, "World History Book Outlet on Two Billion Africans and Non-White People." Below the words were portraits of about a dozen men. I read their names but only recognized a few. Beneath the portraits, another sign read, "Repatriation Headquarters—Back to Africa Movement—Recruiting." I had a sudden fear of being recruited immediately and shipped off to Africa right then and there. I began to sweat as we approached the door. I pictured Dawn, Mom, and Dad wondering what had happened to me. I knew it was irrational, and I chastised myself for being so dramatic.

Around the storefront were so many signs you could barely see through the glass. *The House of Common Sense* and *Home of Proper Propaganda. Harlem Square.* There were innumerable books and pamphlets on display. Men in suits lined the sidewalk. I worried that I would need some kind of identification or password to get in.

The sound of fingertips tapping a microphone blasted from the speakers, followed by a screech. Heads turned and people came out of the bookstore, thickening the crowd, which gathered around the stage. Robbie found us a spot with a clear view past the shoulders of the grown men surrounding us.

A young man in a suit shuffled papers next to the podium. We were so close to the stage that I could hear the tall, red-headed man seated behind him say, "Make it plain, Louis."

The young man—Louis—stood at the podium and gave a short introductory speech. He appeared to be in training, and his job was to warm up the crowd. He welcomed us as his "dear respected brothers and sisters," and at those words, my heart skipped.

There he was, at the back of the stage: Minister Malcolm, drumming his fingers on his thigh. He was introspective, almost shy. And then he was standing, to the whistles and claps of the people. He shook the young brother's hand as they traded places. He arranged and rearranged his papers on the podium. Finally, the applause died down. Malcolm nodded a brief thank-you for the love and launched into his speech.

It can't be described. Standing on the street in Harlem, one drop in a sea of Black faces, hearing Malcolm tell you he loves you. Feeling the weight of the world drop away because he sees clearly and he understands. Finding, for one hour of your short life, that you don't have to pretend.

It was a formal speech and a family reunion. He was a professor and a preacher. He was noble and saintly and then harsh and analytical too. He was a magnifying glass, concentrating sunlight into a beam that could light the world on fire.

Everyone was still, rapt in the grip of his voice. Not one person left while he spoke. I can only imagine it's what hypnotism feels like.

In person, among us, that objectivity that sometimes made him appear cold on television was replaced by warmth, affection, love. And it flowed both ways. The people hung on his words. The audience responded to his declarations, letting Malcolm know we were with him. I wanted to join the back-and-forth, to feel a part of it, to connect with him, to return the love he was offering. I was an outsider here, but he pulled every Black person in. I saw immediately how Robbie had become addicted to this feeling, this bond. If we lived close enough, I would have too. Thanks to my parents, I couldn't.

We don't need the white man, Malcolm said. We don't need his schools. We don't need his neighborhoods. We don't need his women. We used to think we were so pitiful and the white man was so great that we could only get better by being around him and begging for his scraps. But now, Malcolm said, the Black man is starting to wake up. (*Yes!*) The so-called Negro is starting to see things as they really are. (*That's right!*) The white man is the one who put us in the ghettoes, with the broken-down buildings and the crummy schools. (*Speak!*) He is the one who sent drugs into our communities and used our women as prostitutes, and then arrested us for those situations. (*Sure did!*) Therefore, we would have to be insane to go to the one who has been trying to kill us for four hundred years and try to pry our rights and justice from him. (*Say it!*)

The white man hates us, he said. So all that's left to do is to do for ourselves.

It was true, then. The feeling I had always tried to shake: the feeling of being tolerated but not accepted. Of being a dilemma, a trophy, a symbol, anything but a plain human being.

He didn't have to talk about the march to win me over—in fact I hoped he wouldn't—but he went there too.

When the newspapers had called the march a picnic-like atmosphere, it had sounded endearing. When Malcolm said the same, it was an indictment. His analysis made me feel it had been all wrong. Designed to make us think we were doing something when we were only going to get more of the same.

Robbie had been repeating Malcolm's words, then. When Robbie said it, I felt defensive and resentful. Now I felt indignant. I wanted to do something about it. To find out where the real revolution was happening.

The people were angry, Malcolm said. The people were talking about lying down on the tarmacs and not letting planes take off; they were talking about halting business as usual.

The people were angry with the so-called leaders after the failure to integrate Albany, Georgia. They were sick of the so-called leaders criticizing one another and getting nothing done. The people were calling for a revolution. And when the white politicians found out that the so-called Negro leaders weren't in control, they figured, if you can't beat 'em, join 'em. So that's just what they did.

They endorsed the march. They integrated the march. They put the Big Six up front. Everything became official and approved. In for the day, out by sunset. Controlled. In hand. The Black anger was diluted, tempered with the cool, detached goodwill of white liberals.

Malcolm recited facts. He cited names of hotels where meetings took place and dollar amounts that had changed hands. He had followed the developments, researched meticulously, and he had attended the march himself.

As we left the corner to go home to Brooklyn, both Robbie and I were silent, lost in our own feelings.

At home, it took me years to do what Robbie seemed to do in days: decode what Malcolm's words meant for me and my place in the world. That young leader from SNCC who I'd heard at the march—was he a part of the Big Six? I needed to know. With some digging, I found out that his original speech had been even more fiery. The powers that be, having required the speeches to be preapproved, had made him tone it down. Years later, I learned that they had nearly pulled the plug on his speech; they hadn't wanted him to speak at all. SNCC had started with the lunch-counter sit-ins, had endured beatings and savagery for years, so it made sense that they took up where Malcolm left off when his life was cut short.

That was yet to come. In 1963, I was fourteen, newly

exposed. I was still digesting a few weeks later when the terrorist church bombing in Birmingham killed those four little girls.

My perspective had shifted. My politics transformed. Maybe I thought I could change other people the way Robbie had changed me. I didn't care how I had felt about Robbie in the process; the outcome was what mattered. I tried to convert Dawn to my view. Instead, I ended up pushing her away.

### Tuesday, April 23, 1968

I leave the posters of Malcolm and Stokely to preside over the lobby. I find Eddie with the group working on the banners. They're making a mess. Eddie asks me to take over. The letters are enormous, to be seen from across campus. I outline the letters with straight lines and let others help fill them in with black paint. While they paint, I ask Eddie if I can borrow a pencil and use some of the smaller papers. I don't have my sketch pad, and I've already captured some scenes in my head today that I want to get down on paper.

"Of course," he says. "Take whatever you need."

I roll up a stack of papers and put them in my pocket. In the bathroom I wash the paint off my hands. On my way back to the lobby, I smell reefer. I look around to see where it's coming from. Inside a classroom, a handful of white students are passing a joint around. I feel like I should say something. This is not how we behave at sit-ins. Our behavior is supposed to be beyond reproach. In a corner of the hallway, a white couple is making out. Good grief.

Back in the lobby, I find Eddie again. "Do you know what some of these crackers are up to in the classrooms?" I ask him. I tell him what I saw.

"What do they think this is?" He looks around with disgust.

Black students sit in groups, upright, with looks of concern on their faces. White students lounge and chat excitedly.

"We need to get this situation under control," Eddie says, "or we're not going to accomplish anything. I'm gonna go look for Claudius."

I want to follow him, but I'm exhausted. I find a place to sit down and pull out the paper and pencil. I remember Richard's face as he stepped in front of the cop. A chill runs through me as I remember Richard reaching for the cop's hand, trying to calm him down, to diffuse the situation . . .

I'm deep into sketching when a bag of chips flies so close to my head, it grazes my ear. I duck and then look up to see who threw it. A white student standing with a box full of snacks looks at me like he's afraid he's poked a lion.

"Sorry!" he mouths. "Sorry about that!"

The person who caught the chips holds them out to me as a peace offering.

"No, thanks," I say, and go back to my sketch.

A few minutes later, a guitar stops strumming, clapping slows down, and whispers spread. I look up from my sketch to see a group of about thirty Black folks, mostly brothers, filing in from the hallway, checking the place out like they've never been here before. They haven't, I realize. I know the faces of all the Black students, even when I don't know their names. These brothers aren't Columbia students.

They're older, most of them. They wear afros of various sizes. They look organized, prepared, put together, unlike us ragtag students who look like we crawled out of bed and decided spontaneously to sit down in this administration building. Which is essentially what we did.

A sort of awed hush falls over the lobby. I recognize people from the community rally—from Harlem CORE, Harlem tenants' organizations, and people fighting for community control of public schools. There are also some students from City College. The newcomers greet people and take up positions around the room's perimeter. As they spread through the room, I see a familiar face among them. My cousin. Robbie. Here, on my campus.

It takes a minute for Robbie to notice me. He waves and walks over to me, looking delighted, as if he came to visit me. I wish I were as happy to see him. I can't help thinking, every time I get close to being useful, he shows up to remind me he's ten steps ahead of me.

# 9

## GIBRAN
*Massachusetts | September 1995*

On Thursday, throughout the day, we remind the Black boys we see to come to the Brother Bonding meeting. They don't disappoint. The three long couches are filled. We bring extra folding chairs to complete a circle around the coffee table. When everyone's seated, David passes out copies of the letter.

"Okay," I say, "last week when the school denied our request, as you know, I was pissed."

Everyone laughs a little.

"I started this letter as a response to them saying the Day of Absence was irrelevant. We worked on it together—me, David, and James—and added stuff about how the school ignores our needs. There's some specific examples in there, but we also talk about the general atmosphere on campus and how it needs to change. We want to give everyone a basic understanding of how it feels to be Black here, so then we can have some real talk about race."

David adds, "The point is for everyone in the school to

read this. The students, the faculty, administration, the principal. If the board and the discipline committee and whoever else can read it too, that's even better."

"We want to read it together now," James says. "If you see something you want to change or think of something to add, let us know. Then if there's no changes, people can sign it before we post it for the school to read. Cool?"

Everyone agrees, though some of them seem a little alarmed at the whole idea. Chris, who's sitting across from me on the end of a couch, blinks and bites his lip.

"We're not trying to pressure anyone," I say. "If you stand behind it, you sign it. If you don't, it's all good. That's why we're going over it, so you can decide."

"All right," David says, clapping his hands together. "Let's read. Who wants to start?"

I lean forward, elbows on my knees. No one volunteers. "Okay," I say. "I'll read.

"We, *Black men of Lakeside Academy, have observed that the conversations about race on campus have been hostile to, and ignorant of, us and our experiences as Black people. We are giving the school the benefit of the doubt and assuming that this has been done out of ignorance rather than intentionally to harm us. Therefore, there are some basic facts we wish to clarify, which we hope will make conversations about race more realistic.'* Okay, then we get into the points. Someone else want to read?"

James picks up.

"*One. Black people in this country live a different reality than white people in this country. The dream of color not mattering has not been achieved. White people walk around as in-*

dividuals. *Black people do not have that luxury. White people get the benefit of the doubt and are assumed innocent even with evidence against them. The opposite is true for Black people. We walk around with stereotypes attached to us, and everything we do, say, and wear is judged as if it either proves that we're a real-life stereotype, or miraculously sets us apart from the rest of our people.'"* James looks up.

David lifts his paper to eye level. *"Two. In order to separate ourselves from the stereotypes about us and gain the approval of white people—including teachers, administrators, and students here at Lakeside—Black men have to become copies of white people. We are expected to talk like you, walk like you, act like you, and believe your truths, including your ideas about us. Yet, even when we do all of that, we are not fully accepted. The more we act like you, the more comfortable you are, and the less you see us as a threat. But the more we become like you, the more we abandon our right to be who we are. To become nonthreatening, we abandon our needs and the needs of our people. What is the point of an education that teaches us to abandon our people?'"*

All eyes are on the pages in front of their bent heads. I wonder if they're imagining their white peers reading these words. I wonder how many of them are eager for this, and how many are scared or nervous.

Marcus, a sophomore with warm brown skin and a crisp baseball cap on top of his fade, sits to David's right. He looks at David, who nods at him. Marcus reads.

*"'Three. When a Black man in this country tells the truth about what white people have done to Black people, he is vilified. When a Black man in this country puts Black people*

*first, he is persecuted. White people do not acknowledge that they have always put themselves first, and continue to do so. White people are afraid of what could happen if Black people take care of themselves instead of being dependent on white culture and handouts. Black leaders of the past and present who have tried to take care of their own people have been demonized and usually destroyed. This is the true reason for the Million Man March, a nonsectarian event supported by dozens of mainstream Black leaders whose beliefs overlap with the Nation of Islam only in the commitment to healing the Black community.'"*

Silence.

"Mmm . . ." Trey says. "You don't think this weakens the argument? I mean, like, in terms of how they'll perceive it?"

"What you mean?" I ask.

"I'm saying, like, they could read this part and think the whole thing is about the march, when really it's more general than that. You know?"

"For sure," I say. "But I don't think we should hold back based on how they're going to twist it. I mean, if we avoid specifics, it's easy for them to say, 'Oh sure, we agree with this!' It's when you give examples of how it applies in the present day, that's when they try to say, 'Oh, that's not the same.' Nahmsayin?"

"That's true," Trey says. "I don't know. What if people stop reading at this point? Just say, like, 'Okay, this is about the march,' and dismiss it 'cause they already have their opinion about the march. That's what they've been doing this whole time."

"That could definitely happen. Then again, some people

are gonna dismiss it no matter what." I look at James and David. "What y'all think?"

James bites the inside of his cheek. "I mean, no matter how we say it, no matter what names we put or don't put, some people are gonna trip. We know that, and we have to be ready for that. I say, if we're gonna do this, we might as well say what's really on our minds. This may be the only time we let 'em know how we really feel."

"Yeah," I say. "I'm with it."

David asks, "Is this a deal breaker for anyone?"

The boys look around. Trey shrugs.

Before someone's hesitation can lead everyone to back down, I say, "Let's read the rest of it and then go back to any parts people aren't cool with. Aight?"

Jibreel, a sophomore with straight black hair and a hint of a mustache, reads next. "'Four. Instead of vilifying and dismissing leaders who rally Black people to care for themselves and do for themselves, white people should ask themselves why would Black people follow this person, and why do they feel that what this person says is important and necessary?'"

Kwame, a junior from New York, reads with a light accent. "'Five. Instead of assuming that Black students at Lakeside have separate interests and needs from Black people outside of Lakeside, students and faculty should listen to us. We define what we believe and what we need, inside and outside of class. For example, when entertainment is planned for the whole student body, the perspective of Black students should be considered. Will we find it funny when you mock our culture, as in the so-called rap performance at the talent show earlier this year? In fact, that kind of performance is *modern-day blackface, and we should not be subjected to it. How can we learn in a place where we are ridiculed?'"*

Trey shakes his hand and hisses like he's touched something hot. He is grinning now.

Zeke reads: "'Six. *Having a Black principal does not mean that all is well for the Black students.'"* He blinks.

"Yeah," I say, scratching my neck. "I had more to say about that, but they didn't want me to rash on him all out in the open like that, so. Someone wanna read the last bit?"

Chris looks around and then at me.

"Go ahead, Chris," I say.

His voice wavers at first, but he finishes strong. "'We hope the community will reflect on our perspective and come to a better understanding of our position as Black people in America and in this school.'"

A few moments pass while everyone digests what we've read. David pulls out a pen and hands it to me. I take the official copy out of my bag and sign my name at the bottom, big enough to read but leaving plenty of space for others.

I hand the paper and pen to David, who signs and then hands it to James. After James signs, Trey holds out his hand to take the paper and pen. A few more boys sign while others hold back. Chris sits biting his nails and bouncing his skinny leg up and down.

After Marcus signs, no one else reaches for the paper, so I get up and take it from him.

"We'll leave it on the table here," I announce. "No pressure, no rush. We're gonna put it up after the meeting though, so if you wanna sign it, make sure you do it before you leave."

We move on to other topics. We eat snacks and talk about the weekend.

Eventually, athletes trickle out to get to sports practice. Others head to the library, activities, or back to their own dorms. James and I rearrange the tables and chairs. I grab the letter and count the signatures at the bottom. Twelve. I had already counted how many boys were at the meeting. Twelve.

At the library, James and I make photocopies of the signed letter. He should be at rehearsal, but his scenes aren't running today, so he's prepared to make up an excuse for skipping. While the copies run, the late-afternoon sun sends its long rays over the campus and into the floor-to-ceiling windows of the library. Day students get in their cars—Beamers and Jeeps gifted from their parents—and drive home. Theater kids leave the performing arts center, tired from rehearsals and sore from dance. On the other side of campus, athletes are showering and throwing sweaty clothes into gym bags.

When we come back outside, dusk has turned the school's bright grass and white fences, its serious brick and painted doors, into evening shades of gray under a lavender sky. We walk quickly from building to building, each carrying a stack of papers. We use tape on walls and doors, thumbtacks on bulletin boards. Inside each building, our sneakers on the gleaming hallway floors make the only sounds.

When we post the last copy, on the door from Thatcher Hall to the dining hall path, we stand back to admire it. I hope no one will see these tonight. I want everyone to discover them in the morning, arriving at a school transformed.

# 10

**KEVIN**
*New York City | Tuesday, April 23, 1968*

Robbie opens his arms, embracing the scene. The lobby filled with protestors spilling into the hallway and onto the balconies. The funk band playing to keep our spirits up.

"Check y'all out," he says. "Taking over." He grabs my hand and pulls me in for a hug. "I'm proud of you, cousin," he says over my shoulder.

"How'd you hear?" I ask.

"Everybody's heard, man! Word spread after the scene at the construction site. People are planning to send over food and supplies." He scans the room, checking out the entryways and windows.

"Really? That's—that's amazing."

"Hey, we gotta stick together, right?"

"Yeah. I guess so." I still can't believe he's here. That all these community groups with such history in Harlem are here, on my campus, inside Hamilton Hall.

"Hey, sister," Robbie says, waving at someone near one of the doors. Valerie.

She gives him a head nod. He waves her over. She hesitates and then joins us.

"How's it going, sister? Valerie, right?" Robbie asks.

"Right," she says. "It's great to see you all out here supporting us."

"Of course," he says. "We're glad to see you all backing the community's cause. Maybe together we can accomplish what neither group could on our own."

"That's the hope," she says.

I put my hands in my pockets and look at the floor.

"Could you two help me out with something?" Robbie says.

She stiffens slightly, but Robbie doesn't notice.

"Some folks from the community will be sending in food for you all. You think you could help figure out how to bring it inside once it comes?"

"Oh sure," Valerie says. "Do you have any idea what time we should expect them?"

"It might not be until morning," he says. "Assuming you'll still be here."

"All right, that gives us time to get a committee together and prepare. I'll take care of it, Kevin."

The way she says my name without looking at me nearly destroys me.

"I can—"

"Don't worry about it," she says. "I've got it covered."

"Right on," Robbie says.

I watch her walk away.

I hope Robbie won't mention the awkwardness between

me and Valerie. Before he can speak again, one of the other community organizers signals for him.

"Excuse me," he says, patting my arm, "I'll be back."

I find a place to sit and try to quiet my mind by doing some more sketching.

Night falls, and the dean hasn't left his office. The white jocks who were standing outside his door were sent away, replaced by Black students and community members.

Claudius makes his way around the lobby, stopping at groups of Black students and gesturing toward the hallway. He stoops down next to me. "Hey," he says. "We're having a meeting of Black students out there."

In the hallway, the Black students are gathered in a small circle with the Black student leaders from the steering committee. We find an empty classroom and launch a discussion.

"The steering committee has split in two," Wesley says. "The SDS leaders operate differently. We have the same goals, but their methods . . ."

"Are we gonna barricade the building?" someone asks. "People keep coming in and out."

"That's right," someone else says. "We had to get those jocks out of here, and tomorrow people will come in for classes if we don't stop them. Didn't we take the building so we could shut things down?"

"That's what we want," Richard says. "In order to force the university's hand, we have to be organized and decisive. The SDS and the white students use this sort of participatory democracy, which is nice in theory, but with

BLACK & WHITE
DRAWINGS
TO COME

hundreds of students? Trying to get everyone in on every decision? It's . . . unwieldly, to say the least."

"They want to bring more people into the occupation and recruit students to their cause," Wesley says. "But that means keeping the doors unlocked."

"That won't work," another student says. "If we don't control the space, no one has to listen to us."

"Besides," Valerie says, "it's not about numbers. It's about commitment."

"That's right."

We debate our next steps, tossing ideas back and forth for almost an hour. Finally, someone proposes asking the white students to leave the building.

"If we do that," Claudius says, "will we all stay here and occupy Hamilton Hall until our demands are met?"

"Will we keep the same demands?" I ask.

"I think we should," Richard says. "We need to maintain an organized, united front. We still have a common cause. We don't want the administration to think they can divide and conquer."

If the white students leave, our numbers decrease dramatically. We will have self-determination, but we may be more vulnerable. Then again, the community is with us. We're all more aware of the risks we're taking than the white students seem to be.

"We just don't know if we can trust them," a Barnard sister says.

Others nod.

"And let's face it, we have to project a better image than this if we want to be taken seriously." Jack gestures toward the door that separates us from the hallway. We consider how the situation could change if we have the building to ourselves. Tension falls from our shoulders, and we become energized again.

Eddie is the first to say, "Yes. Let's do it."

One by one, everyone agrees.

"Okay," the leaders say. They look exhausted already.

"There's one more thing," Wesley says. "While we are grateful and humbled that community members have come out to support us . . . we need to remember that, although we're here in large part for Harlem, we can't rely on Harlem to the end. This struggle is between us and the school. We'll face the consequences, whether Harlem stands with us or not."

Someone asks, "Why would they be here if they're not with us?"

"Yeah," someone else says. "They have a stake in this too."

The leaders consider their words.

"The community has been fighting Columbia for years before we came along," Richard says. "Decades. They have their own organizations, priorities, and methods. Our goals are overlapping. We are stronger together. But we can't expect them to risk anything for us. They didn't ask us to do this. We feel it's our duty because we're here. We stand in solidarity, but we stand on our own."

It's not what I want to hear. I hoped that working together could unite us with the community. But I know he's right.

Relationships fracture at times of change. You don't always see it coming, but once it's done, you feel the loss.

## 1963–1966

If I could trace the fracture between me and Dawn, where would I find the starting place? Maybe on the day President Kennedy was assassinated.

It was three months after the March on Washington and my introduction to Harlem. Two months after the church bombing in Birmingham that killed those four little girls.

We were sitting in the living room, watching the presidential procession on television. Mom and Dad sat on the couch, Dawn sat cross-legged on the floor, and I sat in a wingback chair with a book in my hand. The president and the First Lady waved from the convertible. Then, a crack. He collapsed, right into Jackie's lap.

Dawn and Mom gasped and held their hands to their mouths. Dawn crawled to the television and touched the screen, as if she could turn back time. Dad leaned forward, listening to the announcer. Then he went to his study, turned on the radio, and stayed there for the rest of the night.

I sat still as a statue while Dawn cried and Mom dabbed at her eyes. Dawn loved Jackie. Everyone loved JFK. I knew this was a big deal. But I couldn't feel.

The next night at dinner, Mom and Dawn poked at their chicken pot pie.

Mom put her fork down and sighed. "What a tragic loss," she said solemnly.

"Why?" I asked.

She looked at me like I had grown horns.

"What did he ever do for our people?"

"Kevin!"

225

"I know what he *said*," I explained. "But what did he actually *do* for us?" I waited for a response.

Mom glanced at Dad, who was riveted by his food. "Well, he didn't get a chance," she said. "Now we'll never know, will we?"

After dinner, there was a soft knock on my bedroom door. When I didn't answer, Dawn said, "It's me. Can I come in?"

Dawn hadn't come to my room for a while. I had been spending more time in there since the summer, since we came home from the march and from the City.

I put my book facedown on my desk to hold my page and opened the door. She hesitated.

"In or out?" I said.

She stepped in cautiously, then plopped down in my desk chair and spun around slowly, leaning her head back and staring at the ceiling. I watched her. Her breath was shallow. She pulled her sweater around her and frowned. Was she seeking comfort? Was she so upset about the president? I wanted to wake her up.

"You know JFK was not our friend, right?" I asked.

She stopped spinning.

"People think this is the biggest tragedy ever," I said, gaining momentum. "We need to realize, Dawn, white people don't want what's best for us. We know this. We've seen this! How many times have white people betrayed us? From day one in this town. Mom and Dad can insist we deserve to be here. That doesn't change the fact that we don't belong here, and we never will."

Dawn let me talk, spilling everything I had been digesting

for months. I felt better afterward. Dawn's expression hardly changed. Or did it? Did her glassy-eyed sadness harden to a stony stare?

This became our routine. Throughout high school, I read constantly and tried to explain my revelations to Dawn, to open her eyes. Dawn kept coming to my room, night after night. Her eyes would go tired and dull, but she wouldn't leave.

Sometimes she tried to lighten the mood. Sometimes she asked where I got my ideas from. When I showed her the deep, heavy books I was reading, she sometimes offered book suggestions of her own. Poetry. Fiction. I told her she needed to educate herself. Maybe I went overboard, like Robbie had with me. With the zeal of an evangelist, I was desperate to make her free.

She watched me and she listened. Maybe she was observing. As if she needed to see what I was becoming. Night after night. Until the last time.

When she stopped coming to my room, I told myself she had gotten busy with other things. I was deep in the college application process by then. By the time I got less busy and started to miss her, I made up new excuses. Maybe I hoped her silence was defeat. Maybe I thought I had won her over and she finally understood.

Maybe I forgot she didn't care about being right. Maybe I forgot she just wanted to be loved.

**Wednesday, April 24, 1968**
I didn't see it coming with Dawn. It could happen as easily with Valerie. Or has it already? I can't stand that thought.

Valerie directs the food committee as they set up a classroom as a pantry, preparing for food supplies to be sent in. Running things, as usual. She doesn't notice me hovering, and the ease with which she goes on about her life makes me dizzy with panic, like I've lost something precious in water too deep.

There's no cool way to play this. I wipe my sweaty palms on my pants and walk right up to her.

"Hey," I say.

"Hey," she says. She keeps moving.

I almost shiver at her coolness. "Let me help," I say. "Give me a job."

"We're okay," she says, picking up a box of fruit and carrying it into the makeshift pantry.

I follow her.

"Okay, you don't need help. I need to be helpful." I step in front of her, willing her not to avoid my eyes. "Please."

She blinks almost resentfully. Like she's thinking, *Now you want to be helpful?* I stay in place. I feel vulnerable but also brave, trying to show her I'm still here.

"All right," she says. "You can find a janitorial closet and bring whatever brooms and mops you see."

"Got it," I say. I wander down the hall and get to work.

The band has gone quiet. The radio toggles between Janis Joplin, Motown hits, and the campus radio station reporting on the sit-in. A breeze from the windows tempers the heat of so many bodies close together.

The luckiest ones in the building have staked their claim to the few couches and armchairs in the lobby. The rest of us are stretched out on the floor, balling up jackets as pillows or lying on the rug.

It's about five a.m. when the members of both steering committees enter the lobby together. Their faces are worn and tense. They ask for everyone's attention. Someone switches off the radio.

"The steering committee members have come to an agreement," Richard announces. "At the request of the Black students, the white protestors will leave Hamilton Hall—"

"What?!" Gasps and sounds of surprise come from every corner of the room.

"In order to respect our process and allow for self-determination on the part of the Black protestors, white protestors are asked to leave this building. If you're committed to the cause, the best thing you can do right now is to take over another building or buildings on campus."

The white students are caught completely off guard. They look at one another incredulously, and then at their Black friends questioningly.

An SDS leader speaks up, desperate to calm them down. "If we hold other buildings, we'll also have more leverage for shutting down campus today. So—let's go plan how to make this move."

Students stand up slowly, gathering books and blankets and putting on their shoes, leaving behind trails of crumbs, trash, and ends of joints. They filter out, red-faced, some openly weeping, all looking shocked and horrified. They must have thought we were creating a multiracial utopia in here. They had no clue how uncomfortable we were. They didn't notice that we weren't here to party.

The new composition of the room asserts itself. There is more space to spread out. The breeze from the windows moves more freely, and it feels a little cooler. We breathe in relief. With the chaos on its way out, we can get organized and focused.

The SAS leaders sit on the floor with the rest of us.

A graduate student addresses the group. "We need a name," she says. "Something accurate and to the point."

"We shouldn't use 'SAS,'" Wesley says. "The group didn't come to an agreement about this protest. And we don't want the group to be sanctioned based on our actions here."

"Right," Richard says.

I'm sure I'm not the only one who's noticed that the most conservative SAS members are absent today. An impressive number of moderates are here though.

"'Black Students of Columbia'?" someone suggests.

"Barnard is here too," Valerie points out, to murmurs and nods.

"How about 'Black Students of Hamilton Hall'? If we're really planning to stay until our demands are met."

Then someone else says, "We should rename 'Hamilton Hall' though."

"Yeah, like Howard did at their sit-in."

"We should call it . . . 'Nat Turner Hall.'"

"Right on!"

"We should rename the whole university."

I study the posters and say, "'Nat Turner Hall of Malcolm X University.'"

"Yes!"

One of the Barnard sisters says, "I'll make a new sign."
Two of her friends get up to help her.

The leaders draft a press release explaining the development. Most of us try to get some rest. As silence settles over the room, faint noises come from the direction of the dean's office. Scraping, then pause. Scraping, then pause. Then a bump against the inside of the door.

It's the movement of furniture. The dean must be barricading himself inside his office. Why? Does he know that the white students left? Is he afraid of us? Has he heard the rumors that the community supporters here are armed militants?

I wonder if we should have taken a different building and left the white students here with their "hostage." Knowing he's in there makes this place feel like a ticking time bomb.

# 11

## GIBRAN
*Massachusetts | September 1995*

Friday morning, I wake up early with that feeling that I'm late for something important. Then I remember what we did. Our letters. Posted on campus. It's time to find out how they're being received.

I've never been so early for morning assembly. I pause to admire our letter on the door into Thatcher Hall.

Inside the assembly hall, the loud, immature chaos that usually reigns until Mr. Clarke arrives is subdued. I hope this is not my imagination. And I hope it is because of us.

The rows of seats form a semicircle around the stage and rise up toward the back in the shape of an amphitheater. James sits at the back in the dead center, alone. I march across the room and climb up the aisle to join him. I put my backpack at my feet and lean on my thighs, watching, listening. David rushes in a minute later and sits on my other side.

The other Black boys look for us as they walk in. We nod at them. They nod back and find seats. We all wait.

Mr. Clarke is an eerily punctual person. Every day he steps onto the stage in the assembly hall as the clock strikes eight o'clock. Today, he's one minute and twenty seconds late. He rushes in, short of breath, red-faced beneath his brown skin, gleaming with sweat.

Before he reaches the microphone, the room fades to silence. Another thing that never happens. Mr. Clarke looks startled, as though he wasn't ready for our attention.

Tick. Tick. The clock on the wall high above our heads announces the passage of time.

A few teachers who normally aren't at assembly slip in. They tiptoe toward a seat, or they stand just inside the doors.

Mr. Clarke arranges his face with a practiced smile. "Good morning, students."

With a tug at his collar and a deep breath, he launches into his routine.

"Our football team had a victory yesterday!"

On cue, students clap. Athletes stomp their feet and give high fives.

"Some reminders and announcements." He begins to pace, falling into his actor's rhythm. "The French Club would like to remind everyone that they meet on Thursdays at four o'clock in the Cabot Common Room. New members are welcome throughout the year. It's a great way to practice for the French trip, for those of you who will be going to France in March.

"The field hockey team has their second game of the season today after school on field three. They would love to have more support on the sidelines for the home team.

Please consider stopping by to cheer them on.

"Seniors, please sign up for your meetings with a college counselor by the end of the day if you haven't already."

I tune out the rest of the announcements and reminders, willing him to get to the point, to address what I hope is on everyone's minds.

I focus again when he pauses. He clasps his hands together, his starched white shirt gleaming beneath his navy blue suit.

I think he's going to do it. I think he's about to address the most crucial topic of the day. For a moment I think he's going to acknowledge us and our message. For a moment I think he finally sees that we're more important than starting classes on time.

For a moment. But only for a moment.

"That, my friends, is what I have for you this morning." He opens his hands as if releasing fireflies into the air. "Please have an excellent day."

Is there a collective pause before the students stand up? Do they wait one extra second to see if there's anything else?

In slow motion, the students pick up their backpacks, sling them over one shoulder, and mill around, chatting. Lisa looks at us as Malika whispers furiously at her and Tanya. I nod to say what's up, but she turns back to Malika.

James, David, and I stay in our seats. Mr. Clarke speaks with a handful of teachers by the door. All business, no passion, he nods like a robot. I fantasize about getting in his face, releasing a primal scream, a roar, beating my chest, stepping on his shiny shoes, to terrify and embarrass him.

*You could have been like me*, I want to tell him. But I know his answer. *You can still be like me.*

Mr. Clarke hurries out of the assembly hall, down to his office, probably to avoid us. In a few minutes, the room is cleared. Students spread throughout the campus for their morning classes.

David, James, and I stand and give each other pounds.

We don't need to talk about it. We know everyone has seen the letter. They are stewing on it, like we've spent days stewing—years of our lives.

We head to our separate classes.

Two words in my mind.

*Bring it.*

I am the last to enter the classroom for honors calculus. Kids are talking, and Mr. Seaver shuffles papers at his desk. When the door clicks shut behind me, he looks up, out of habit. His face falls, and then his mouth twitches with an aborted smile. He manages a curt nod before turning back to his papers.

Everyone else goes still for about two seconds. Just long enough to be unmistakable. Students glance at me quickly and then avert their eyes.

It's as if I have a stage to make a speech. Like they're waiting for some sort of live follow-up to the letter.

I've said what I have to say. It's their move.

It happens this way in every class.

Physics.

AP English.

Spanish.

Silence. Shifting eyes. Slow coughs. Meaningless shuffling

of notebooks and tapping of pens. Tentative voices resuming conversations, leaving space, as if listening, waiting, and talking at the same time.

Teachers watch me openly. Are they seeking warning signs? Are they trying to map something from my words onto my body? Radicalism? Intent to harm? I'm tempted to jump at them and whisper, "Boo!"

They begin their classes without acknowledging anything out of the ordinary, just like Mr. Clarke. But in the small space of the classroom, it's harder for them to conceal the tension than it was for Mr. Clarke from the stage of the assembly hall.

After each class, I pick up my books slowly, daring anyone to take the opportunity to speak to me. Ask me something. Bring it on.

Nothing.

In the hallways between classrooms and on the pathways between buildings, I look for brown faces. When I see any of the younger students, I put an arm around their shoulder and make jokes to get them to lighten up. Chris looks straight shook. I walk him to his class.

"Anyone giving you any trouble?"

"No."

"Aight. It's all good. If anybody bothers you, come straight to me. I got you."

At lunch, we sit together at the end of the Black table, where David, James, and I always sit. Being together helps shed some of the mental exhaustion from staying on high alert all day.

I eat hungrily—I'd skipped breakfast in my rush to get

to school. Some of the younger boys pick at their food and force it down.

The girls ignore us as they push past us to the other end of the table with their trays. I wonder if they're always so silent and I don't notice, or if there's extra attitude today.

"So," David says between bites, "is it me, or is everyone trying to act like nothing happened?"

"That's exactly what's happening," James says. "The first step is denial, right?"

"Word," I say.

Chris raises his eyebrows. "Wait," he says, "what if no one ever says anything?"

"Yeah," Trey says, "and then if we get in trouble, there'll be no point in having done it."

"Oh, they're talking about it already," I assure them. "Can't you tell?" I chug my juice and reach for a napkin from the black metal box in the middle of the table.

The boys look around the lunchroom as if they'll see signs of surreptitious conversations, whispering and pointing at us.

"Nah," I say. "They're talking about it with each other when we're not around. That's why it's so awkward when we walk in the room. Same way we had to meet with our peoples to figure out what to say and how to say it. That's what they're doing now. But they don't know it."

"Yeah," James says. "They're probably acting offended. Or cracking jokes."

"Definitely," I say. "Forming a united front by complaining about us. They'll bring it up eventually." What I don't say is that I'm itching for that to happen today. The silence is beating me down. I can't help but feel disappointed.

We've mostly finished eating and some of the boys have left when Malika takes a seat closer to us. Tanya and Lisa and some of the other girls are still here too.

"So," Malika says. "Y'all really did that, huh."

"Yeah," James says. "We did. What you think?"

She looks at the ceiling like it will help her form her next words. "One day you're 'defending our honor' with threats. The next day you're completely ignoring us and acting on your own out here." She leans in, dropping the sarcasm. "You didn't even run it by us before plastering this around the school."

"Hold up," I say, "when I tried to defend Tanya, y'all made it clear that you don't want us speaking for you. Plus, we signed it the Black *men* of Lakeside. You want us to ask your permission before we even speak for ourselves now?"

"Um, yeah," she says. "You know everything you say as Black students reflects on us too, whether we like it or not. You think my roommates won't be asking me about this?"

"Just say you weren't involved," David says.

Malika scoffs. "Right. The head of the Black Student Union had nothing to do with this letter about The Black Experience at Lakeside. That's easy for them to believe." She folds her arms across her chest and leans back in her chair, setting her jaw.

Lisa moves closer too. "You said yourselves in the letter that we don't get to be individuals. Does that only apply to men? Do you think Black women get that luxury?"

"Okay, I'm sorry, I can't keep up with y'all." I throw my arms up in the air. "I don't know what you want from me. We weren't trying to speak for anyone who didn't sign it. But it could help all of us."

Tanya's soft voice makes us strain to hear her. "You could have just asked us before you posted it. Or told us. A heads-up would have been nice."

"All right," David says, "point taken. We'll try to keep that in mind."

"Thank you," Malika says, in a tone that really means she's still fed up with us.

A minute passes. Malika rips a napkin into small pieces and stares into the distance. David, James, and I exchange glances, wondering what to say next.

Malika asks, "So what have people been saying about it?"

"Oh," James says, "she comes at us with attitude, and now she wants the intel."

"Boy!" She grabs a French fry from Lisa's plate and throws it at him.

He ducks, covering his head, and we laugh.

David says, "We were just talking about how nobody's saying nothing. It's as if nothing happened."

"Hm," Lisa says. "Well, you know that's not the end of it."

"No doubt," I say. "Reactions are coming. I'm ready for it."

After lunch, I don't hear another word about the letter. The white students and the faculty avoid me. If they're speechless, I can live with that. If they're thinking about what we wrote, or if they respect our right to have an opinion, then maybe I can survive this year.

When I get home, I'm hungry again. There's not much to snack on, so I pull out a leftover casserole and stick it in the oven. I go up to my room and pull out my notebook of rhymes for the first time in over a week.

I'm bobbing my head to the beat in my mind and flowing under my breath. I don't hear Mom come in the front door and climb the stairs. She opens my bedroom door, and I jump. Her coat and shoes are still on. Her bag hangs heavily on her shoulder.

"I need to talk to you," she says breathlessly. "Now."

She stops in her room to shed her jacket and pull off her tall suede boots. I wait as she pulls folded papers from her big bag, then follow her as she stomps down the stairs in her slippers.

She sits at the kitchen table, opens the papers, and places them facedown in front of her. Her eyes are a little puffy. I hope she hasn't been crying.

"You okay?" I ask. "You want something to drink?" I take a glass from the cabinet, fill it with water from the pitcher in the fridge, and place it in front of her. I turn off the oven and pull out the casserole so it doesn't get dry.

I sit down with her and try to look attentive.

She doesn't speak. Her eyes rest on the papers between us.

I start to fidget. Finally, I say, as softly as I can, "Ma? What's up?"

She looks at me suddenly, as though remembering I'm in the room, then she flips the papers over and pushes them toward me.

A copy of our letter to the school faces me, so strange on our kitchen table. Small lines of text on the top and bottom of the pages show that it was faxed to her at work today, our signatures grainy from the machine.

"Tell me about this," she says.

She doesn't sound angry. She doesn't sound disappointed. I let myself hope that she understands what we wrote and why we wrote it. That maybe she's even proud. I know she feels the same way I do about the school.

I pick up the paper and scan the letter, admiring our words and our courage again.

*Tell me about this.*

It occurs to me that I hadn't discussed any of this with Mom. Maybe she is angry, like the girls were at lunch. Maybe Mom has a right to be.

"I'm waiting," she says. She tilts her head.

"Well, it's a letter to the school that I wrote up with James and David. A bunch of other Black boys at school signed it too. We put it up around the school so everyone could read it. And . . . that's pretty much it."

She raps her fingertips on the table.

"So . . . ," I say. "Did you read it? What do you think?"

"Don't you want to know who sent it to me?" she asks.

I frown. "I don't know," I mumble.

She makes a pained face. "Don't you care?"

I know the right answer, but I can't say it. "Not really."

She takes in a sharp breath and looks at the wall seeking sympathy from that invisible audience witnessing her hardships.

"Does it ever occur to you," she says, "that actions have consequences? Huh? Do you ever stop and think, 'This may seem like a good idea right now, but how might it affect my future?'"

I blink slowly to force myself not to roll my eyes. It sounds like I'm in for a lecture. I wish I had served myself a plate.

She holds out her hands as if asking for more of an explanation.

"I mean, what you want me to say, Ma? We spent a week writing this, and we put it around the school just to piss people off and get in trouble? I wanted to get a rise out of you? Come on, Ma."

She makes a tight line with her lips and folds her hands on the table in front of her. "I want you to guess who sent this to me."

"Did you even read it?" I ask.

"Guess!" she shouts, slamming her hand on the tabletop.

I lean back in my chair, sulking. "My advisor."

"Wrong. Guess again."

"Ma, come on—"

"Guess. Again." Now her eyes are shining and her voice shakes. "Who do you think paid so much attention to this that they contacted your mother, *at work*, with concerns?"

My day flashes through my mind, beginning with morning assembly. I remember how persistently Mr. Clarke avoided seeing us, even though we were right there in the middle of the room. I didn't see him again during the day. Not at lunch, making small talk with the faculty. Not at the pick-up line, waving to parents as I walked to the bus stop.

Now I imagine him sitting at his desk, calling our parents, sending them faxes, expressing his "concern." Making check marks next to each student's name as he went down the list.

I suck my teeth and mumble, "Mr. Clarke."

"Bingo," she says. "Now. Does this surprise you?"

"I mean, not really. I'm not surprised, but I am disappointed. If he was so 'concerned,' why wouldn't he talk to us? We didn't do nothin wrong. We're expressing our opinions. That's supposed to be good, right? We're trying to get things out in the open, handle stuff like men. He's hiding out, callin you behind my back, getting you all worried. Acting like a punk—"

"Okay." She makes prayer hands and puts them in front of her mouth. She looks toward the ceiling and then back at me. "I get it. Okay? I do. As a Black man, he really could have brought you together and talked with you directly. But Gibran, you've been at that school for three years now. We know what we're dealing with. That's just not who he is." She separates her hands. "If you can't anticipate the outcome of your actions by now . . . well, life is going to teach you. And trust me, life is a much harsher teacher than me, or than your school or your principal." She covers her eyes with her palms.

I could smack Mr. Clarke right now. What's the point of getting parents upset? Why doesn't he do his job and fix the school he's in charge of instead of blaming us for pointing out what's happening?

She pulls her hands down. "He's going to call an all-school assembly."

"Really?"

She glares at me, and I try to suppress my excitement.

"Yes, really. It's on Monday. He called 'just to let me know.' In case I want to be there." She studies my face. "Do I need to be there?"

"*Need* to? I don't think you need to be there."

"Are you going to need help controlling your emotions?"

"I mean, if they respect me, I'ma respect them."

"Yeah," she says. "I guess I'd better come."

"If you insist."

It's true that she might keep me from saying something that will get me in trouble. But she also might keep me from saying what needs to be said.

She rolls the corner of the paper. "The thing is, Gibran, he talked to me as if I was familiar with this. And I was too embarrassed to tell him I had no idea what he was talking about."

"I mean, I didn't purposely hide it from you," I tell her. "I guess . . . I wanted to say what we had to say, in our own words. I didn't want anyone telling us to tone it down or whatever."

I want to apologize for making things awkward for her, but I'm not sorry for the letter. I can't always tell her what I'm thinking about, because I don't know how to complain without sounding like I'm blaming her. But with other people, I'm not trying to hold back.

While she gazes at the paper, I get up and serve us plates of the casserole. It's room temperature and stiff, and I know she's not going to eat hers, so I give her a tiny portion.

I sit down and take a bite. While she pokes at her plate, I ask, "Did you read it?"

She purses her lips and shakes her head no.

I eat quietly. She watches me for a minute, as if she's learning who I am. Then she picks up the letter and reads. I try not to stare, but I keep glancing at her to catch her reaction. She bites her cuticles while she reads, and when she finishes, she stares at her plate.

"What you think?" I ask.

She nods slowly. "I think . . . the world isn't ready for you, baby."

I don't know if that's good or bad. She doesn't seem happy.

She pushes away her plate and says, "I'll eat later." Lies.

When we were small, after we left our father, we were so poor that she fed us everything and ate nothing. She got used to not eating, and now that we're doing okay again, it's like she doesn't remember how to eat. Especially when she's stressed. Which seems like all the time lately. I make a mental note to make her a milkshake later.

She gets up and pats my shoulder. Before she walks out, she smooths my hair and says, "Gibran. I really, really hate surprises."

"Noted."

*What I don't say*

If I had told you everything all along, I guess I would make more sense to you now. When I was younger, I didn't have the words, or I didn't trust my own perception. As I got older and started to understand more, I probably didn't want to admit you'd been right about not trusting people.

By the end of middle school, I started to see more clearly. I let some friendships fade. I didn't go to Luke's house every day anymore. You must have been relieved. You had always worried that he was bad for me, the kind of white boy who gets into all sorts of trouble but only earns a slap on the wrist, while I would get serious consequences for being guilty by association. You resented his freedom and feared

245

where its illusion could lead me. Only now you were also worried about the new friends I was making around the way.

One day, I was waiting for you to be ready to leave school. You were cleaning up your classroom, or maybe there was a faculty meeting, or maybe you were writing comments for your students at the end of the term. Luke saw me waiting and asked if I wanted to come over and play video games. Anything would be better than sitting in the school lobby for hours. I was restless, and so I went with him.

As we walked the half mile to his house, he talked non-stop about his new speaker system and the latest games he'd bought. When we got inside, I went straight to the den and sat in front of their biggest TV. I took off my backpack and sat on the couch like I always used to do.

Luke stopped in the kitchen and brought an entire plate of freshly baked cookies, a big bag of Doritos and two empty glasses. While I stuffed a cookie in my mouth, Luke went over to his parents' bar and opened cupboards.

We had spent countless hours on that sofa, in that room, drinking can after can of soda, playing games. He had never gone into the cupboard before. Not with me around.

I had never seen alcohol up close. You didn't drink, so there was none in our house.

He placed two bottles on the coffee table between us and the TV. His sky-blue eyes gleamed.

"Pick one," he said.

I read the labels. Whiskey and a beer.

I imagined getting in our car with alcohol on my breath. I heard your lectures in my ear. *They can do what they want. We have to work twice as hard to get half as far.* I looked at

Luke with his mischievous smile. Luke, in his spacious den with his huge TV and his brand-new console. I wondered what was the worst that could happen if he got caught. Was this one of the moments you had been preparing me for?

But what was the worst that could happen to either of us? This was probably the safest place for me to experiment.

They kept a spare toothbrush for me in Luke's bathroom. I wondered if brushing my teeth would mask the smell or protect me from your psychic powers.

Luke counted down. "Five. Four. Three. Two."

I didn't want to get stuck with the whiskey. I had seen enough TV to know it wouldn't go down easily.

"Okay, okay!" I said to shut him up. I grabbed the beer.

Luke poured himself a shot. I watched him throw the liquid into his mouth. His eyes watered as if he'd eaten a hot pepper. He poured himself another. He saw me watching him and laughed. Was he drunk already? Did it work that fast?

I took a small sip of the beer. It was nasty. I made a face. I wanted to drink more to feel the effect and find out what the appeal was, but I couldn't get past the taste. I set the bottle down. He laughed at me. I didn't care. He didn't have to go home to you.

I turned on the TV. "Let's play," I said.

We played *Super Mario Brothers*, and he was sloppier than ever. It wasn't even fun, though he appeared to be having the time of his life. I almost wanted to have some whiskey too so I could see what was so funny.

Then a voice came from behind us, loud and shrill. "Luke!"

We both jumped.

"Holy shit, Mom! What the hell?!"

She glanced at me and then back at her son. "Don't be rude." I knew she wouldn't comment on his language if I wasn't there.

I paused the game and then regretted pressing pause. It got too quiet. In the silence, the bottles on the table grew larger, til they were the only thing in the room, as if we had been sitting there doing nothing but chugging drinks.

Luke's mother didn't know what to do with her face. Her red cheeks seemed to tremble. She squinted, as if all of this—the scene in front of her, me, maybe her son, maybe her whole life—could disappear if she willed it away.

Luke didn't notice. He didn't even look at her.

"What do you want?" he asked, impatient.

"I want to know," she said slowly, as if she wasn't really sure, "what you think you are doing." She gestured toward the coffee table and then folded her arms across her thin body.

Luke made a sound of supreme annoyance.

I wished I hadn't come. I should have listened to my instinct and stayed at school, staring out the window.

I rose from the couch and spoke to fill the silence. "I'm sorry, Mrs. Anderson." She tilted her head toward me, and I stumbled over my words. "It was . . . a dare. I dared him to try some of your drinks. So he did, and he offered me some too. It was my idea. I'm sorry. It won't happen again." The last part was the truth.

She blinked hard. She had to know I was lying. It came as such a relief, I guess, she relaxed into the story and accepted it gladly.

She gave the slightest nod. "Luke, put it away," she said, and turned to climb the stairs.

Her footsteps faded. I became aware of the adrenaline pulsing through my body. I sank into the couch. My heart knocked in my chest and pounded my ears.

Luke unpaused the game and kept playing. "Aaaah man!" he screamed when his player died. He started a new game.

I guess I had expected someone to protest. But the way she had looked at me—like I had restored order by claiming responsibility. She knew I hadn't done this, but I must be guilty of something, so it was right that I take the blame.

And then there was the way he didn't look at me at all.

The way my heart had been generous, and had flipped already to something else, something that would soon become bitter resentment.

I stood up and grabbed my backpack, mumbling, "I gotta go."

"You're missing out!" he said to the screen.

I took the stairs two at a time. I peeked into the kitchen to see if Anita was there, hoping I wouldn't see his mom again. Anita waved to me from behind the stove. I waved back and lingered, wanting to say a proper goodbye. She came over to see me out.

At the door, I faced her. I opened my mouth, but I didn't know what to say. Would I sound crazy if I said I wasn't coming back here, that I might never see her again?

She cupped my cheek in her hand and looked into my eyes. I was as tall as her now, but she had known me since I was five. She knew Luke better than Luke's mom knew him, and now I saw what a situation that put her in.

Anita gave me a tight hug, and I squeezed her back. I ducked my head to walk out. She stood in the doorway and watched me walk down the graveled driveway, shaded by so many trees.

I spend the rest of the night in my room. I listen to music and consider doing homework to free up my weekend, but my mind is too full. I'm thinking about what people might say at the assembly and how I'll respond.

I flip through *The Mis-Education of the Negro*, stopping at the highlighted parts. I love reading where someone underlined and scribbled in the margins years ago as much as I love reading the author's words. The name in the front of *Mis-Education* is Grandpa's, but the writing in the margins matches Uncle Kevin's dedication in *Black Power*. Maybe Uncle Kevin took books from Grandpa's shelves the same way I take them from Mom's.

I wonder if Uncle Kevin and Grandpa went through the stuff I'm going through. I don't hear them complain about their struggles. I can't imagine getting out of Lakeside and being over it. It's taking something out of me. But maybe once it's over, I'll never want to talk about it again. Maybe that's why they don't talk about their past.

In the few photos I've seen of Uncle Kevin as a young man, he's never smiling. Which is weird because whenever I see him at the holidays, he's always smiling and joking with us. I figured it was his way of looking cool for photos. Maybe that's not it. Maybe he changed. I'm glad I'll be near him next year. I can't wait to hear more of his stories.

In the black-and-white photos of Grandpa in his doctor's coat, he looks like a suave Langston Hughes. He's always been quiet, so most of what I know about his history came from Mom. How his father passed as white at work to get a good-paying job, then came home to his Black family. The calm way Grandpa dealt with people either calling him a credit to his race or refusing to be treated by him in the hospital because he's Black. I've sometimes felt jealous of the times he lived in. I know that sounds backward, but I imagine knowing who your enemy is would be easier than not knowing. This color-blind lie is exhausting—learning to be on high alert because your closest friends could be your worst enemies.

The phone rings. Mom picks it up and talks for a while. Then she calls my name. I open my door and call down the hall, "Yeah?"

"Phone!"

It must be family.

I get the cordless phone from the hallway and bring it in my bedroom. I turn down the music.

"Hello?"

"Hey, Gibran!" It's Ava.

"Hey, sis. Whaddup?"

"Not much. How are you?"

"I'm aight. What's goin on?"

"You know. School and work. School and work."

"Sounds fun."

"A blast. But I'm coming home tomorrow."

"Oh word?"

"Yeah. Will you be around?"

"I mean, I'm sure I'll see you. I don't have big plans. Just chillin with my boys." I lie back on my bed and pick at the blue tack in the corner of my Wu-Tang poster.

"Okay. Good." She hesitates.

"What's up?" I say. "I can hear you thinking."

She chuckles. "Well . . . are you okay? Like, for real. Mom told me about the letter. . . ."

"Aha. I knew it. Actin like you're just calling to say hi. What she say? She got you all worried too?"

"I mean, I don't know. Should I be worried? The letter doesn't sound like such a big deal. What about the meeting though?"

"Yeah, she's coming to the meeting."

"Right. And you're gonna be careful, right?"

"What does that mean?" I suck my teeth. "Man, y'all are the worst. You want me to watch what I say while everyone else says exactly what they think? Why should I do that?"

"I don't know, maybe so you can graduate?"

"Y'all act like graduating from this stupid school is some kinda ticket to heaven."

"It's not that. It's just that if you get kicked out, everything else will be harder. Maybe for the rest of your life."

"I'm not tryin to let a school have that kinda power over me. My whole future? Hell nah. I'd quit right now if I could. I'm definitely not tryin to stay *and* keep my mouth shut too. That's crazy."

She makes a sound of exasperation.

"It's okay. I'll tell Ma you tried."

She chuckles. "Thanks."

My cassette tape ends, and I flip it over to the other side and press play.

After a pause, she says, "Can you tell me about your letter?"

It's cool that she wants to hear what I have to say about it. It feels different than Mom asking me to explain myself. But still, I'm not sure I want to do this again.

"Basically," I tell her, "we'd requested a day off for the Day of Absence—"

"The what?"

"The Day of Absence. You know, for the Million Man March. That's what people who can't get to the march are doing. To show our support for the idea and everything."

"Oh, okay."

"You didn't hear about it?"

"Uh . . . I don't really pay attention to the news."

"Figures."

"Well, I'm sorry, some of us are busy studying and working, you know?"

"Mm-hm. That's the problem. People too busy getting fancy degrees to be involved in making noise."

She says nothing. She moves around her tiny dorm room.

"You there?" I ask.

"Yeah, I'm here."

"I wasn't trying to—"

"No, it's fine. I mean, it's kinda true."

"What you doing?"

"I'm packing for tomorrow. Go on. You wanted to do the Day of Absence. Then what happened?"

"Yeah, so, basically, Mr. Clarke came to the Brother

253

Bonding meeting and told us the Day of Absence wasn't a worthy cause. . . ."

"He said that?"

"Basically."

"Huh."

"Yeah. I was pissed, 'cause what we really wanted to do was to go to the march. We couldn't hook that up, so we asked for the day off classes, which is nothing. And even that was treated like some radical, inappropriate request. So I just wanted to explain that being Black isn't radical. That's what the letter's about. Explaining that we're expected to be carbon copies of white people, and we're not havin it."

"Wow. That actually sounds pretty cool."

"Yeah," I say. "It was. We posted the letter around school, then Mr. Clarke ignored us to our faces and went and called our parents as if we did something wrong."

"Oh. Maybe he didn't know what to say to you?"

"Yeah, he a punk anyways."

"Nice."

"You know it's true."

She laughs. "Okay. Well, I want to read this letter. You have a copy?"

"Yeah, we got a couple copies here at the crib."

"Cool. Hold on to one for me. I'll be home in the afternoon."

"Aight. If I go out, I'll leave it on my desk."

"Don't go out. I want to see you."

"Don't front. You know you're coming to comfort Mom about her incorrigible son."

"Ha. Yeah, that too."

"See?"

"Kidding! Kind of."

"Foul."

She laughs. "Be good for one night, will you? No more stress til tomorrow. I'll see you soon. Can you put Mom back on for a sec?"

"Aight, peace."

Mom and Ava talk for a while longer. Probably about me. What are they going to do about me? At least Ava wants to read the letter. Maybe she could help Mom see it the way I do.

# 12

## KEVIN
*New York City | Wednesday, April 24, 1968*

The white students are gone. The dean is barricaded inside his office. We have a statement to share with the administration, and with the news reporters too, if we can get the word out. We settle in for a few hours' rest before the university starts its day; a long day of negotiations lies ahead.

I find a blanket left on a chair and shake it out. Valerie is looking for a place to rest too.

"Here you go," I say softly, offering her the blanket.

"Oh. Thanks, but I'm good. I've slept many a night with nothing." She eases herself against the wall and nestles her head in the corner.

I step away.

In the hallway, Robbie and a few other Muslims recite their early morning prayers. Robbie leads, standing in front of a row of men, and the steady hum of his voice praising God captivates and calms me even though I don't understand the words.

Valerie drops quickly into sleep, breathing deeply with her jacket wrapped around her. Gently, I drape the blanket over her. She stirs but doesn't wake.

Only a few hours pass before everyone is up again. The sun is shining, campus is stirring, and the reality of our situation is upon us. Our all-Black building is a danger and an opportunity. On the one hand, we are dispensable. On the other hand, Columbia can't afford to bring the police down violently on a group of Black students. Not in Harlem, not so soon after King's assassination. The city is still on edge.

A scout climbs over the barricade and slips out to collect morning newspapers. While we wait for him to return, we listen to the radio.

*Radical white students, militant Negroes, and outside agitators barricaded themselves inside a building at Columbia University, halting classes yesterday evening. Amidst controversy over Harlem residents' rights and the growing unpopularity of the Vietnam War among youth, protestors are demanding that the university halt construction of a gymnasium in the community, pull out of the Institute for Defense Analysis, and change policies to benefit student protestors. University administrators say they will not give in to demands of lawless students.*

After the reports, someone changes the station to music. Nina Simone's voice floods the lobby, and some of the sisters sing along.

The phone rings with calls from concerned parents. Jack works to keep up with the calls. When parents of admitted students want to know what will happen in the fall, he tells them, "We're not sure there will *be* a Columbia University in the fall, dig?"

A runner comes down to the lobby to fetch people who are in the building when their parents call. Some return with stubborn determination, some with relief written on their faces. Every time the runner comes in, I stiffen, wondering if my name is next, wondering what I'll say to my parents and how I'll respond if they ask me to leave the protest.

The worried calls increase in number and intensity, reaching a frenzy. Supporters come out in greater numbers too. Trays of food are sent up through the windows, along with utensils and plates. Thank God. I'm starving.

The food committee rations out meals, planning ahead in case we're in here for days.

Scattered on the floor of the lobby and in classrooms, we eat our first hot meal in twenty-four hours. Homemade eggs, grits, and pancakes make me glad to miss a dining hall meal. Even students who live off-campus say it's the best meal they've had in all their years here.

As we clean up, Wesley announces that classes are canceled for the day.

"Yes!"

"Right on!"

We cheer, and the community members applaud. Every victory energizes us, though the awareness of danger never leaves.

To prepare us for all scenarios, a community member and a graduate student lead training drills. They line us up in rows and then stand in front to demonstrate a protective crouch.

"The lower you are to the ground, the harder it is to knock you down. You'd be surprised how many head injuries happen from the fall, not from the blow itself. If you're standing, bend your knees to stabilize yourself. Better yet, come way down into a crouch."

I fold my torso over my bent legs and try to balance on my feet. It's not easy.

Harder than the physical drills are the mental ones. Could our school really turn on us and make all this necessary?

Some of the students have been trained before and survived protests that got ugly. They still practice with us to prepare psychologically.

"Cover your head completely. Get yourself into a tight ball with your arms over your head. Tuck your face into your legs. That's right."

I hold my breath as if bracing myself for blows.

"Protect your organs too. If a kick, a fist, or a billy club comes at you—there you go—a broken arm is better than a broken rib or a punctured lung. And guys, make sure to keep those family jewels covered."

I'm in position, but this feels surreal. I can't imagine any of what we're preparing for happening in the same building where our classes are held.

"Good. Okay, let's take a break."

I relax my arms and drop to the floor, marveling at my intact body.

"Now," the graduate student says. "It's hard to keep your cool when you're facing a blue uniform and weapons. If you remember one thing, it's this: Don't run. Don't turn. Don't walk away. They can always fall back on 'resisting arrest' as an excuse to tackle you or even to shoot."

"Sitting down is bad news too," Richard says. "You want to stand and offer your hands. We'll organize ourselves in rows if it comes to that."

"Absolutely," another brother says. "In crowds, they might use tear gas. We've sent for cloths, and we'll hand them out ahead of time. You'll wet the cloth and hold it over your face. Then try to get outside as quickly as possible. We don't expect them to do that in here, but we want to be prepared."

"What about that Black inspector we met in the fall?" Eddie asks. "He was cool, right?"

Some of the brothers met Inspector Waithe, the highest-ranking Black officer in the NYPD, at a community event. A few weeks later, he scared the shit out of them by showing up at their apartment door with four other officers. Turned out he just wanted to talk to them more about community relationships. They talked for hours.

"We told him what we expect from a Black officer," Richard says. "He heard us. I think the fact that he knows us might help de-escalate things if the police do come in."

"Still," Wesley says, "he's just one officer. There's no telling how many would come in and how rough they might get. Sisters, if there is an arrest, I hope you'll consider making a safe exit beforehand."

The sisters make sounds of annoyance and protest.

"Uh-uh."

"You can go on with that."

"Nope."

Wesley's shoulders sag.

I know there's no convincing Valerie to leave early, but I worry about violence coming to her. It will be hard to keep calm if they get rough with us, but impossible if they get rough with the sisters.

"Well," a community organizer says, "at least make sure your hair is covered if it's long enough to be grabbed in a fist. Let me tell you, it hurts like hell to be dragged by the hair or to have a fistful of hair ripped out of your scalp." He fluffs his wide afro fondly. Most of the sisters have already found scarves to tie up their hair overnight.

The students huddled around the radio shush the rest of us. They raise the volume as an announcement comes through.

*Black students at Boston University have taken over the administration building on Bay State Road in Boston. This is one of a dozen or so similar actions taken by college students around the country this month.*

Whoops and cheers fly around the room.

*The student group called Umoja has shared a list of demands directed at BU president Christ-Janer. At this time, it is unclear whether students at different schools have coordinated the timing of their protests, or if the idea is spreading. Nearly three weeks have passed since the assassination of the civil rights leader Dr. Martin Luther King, Jr., and the urban riots which followed the announcement of his death.*

Before I have a moment to digest this news, Robbie is at my side, clapping me on the back. "Can you believe that? Two Wilsons on the same day! Sticking it to the man!"

Valerie surprises me by approaching my other side. "Isn't that where your sister goes?"

"Yeah, it is," I say. My throat feels dry.

"Right on," she says, smiling proudly.

"Right—right on."

I'm proud of Dawn; I know she's there at the sit-in.

I run my mind over our phone call a couple of weeks ago, its hollowness. Did she know they would be sitting in? If she'd had more time, would she have told me about it? Will I ever get to hear her retell this day, acting out the parts of everyone involved, giddy from the excitement of it? We have so much to talk about, but will we ever get the chance?

A few hours later, around noon, another update comes through on Boston University. Their president has accepted their demands. Everyone cheers and claps, raising fists in the air.

Robbie shakes my shoulders. "They did it! Check out little Dawn!"

I try to smile.

Valerie makes a face at me from across the room. *See that?* it says. *We can change the world.*

I nod.

I want so badly to call Dawn again. No—I want to be the person she'd want to call right now. I want to go back to the time when she knew I'd be just as excited as she is about her victory, her part in the movement, both of us finding our place to belong.

Who is she celebrating with now?

The rest of the students in the building chatter excitedly about BU's success. Their battle isn't the same as ours; their demands are focused on campus issues: more Black students, Black faculty, and Black studies. Still, their outcome is encouraging.

We allow ourselves to hope. Maybe the university administrations will topple like dominoes. Even ours.

The white protestors have settled into other campus buildings. They've taken Low Library, which is the university's headquarters, and other buildings too, which will make it hard for classes to run. Now our group can run smoothly, on consensus, and if theirs devolve into disorder, it won't destroy the movement. But we still have the challenge of Dean Coleman in our building. Why hasn't he left?

By the afternoon, we decide to make sure he knows he's free to go. Richard knocks on his office door and waits. When it cracks open, Richard steps inside, and after a few minutes, Dean Coleman emerges warily. His eyes are red, and he stumbles a bit as Richard escorts him to the front door and sees him out.

News reporters from the campus paper, the local news, and the *New York Times* accost the dean on the steps. He speaks briefly and excuses himself. They follow him a few paces down the path before returning to the steps of Hamilton Hall.

By late afternoon, crowds of students fill the campus, milling around on the green, with no classes to attend. White protestors in the other buildings sit on the ledges of windows, holding huge banners to beckon the uncommitted: "JOIN US."

Angry students organize a counter-protest. They call themselves the "Majority Coalition"—a clever way of pretending they outnumber the protestors. As their numbers grow,

BLACK & WHITE
DRAWINGS
TO COME

they become bolder. They interfere with student supporters, trying to intimidate them and prevent them from bringing food and supplies to those of us inside the buildings.

Faculty members insert themselves between the counter-protestors and the supporters. They try to diffuse the tension before the situation explodes into violence.

I watch from the balcony. I think about how Dean Coleman looked when he left the building. Is he surprised that the students he went out of his way to recruit are dissatisfied with this school? I think about Dawn. Does the fact that we're involved in the same action on the same day mean something to her like it does to me?

When I'm too disgusted with the counter-protestors to watch the scenes on campus any longer, I go back inside. Across the hall, the door to the dean's office is slightly ajar. I push the door open and peer inside the room.

Two upperclassmen stand over the dean's desk with open files and papers spread out in front of them. Behind them, a file cabinet drawer sits open. They don't speak. I step inside and shut the door behind me.

Melvin stares at the papers, but his eyes are unseeing. I walk around the large mahogany desk to stand next to him. The folder in front of him, labeled with his name in typed black letters, is open to the last page. Details about Melvin's family and background snake through the page. But at the top is a stamp in block letters: "Unlikely to succeed."

The paper is dated August 15, 1965. That's before Melvin got to campus to start his freshman year. I shake my head, not comprehending. This determination was made before he even got here?

Melvin looks like a sculpture, like he will never move again. I am dazed, but I need to understand. Riffling through the open file cabinet drawer, I recognize name after name. A catalogue of the Black undergraduate students on campus. This must be where Dean Coleman kept track of us while recruiting.

Is this the reason they don't want to change the school's culture to accommodate us? Are we destined to fail, not worth the effort? Then to be blamed for our inability to overcome the hurdles that are invisible to them?

I don't want to know, but I need to know. I pull folders out of the drawer, one by one. My heart races. I flip through folder after folder, searching for that ugly stamp. Many files contain it, but not all. A pattern emerges.

The detailed profiles of the students include parents' education, income, areas of residence, and secondary school attended. Students whose parents are professionals, who come from middle-class backgrounds and live in "quality" neighborhoods are not stamped. Is this why Dean Coleman recruited us in person? To see for himself what backgrounds we were coming from?

I think of Charles. This is what he's been trying to tell me. I always thought he was too hard on himself. He can't have known that his file was literally stamped, that his fate was all but sealed. He does know that he can't afford to take any chances. That he's walking a tightrope here. He's squeezing in, trying to justify his presence.

I look for Charles's name and quickly find it. I pull out his folder and brace myself before opening it.

Charles. Always in the library, studying.

Charles. Not here protesting because he can't afford to risk losing his opportunity to graduate from college.

Charles: determined to get what he came for—a degree, with the respect and privileges it supposedly confers. A chance to lift his family out of poverty. What does Columbia think of his chances?

"Unlikely to succeed."

I double over like I've been punched.

I want to tear up this folder and the others too.

I want to set fire to the cabinet. I want to go home.

Home. The home I took for granted. The home Charles visited and adored. "Man, it's so nice out here," he kept saying, smiling and looking around. The bird feeder. The quiet. The jazz floating out from my father's study.

I had to stop myself from complaining. *If you only knew,* I wanted to tell him. *If you lived here. If you went to school here.* But he could never know.

Now I need to see my file, even though it can't relieve my madness.

Melvin stands still at the desk. Probably running the past few years of his life through his mind. Meeting Dean Coleman. Deciding to enroll. His family's excitement. The encouragement he received before he arrived. The abandonments and humiliations once he got here.

I don't want the contents of my folder to tell me who I am. This institution doesn't know us, and doesn't care to. Yet I need to see how it judged me.

I hook my fingers on the cool metal of the second drawer

handle and pull it all the way out. Washington. Webster. Wilson, Kevin. I pull out my file, breathe deeply to slow my heartbeat, and open it up.

Here are the facts of my family in black and white.

Father: medical doctor.

Mother: housewife.

Community: quality.

What does that mean? White?

I flip through the pages. There is no stamp. Nowhere am I marked a risk. I am expected to succeed, then. Am I also supposed to belong?

I flip through the papers carefully one more time. Then I close the folder. I consider taking it with me, but we have vowed to leave everything in the building intact. Our actions reflect on our entire community, the entire Black race. We must be orderly, purposeful, responsible, mature. Only I don't feel mature or responsible right now.

I grip the folder tightly, willing myself not to tear it in two. I slide it back into its place in the drawer.

Like Melvin, I stand there, seeing not what's in front of me, but what's beyond. I see the details of my life, of this campus, of this city, of this nation, as one big design, a life-sized game of chess. What does it take, and what does it mean, to win?

Evening classes are canceled. Faculty are organized. They wear white armbands and form a ring around the occupied buildings, trying to establish a barrier, trying to prevent insults from becoming violence and violence from becoming riots. We admire their involvement, though we wish that instead of being an impartial voice of "reason," they'd take a principled stand. If there's anything we're

268

trying to show, it's that there is no objectivity when injustice is being done in your name.

Richard and Wesley call another strategic meeting.

"We have an offer," Richard says, "from the administration. They say if we leave tonight, we can avoid suspension."

"And?" Valerie asks.

"That's the only concession?" Jack asks. "None of our demands would be addressed?"

"That's right," Wesley says.

"They're playing on our fears," Claudius says. "It's a test. To see if we're serious."

"It's been over twenty-four hours," Ed says. "Other schools have had their demands met within the same day. They're not even opening negotiations about our demands."

"You saw the *New York Times* article," someone says. "They're depicting this as some spoiled kids throwing a tantrum."

Someone else grumbles, "It doesn't help that they got pictures of the white kids in the president's office smoking his cigars with their feet up on his desk."

Nearly everyone has something to say about that.

"They're barely mentioning the Black students. When they do, they imply that 'outside agitators' are the real cause and danger of our occupation."

The community members don't try to impose on our strategizing and decision-making. But their presence intimidates the administration and even the white protestors who were here before.

"We need to respond to the administration about their offer," Wesley says.

It doesn't take long for a consensus to emerge.

"Are we ready to vote?" Richard asks.

Everyone agrees.

"All in favor of accepting the offer to leave the building tonight in exchange for escaping suspension?"

No hands are raised.

"All in favor of rejecting the offer and staying put until our demands are addressed?"

We all raise our hands.

"All right," Wesley says. "We'll let the protestors in the other buildings know, and then we'll respond to the administration."

Robbie catches my eye and gives me a little Black Power fist.

We send for the evening papers. We keep the radio on.

I think of Charles, and I think of Dawn. I think of my parents, of Finchburg, of Brooklyn.

We do another self-defense practice drill, trying to embed the moves into our muscle memory.

Each time we practice, the leaders ask the sisters to leave if police are mobilized. Each time they are asked, the sisters say no.

I've been thinking of my parents since I read the files, but I'm still not prepared when the runner comes for me. I'm not ready to talk to Mom. But she's on the line, waiting for me. I march up the stairs to the telephone, where Jack waits to hand me the receiver.

"Make it quick, man," Jack says. "We've got lots of calls coming in."

He leaves the room to give me privacy.

I hesitate, take a deep breath, and put the receiver to my ear. "Mom?"

"Kevin! Oh, thank God. I've been calling nonstop. I hardly slept last night. Tell me what is going on."

"Everything's fine, Mom. I'm here in Hamilton Hall with the Black students. We're staging a sit-in. The administration has our demands. We're waiting them out."

"I knew you would be in there. Kevin, have you seen the papers? You students are in the news every day. Destroying property in the president's office? We raised you better than that."

"No, no, Mom. Don't believe what you see in the papers. I'm not even in that building. Here in Hamilton Hall, we *are* being careful and respectful. I promise you that. Look, the president has the *Times* in his pocket. He's pulling strings over there. This is their game. They use their power and influence to get public opinion against us so no one has to think about what the university is doing wrong. It's a distraction."

I know she doesn't want to believe that the *New York Times* could be spreading lies. We didn't want to believe it either. But now that we know, we can't unsee it. Just like the dean's files.

She takes a deep breath. "How did it come to this, Kevin? Couldn't you petition, or ... I don't know. ..."

"We've tried for months—years—to make them listen. They refuse. That's why we're in here. To force them to negotiate."

She moans like she feels queasy.

"Did you hear about BU?" I ask.

"Yes, I did," she says eagerly. "That was a student protest. The papers say you have militants in there, and that some of them may be armed. Is that true?"

"Mom. Don't believe the papers, please. The students are in charge here. There are no weapons." I have probably one more minute before Jack takes back the line. "Robbie's here." I don't know if that will help or hurt. Mom knows his parents took a long time to accept his path as an activist and his conversion to Islam.

"You can't force an institution like Columbia, Kevin. This is a setup for disaster. Think about your future. Getting expelled is a best-case scenario here." She lowers her voice to a whisper. "You could be killed!" As if speaking it aloud could make it happen.

Nothing I can say in these brief seconds will calm her fears. What's strange is that I don't feel frustrated or angry with her and Dad right now. I want to let go of that. And the judgment too. They made their decisions, and now I'm making mine. Our methods are different, but maybe our goals are closer than I thought.

"Do you remember that poem you taught us when we were young?" I ask my mother.

She pauses. "What . . . which one?"

> *"If we must die, O let us nobly die,*
> *So that our precious blood may not be shed*
> *In vain; then even the monsters we defy*
> *Shall be constrained to honor us though dead!"*

"Kevin . . ."

*"O kinsmen! we must meet the common foe!*
*Though far outnumbered let us show us brave."*

"Kevin," she whispers. I think she is crying.

*"Like men we'll face the murderous, cowardly pack,*
*Pressed to the wall, dying, but fighting back!"*

"Kevin, please."

"Mom, it's okay. We're not going to die in here."

"How do you know that?"

"Because." I sigh. "I know. We're prepared. We're using every resource we have. Lawyers from the NAACP. Political leaders. Community contacts. We know what we're doing. Mom, we have to do this."

She takes a shaky breath. "Why are you reciting that poem then?"

"To remind you . . . that you taught me well. Who I am . . ." I swallow. "I owe a lot of it to you. And Dad."

Jack raps on the door. My time is up. He cracks it open and signals to me.

"Mom. I have to go. I have to free up the line. Listen to me, okay? Columbia doesn't want to go to war with us. They don't. But in case anything happens . . . the poem is true. I'd rather die on my feet than live on my knees."

"Be careful, Kevin."

"And Mom? If you talk to Dawn, tell her . . . tell her I'm proud of her."

"Yes."

"I love you, Mom."

As I trudge back down the stairs, words roll through my mind. Words I could say to my parents. *I'm sorry. Thank you. Forgive me. I forgive you.*

I don't know how to say these words. Maybe I can show them. At home, after all this is over.

"How's my auntie doing?" Robbie asks me when I reach the lobby.

"Worried," I say. "I guess from the outside we look like a powder keg ready to blow."

"Right," he says. "She can talk to my parents. Get some tips on parenting activists."

I try to smile. I appreciate the sentiment, but I can't really be compared to Robbie.

"Don't worry, man," he says, putting his hand on my shoulder. "When this is over, your folks will be proud.

# 13

## GIBRAN
*Massachusetts | September – October 1995*

Ava arrives early in the afternoon on Saturday. I'm still in my boxers and a T-shirt when she knocks on my bedroom door. I pull on a pair of sweatpants.

"Enter," I call.

"Hey!" she says.

"Ay! Ava's in the house! Whaddup, sis?"

She gives me a hug, then sits on my bed, crossing her legs beneath her like it's a slumber party. She wears loose pants with a button-down shirt, her shoulder-length braids in a ponytail. "I'm glad I caught you before you went out. You have to be back by six for family dinner. Seven at the latest."

"What? Man, nobody tells me nothin. I got plans!"

"Aw. Cancel them?" She blinks at me.

"Y'all are the worst, for real. It's my birthday weekend. How I'm supposed to stay home tonight?" The alarm clock on my desk says 1:15 p.m. "I'm meeting up with Supreme in a hour."

"Well, I came all the way from Connecticut to see you," she says.

"You ain't come to see me."

"Are you calling me a liar?"

"I call 'em like I see 'em."

She pushes out her lips in protest. "Why else would I come specifically this weekend?"

I just blink at her.

"Okay, fine, maybe I get a two-for-one."

"Mm-hm."

"Hey, don't be grumpy with me. If you're nice, I might make you a cake."

"Oh, aight, now you're talking. Why didn't you say that?"

"So you'll stay for cake but not for family. Greedy."

"Hey, it's about time somebody else cooks up in here."

She runs her hands over my comforter. "Okay, where's this infamous letter?"

I pick through my backpack for a copy. I hesitate before handing it over, like it's a precious thing she might break.

She holds the paper with both hands. As she reads, her eyebrows jump and press together. Her eyes go wide and then blink back to normal size.

When she finishes reading, she lowers the paper and lays it on her thighs. She picks at her clear nail polish, staring into space.

"So?" I ask. "What you think?"

"I mean . . . wow. I'm trying to imagine finding this on campus. I guess it would seem . . . pretty aggressive?"

"Yeah, well, being passive hasn't done nothing for us.

And being passive-aggressive is stupid. So it's pretty much the only way left."

"Okay," she says. "What were you hoping would happen next?"

I chew on my lip. "I don't know. We just had to let this out. It's too much. I can't stand the arrogance. The assumption that we should feel lucky to be there. Like we have nothing to complain about. Like Lakeside is the best thing to ever happen to us. When really, it's crushing us. Or trying to."

I stab my notebook with a pen.

She leans back against the wall and rests her head between my magazine cutouts of Tupac and The Roots. "It wasn't easy for me there," she says. "But it seems so much harder for you. I guess I got used to it and sort of navigated around it. I didn't think anyone meant any harm, so . . . I guess I didn't blame anyone or get angry about it." She bites the inside of her cheek, thinking.

"That's the thing," I say. "They don't have to *mean* harm to *do* harm. Half the time they think they're helping, or joking, or 'just trying to understand.' That's why we had to start from scratch. Make 'em think."

"Yeah," she says, "that makes sense, I guess. But when did it start to get to you so much? I mean, the school didn't change. You changed. When did that happen?"

I grab a pillow from the bed and lie on my back on the floor, resting my head on the pillow.

"I been *feeling* this way for the longest," I say. "You mean when did I start to let it show that stuff was bothering me."

There was a time when this fire was just a spark inside of me. Maybe my breaking point was the LA riots. For almost a year, you couldn't watch the news without seeing that video of those police officers beating Rodney King as he lay on the ground, begging for mercy. They tried the officers, and then they let them off. People went out in the streets and burned LA to the ground.

We had never seen anything like that in our lifetimes. We didn't know it was routine for our parents growing up.

"You remember when the Rodney King verdict came out," I say, "how everyone went to school like everything was normal?"

"Yeah," Ava says. "I remember."

"What was we supposed to do wit that? If people thought King deserved that beating from all them cops, they musta thought he was a straight-up animal. Some kind of wild beast. A 'danger' til he stops moving."

An image invades my mind. Live footage from a helicopter on a bright, sunny day. These Black guys pull a white guy from a truck and just pound him. Like they want to kill him. They didn't stop. They got bottles and bricks. Beating his head in. Blood running down his face, soaking his blond curls.

"So dudes in the hood was like, 'Okay, fine, we're animals? Bet. This is what animals do.'"

The whole way to school I was thinking, *We're gonna talk about this in morning meeting. What am I gonna say? What's everyone else gonna say?*

"I remember . . . I went into school feeling mad nervous that day," I tell Ava. "For me, the world had changed. But at school, nothing changed. Nobody talked about Rodney King, the verdict, the riots, nothing. Just leave all that outside the door. Everything's still perfect up in here."

They didn't bring it up in morning meeting. No one whispered about it between classes. No one seemed to be thinking about it at all. I wanted to scream, *Did anybody watch the fucking news?*

"I guess I always knew they saw me as different. But that day, with everyone else laughing and joking like it was any normal day... I was feeling like I really *was* different." I pick up my head to look at Ava. She's staring out the window. Her eyes are wet. "You remember that?" I ask.

"Of course," she says.

I settle back onto the pillow and stare at the ceiling.

After a minute, she says, "I guess it never occurred to me ... that I could do something about it."

When I get back from Supreme's friend's crib, Ashanta's car is in front of the house. Inside, the smell of vanilla cake, thick and sweet in the air, makes my stomach grumble. I jog up the stairs to my room and change my clothes, stuffing the ones I was wearing inside my hamper. I check my eyes in the bathroom mirror. Not too bad, but I put a few drops of Visine anyway.

Ashanta, Kareem, and the baby are in the living room.

"Whassup, everybody?" I say.

Zakiyyah crawls around on the rug.

"Oooh shoot! Check you out!" I say.

She stops and stares up at me.

"Yeah, that's right! Uncle G's in tha house!" I pick her up and dance with her, trying to get a giggle, but she stares at me straight-faced. "Oh no, you forgot how to smile?"

Ashanta laughs. "I think she's scared 'cause you're so

tall, you've got her so high up from the ground."

"Oh, aight," I say, "we can fix that." I bend at the knees and bounce to a beat, singing to babygirl from Black Sheep's "The Choice Is Yours." I bounce low and then high, rising back up to full height on the last line. Finally, she laughs. "Yes!" I raise my free hand in the air and show off her dimpled smile. In three seconds, it's gone. "Dag, girl!" I tickle her. Nothing. "You too much work. Forget you." I put her down with Ashanta, who's laughing at me. "I'll be back. Lemme see what smells so good."

I go to the kitchen, where Mom sits with her legs crossed while Ava sets out cups and forks. Containers of Indian food are arranged on the table.

"There you are!" Mom says.

"Y'all didn't hear me come in? I been here for a minute."

"You should have told us," Ava says. "The food's getting cold."

"I'm starving," I say. "Let's eat."

Ava opens the containers, and Mom calls Ashanta and Kareem. Kareem stays with the baby while Ashanta makes two plates.

We bring our plates and drinks into the living room and sit on couches, chairs, and the floor. I eat like a starving person. Chicken tikka masala, lamb samosas with that sweet brown sauce, puffy poori bread that leaves oil on my fingers. Mom may not cook often, but she sure knows how to order.

The oven timer dings. Ava puts her plate down and skips into the kitchen. I hear the oven open and close.

"I hope that's my cake!" I call.

She comes back into the living room. "Yes, that's your cake."

"Aight! That's what's up! Thank you."

"You're welcome. I'm only gonna take half of it back to school with me."

"Oh, you mean the half I don't eat?"

I haven't had a birthday cake in years. We fell out of the habit as my sisters left home and I started spending my birthdays with my boys. I thought it would feel silly to have one when I'm turning eighteen, but it's actually pretty cool.

We don't bother with icing. We cut into the golden cake while it's warm, even though everyone's still full from dinner. The sugary crust surrounds two inches of fluffy, golden deliciousness. I decide I need to learn the recipe.

We sit around, talking and joking, Mom rapping her old-school rap songs and trying to teach the baby to dance. Mom is so happy having everyone home, I can't help but feel it too.

Later, after Ashanta and family go home, Ava hangs out in Mom's room. I have time to go back out with my boys, but I'm stuffed and tired. I go to my room and turn on some music.

There's an envelope I hadn't noticed earlier on my desk, mailed from Nana and Grandpa in Finchburg, NY. I tear it open and pull out a thick card with a printed drawing of a young Black boy on the cover. *On your birthday*, it says in blue letters. When I open the card, a hundred dollar bill floats onto the desk. Nice. Nana's handwriting fills both sides of the page.

Dear Gibran,

It's hard to believe our youngest grandchild is becoming a young man! We wish we could see more of you, but we know how busy you and your mom are. We are keeping busy too. Even though Grandpa is retired, he is constantly asked to serve on boards for organizations. As for me, I am still teaching art in the after-school program. There are more Black families than ever before. And the program is needed more than ever. We may turn it into a nonprofit soon.

We would love to have you come stay with us again. We have your move to college on our calendar for August. Grandpa will bring down the van. We are so proud of you.

Love,
Nana and Grandpa

I read the letter twice and lay the crisp bill on my desk. Maybe I should visit them again before I go to college. I was so bored in upstate New York though. Mom left me there for a month the summer before junior year, probably hoping I'd be reformed afterward. That didn't work. I just got restless. When I came home, I was running the streets more than before.

It's obvious that Mom and Uncle Kevin both got their love of Black people from Nana and Grandpa, even though they live it differently. Nana and Grandpa are so calm though. They seem so sure of their purpose. So comfortable with themselves. Like it doesn't matter what the world thinks.

282

I wonder how that feels. How long did it take them to get there?

I pull out my notebook and a pen to write down some lyrics.

Before I get a full line down, Ava comes in, wearing her pajamas. "Whatcha doing?" she asks.

"Nothing," I say. "Writing down some lyrics."

"Ooh, can I hear?" She lies sideways on my bed, cradling her head in her hand.

"Don't you got schoolwork to do?" I ask her.

"Yeah," she says. "Don't remind me. That's why I'm in here instead of in my room. Come on, let's hear it. Want me to beatbox for you?"

"Oh God, please don't," I tease. "Okay, okay." I flip to the last full page and start a beat in my mind. I bob my head to keep time and start flowing.

*This life real*
*It could take a toll on the feeble minded*
*I read the science*
*And know that it's something deep behind it*
*Police and riots*
*Is ingredients for heated climates*
*Might find fatality if you choosing to seek the violence*
*I'm speaking silence*
*Alignment with all your higher hopes*
*3rd eye vision admitting I'm living wide awoke*
*Nah I don't try to cope*
*I got no choice to survive*
*The price of life ain't never close to the price you quote*

*We just here fighting broke and still we righteous teachers*
*Give all praises and thanks before I light my rifa*

"Yeah . . . I'll stop there," I tell her.

"Why?"

"You can't handle the realness."

"Hm. Okay. That was good." She yawns. "You wanna hear mine?"

"What, you join the hip hop club of Yale or somethin?"

She cracks up. "Yes. We're touring nationally. We're amazing."

"Oh shoot. Check you out."

She bunches up my pillow and snuggles into it.

"Make yourself comfortable," I say.

"Thanks!" she says, and pulls my blanket up over her shoulders.

"You really are hiding from your homework, huh?"

She groans and turns her face to the wall.

I go back to my rhymes. After a few minutes, she's breathing deep and regular.

I gently pull off her slippers and spread the blanket to cover her feet. I click off the desk lamp and bring my notebook to her room across the hall.

Ava leaves late Sunday morning. She hugs me and then holds me by the shoulders.

In a low voice, she says, "Promise you'll try to behave at the assembly tomorrow? For Mom?"

I fold my arms. "Promise me nobody's gonna say something stupid and need to get checked?"

She narrows her eyes.

I shrug. "They don't start nothin, won't be nothin."

"You're impossible," she says.

"I know."

Mom appears in the hallway, putting her coat on. "You ready?" she asks Ava.

"Yeah," Ava says. "But you really don't have to drive me all the way to South Station . . ."

Mom waves her off and kisses me on the cheek. "I'll be back soon."

"Okay." I stand at the front door and watch them go. "Thanks for the cake!" I call to Ava.

I wander into the kitchen and eat a piece of cake for breakfast. I think of calling up James and David to make a game plan for the assembly, but I don't want to cut my weekend short.

In the quiet, my throat gets tight and something comes over me.

Maybe because it's my birthday. Maybe because I'm eighteen now. A man.

I know my father's not going to call the house, even if he's thinking of me. I decide to go over there and see him and my aunt and my grandparents.

As I walk to the station and wait for the bus, I try to remember the last time I saw my father. Mom stopped taking us to visit them years ago, probably afraid he'd be a bad influence once we were old enough to notice details, like dime bags lying around his apartment. I've only been there on my own a few times. I never tell Mom when I go.

Everything's running slowly because it's Sunday and the MBTA is ridiculous. When the bus finally comes, I ride ten minutes and get off at the end of Dumas Street. I walk up the block and pull off my headphones as I approach the door of their triple-decker. I ring my aunt's bell.

"Who's that?" Her voice comes through the metal box like a bell, her light Caribbean lilt barely audible after decades in the States.

"It's Gibran," I say into the machine.

The loud buzz startles me every time, even though I know it's coming. I climb the stairs to her apartment on the second floor. She's already flung the door open, and she spreads her arms out wide to embrace me. She wears a thick beige sweater and house slippers.

"Gibran," she says. "We haven't seen you or your sisters in ages."

"I know, my bad, Auntie." I hug her back.

"Come on in, come in and see your grandparents."

I pass through the entryway into the living room, where Papa and Mama, my father's parents, are installed in their usual spots on opposite ends of the couch in front of the TV, legs tucked up on the cushions. Papa is tiny, but his voice is strong, and his accent is so thick, I have to focus to understand him.

"Who's that there?" Papa calls out, his milky eyes peering at me through thick glasses that hide half his coffee-black face. He reaches out and pulls me toward him. "Dis Gibran? Winston's boy? Look at you, how you done grown." I lean down for a hug.

"Oh yes," Mama says, beckoning me. "He's a young man now."

I bend over and kiss her cheek. Even though I tower over

her, I feel as if she's looking down at me. She holds her head like she's wearing a crown.

I sit in an armchair in the corner, facing them.

Aunt Letitia emerges from the kitchen holding a tray, balancing four glasses of iced tea and one small plate with a generous piece of Entenmann's coffee cake topped with a lit candle. "Happy birthdaaay tooo youuuu," she sings. Mama and Papa join in.

I cover my mouth with my hand. "Oh wow."

I let myself smile while they serenade me. They finish with a flourish, and I blow out the candle.

"This is so nice of you," I say, taking the plate from my aunt.

"Did you think we forgot?" she asks. "You may forget about us, but we don't forget about you."

"Aw, I never forget y'all," I say. I make a mental note to come by more often. I don't have to see my father every time.

The cake is good, and I wash it down with the iced tea. "Thank you so much," I say again.

"How old you now, boy?" Papa asks me. "Seventeen?"

"I'm eighteen."

He whistles. "Eighteen!" He starts talking about what he and Mama were doing at eighteen. Images of a young, handsome couple courting at dances in the warm island nights bloom like an old movie in my mind. Mama giggles and tells him to stop exaggerating. He rubs her foot in response. They are too cute. I don't know how my father missed learning how to be a good husband when he was raised by these two.

After a while, Papa and Mama start closing their eyes in front of the TV.

"I should get going," I say to my aunt.

"Are you going upstairs to see your father?" she asks.

"I figured I would," I say. "Is he home?"

"Where else would he be?"

She sees me to her door. I climb the creaky stairs to the top floor and knock three times on his apartment door.

"Yeah!" he calls from inside.

I get the jittery feeling I have every time I'm at his door. He pulls it open dramatically, and I take a step back.

"Gibran!" he yells. "My man! What's happening?"

My father is one of the only people I know who's still taller than me, even though I've gained an inch or two since I saw him last. I'll never have his deep brown skin tone, but being almost eye to eye with him has me feeling some kind of way.

"Just stopping by," I say.

"Come on in," he says, slapping me on the back. This echo of love, of fatherhood, this thin presence, gives me chills. I remind myself not to expect anything at all.

Papers and books cover every surface.

"Let's see . . ." He moves a stack of papers and notebooks from a vintage wooden rocking chair and motions for me to sit down. "What's new with you?"

"Not much," I say, drumming my fingers on the arms of the chair. "Last year of high school."

"That's a big milestone! You have plans for next year? You thinking about college? You know, if your mom had let me teach you tennis, you would have been set. You'd have your pick of full scholarships. But I guess she didn't want that for you, so here we are." He barely takes a breath before moving on. He jumps up and plucks a stack of typed pages from the table and waves it at me. "I'm almost done with my screenplay. Yep. It's gonna be big. Once I get it out there, it'll make millions. You and your sisters won't have to worry about a thing."

"Mm."

"I know, I know." He laughs, smooth and confident like the Hollywood actor he could have been. "You're thinking, 'Man, this jive turkey, always talking bout making it big.' But this time, I'm telling you, I mean it. It's gonna happen. I'm this close!"

"Okay." I don't give a damn about his dreams of making it big. He could be dead broke and still be a dad. But I don't bother to tell him how I really feel.

Instead, I let him go on about himself, his "work," and his dreams. He's not running out of steam anytime soon.

The sun streams in through the window, low in the sky.

"I better get going," I say, pushing myself up to stand.

"Oh, all right, no problem," he says. "Thanks for dropping by." At the door, he asks, "Oh, hey, any chance you got some reefer on you?"

"Oh. Yeah, I got you." I dig in my pocket and hand him the last of my stash. I brought it in case he asked, but I still feel some kinda way that he did.

"Thanks, man, I appreciate it," he says. "I'll get you back!" He laughs. We both know that's a lie.

"It's all good," I say.

As I head toward the stairs, Aunt Letitia opens her door

on the next landing. "Winston!" she calls. She must have been waiting.

"Yeah? What do you want?"

"Did you say happy birthday to your son?"

His face freezes for a second.

I focus on the stairs and count my steps.

Then he laughs. "Boy, is that why you came here today? You know I'm not studying no calendar."

"I know," I say. "It's fine." I feel hot, and I want to get outside.

"I can sing for you if you want me to," he says. "Happy biiirthdaaay to youuuu," he croons, and then cackles.

I keep trudging down the stairs, trying not to make it obvious how eager I am to get out of here.

Aunt Letitia calls me over before I round her landing. She stuffs a twenty in my pocket. "That's from me," she says. She stuffs a fifty in my other pocket. "That's from Mama and Papa."

"Oh man. You didn't have to—"

"I know," she says.

The door upstairs slams shut, and she glares upward.

I hug her again. "Thank you."

The cool air outside feels good on my face and neck. I rush down the street to the bus stop. If I get home before dark, Mom won't ask where I've been. I bounce on my toes, waiting for the bus. The wind chills my sweat, and I shiver. I wipe my eyes, put my earphones back on, and press play on my Walkman.

At home, we eat leftover Indian food for dinner. Mom works on sketches for a painting, with the TV on in the background. I can't focus on my homework, so I pick through the box of books I took from the attic. I flip through *Black Power* again. I want to ask Mom about the letter I found in it, but she's in the zone, and I don't want to stress her out any more than she already is with the school meeting tomorrow.

I think about my history project. I could use it to school white kids again, but I spend too much time doing that. What if I did this for me? To actually learn something instead of to teach?

I pick up *A Raisin in the Sun* and read it from beginning to end. It's Mom's old copy, all marked-up and highlighted from decades ago, when she played Mama to my father's charismatic Walter Lee. I'm sure Mom later saw the irony in that. I'm sure he didn't.

Maybe I'll do profiles. Learn more about the intellectuals who wrote these books. Everybody knows about the Harlem Renaissance. What about the writers and activists of the fifties, sixties, seventies? And where are they now? Some of them are dead of course, but some of them must still be around. I'll have to go to the public library to do some of the research, since the section on Black culture at Lakeside isn't exactly robust. I'll go next weekend.

Now I have two things to look forward to. The assembly tomorrow and my history project. It's gonna be tight.

# 14

## KEVIN
*New York City | Thursday, April 25, 1968*

The police have been called to campus, but they haven't been sicced on us yet. They surround our campus in a ring. Their show of force is impressive. Rows and rows of blue uniforms, with weapons hanging from their hips.

Drilling to prepare for police action was one thing. Seeing them line up outside our building is another. All that stands between us and those weapons is a phone call from our president, who is surely fed up with us already. These brick walls, those iron gates, those campus guards—all meant to protect Columbia students and staff—now close in on us. We've blocked the institution from conducting business as usual, so now we are the target.

It's time to reaffirm our commitment, and it's time for those who aren't ready for all this to pack up and go. Some do. There's no judgment on them. I don't know if I am ready. But I know that I am staying. I have to.

I think again of Orangeburg. I think of our leaders. Dr. King. Malcolm. Medgar Evers. The freedom fighters. The assassinations. The murders. The violence to hold people in line, to keep the status quo. Are we next? Would Columbia allow it?

Thursday night, Harlem comes out to meet the police line.

"Check it out!" Claudius announces. "There's a rally outside!"

We jump up like a swarm of butterflies and flow toward the classrooms with windows facing Amsterdam Avenue outside of campus. We take turns leaning out the windows to see down the block. A crowd of people from Harlem marches in front of the police barricade. Some of them hold signs that say, "Support Our Black Students" and "Columbia, Hands Off Harlem." A few reporters with cameras and notepads stroll between the protestors and the police line.

We make some noise from our windows. When the demonstrators see us, we raise our fists in the air. They return our gesture.

"Do you know who's out there?" I ask Robbie.

"I see some folks I know," he says. "And there are more where they've come from. If the university knows what's good for it, they'll sit up and pay attention."

The energy from seeing our supporters charges the space as hours pass. Everyone knows Columbia can't afford to anger the people of Harlem. Just because the riots haven't reached here yet doesn't mean they never could. A police crack down on a group of Black students could wake a sleeping giant. We don't have to speak it, but we all know that separating from the white students was the best strategic

BLACK & WHITE
DRAWINGS
TO COME

294

move. Harlem wouldn't be out here defending hundreds of white students and a handful of Blacks. Community members have kept us well-fed and well-stocked with toiletries, blankets, supplies.

No one knows what will happen tomorrow, but in this moment, I indulge the feeling of being a part of something vast. Right now, in this building, we are a symbol of solidarity, and a doorstop preventing the president from clearing out all the buildings.

We take turns napping in chairs, on floors, on tabletops.

The president meets with the faculty throughout the night.

The police hold their positions, stationed in a ring around the campus.

**Friday, April 26, 1968**
At four a.m., Richard bursts into the lobby. "Everybody, listen up! We've got a message from President Kirk."

I sit up and hold my breath.

"The university has canceled the police action that was threatened against campus protestors—"

"Yes!"

"Right on!"

We clap and holler in relief.

Richard holds his hand up. "And . . ." He waits for us to quiet down. Then he yells, "They have suspended the construction of Columbia Gym!"

I stand up. Others get up too. We scream and hug and slap hands and cry.

Robbie claps, and so do other community members.

"Also," Wesley adds as the noise settles into an excited buzz, "The university will remain closed until Monday."

The room breathes a collective sigh of relief.

We have three days to hope for change without direct confrontation. It's still tense. But for now, at least, our necks aren't right in the guillotine.

We take a few minutes to celebrate and soak in the good news. Then Wesley says, "I don't have to remind you that this is far from over. Our other demands have yet to be addressed. We also want to make sure the 'suspension' of the gym construction becomes *cancellation*. We don't want them to placate us to get us out and then go right back to their plans."

"That's right," Richard says. "The administration is angry and embarrassed, and they're still planning to win. Let's enjoy this moment and get some rest. We'll reconvene later this morning and discuss next steps."

Valerie appears in front of me, carrying the blanket I laid on her last night. "Here you go," she says, holding it out to me.

"I'm fine," I say. "I couldn't sleep right now if I wanted to. You hold on to it."

She hesitates, then folds the blanket over her arms. "Thank you," she says.

"Of course."

I wish she would sit with me, but before I find the courage to ask, she crosses the room and settles into a couch next to a friend, who gladly shares the blanket. Her smile returns. That brilliant smile I used to draw out so easily. I give myself three days—the three days we'll likely remain in this building—to make things right with Valerie.

For now, I climb out on the balcony to get some air. Some students and community folk are rapping revolution. Robbie sits on the ledge overlooking the campus. I walk over and lean on the ledge beside him.

He takes in a deep breath. "You know the air smells different here? Isn't that something?"

"It is." I've noticed it too. The air inside Columbia's gates is different from the air in Harlem. It must be the grass.

The counter-protestors in suits circle the faculty members wearing white armbands.

"You still worried about your parents?" Robbie asks.

"Not too much. I'm more worried that . . . we'll do all of this and it won't make a difference. The powers that be will just deal with us and continue on with their plans, business as usual. You know?"

"Yeah," he says. "I know. That's why you don't stop with one action. You keep escalating. You keep agitating. You get in the way. I mean, this is really something, what you all are doing right here."

I look at him. "You think so?"

"I *know* so. This is the man's worst nightmare. The common people building a movement, and the elite lending whatever power they have to bring the message inside?" He nods. "And if it doesn't succeed, you're gonna keep on trying. And so will those that come after you. Just like the community's been doing for years." He looks down. "If there's one thing we learned from losing Malcolm, it's that the work can't start and end with one man. We each do what we can with what we have from where we are. That's how we keep moving in the right direction."

Malcolm X's murder feels long ago, but it's only been three years. Robbie changed so much in the year before it happened. Elijah Muhammad had silenced Malcolm because of his comments about JFK's assassination, so Malcolm wasn't giving speeches anymore. When he broke from the Nation of Islam, made the hajj, and traveled around the Middle East and Africa, he was welcomed by laypeople and world leaders alike. He came back to New York an orthodox Muslim and a Black nationalist. A changed man. El-Hajj Malik El-Shabazz.

For Robbie, it all clicked then. He had wanted an explanation and a way forward. Now he had both. An explanation for everything that is. And a way forward as a Black man in America.

Robbie converted to Islam. He spoke with reverence about Malcolm's new organizations. The plans to sue the US government on behalf of twenty million Black Americans.

That was when Robbie started to bring me along as he learned. No more showing off and leaving me behind. I couldn't wait to be old enough to visit Robbie on my own. I wanted to go with him to the mosque and to the political meetings and see the changes happening in real time. I was ready for direction too.

But then. Then Malcolm was killed. And who was there to take his place?

Robbie and I didn't talk as much after the assassination. He was rarely home. When we visited, he would try to catch me up, but it wasn't the same.

Here on the balcony at the school that I hate, we talk like we had started to back then. Only now he's a man, and I'm becoming one.

"I could have given up after Malcolm died," Robbie says. "It would have been the easiest thing to do. I was so angry. I didn't know . . . how to keep going. What to do next." He sighs. "We had to realize—our work, each of us, we're only adding pieces to the puzzle. You may not see all the change you're working for." He looks at me. "You may fail. This"—he gestures to the upside-down campus below us—"it may not work. You may not get your demands met. You may get kicked out. Arrested. Beaten. Shot. That doesn't mean you did nothing. It still matters. Regardless of the outcome you get to see. What's important is to be involved. To do something. You dig?"

I nod.

"I know how it feels to be wandering blindly," he says, "not knowing if your actions will make a difference. It's enough to make you want to quit sometimes." He swings his legs gently, and I worry he'll fall to the ground. It's only a twenty-foot drop, but it makes my stomach lurch. "Don't quit, Kevin. Do the best you know how today. Right here, right now. You'll be guided to the next step when you're ready."

Robbie and I stay on the balcony as the sun lifts into the sky.

The crowds around the buildings thin and thicken again.

Late in the morning, a small group of young people appears on the path heading toward our building. They are Black and Puerto Rican. I stand and shield my eyes. Their

299

voices reach us before their forms and faces are clear: chanting, loose and spontaneous.

"Power to the people!"

"Black Power!"

They pass the sundial.

Robbie calls inside, "You all need to see this!"

Students pour out of the windows.

The new arrivals get closer: Black and Puerto Rican teenagers, looking serious and ready. Their numbers grow as they approach the occupied buildings. Some of them wear hats cocked to the side, with cool gazes to match.

They approach the counter-protestors and stare them down. The counter-protestors, many of whom are athletes, shrink under the gaze of these Harlem teens. I relish the sight. I don't know how they got through the police line, but if it was anything like this, I wish I had seen it.

Up on the balcony, we wave and call out to the teens. We raise our fists in the air, and they raise theirs. Their faces brighten, and to me they look young again, less intimidating, but the counter-protestors have already shuffled out of their way.

A familiar tan jacket in the crowd of teens pulls my focus. It's Mike! And he's not the only one from the tutoring program in the group.

I hear a squeal next to me and feel a slap on my arm. Valerie stands beside me, wiping away a tear and smiling her proudest smile.

"Can you believe this?" she says.

I shake my head. But then I say, "Yeah. Yeah, I guess I can."

The students from their high school are always organizing for activist causes. The surprising part is seeing them *here*.

We stand together, saying nothing, watching our mentees intimidate our opponents.

Then another small crowd of brown people crosses the green from the far gate. Another group of teens, forming a circle around a couple of Black men.

Someone on the balcony has binoculars. He pulls them down from his eyes and whispers, "No way." Then he laughs out loud. "Open the door!" he shouts, hopping down from the ledge and running inside to the guards at the front door.

Valerie and I keep watching from the balcony.

As they approach, I recognize the two men in the middle of the circle, but my brain can't compute. One is slim and brown-skinned. The other is light-skinned with a full mustache and a beret on top of his short afro. Is it really?

I look at Valerie, wide-eyed.

She looks stunned too.

As the men reach Hamilton Hall, the "Majority Coalition" scrambles to get out of the way. No more pushing, no more yelling, no threats, no blocking. The faculty step aside too. The teens join the other high schoolers on the green—there must be nearly a hundred of them now—and the two men climb the stairs to our building and knock on the door. We all race to meet them.

It takes ten minutes to pull enough furniture out of the way so they can climb over the barricade. I look at the posters on the wall and then back at our guests. Stokely

Carmichael and H. Rap Brown are here. To see us!

Wesley shakes their hands and thanks them for coming out. I remember hearing that Wesley's father represented Rap in court before. They must have already met. Robbie greets them like old friends.

I am starstruck. I have seen them speak before, but this is different. They are here because of what *we're* doing.

We sit quietly, eager to take in their words.

"Those young brothers out there," Rap says as he joins us on the floor, "they're fearless! You know they broke through the police line twice? They got themselves through, and then they came back to break us through and show us the way over here."

We all laugh.

"The oppressed people around the world are rising up," Stokely says. "Everybody's doing their part. You all right here in the 'master's' house."

"We came to ask how we can support you," Rap says. "And we needed to talk to you in person. So let's talk strategy."

Anyone who has heard the sound bites reporters use to represent these two men would think they came here to get us riled up, to agitate, to instigate a race war. Honestly, when I saw them striding across the campus, I half expected a jolt of militant energy to overtake us when they arrived. Their presence is electrifying, but not in the wild way the media projects. Instead, a calm spreads through the room.

"You all know you're on your own in here," Rap continues. "The people of Harlem support you. But the people have bigger problems to deal with than protecting some university students from your board of trustees or even from

BLACK & WHITE
DRAWINGS
TO COME

the police. You all know that. We know that. But Columbia doesn't know that."

He and Stokely smile.

"So as long as we're on the same page about what's really going on, we're happy to support you however we can. We have a reputation, and we have no problem using it. You want us to go out and tell them Harlem's ready to tear this place up, just say the word. We know how the man thinks. They won't call our bluff. They can't afford to risk it."

Richard, Wesley, and Claudius update them on our demands and the administration's responses, including the concessions earlier this morning.

"We want to stay in here until all the demands are met," Claudius says. "Our strategy has been to keep repeating our demands and insisting we aren't leaving until they're all addressed. But it's been hard to keep the media's attention on the issues."

"The *New York Times* sympathizes with the administration," Richard says. "We can hardly get our perspective out to the public. The press is trying to discredit the whole occupation as anarchy, a disruption caused by rowdy, privileged kids. They don't even talk about our Black-held building."

"No surprise there," Stokely says. "They probably can't believe you have the discipline and commitment to organize this way."

Wesley pulls out a sheet of paper. "Maybe if you would read our demands to the press?"

Rap skims it, nodding, while Stokely reads over his shoulder.

Rap smiles. "So you need to get some attention. I think we can help with that."

The crowd of news reporters has already grown outside the building in the hour our visitors have been here.

Rap and Stokely climb back over the barricade and slide out the door to face cameras flashing and microphones stuck in their faces. Rap looks at the cameras through his shades and reads our demands to the reporters. The smile he wore with us a few minutes ago is gone. He. At the end of our formal statement, he adds, "If Columbia doesn't deal with the brothers in there, Columbia's going to have to deal with the brothers out in the streets."

They haven't been gone long when the phone begins to ring again. Parents of protestors, parents of admitted students, parents, parents, parents . . . and finally, the press.

Our spirits are high since the visit from Rap and Stokely. We move around and spread out, chatting excitedly about the visit, speculating about what comes next.

I keep an eye on Valerie, waiting for an opportunity to talk to her. When the sister she's talking to gets up, I take her place before I can overthink it.

"Hey," I say.

"Hey," she says. She's still smiling contentedly, and so am I. Even though we're not exactly smiling at each other or because of each other, it feels like enough common ground to build from.

"This has been a day, hasn't it?" I ask.

"It sure has," she says. "When I saw our kids out there, in the middle of campus? Facing down the jocks?" She makes an O with her mouth and shakes her hand like she's burned it.

"They are something else," I say.

"Mm-hm." She nods.

I take a big breath. "Listen. Um . . . I've been thinking."

"Mm. What's new? That's all you do." She smirks.

I'm not sure if she's laughing at me or with me. I take a breath and try again. "Well . . . I've been thinking about what you said to me. About . . . focusing on doing the work, instead of, you know . . . blaming people for why I can't."

She tilts her head and watches me.

"Well, I guess, I think, you were probably right. . . ."

"Probably?" She presses her lips together.

"Maybe?" I pick at the rug.

She sucks her teeth slowly. "You're gonna have to do better than that, Kevin."

"All right." I sigh. "I'm sorry. I . . . took you for granted, and I let my issues get in the way of our work, and . . . I messed up. I'm sorry." I sneak a look at her.

She lets me suffer in silence for a moment longer. Then she says, "Okay."

"So . . . ?"

"So what?"

"Can we be cool again?"

"Maybe," she says.

"You're cold!"

"I have to be, to deal with you brothers."

"Hmph." I relax a little bit.

"So what made you come to your senses?" she asks.

I shrug. "You."

"I could have talked til I was blue in the face; you weren't listening before. Why now?"

I look around. Wesley, Richard, and Claudius are huddled together over a pad of paper. Robbie is rapping with some brothers from the community. Students sit in circles predicting how much longer we'll be in here. The door to the dean's office is closed, and I wonder who else saw or heard about the files and the stamps.

"I guess being in here, taking this stand, being supported by the community while we're trying to support them . . . I feel different . . . hopeful, I guess. And . . . I'm only here in this building because I'm here at this school. So . . . I don't know. There's still a lot I'm trying to figure out. But like my cousin said, you do what you can from where you are. And then you figure out the next steps. You know?"

She smiles. "That sounds like a man of action."

"Yeah. He's pretty cool." Normally I'd be resentful admitting that my cousin taught me something. But I'm feeling closer to him too. He's proud of me, and now I can be proud of him.

"I'm talking about you," Valerie says.

"Oh. What?"

She chuckles. "You're *starting* to sound like a man of action. This is the Kevin I've been waiting for. You're almost there, anyway."

"Oh, almost."

She pinches her fingers together. "This close."

# 15

## GIBRAN
*Massachusetts | October 1995*

Our letters have been removed from the walls, the doors, and the bulletin boards.

Finally, someone talks about it.

"As you know," Mr. Adrian says once we're settled around the table, "there is an assembly this afternoon to discuss the letter that was posted around campus on Friday." He doesn't avoid looking at me, James, and David, but he doesn't stare us down either. "I want to take a few minutes here to foster a discussion of the letter in the context of African American history."

People squirm in their seats.

"We've talked about the origin of American ideas about race, how those ideas served the perpetuation of the Transatlantic Slave Trade. Later in the semester, we'll talk more about how those ideas haunt our present. This has been broached in a very immediate way on campus, so I think it's appropriate to discuss it, at least briefly, now. I wonder how many of us were surprised by the letter and/or its contents? Show of hands?"

All of the white students raise their hands almost immediately. Lisa lifts her hand to her shoulder and then folds her arms.

Mr. Adrian surveys the responses. "To be honest," he says, "we had a similar situation among the faculty. And yet . . . there are issues mentioned in this document that have apparently been plaguing the writers for months. Years, even." He checks our faces for confirmation. I nod. "Now, if these are long-standing concerns for some members of our community," he continues, "how is it that so many others are completely unaware?"

Mr. Adrian folds his hands on the table and waits, unafraid of a long pause.

Finally, Kate raises her hand. "I don't mean to be, like, rude or anything, but . . . how this is related to history?"

Here we go.

Mr. Adrian opens his mouth, closes it, and opens it again. "Okay. Let's back up a bit. Does anyone want to respond to that?"

David raises his hand. "I can." He turns to Kate. "Basically, the letter was about how it feels to be a Black man today, especially here on this campus, which was designed for white people. Everything we've been talking about in history—how white people made themselves think of Black people as uncivilized, without culture, all of that? That's the reason why it's still hard for us to be in a place like this. It's directly related."

Kate twists her mouth and pulls on the ends of her hair. She's obviously not convinced.

Hunter responds. "But most of the people in this room

right now are interested in Black history but wouldn't support the Million Man March. The march isn't Black history. It's . . ." He searches for words. "Current-day extremism. I mean, were Lakeside students going to Black Panther rallies in the sixties?" He looks at Mr. Adrian for backup.

"How is that the same?" I ask. "That's such an ignorant comment. I mean, the Panthers and the Nation are both for Black independence and liberation. That's pretty much all they have in common."

Hunter scoffs, and I can tell he's about to defend himself. I cut him off before he gets even stupider.

"This march is not militant. Not that there's anything wrong with being militant. But this is actually anti-violence. Rival gangs are squashing beef in order to go and be in the same place. How is that 'extreme'?"

Hunter says, "I just don't see why it has to be only Black people."

I take a deep breath. James rescues me.

"Remember how we learned that enslaved Africans weren't allowed to gather in groups? Well, maybe the idea of Black people getting together without white people still scares the majority. Even though it's a public event, out in the open, maybe there's still a fear that we're plotting to overthrow the white power structure and break our chains."

*Thank you.* I want to give him pounds, but I hold back to let his words settle. After a few seconds, I add, "That's exactly what it is. White people are afraid of what we could do if we unite. That's the real reason the government dismantled the Panthers. And that's the real reason this march is getting so much bad press."

Skeptical faces blink at me. I could go on, but I'll save the rest for the assembly.

Mr. Adrian lets us sit in silence for a minute.

Then Andrew, a white senior with short brown hair, raises his hand. "I'm not trying to be combative. I just thought that the goal of, like, civil rights and reaching equality was to not see race. You know, 'I have a dream' and all that. We're making all this progress getting over racism, and then . . . this letter and the march . . . I don't know, it's like some people don't want to put it behind us."

Did these people even read the letter?

David kind of chuckles. "Everyone wants to put *racism* behind us. That's not the same as putting *race* behind us. We're saying, pretending that race isn't a thing anymore is actually another way of being racist."

Andrew screws up his face. A bunch of the white students draw their eyebrows together and frown. Kate's cheeks are bright red. Lisa stares at her notebook.

Mr. Adrian surveys the room. When no one volunteers to speak again, he tries to close out the discussion. "These conversations are not easy to have. But they are important. We broaden our views and hopefully get closer to being that inclusive community we strive to be." He looks unsure he should have brought it up, but he adds, "I'm here to discuss these issues with you at any time, inside or outside of class."

He asks us to pull out the reading. A few people participate eagerly, glad to push the hard stuff away. I'm still turning the comments over in my mind, wondering if the assembly will go the same way.

After class, Mr. Adrian asks the three of us to stay for a

minute. When the other students have left, he says, "I want you to know that I'm here to listen. I said it to the whole class, but I want to make sure you know I mean it."

"Thank you," I say.

"Yeah," David says. "We appreciate that."

He nods.

We take a side path to the dining hall for lunch. We walk a few paces without speaking. Then I say, "Can you believe them white kids?"

"Can't wait for the assembly," James says sarcastically.

Over lunch, we try to guess who will have the most asinine comments.

"Definitely Kate," David says.

"This'll be her," I say, and raise my voice into a high-pitched Valley girl accent. "'Like, can you imagine if white people had a march? It would totally be called racist.'"

James almost spits out his food laughing.

"They better not come with that nonsense," he says.

"You know it's coming," I say. Without meaning to, my tone turns serious when I add, "We better be ready."

I get to the assembly early to watch people arrive. Mom shows up a few minutes after me. She is never early. She must be trying to beat the crowd. She stands inside the door, clutching her big bag like a shield. I remember her saying that groups of white teenagers make her nervous. She would chase down a group of Black boys who stole my bike and chastise Black teens in our neighborhood for littering. But on white territory, she's in survival mode.

I meet her where she's standing inside the door and walk her to a seat. David and James join us. They each hug Mom before sitting down. Mom sits up straight, her big purse in her lap, and fusses with her jewelry. As the hall fills up, I see it through her eyes.

Hundreds of teenagers wearing jeans and T-shirts with beat-up sneakers or shorts with sandals and sweatshirts around their waists. White girls sit with their arms crossed or play with their hair. White boys stretch their legs out in front of them. Within the rows and rows of white students, pockets of Black students sit together, not speaking, scanning the room. They bite their nails, their lips, and the insides of their cheeks. They press their knees together and sit on their hands. Faculty stand at the sides of the room or sit at the ends of the rows of benches. The assembly must not be required for faculty. I notice which ones choose to come.

The door at the front of the room swings open one more time, and in walks Mr. Clarke. His glasses reflect the afternoon sunlight and so do his shiny black shoes. Students' last jokes, giggles, and whispers echo in the high ceiling and then fade to nothing. Mom takes a deep breath and a shaky exhale.

Mr. Clarke begins with a serious expression. "Good afternoon, Lakeside community. Thank you for being here. As you know and no doubt read, a small group of students wrote a sort of manifesto, if you will, and posted it around school on Friday."

James, David, and I exchange looks. I'm not sure when it got the title of a manifesto, but I like it.

"Since the document was addressed to all, we felt it appropriate to have a community discussion in response. The contents and the tone of the address were . . . provocative. In this discussion, everyone may respond without judgment.

We will treat all statements with respect." He takes a breath and pushes up his glasses. "Now. With that understanding, I open the floor to you students to share how it felt to read the document. Perhaps how it compares with your view of our community?"

My muscles tighten and I brace myself. He's not asking those of us who wrote it how it felt to put ourselves out there like that, or what we were hoping to gain. I didn't realize how much that would bother me.

After a few moments, Colin stands up, hands in the pockets of his cargo shorts and baseball cap to the back. "I'll start," he says. "I was pretty surprised. I don't think it reflects what our school is really like. It made it sound like it's racist and hostile, and I don't think that's true. This is a totally open community. Plus, they made it sound like African American culture is only for African Americans. That seems really divisive and pretty touchy." He sits down and stretches his legs again. He's chewing gum visibly, and all I can think about as I stare at him is how many times I've been reprimanded for chewing gum inside school buildings.

Mr. Clarke's voice pulls me back. "Thank you for sharing, Colin."

I look sideways at my boys.

A junior named Melissa stands up next. She waits until all eyes are fixed on her before flipping her dark blond hair over her shoulder and speaking. "I agree with Colin. I don't see color, and that's an important value here. I've been going here since kindergarten, and we believe everyone is equal and everyone is the same. I felt . . . insulted, I guess, by the . . . letter or manifesto, whatever. It was basically accusing us of thoughts we don't even have." She sits down and crosses her legs, flipping her hair to the other side.

Mom looks at me, and I hold her gaze. I try to tell her mentally, *Do you see what we're dealing with?* Her looks says, *I know. No one said it would be easy.*

A senior named Tom says, "I was just kind of confused. I mean, why was it addressed to everyone?" He looks between us and Mr. Clarke, unsure if he's supposed to address us directly or not. "They were mad about certain events and attitudes, and I had nothing to do with those things, so I don't know why I had to be dragged into it."

Others nod and murmur in agreement.

"Yeah," Andrew says. "They're doing the same thing to us that they don't want done to them. Grouping everyone by color and stuff."

"Okay," Mr. Clarke says. "I'm hearing people say that the manifesto runs counter to our vision of our community and our values around racial equality."

My forearms are folded on my knees, and my head is down. My pulse pounds in my neck and my temples. My mind swirls with what I could say. More kids brag about how little race matters to them and whine about being accused of white supremacist thinking.

I have to decide if we're going to participate, if we're going to bust up this pity party, or if we're going to sit on the sidelines again. The more complaints I hear, the more I want to scream.

Another voice catches my attention. It has a different tone than the complaints and the claims of purity. It's mock-humble. I can tell it's an act. I look up. It's Nick, one of Colin's friends.

"I just want to apologize," he says, barely hiding a smirk. "I was part of the rap performance at the talent show, and apparently that caused some offense." He waves his hands in front of him like we're so unpredictable in what we're sensitive about. "Even though I don't see any problem with it, if I had known it was going to cause all of this . . ." There's nervous laughter. "Anyway, from now on, I'll keep it totally PC. Actually, maybe there should be a PC committee or something. They could, like, preapprove everything . . ." His friend hits him and he laughs. "Okay, I'll shut up now." He sits down.

"You should have shut up a long time ago." It's out of my mouth before I realize it, and it's a little bit louder than I intended.

Nick looks at me like he's not sure I was talking to him.

"Uh—" Mr. Clarke raises a hand in my direction. "We have established that we're not going to judge—"

"Right," I say. "We're not supposed to judge. Tell me this. If you're not gonna call people on it when they judge *us* and make fun of *our* feelings, then what are we supposed to do? Sit here and take it, right? Like we always do?"

"Well . . ." He pushes his glasses up and looks around nervously.

I stand up and face everybody. "Here's the thing. Right now, you all are showing exactly what's wrong with this place. You're proving everything we wrote down." I count on my fingers, and point at kids who have spoken, starting with Nick. "You don't take us seriously. You don't believe us when we tell you what we're going through. You're too busy feeling offended to open up your ears and learn something from us." I spread my arms. "You don't want to spend one hour of your life talking about real issues that we've had to live with for years."

"Let's stay calm," Mr. Clarke says.

"I am calm," I say, turning on him, but my voice rises steadily. "I was calm when I wrote the proposal for the Day of Absence. I was calm when I wrote the manifesto. You all don't hear calm. You want to stay comfortable. Pretending you're doing something when you know you're not!" I don't feel calm anymore.

Mom reaches out to touch my arm.

"We're not here to attack anyone," Mr. Clarke says.

"Yeah, right!" I say.

Mom springs to her feet and tries to pull me toward the door. But I'm not done.

"This whole thing is an attack! On us!"

She looks to James and David, who jump up and surround me.

"Man, fu—"

"Enough," Mom says. Her voice shakes, but it's strong enough to cover mine.

They get me through the doors.

In the hallway, I shrug them off. I pace back and forth, muttering to myself. I could say everything, and it wouldn't make a difference.

I stop pacing, face the wall, and punch it right beneath one of those ten-foot-tall portraits. Pain radiates from my knuckles up my arm. These walls are heavier than the ones at home. Still, there's something oddly satisfying about feeling physical pain. At least it can't be denied.

I turn on Mom. "Why do you care so much what people think?"

She makes a shocked sound. Lifts her hands to the sides and then lets them fall. Her silver bracelets jangle as they hit her hips. She shakes her head.

"You, Gibran. I only care about you." Her voice is tired and defeated.

I snort. It's cruel, but I can't help it. I can only laugh or cry right now, and I'm not about to cry in here. I want her to admit that I embarrass her. "It's not *me*," I argue. "It's my image. It's how I look." I point at my close-shaven head. "What degrees I get. Your bragging rights. That's not the same as caring about *me*. You don't even see me."

She tilts her head like this doesn't compute.

David and James look at each other and then down at the floor.

Mom turns and walks out of the building alone. The door falls closed behind her, and a wave of shame washes over me. I lean against the wall, and David and James join me. My knuckles are red and starting to swell.

"I could go back in there," I say in a low voice, as if Mom might be listening from outside the door.

"Man, it's not even worth it," David says.

"For real," James says. "They're not trying to hear it. They just wanna hear themselves talk."

I know they're right. Still, part of me wants to exhaust myself trying.

"You should go check on your moms, dawg," James says.

I suck my teeth. I'm not ready. I still want to fight with her too. She should have cussed out Mr. Clarke. But the thought of her sitting alone in the car, waiting for me, stabs my chest.

I put out my fist to give my friends pounds. I wince when David's hand lands too hard, and switch to my left hand for James.

I head toward the door, then turn around to walk backward. "Yo. Say somethin, aight? Even if they're not tryna hear it."

We don't speak on the way home. El DeBarge sings in his high-pitched voice, but Mom doesn't sing along, even when her favorite songs come on. When she parks in the driveway, she turns off the ignition and sits for a few seconds, staring out the windshield into the neighbor's yard.

I wonder if this is the time to tell her I'm sorry. Speaking could unleash the wrath that I know is brewing inside her. She gets out of the car, and I follow a few steps behind.

Before heading up to my room, I stop in the kitchen and grab a banana. I know Mom won't want to cook or even eat tonight, so I pull out some shrimp from the freezer and let it sit in a bowl.

In my room, I pick up clothes off the floor and sort my dirty laundry. I move around to keep my mind still and calm the rage. I can't smoke with Mom home, and I can't sit with my thoughts yet.

Mom knocks softly and opens my bedroom door. She's carrying a shoebox, tattered and dusty. She sits on my chair, cradling it in her lap.

I toss more clothes into the laundry basket and then sit

on my bed. I look at the box in her lap and then at her face. "Ma," I say.

She meets my eyes.

"I didn't really mean what I said." I look at my hands. "I know you care about me. It's just—there's some things you don't get."

"I know," she says. "I can accept that. Gibran, there is so much you don't know too. You have your whole life to fight. You don't have to get it all out now. I know it feels like everything is urgent, but . . . I've seen so many people burn themselves out while they're young and end up . . ." She frowns and shakes her head.

"What? Like you? Like my father?"

She looks confused. "What does that mean?"

"I don't know, Ma. I mean, you have all these stories from back in the day. Pictures of you with your afro. Black Power? What happened to changing the world? It's like the revolution was a phase and everyone forgot about it."

She gazes into the distance.

"I'm not trying to be disrespectful," I say. "It just . . . seems like people mellow out and give up. I don't wanna do that. And I don't want to be afraid to speak up."

"It's not a choice between giving up or speaking up," she says. "It's not yelling the loudest that gets you heard."

She lays a hand on the box in her lap.

"What's that?" I ask, nodding at it.

"Clippings," she says.

"Clippings?"

"Yes. Newspaper clippings. I think . . . it might be time for you to get to know your uncle."

"Oh word? He was in the newspaper?"

"In a way."

"When was this?"

"1968. April. A month I will never forget. I've told you about my sit-in at BU. But I don't think you've heard about his occupation at Columbia."

"Nah, I haven't."

"It was a very hard time for our family. He was with a group of student protestors who occupied multiple buildings for a whole week. The police got involved. It was . . . pretty scary. These," she says, holding up the box, "are all the articles I could find that week. I could hardly sleep. I searched the papers every day to see if he was still safe." She shivers like the memory gives her a chill. "We never really talked about it afterward. Kevin and I had already sort of drifted apart."

"Why?"

"Well . . . He had made it clear that he cared more about politics and being right than he did about relationships. Some people are like that. And I didn't want to be vulnerable to that anymore." Her voice trembles slightly. "Anyway," she says, trying to sound more upbeat as she offers me the box, "you can read these. I'm not ready to revisit it yet, but . . . we can talk about it sometime."

She stands up. At the door, she turns around. "You know, I've tried really hard to shelter you, and maybe that was in vain. I've always blamed myself for Kevin's turn in politics, because I was the one who got our family to go to the March on Washington. I never figured out exactly what it was that changed him. But when we got home from that trip, he was . . . different. He had this . . . edge. I guess that's part of what came between us too. Every time he fought with Mom and Dad, or hurt me, I knew it was somehow my fault for planning that trip." She grips the doorknob. "I guess the only thing harder to face than anger is guilt."

# 16

## KEVIN
*New York City | Saturday, April 27, 1968*

The weekend is a waiting game.

Despite the reality check from H. Rap Brown, the support from Harlem has boosted our morale.

The board of trustees issues a statement condemning the occupations and reaffirming the president's authority.

The counter-protestors take a poll of students. Supposedly they find that the majority are for our cause but against our tactics. Emboldened, the "Majority Coalition" surrounds Low Library again and prevents people from entering to join the protest or help those inside.

Faculty sympathetic to our cause have formed an ad hoc committee to attempt negotiations. They meet all night long, with and then without President Kirk. They approach us with a compromise plan which they call the "Bitter Pill" solution. They should know we're not occupying these buildings so we can swallow a bitter pill.

Our policy is consensus, and no decision comes quickly. We discuss the proposed compromise for hours.

It may be a last chance to consider meeting in the middle. We communicate with the striking students in the other buildings. We agree to reject the compromise and stick to our demands. We encourage faculty to do the moral thing and take a political stand on the issues. We won't accept cowardice and complicity under a cover of neutrality.

So our standoff with the administration continues.

Harlemites continue to bring us food, but they also bring us Vaseline and rags. Some students' parents come in to visit. They support what we're doing, but their relief when they hug their children is tangible. So is their worry when they leave.

In between meetings and meals, visits from supporters and parents, and communications with faculty, we drill our self-protection stances until they become reflexes and review our plan for submitting to arrest. We have sponta- neous dance parties to shake the tension away.

Thank God I can talk to Valerie now. There is too much to digest. During a break, we sit together again, finding a spot against the wall near the open windows. I tell her about the files in the dean's office.

"That is unbelievable," she says.

"Tell me about it."

"Does it make you see your parents differently? Less bitter? Maybe even a little bit grateful?"

"I don't know. I mean, yeah, kind of. But . . . I still hate that we had to participate in a system that judges us that way."

"Of course. That's not your parents' fault though, right? They were making do with what the world gave them."

"While also trying to make the world a better place . . . ,"
I add.

"Oh! Check you out!" Valerie exclaims. "I don't think I've
heard you praise your parents before! Tell me more."

"I was so stuck on the fact that we were out there in the
suburbs. . . . I couldn't give them credit for anything positive
they did. But the fact is . . . we did a lot. Considering." I get
animated as I talk. "I mean, we marched. We picketed. We
learned our history and culture. I must have read hundreds
of books, and most of them I found on my dad's shelves."

Valerie smiles so hard, her eyes crease.

"When my mom called here, I recited a poem to her. One
she'd taught us when we were younger."

"What poem?"

*"If we must die—"*

*"Let it not be like hogs,"* Valerie joins in.

*"Hunted and penned in an inglorious spot,"* we continue
in unison.

*"While round us bark the mad and hungry dogs,*
*Making their mock at our accursèd lot.*
*If we must die, O let us nobly die . . ."*

We recite the poem to the end.

"I love Claude McKay. He was Jamaican, you know," she
says.

"I do know."

"Just making sure."

I lean my head back against the wall.

"My dad taught me that poem," Valerie says.

"He must be one cool cat," I say.

"Yeah, I'll tell him you said that."

"Not in those words, please."

She laughs. Then she starts tapping her foot.

"Have you talked to him since we've been in here?"

She shakes her head and bites her lip.

"He may have tried to get through," I say. "The phone line was constantly busy. And now it's been cut off. I guess they got tired of Jack fielding calls for the college."

"I know," she says.

"What are you worried about?" I ask.

She plays with her hands. "My brother. I usually talk to him every week. I know my dad knows I'm in here. If he's been following the news, he knows why I haven't called. And I'm not worried about him disapproving. He raised us to fight the man. It's my little brother." She shrugs. "If anything happens to us . . ."

"It won't," I say. "And . . . there's nothing wrong with leaving early."

She cuts her eyes at me.

I wince under her glare. "Sorry," I say. "I had to try. I'm worried about you."

"Worry about yourself."

"I can do two things at once." A lot of things at once, when it comes to worrying about people.

"What about your sister?" she asks, as if she read my mind.

I shrug. "She's not concerned about me."

"How do you know that?"

"I know."

"Well, that's not normal. You should do something about that."

"I've tried."

"Well, try again."

I look at her. "You are really bossy, you know that?"

"I've been told that before. I mean it though. Every girl wants a big brother. If your little sister doesn't adore you, you're definitely doing something wrong."

Valerie gets up to use the bathroom, leaving me to think about my sister. I know she's right about Dawn, and I let myself hope that, if I could make things right with Valerie, maybe I can fix things with Dawn too.

I have to remember what I did, and figure out why, and explain myself to her.

I sneak into the dean's office for more paper and a pen. I sit in a corner of the lobby, tapping the pen on my knee. Memories flood my mind, ones I've pushed away or justified to myself or hidden from.

When I have some idea of how the memories that burn the brightest are connected, I start to write a letter to my sister.

### Monday, April 29, 1968

Classes are canceled again.

A change is coming, for better or worse.

It takes hours, not days, this time.

Monday evening, the stalemate ends with an ultimatum.

"The president wants us out of the building by midnight," Wesley announces. "If we don't comply, he says he will cut off the power supply and have us forcibly removed."

There are no sounds of surprise, but somber faces register

disappointment and worry. He lets the news sink in before continuing.

"We agreed we won't leave willingly and that we won't resist arrest. It's time to reaffirm that commitment. Or reconsider."

"We have parents experienced with the courts ready to defend us," Richard reminds us. "There are members of the NAACP outside, and community leaders as well, prepared to witness our arrest. We can do this." He pauses. "But . . . everyone doesn't have to stay. Now is the time for us each to decide if we have the stamina to go through with this."

Wesley says, "Let's be clear. We know that anyone not affiliated with Columbia is at a greater risk."

Only a handful of community members are still here. Robbie is among them. He makes eye contact with the others as Wesley continues.

"Brothers, we hold you all in tremendous respect. Your support has been critical in helping us hold our stand for this long. We don't want you to suffer serious consequences over this. Students can be disciplined without criminal charges, which we hope will be the case. But any so-called outside agitators arrested on campus could face criminal charges, such as trespassing. We'll have someone ready to escort community members to a point beyond the police line tonight."

Robbie and the remaining community members form a huddle and talk among themselves.

"And sisters," Richard pleads, "we know you're every bit as dedicated, and we hope the officers won't get rough. Still, I'd be remiss if I didn't try one last time—"

A graduate student named Angela cuts him off gently. "Richard. For the last time. We're staying."

I glance at Valerie. Our eyes lock for a moment. She raises one eyebrow, daring me.

Noise from the street floats up into the windows facing the outside of campus. We all fall still, straining to listen. It's coming from Amsterdam Avenue. We flock to the windows.

Darkness has fallen, but a crowd of people from the community has gathered outside the police line. They keep coming. There are hundreds of people. Almost outnumbering the police. A person holding a megaphone addresses the crowd.

"This is perfect," someone whispers.

As long as the community is watching, the police will have to stand down.

We wave and shout. They see us, and they move closer. The police line pushes them back, but the people in the crowd stand their ground. In a few spots, people grapple with the police, who must have orders to stand down. They push the protestors, but they don't strike, and they don't pull out weapons.

The protestors can't get into campus, and we can't get out. We hold vigil at the windows, hoping they'll stay stationed on the street, protecting us from the police with their presence.

Enormous buses marked "Police" slide down the avenue, one after another. When the side of the road is filled, more buses park in the middle of the street. The cops who descend from these buses look different from the local police who have surrounded the campus for days. These ones are huge, intimidating even from our second-story window. They wear helmets instead of hats. They carry shields and extra weapons.

"Shit. That's the tactical police force," Eddie says.

For two hours, the people from Harlem stay in the street. We call out to them, and they gesture back, but between the noise of the crowd and their distance from our windows, they can't hear our voices. We motion for them to send up the megaphone. We need to get our message down. We need them to stay overnight. We don't know if they know about the ultimatum. That we only have a few hours.

We throw written notes. We flail our arms. We yell in unison. We wear ourselves out. It's as if the two men sharing the bullhorn don't want to give it up.

Finally, one of them says, "Aight, everybody, let's go home. We'll come back in the morning."

No. No! We wave frantically to stop them. It is no use. They disperse.

In less time than it took for them to gather, they are all gone.

The street looks like it did before they came, only the number of police has multiplied. There must be a thousand blue uniforms milling, marching, at the ready.

For a minute, we stand still in the classroom, unsure what to do next.

The reality of our situation sets in with a chill. It's time to get ready for the police to move in.

Claudius claps his hands once. "We need the clean-up committee to show us where the supplies are."

Our daze broken, people move, spreading through the building with trash bags and cleaning supplies. I help some brothers move furniture back to original layouts. While they go find brooms, I tell Robbie I'll walk them out.

"Great," he says. He scans his crew. "Everyone ready?"

We head to the hallway, and I almost collide with someone rushing in from outside.

Charles. He stands there, catching his breath, taking in the scene of people rushing around to clean up.

"What are you doing here?" My pulse throbs, and the activity around us fades.

"I heard they're sending in the police to clear you all out," he says. "Are you really going to stay here and get arrested?"

"Yes. That's the plan. But why did you come?"

This space can't hold Charles. There's a target on his back. The expectation that he will fail. I want to push him back out the door.

"Don't worry about us, Charles. We'll be okay. We have witnesses. But you—you need to go back out, now."

"The administration is fed up with you," he says. "The police out there—it's really tense. The ones who've been on campus all week, getting yelled at by students? They're mad as hell. Once they're set loose . . ."

Charles looks sick. Almost panicked. I still can't believe he's here.

"I wanted to ask if you need anything," he says. "Like, any messages you want to send to anyone . . ."

He really thinks we may not make it out alive.

I feel the pocket that holds my sketches and the letter.

Should I give him the letter to send to Dawn? I haven't finished writing, and I don't want to give into pessimism. I will make it out of here. I will be with my family again, and I'll give Dawn this letter myself. I need to believe that.

"There is one thing you could help with," I say. "We need to get these brothers out, off school property, quickly and safely, without a lot of pictures and stuff, before the police come in."

Charles guesses the plan. "The tunnels."

"Exactly. If you could get them out past the police line, that would be really great."

"Sure. I can do that."

"Thank you. Brother. I appreciate you coming out."

He shrugs. "You'd come for me if I did something crazy. Not that I would."

"You better not," I say.

He looks at me as if he's not sure who I am.

I wonder if I'll ever tell him about the files.

"All right," I say. "Let's get these 'outside agitators' out of here."

"Let's move," Robbie says to his folks.

Charles and I lead them into the tunnels beneath the building. Our footsteps echo, and somewhere, water drips steadily. I've been down here before in a spirit of exploration. Now, though, the sordid history of these tunnels haunts me. Before Columbia University was here, there were insane asylums, and these tunnels connected the buildings. I wonder if any mental patients escaped through these walls. I wonder how they sweated and how they caught their breath, knowing the authorities were hunting them down.

When we reach an intersection, I stop and face the group. "Charles is going to lead you the rest of the way," I tell them.

I reach for Robbie's hand. He pulls me in and hugs me tight. So tight and for so long I'm afraid he also believes I am about to die. I hold on longer than I ever have to my cousin.

"Thank you," I tell him.

Finally, he pats my back, and we let go.

"You'll get out on 116th Street, beyond the police barricade. From there you should be fine. Get home safe, everyone. Thank you for being here."

I want to thank Charles again, but words are inadequate. I spread my arms for a hug. He squeezes me and pounds my back. "Don't get killed," he grumbles in my ear. Then he turns away to continue their march.

For a few moments, I watch them. A spark of fear for Charles seizes the nape of my neck when I realize he'll have to enter campus through the police barricade to get back to the dorm. I know he can handle himself, but I also know he gets more nervous than most around police. I hope he has his ID. I've never known him not to carry it.

I tell myself he'll be fine. I tell myself we all will. I chant this as their backs fade from view, their wrinkled clothes and weary gaits retreating through the tunnel. I rush back to the lobby before the sound of their footsteps can leave me all alone.

Upstairs, the jobs are done. The rooms have been checked. The supplies collected. Trash bags tied. The windows are closed, the rugs swept, the floors mopped.

Janitorial supplies are returned to closets. No one can say we've disrespected this space.

Only our posters of Malcolm and Stokely remain, looking down on us approvingly, telling us not to give up. No one wants to be the one to take those down.

The leaders talk in low tones and then face us.

"Okay, listen up, everyone," Wesley says. "It's almost midnight. We're going to let in the lawyer now and some community leaders who will witness our arrest."

An undergrad coming from the bathrooms says, "Did they shut off the water? The faucets aren't running."

Everyone looks around as if someone can tell us what happens next.

"What if they cut off the lights?"

"We should prepare for that possibility," Wesley says.

"It doesn't make sense to make the arrest in the dark," Richard says, like he's thinking out loud.

"They may try to smoke us out," Claudius says. "Giving us one last chance to surrender before they send the pigs inside."

"Okay, let's get organized," Wesley says, "while we still have lights."

Claudius goes to the campus side of the building and guides the lawyer who's representing us inside, along with a handful of leaders from Harlem. The safety crew passes out wet rags and circulates jars of Vaseline, which we smear all over ourselves.

Ed reminds us, "If you hear 'put your hands up' or any other direct command, do as you're told."

My hands tremble as I accept the rag. I repeat the mantra

in my head. We are going to be fine. I see other brothers remove their ties, and I take mine off too, roll it up and put it in my pocket. Anything that can be yanked or pulled has to go.

I have never been touched by a cop before, and I have never been attacked. People train for months for nonviolent resistance, and some don't make it through the training. I always thought that would be me—that I wouldn't be able to resist fighting back.

And now here I am. With one week's training under my belt, our success and our safety depend on not resisting. If one of us resists, they could crack down on the whole group. They may be looking for an excuse. They may not even wait for one.

This feels so far from the stand I used to think I'd take whenever I envisioned my turn on the front lines. Now that I'm here, it's clear that this is the way to make our movement last. Playing the end game, as Valerie would say.

Across the room, Valerie tucks her hair inside her headscarf. She removes her earrings and necklace and buries them inside her socks. She works with a friend to tape their bracelets to their skin.

There was a couple who got married in the president's office this past week. We all laughed and shook our heads when we heard about them. It was something only white kids would do. Except now, facing our uncertain future, I think, *Why not us?* I would marry Valerie right now if she'd have me.

Lookouts are stationed at the front door, on the balcony, and near the tunnel. The rest of us stay in the lobby, waiting.

There's no privacy in here, but I don't care. I need to tell her what I know. That she makes me a better person, and I want to be the man she sees in me. That I want to build something together—not just a program. A life. She might laugh. I don't care how long it takes to show her I mean it. I need to say it now.

I try to remember the prayer Robbie taught me to untie my tongue. I can do this.

Valerie sees me. I walk toward her.

Then, all at once, every light in the building goes out.

# 17

## GIBRAN
*Massachusetts | October 1995*

Mom wasn't kidding about checking the papers every day for news about Columbia. Some of the articles are from the *New York Times*, and others are from college newspapers, Marxist newspapers, and a few from *The Boston Globe*. Each dated from the same week in April 1968. They are delicate like butterfly wings, thin at the creases. The dust makes me sneeze.

I open *Black Power* again to check the date inside the dedication. May 1968. The month after the sit-ins. I turn the unopened letter over in my hands and wonder if it was written back then too.

I read the articles in chronological order, imagining this story unfolding for Mom and my grandparents hours away. That must have been intense. And it must have been amazing for my uncle.

After the last article, I stare at the wall, imagining how it must have felt. Mom's not ready to talk about it yet, but when she is, I have a way to ask about the book and the letter.

On Tuesday, the day after the assembly, I don't speak to anyone at school until lunch. In the dining hall, I sit in my usual spot with a big bowl of pasta and a salad.

"Aight," I say to James and David. "Tell me what I missed."

James shrugs. "There's not that much to tell."

"Well, tell it," I say, stabbing some pasta with my fork. "Did y'all get any points across?"

"Not really," David says. "It got kinda quiet after you left. I guess the white kids got afraid to talk. Someone said something like, 'This is why people don't want to talk about race,' or some nonsense."

I suck my teeth. "So y'all didn't say nothing?"

"I mean, it's not worth it at that point," James says. "We said our piece in the letter. It's obvious nobody's trying to hear us."

"Now we're back to square one," I say.

"Or worse," David says, wiping his mouth with a napkin. "The more they defend themselves, the more they convince themselves they're perfect, nothing's wrong, and we're just hypersensitive, complaining over nothing."

"Yeah," James agrees. "The only person who said anything at all supportive was Todd."

"Who?" I ask.

"Todd," he repeats, turning around to look for him. "He's a junior. White kid, part of the Gay-Straight Alliance."

"What he say?" I ask.

"Some ole kumbaya stuff about respecting differences and getting along," David says. "I mean, it was better than what the others were saying, but . . ." He shrugs.

"We don't need words," I say. "We need action. This ain't some after-school special."

"Yeah, well, Mr. Clarke thought it was the perfect note to end on," David says. "He couldn't get outta there fast enough."

"He thinks it's over," I say. "Nah. We can't give up like that."

Around us, it looks like a regular day. Kids throw half-eaten plates of food into the trash and toss their trays on the conveyor belt. They laugh and shove one another, share secrets and plans. How many of them have changed? I want this place to grind to a stop. I think about the occupation at Columbia. That took guts. I'd love to see Mr. Clarke's face if we pulled something like that here.

I poke at my pasta again. Trey appears at our end of the table. "Yo," he says, "y'all hear about the OJ verdict?"

We turn towards him.

"Not guilty!"

"For real?" James asks.

"If I'm lyin, I'm dyin! I can't believe it!"

"Daaaaayum!" David says. "I was ready for the death penalty."

"For real," I say.

None of us are OJ fans, but I'll be the first to admit I feel a little lighter seeing a Black man go free for once.

"I guess money trumped race this time," I say. "He better watch his back though. If I was him, I'd get the heck outta the States. You know there's a lynch mob waiting to get their hands on him."

"Dag," Trey says. "You can't let us enjoy it for a minute?"

"Just keepin it real," I say.

My food is cold, and my stomach feels funny.

"So what's our next move?" I ask them.

James and David eye each other.

"I don't know, dawg," James says. "My moms is on my case. College this, college that. If I get in trouble, she will murder me, for real."

"I don't know what more we can do," David says. "What's left?"

The clatter of trays and silverware gets louder as people head to their next classes.

"We could use more people," I say, thinking aloud.

"You wanna see if the BSU wants to collaborate on something?" David asks.

I wave that away. "You saw how they reacted about the march. And even when I tried to defend Tanya. Nah, they too worried about what white people think. We can't get nowhere working with them."

The sounds in the room merge for half a second. I sense something coming at me fast. I turn away from it, putting my hand up to shield my head, but I'm too late. Something heavy hits my head and then the wall behind me. My head explodes in pain. My eyesight blurs at the edges, and my fingers go numb. There's blood on the hand that tried to block my head.

Malika stands at the middle of the table with her hands over her mouth, chanting, "Oh no. Oh no. Oh no."

James runs to get a teacher.

David's at my side, holding napkins to my head. "You aight, man?" His voice is gentle. "It's okay, you're okay. Hold on, G, hold on."

It takes too much effort to keep my eyes open. I close them and rest my head on the table.

When I open my eyes, I'm in the emergency room. Mom holds my hand while James tells the doctor what happened.

"We were sitting at lunch, and someone threw something that hit him in the head."

"What was thrown?"

"A napkin holder."

The doctor holds his pen above his notepad.

James makes a square shape with his hands. "It's only like this big, but it's made out of metal and it's heavy."

"I see."

Mom shakes her head.

"And what school did you say you're coming from?"

"Lakeside Academy," James answers.

The doctor arches one eyebrow, surprised and amused. Pretty scandalous for a prep school, I guess.

He examines me gently. They give me stitches and pain-killers and send us home.

In the car, Mom makes me drink soda and tells me not to go back to sleep. She thinks she's some kind of expert on concussions.

"He didn't say I couldn't sleep, Ma," I protest, leaning my head against the window.

"Boy," she says. "Do not test me." She looks in the rear-view mirror. "James, do you want to come over?"

"Um . . . I didn't bring any of my stuff since we left school so fast," he says. "I'm only signed out until dinner, so . . . I guess I should go back to school. If you'll be all right." He pounds my shoulder.

"It's cool," I say. "Good lookin out."

"No doubt," he says. Then to Mom he says, "I can actually walk back to campus. It's a straight shot down the street."

"Put your seatbelt on," she says, ignoring him.

"Yes, ma'am."

Marvin Gaye sings "What's Going On," and Mom sings along like it's the soundtrack to her life.

When we pull up outside James's dorm, Mom lets the car run.

"James?" she asks. "Can you tell me who did this to Gibran?"

James scratches the back of his neck and looks down as he mumbles, "It was this girl Malika."

"Malika," Mom repeats. She knows a lot of the Black students from when Ava was here. "Any idea why she did this?"

"No, ma'am," he says.

"Hm," Mom says. "Okay. Thank you for staying with Gibran."

On the ride home, Mom checks me every few minutes, scrutinizing my stitches and leaning over at red lights to check the dilation of my pupils.

"I'm good," I say, fending her off. "Stop worrying."

"Yeah, well, I'm not," she says. "I am not okay at all."

At home I change into sweats and get straight into bed with a pack of ice on my head. Mom checks on me one last time.

Stroking my head, she asks, "What happened today, Gibran?"

I stare at the wall. "I don't know. Random act of violence?"

She scoffs and reaches back to massage her neck. "I don't understand," she says.

"Me neither," I say.

She looks at her watch. "And no one from the school has called me to follow up. I checked the voicemail. This is ridiculous. If you were some precious white boy, they'd have someone's head on a platter right now."

I didn't even think about that.

"What do you think I should do?" she asks.

"Nothing," I say quickly.

"Well, I want answers. I need to know you're going to be safe on that campus."

"I can handle myself. I'll be fine."

"Says the boy who just woke up in the hospital."

I roll over to my other side. "Could you turn off the light?" I ask.

She sits there for a second. Then she gets up, checks my stitches again, and pulls my blanket over me, before shutting off the light and closing the door.

As I drift in and out of sleep, Mom calls Nana and Grandpa. She tells them what happened to me like she's about to storm the school. After she hangs up though, I think I hear her sniffling.

The next day, Mom makes me stay home from school. She leaves the cordless phone in my room in the morning so that I'll answer if she calls. I guess I'll be getting periodic concussion checks while she's at work.

The phone rings before I'm up, and I wonder if she's calling as soon as she got to work.

"Gibran?" It's not Mom's voice.

"Yeah," I say, gravel still in my voice from sleep. "Who dis?"

"It's me, Malika."

"Whassup." I lie back down and hold the phone to the side of my head that's not stitched up.

"Are you okay?"

"Yeah, I'm aight," I say.

She lets out a breath so long, it sounds like she's been holding it since yesterday. "I . . . was so worried. Gibran, I am so sorry. Seriously. I can't believe I did that."

"It's all right."

"What do you mean it's all right? It is not all right!"

"Well, I don't want you to feel bad about it forever."

She groans.

"Can you tell me something though?" I ask. "Why'd you do it?"

"Oh." She hesitates. "I guess you don't remember what you were saying?"

"I mean, nah, not really. I remember that I wasn't talking to you. . . ."

"I know, I know. I should mind my business. David mentioned the BSU, so my ears perked up. And then I caught what you were saying, completely dismissing us, like we're worthless to your 'cause' or whatever."

"I said you were worthless?"

"Well, not in so many words, but you were basically calling us sellouts. Oh, you said you didn't want to work with us because we care too much about what white people think. Basically because Tanya didn't want you beating someone up for her and because we didn't support the march."

"Oh. Okay. So . . . therefore you tried to knock me out?"

"I don't know, Gibran, I got so mad for some reason. I wasn't thinking. Obviously."

"I mean, I wasn't trying to judge you," I say. "Some people just care more about what white people think than I do. It doesn't make you a bad person or nothin."

"Well. It sure sounds like a judgment," she says. In the background, doors slam shut, and girls' voices come and go as they leave the dorm for classes. "Besides, how do you know we care more about what they think? Maybe it's that we don't want to spend our time and energy fighting? I mean, you talk like you're the official spokesperson for Black people. That's what drives me crazy. Like when you posted the manifesto. People kept asking us what we thought about it, but you didn't have to deal with that, 'cause they're scared of you." She takes a breath and slows down. "I guess I've been kinda mad at you for a while."

"Okay." I try to sit up in bed, but my head pounds, so I drop back down.

"I'm not defending what I did," she says. "I just lost my temper. We work hard in the BSU. You don't even come to the meetings. How would you know what we're capable of?"

"My bad. I just thought y'all weren't really seeing things the way we did, so I figured I'd let y'all do your thing."

"Well," she says, "part of working together is compromise."

"Yeah . . . that's not my favorite word."

"I noticed."

The pay phone gives her a thirty-second warning, and she adds more change with a clink. Then she says, "I should go. I really wanted to apologize. And also? Um . . . this is gonna sound really bad, but . . . you know, I could get in serious trouble . . ."

"Oh, don't even worry bout that. I'm not sweatin it. As far as I'm concerned, it was a accident. Nobody cares about me anyways. You're lucky you didn't hit someone else."

"That's not true! But . . . you're not gonna tell on me?"

"What I look like? I ain't no snitch."

She laughs.

"For real though, I wouldn't do that to you. You're still my peoples."

She groans again like she feels even worse. "Thank you. And I really am sorry."

Mom wants me to stay home again on Thursday, but I insist I'm fine. I want to get to the Brother Bonding meeting and salvage any bit of momentum we might have from the manifesto.

I wait while people talk about classes and sports and college applications. I wait while they talk about parties and girls. I wait and watch, scanning their faces for stubbornness to match my own.

During a lull in the conversation, I raise my voice so everyone can hear me.

"I got a question for y'all. How do y'all feel about the way things went down with the letter and the assembly and everything?"

No one answers. They busy their hands and mouths with snacks.

Finally, David speaks. "If change is gonna happen, it's gonna be a long fight. I don't think everyone who signed was trying to start that kind of struggle."

"Yeah," Trey says. "Most of us can't handle having as many enemies as you have."

No one laughs. I guess because it's true.

"It doesn't have to be a war," I say, even though in some ways it already is. "But we shouldn't back down. That's the only power we have, is if we stand our ground."

A senior named Adam says, "You do realize teachers are writing our college recs as we speak, right?"

Adam is one of those kids who hangs with everybody all over school. He only comes to Brother Bonding meetings a few times a year. He wasn't there when we signed the letter, and he shouldn't be talking right now. I study his chiseled face. I picture Malika telling me to be patient with people. I say, "Maybe they'll be impressed when you show some conviction instead of rolling over."

"Or maybe they'll call you troublemakers and not let you in anywhere," he counters. "How do you not care?" He waits for an explanation.

"Yeah," Trey says, "who's writing your recommendations?"

I don't know how this got to be about me, but I answer their questions. "I don't need no letters."

"You're not going to college?" Chris asks in a small, astonished voice.

"I am," I say. "I'm going to Howard. I got in early."

No one bothers to hide their surprise.

"No wonder you're so done with this place," Adam says. He sounds annoyed.

"I *been* done with this place, long before now. I still have to graduate. I have to keep my grades up and stay out of trouble, or they'll revoke my admission and my scholarship.

I'm not trying to burn this place down. I just wanna leave a mark. This is the closest we've gotten. If we don't take it further, nothing changes."

Silence. Everyone seems to be avoiding my eyes.

Then Trey says, "Well, we tried. When the principal shuts you down, what's left after that?"

I turn to James and David, then I look around the rest of the room. "So no one wants to take it further? Everyone's ready to let it die?"

No one speaks. Down the hallway, doors open and close as students come and go. I tap my feet.

"Aight, then," I say. "Carry on." I sit back and drink my soda.

Slowly, the boys go back to talking. Conversations turn back to the mundane.

There's nowhere to go. There's nothing to do. No big last stand to take like my uncle did at Columbia, going out in a blaze of glory, not backing down from the school.

We've given up voluntarily. We've lost.

# 18

## KEVIN
*New York City | Tuesday, April 30, 1968*

"Everybody in the lobby," Wesley says.

The lawyer helps direct us and makes sure no one is left behind. Our eyes adjust to the dim light filtering in through the windows as we file into the lobby and face the building's front door. The brothers line up in front, the sisters behind us. We don't plan to fight the cops, but if they lay hands on the sisters, we will defend them. We place our hands on our heads and wait. Two orderly rows of surrender.

"Do not talk back," our lawyer reminds us. "I will speak for you."

*You will have to arrest them,* he will say, *but they will not resist arrest.*

A Black politician and a handful of community leaders stand to the side, ready to witness.

We all watch the front door. In the still, cold silence, we hear sounds behind us. Is that real? It sounds like footsteps. It sounds like marching. Heavy boots marching up the stairs from the tunnels. In the dark, we strain our ears.

It sounds like the approach of an army. The police are coming from underneath the building. The witnesses out front won't see.

I think of Charles, and my legs go weak. What if they found him coming out or caught him trying to get back into campus? No, no—he must have left in time. As long as they weren't waiting inside the tunnels.

The entry from the tunnels is behind us. We turn around slowly, and now the sisters are in front. We don't want to be moving when the cops enter, so we stay where we are and breathe.

The first cop who enters looks like a soldier from a nightmare. He must be seven feet tall and at least three hundred pounds. I can barely make out his face, but I can see that he is white. He wields a crowbar in one hand and a flashlight in the other. The way he holds that crowbar in the air looks like he's ready to use it. Where is the Black police inspector? Why isn't he at the head of this group?

Our lawyer from the NAACP steps between the officer and us. "Good evening," he says. "I'm the defense attorney for these students. I'm here to ensure their constitutional rights are respected. You won't need any weapons tonight. They are submitting to arrest."

The officer sweeps his flashlight over us. More cops arrive behind him, and they spread through the room, surrounding us. They look us over: our straight rows, our stoic expressions, our still bodies. They must wonder if they're in the right place.

The giant walks the length of our rows. We watch him pass without moving our heads.

Finally, he shouts to his men, "Cuff 'em."

On command, they move.

My hands start to shake again. I breathe deeply and try to find Valerie through the bodies, through the dark. I watch her instead of anticipating my arrest. If she doesn't get hurt, I can maybe, possibly, go through with this.

The officer who approaches her moves slowly. His touch looks almost gentle. He has no weapon drawn.

Valerie was braced for roughness, but there is nothing to strain against. He searches her gingerly and then pulls her hands down behind her back.

The officers on the brothers' side take their time.

"You want to sit down?" an officer asks.

"No," Richard says loudly, cueing all of us not to fall for it. "We're submitting to arrest."

"You can sit down," the cop teases.

"You can jump out the window," another one says. "We won't follow you. Last chance."

"They're not going anywhere," the lawyer says.

In my mind, they grab me and I struggle. I fight. I resist.

But no. I clear my head and focus on now. My body. My hands. The cold steel handcuffs enclosing my wrist. The pull of the handcuffs as they draw it to the brother beside me, chaining us together.

The fear, the tension, the ready rage—all of it drains from my body.

I finally understand an ounce of what the brothers and sisters felt when they got jailed and kicked and tortured at lunch counters, hosed and bitten and beaten on marches and freedom rides. It was not just strength. Not just determination. It was power. Moral power.

Their power drew out angry crowds.

Their power turned people into animals.

Their power made the upholders of the old ways afraid. Afraid of the winds of change.

The world is in our hands. They are trying desperately to grab it back.

Officers pull us to our feet and steer us to the stairs. We stumble a bit, each of us trying to keep up with the student we're sharing handcuffs with.

Before they get us down into the tunnels, Inspector Waithe shows up, out of breath, coming from the campus side. He must have just gotten through the barricade.

"Who's calling the orders here?" he barks.

The other cops freeze. Someone beckons the giant, and he walks through our rows to face the inspector.

"Did you lead this?" the inspector asks.

The giant puts his hands on his hips.

"I'm in charge of this arrest," the inspector says. He turns to the others. "Uncuff them!"

The officers obey the command. Inspector Waithe then leads us all down into the tunnels.

Our hands freed, we march single file through narrow passageways lined with pipes. Our footsteps echo in the dark. The officers' flashlights sweep from wall to wall. I try to keep my eyes on Valerie and steady my breath. I rub my wrists against my pant legs and check that my papers are still in my pockets.

After what feels like an endless march underground, the fresh night air shocks my lungs.

A small crowd lines our path from the building to the police vans. A few eager journalists call out questions and take photographs. Flashes of light blind our eyes. When I picture my parents reading the morning paper, I duck my head to hide my face.

"Do you expect your demands to be met?"

"Will you still graduate?"

"What is the future of your strike?"

"Is it true there were militants inside with you?"

"Were they armed?"

A handful of jocks, supporters of the gym, stand out of reach and sneer.

Rage boils up from that old place inside. I train my eyes on the feet in front of me.

Under the streetlights, police vans and paddy wagons open their doors hungrily to let us in. We fill three vehicles.

As we pull away from campus, we see hundreds of policemen lined up inside and outside the gates. The tactical force with helmets and shields tower over the others.

Some students are yelling at them.

"Cops must go!"

"No pigs on campus!"

The cops wait. Many are swinging batons, nightsticks, even blackjacks. They pose and strut like they're gearing up for a street fight.

"I hope those kids realize how much these cops hate them," Jack says.

We round a corner and see officers on horseback, waiting for their turn to move in.

Our caravan moves down the dark, quiet streets while

the City sleeps. They couldn't have done this in the middle of the day or even a few hours ago, with Harlem supporters watching. For fear of Harlem riots, the mayor held off the president this long, and the cops arrested us gently.

Harlem saved us. I hope to God we helped save Harlem too.

# 19

## GIBRAN
*Massachusetts / October 1995*

I want to skip school on Friday, even though I have free periods for most of the day. I think about telling Mom my head hurts, but I don't want her to get Malika in trouble, so I'm trying not to remind her about my stitches.

The march is coming up a week from Monday, and I'm definitely not going to school that day, so I decide to save skipping for my Day of Absence. That way, if—when—I get in trouble, they can't say it's a pattern. I can insist it was on principle.

After English, I spend the rest of the morning in the library, working on my history project. I wonder if I could do an independent study project next semester with Mr. Adrian. Maybe I can make it to graduation without going crazy.

At lunch, I sit at the Black table for a couple of hours while people come and go. I try to act normal with James and David, but it takes some effort.

Trey rushes over to us, breathing hard like he's been

chased. He leans over the table and whisper-yells at the three of us.

"Did y'all hear what happened to Chris?"

My stomach turns, and my blood freezes. I put my glass down slowly and steel myself for devastation.

"What happened?" James asks, looking ready to slap Trey if he doesn't come out with it.

Trey looks around like he's afraid someone might overhear him. Then he pulls up a chair and sits on its edge, keeping his backpack on. We lean toward him.

"He was minding his own business in the dorm, right. In the common room, just doing homework or something. Some seniors came in and started clowning him. They're like, 'Hey, are you happy about OJ?' He's not answering 'cause . . . you know Chris. So they just keep talking at him. And then one of them called him 'nigger.'"

There's a dramatic pause while we wait for him to continue. He doesn't. That's it. He looks at us expectantly.

I let out the breath I've been holding. I can handle this.

"What's dude's name?" I ask.

Trey hesitates. Probably thinking he could get in trouble for telling me.

"Who said it?" I repeat a little louder. If he acts like he doesn't want anything to come of this, I swear.

"Uh, that dude Nick," he says quietly.

"Aight." I rise from my chair and pick up my tray, scanning the dining hall for Nick.

"Wait," Trey says, standing and facing me. "You're not gonna, like . . . I mean . . ." He turns to David and James for help, but they're standing too.

Trey blocks my way. I stare at him until he moves aside. I bus my tray and scan the hall. I spot the jocks' table, and there's Nick. This is the last lunch period, so he'll have to leave soon. I'll catch him outside. James and David come with me.

We don't talk as we wait. I think about Chris. Small, shy Chris. I wish I had taught him to defend himself already. But I'll take care of this. It won't happen again.

We watch the doors burst open and fall shut, over and over, until finally, I spot Nick and his friends. James and David hang back as I approach him so we don't look like a gang or something.

"Hey, Nick," I call. "Lemme talk to you for a second."

Nick keeps walking. "Why?"

I stand in front of him, and he stops. I watch his face while I tell his friends, "The rest of y'all can go. Don't worry, I'm not gonna hurt him." His friends look unsure, but one of them checks his watch. "You can stay if you want to," I say. "It don't matter to me."

Nick clenches his jaw and watches me with ice-blue eyes. He tells his friends, "I'll be right behind you."

I step backward to draw him off the path, which will soon be crowded with students leaving the dining hall for classes.

I get right to the point. "So you called Chris a nigger?"

"What?" His mouth hangs open. "Who told you that?"

"It don't matter. It wasn't Chris who told me."

He looks at James and David, then back at the dining hall doors. Kids stream out and walk toward the class buildings. I let him squirm for a minute. This is my favorite part.

Let him feel that heart-pounding fear and discomfort Chris had to feel when Nick and his friends said that to him. Let him know his freedom has limits.

"It wasn't even like that," he says.

"Well, I don't care what it was like from your point of view. You're not allowed to say that. Ever. Under any circumstances. You're not even cool with him, so don't act like he's okay with it. He's practically a little kid. If you want to say that to somebody, say it to me, to my face."

I wait. Let him try.

"That's what I thought. You know you won't say it to someone your age and size. So keep your mouth shut and we won't have a problem. You feel me?"

I stand close enough for him to feel the force of my words, but not close enough to threaten.

Nick sputters and pulls at his sagging jeans. "I didn't even—"

"We good?" I fake a cheerful voice.

No answer.

I harden my voice. "Do you understand?"

He makes a sound like he's disgusted and turns to walk away.

"Tell your friends," I call after him. "None of y'all better make that mistake again."

I'm impressed with my own self-restraint.

*What I'll never say*

Once upon a time, there was a six-year-old boy with wiry hair and one crooked tooth and skin that turned copper in the summertime. He smiled all the time, and his sisters and his mom would poke at the dimples in his cheeks.

He went to a new school in a new town where he was the odd one out. He smiled a little less. He made some friends, but no one at school seemed to notice his dimples.

One day in January, when the boy was in first grade, his teacher talked about Dr. Martin Luther King, Jr. He showed the class slides of water fountains and bathroom doors labeled "White" and "Colored."

He showed a teenager wearing a dress and sunglasses, holding her books to her chest while angry white women shouted at her, their faces twisted with hate.

He showed a little Black girl with frilly white socks walking into a nearly empty school, surrounded by armed guards and screaming crowds of white people. The girl in that picture was six, like the boy in this class, but her bright eyes, dark skin, and button nose reminded the boy of his own sister, Ava, who was eight.

"Back then," the teacher said, "white people didn't want to live with Black people. They didn't want to share restaurants, movie theaters, neighborhoods, or even schools with Black people. Sometimes they called Black people names, like *nigger*."

The boy didn't know this word, but he felt his gut twist when his teacher said it.

As his teacher talked about the old days of segregation, the little boy felt as if everyone was watching him. When he caught someone looking, they would quickly look away. So he stared at his desk and played with his hands. He felt hot, and he waited for recess.

Finally, class was over. The boy went to the cubbies in

the hallway with everyone else to get his coat and mittens for recess. The boy's friend Luke ran up to him. Luke said to the boy, "Hey, Gibran! You're a nigger!" And Luke laughed. A wild, airy laugh.

The boy stared at his friend.

Luke said, "Meet you at the slide!"

And Luke ran away.

The boy stared after him. His stomach twisted in knots. He didn't understand why he wanted to cry.

The boy put his coat and mittens back in his cubby. He didn't follow his classmates outside. Instead, he pushed through the doors to the upper-elementary hallway. Some girls in his class watched him go.

He reached the stairwell, heaved open the door with his skinny arms, and climbed the cement stairs. He reached the middle-school hallway already out of breath.

The middle-school hallway was loud and crowded. Metal lockers clinked open and slammed shut. The boy dodged elbows and backpacks as he ran.

At the end of the hall was the art room. The boy tiptoed in through the propped-open door. Tall windows overlooked the sky and treetops. He stopped inside the door, slowed down by the flood of light.

You were reading aloud to your students as they shaded shapes with graphite pencils. When you heard sneakers on your shiny floor, you looked up from your book. You continued reading as you stood from your stool and walked toward him, your arm held out to receive him.

He grabbed you around the middle, nearly knocking you over. You kept reading as you felt his forehead and neck to see if he was hot. You stroked his head as you read with dramatic intonations and suspenseful pauses. When you finished reading the section, you put a pencil in the book to hold your place and laid the book on your table at the front of the room.

Your students looked up, their pencils hovering above their drawings.

"Awww!" some of the girls exclaimed when they saw the boy. "He's so cute!"

Their braces caught the sunlight.

"I'll be right back," you told them gaily. "Keep drawing!"

You walked him into your office, stumbling under the force of his embrace. You sat at your desk and pulled him off your waist to hold him at arm's length and examine his face.

"What's the matter?" you asked.

He shrugged. He couldn't speak.

"You feel sick? Again?"

He nodded.

You sighed. "Okay."

You looked around your office. You picked up your jacket and spread it on the floor underneath your desk. He crawled down and curled up on top of it. You reached around the kiln and pulled out the thick emergency fire blanket and spread it over him. You tucked him in like he was in bed. He shut his eyes tight.

The phone on your desk rang.

"Did you tell your teacher you were coming up here?" you asked the boy.

He shook his head no.

You sighed again, then put on your acting face to answer the phone.

"Art department! . . . Yes, hi, Steve. Yes, he is here with me. He's not feeling well. It's all right, he can stay here for now. Yes, I'm sure. No problem. Of course I'll tell him. Thank you. All right. Bye-bye."

You knelt on the ground and tried to sound stern.

"Gibran. You can't disappear on your teachers, baby. You have to say something, okay?" You stroked his leg. "I'll be back."

You turned off the light in the office and softly closed the door.

I stayed curled in a tight ball under your desk, between your jacket and the fire blanket. The sound of your voice reading stories floated through the drawers that held your students' drawings. I didn't follow the stories. I only followed the sound of your voice, so brave and so vulnerable. I listened to your voice, and I couched myself in the silence all around, and in the dark, safe space underneath your desk, I began to loosen my body. I waited there, listening for your voice, until it was time for you to take me home.

# 20

## KEVIN
*New York City | Tuesday, April 30, 1968*

I've heard about the Tombs of Lower Manhattan, but I never thought I'd be inside. They book us at the precinct. The officers who brought us in are gone. The ones at the station grumble and sneer. I'm no longer Kevin. They call us "nigger" and "boy." We are fingerprinted and processed and then placed in holding cells. I catch a last glimpse of Valerie as she is led away with the women.

For hours, we sit in the dark. No one can sleep, but we rest our heads against the dirty walls and try to close our eyes. The phones ring constantly. Parents and lawyers are calling, but we are not brought to the phone.

I don't know how long we've been here when a commotion in the hallway grabs our attention. My eyes flutter open.

"You can't get away with this!" someone yells.

"Get your hands off of me!"

"Look at him! He should be in the hospital! You can't keep him here."

A new set of police officers, snarling with contempt,

shoves a crowd of rowdy young white people toward the holding cells. Some of them are pushed inside our cell, and others are brought farther in. They are Columbia students. The protestors from the other buildings. They look as surprised to see us as we are to see them.

We all wear the wrinkled clothes we showed up in a week ago at the rally. With our skin covered in Vaseline, everyone is a mess. But these kids look as if they've been through a massacre. They are bruised and bloodied. Their hair is matted and sticks up in clumps. Their clothes are ripped and disheveled. Someone limps in barefoot.

Richard breaks the silence. "What the hell happened to you all?"

"How did you miss it?" a white student responds, marveling.

"We've been here for hours," Wesley says. "They took us out through the tunnels. We didn't see anyone else."

The white students shuffle closer and find places to sit.

We circle around them to hear what happened.

A student with black hair and blue eyes stares vacantly at the wall behind us, dazed. There is so much blood running down his face and hair, I can't believe he is conscious.

"We built a barricade. We piled all the furniture we could carry to the inside of the front door. We wanted to make it hard for them." His voice cracks. "They used axes to get through the doors. By the time they got through, they were pissed. They went crazy. They took the furniture from the barricade and threw it at us. Across the room, desks, chairs, flying." He makes a sound that might be a disbelieving chuckle or the beginning of a sob. "They were monsters.

Huge. Enormous. And their faces? Full of hate. They picked us up like rag dolls and tossed us around." He rubs his eyes. We wait.

A blond kid, the one without shoes, says, "They beat the shit out of everyone they could get their hands on. They started with the people who sat in front of the building to defend us. Students and faculty. Sympathizers, you know? They weren't protesters. They just wanted to protect us. Beat them, threw them, literally threw them, out of the way. Walked over some of them, trampled them. Then they came inside the buildings. The protestors who wanted to walk out peacefully were standing in the lobby, ready to go. They got the worst of it. The pigs beat them without mercy. They pulled them down the stone steps by the feet. Dragged girls by the hair. God." He wipes his face. Tears, sweat and blood streak together on his skin. "Then they came upstairs, axed the doors, and saw us. We were sitting down with our arms linked, singing 'We Shall Overcome.' We wanted to be carried out. We thought . . ." He blows out a long breath and places a hand gently on his ribs. "The ones who wanted to hide and fight and stand their ground were upstairs. I didn't see what happened to them."

Another student speaks then. As if in the telling they are both exorcizing the experience and making it real. His shirt is torn, and his eyes, wide with terror, well with tears. "People heard the screaming and came out of their dorms to see what was happening. People who weren't striking or protesting. But the cops didn't care who was who. They treated everyone like part of a mob. Guys, girls, professors, bystanders. They said they were clearing the campus. They lined up with their shields, pulled down the masks on their helmets. And charged. They trampled people with horses. Bashed people's heads in. There was so much blood. God. They used everything. Everything. Nightsticks. Flashlights. Blackjacks. Steel-toed boots. Fucking handcuffs wrapped around their knuckles like a brass fist." His voice shakes, and he trembles, breathing hard. Finally, he blinks, and his tears fall neatly to his chin. He wipes at them with his sleeve.

It's surreal to imagine the scene at our school. There had been about five hundred local police on campus throughout the week. With the tactical police force that came in last night, they must have totaled a thousand.

This violence is an outcome that never crossed the minds of the white kids. It was the very thing that constantly haunted ours.

We sit together in quiet solidarity. Us imagining. Them reliving. All of us wondering what happens next.

Will the bystanders who got attacked blame us for causing the police to come to campus? Or will they turn against the authorities who sicced the police on their own students? Become more sympathetic to our cause after seeing the end result of tyranny?

Prayer still doesn't come naturally to me, but I ask God to protect Charles. I know he wouldn't have come outside. As long as he was inside before the melee started, I know he's safe.

The students who were high on adrenaline when they arrived, yelling at officers even as blood ran down their faces, are quiet now. Eyes closed, some tremble, and a few cry quietly in the dark.

The Barnard women are not far away. The sisters sing freedom songs, and some of the brothers join in in harmony.

It feels as if this night has lasted forever and will last forever still. But dawn is coming. There will be another day.

The phones ring more and more feverishly. The news must be spreading about the violence that took over campus. Have my parents heard? Has Dawn? Do they think I got caught up in it? Are they angry with me? This is the kind of outcome I could never live down.

I have so much to explain. I need to get my sister back.

I get up from my spot in the back of the cell, where I've been leaning on the wall. A shaft of light shoots in from the hallway, and I step over outstretched legs to reach it. People follow me with their eyes, probably curious to see if I'm going to ask the guards for something—a phone call, a meal, my freedom. I find a spot near the bars and settle in.

I search my pockets for the pen and the letter I started writing to Dawn in Hamilton Hall.

I push away thoughts that it's no use, that she can't hear me anymore, that our days as best friends are over.

Time passes as I write. Lawyers arrive, and parents, raising hell.

Students start to leave. Some on bail, some on recognizance. They give hugs and nods as they make their way to the door.

I stay in the shaft of light. I write small, and I think big, and I try to fit everything onto these pages.

# 21

## GIBRAN
*Massachusetts | October 1995*

I've spent the weekend at the Boston Public Library doing research for my project, and what I've found has blown my mind. I wanted to know what happened to that generation of freedom fighters. Where are they now?

Some of the research was hard because people have changed their names. Stokely Carmichael is now Kwame Ture. H. Rap Brown is now Jamil Al-Amin. I filled notebooks with dates, facts, and quotes; checked out a stack of books; and got access to some archives. I brought home photocopies and stayed up late, reading. I couldn't stop.

Now I'm putting everything together. On oversized poster board from Mom's supply cabinet, I make collages of pictures and words. Each personality gets a small poster-sized profile. I make half-face drawings like I learned from Mom, cutting a photograph in half and drawing the missing half to make a whole. Somehow it feels right for this project. Part of each person from the past, part from the present, as I see them now.

For each personality, I write up a short description of who they were and where they are now. It's kind of depressing. Too many are dead, killed too soon. Others are in jail or in exile. But this is what I want people to understand. That our struggle for liberation is life or death.

Malcolm X: killed when he was gaining international support and planning to sue the US government for human rights violations against African Americans.

Dr. Martin Luther King, Jr.: killed when he spoke out against war and capitalism.

Huey P. Newton, cofounder of the Black Panther Party: found shot to death in the street in Oakland in 1989.

Bobby Seale, cofounder of the Black Panther Party: still speaking out as a community organizer.

Kwame Ture, formerly known as Stokely Carmichael: moved to Guinea in 1969 to escape government persecution; works for Pan-African liberation.

Jamil Al-Amin, formerly known as H. Rap Brown: converted to Islam while in prison in the 1970s for trumped-up charges. Currently leading a Muslim community and constantly harassed by the FBI and police. Arrested in August of this year, awaiting trial.

And then there are the women.

Angela Davis: acquitted in 1972, still an activist and a professor. Organizes for prison abolition.

Maya Angelou: writer and activist, on dock to perform at the Million Man March.

Kathleen Cleaver: lived in exile for twelve years, then went back to school for her undergraduate and law degrees from Yale. Teaches law, writes, and speaks.

Assata Shakur: escaped from unjust imprisonment, lives in exile in Cuba.

There is a pattern. What does the pattern say? I'm not sure, but at least I've posed a big question.

Looking over my work, I'm amazed that I've gotten so far in one weekend. I've never done a school project in such a short time, and I've never worked this hard on a school project, period.

I stand up and stretch my back. The profiles are scattered on the floor. I arrange them in rows.

It's Sunday night, so Mom is probably resting up for Monday. I knock softly on her door.

"Come on in," she says.

She's sitting on the edge of her bed with jewelry tools and wire, working on a beaded necklace.

"Can I show you something?" I ask.

"Sure!" she says. She doesn't move. Her eyebrows are drawn in concentration, the tip of her tongue poking out slightly like it does when she's perfecting something.

"It's in my room," I say.

"Oh, okay." She finishes pinching a piece of wire and sighs with satisfaction. She puts her work down on her cluttered nightstand, gets up, and follows me into my room.

I stand aside to let her in. She gasps as she recognizes the faces.

"It's my history project," I tell her.

Mom kneels to get a closer look. She examines each piece carefully, crawling between them one by one. She reads the titles and the updates on where they are now. She admires each face, touching them lightly. "You did the half faces!

I've never seen anyone use them outside of my classroom."

"Well," I say, "I found this upstairs." I show her the half-face drawing I found in the attic.

She takes it from me. "Nana," she whispers.

I shove my hands in the pockets of my sweatpants. "Did you learn the half-face drawings from your mom?"

"Yep. I never told you about that? She taught me and Kevin to do these. I hated them at first."

She hugs her old half-face drawing and finishes studying my project. Then she sits back on her heels, smiling with sad eyes.

"What do you think?" I ask.

"It's . . . incredible. It's *beautiful*."

I don't notice the tears falling down her face until she sniffles.

I get down on my knees and put my hand on her shoulder. "You okay?"

She nods, wiping at her eyes and her nose. "It's been so hard."

I keep my hand on her shoulder because I don't know what else to do.

"We were so hopeful," she says, gesturing to the profiles. "It was . . . exciting. Exhilarating. And . . . scary, sometimes. Then . . . I don't know . . . everything fell apart." She sniffles. "When you have kids, you know, you want the world to be better for them. But first you need your kids to be okay right now. At some point, it's like, 'Fuck the revolution. My kids need to eat. They need an education. They can do better than we did if we can give them the tools.' That becomes the priority. And it's hard. How do you give your kids everything without giving up . . . everything else?" She looks at me. "Raising you kids was the real revolution. At least for me." She takes a big, shaky breath. "I think for my parents too."

I rest my chin on my knee.

"That's why it's so important to us, Gibran." She takes my hand and squeezes it. "I know you don't like the choices we've had to make, and you know I don't either. But you and your sisters . . . you're my contribution to the world. Giving you the best of everything—that's my revolution. It is rebellion. It is political. If you self-destruct . . ."

"I won't."

I get it now. At least, I think I do.

She sighs. Leans over my papers again. She traces the face of Maya Angelou. "You could add more shading here," she says.

She gets a faraway look in her eyes as she gazes at the portraits and then at the drawing in her hand. Her eyes travel to my desk, where her shoebox of clippings sits in one corner and her book, *Black Power*, sits beside it, with the unopened letter tucked inside.

After another minute, she stands up and leaves my room. She rummages in her closet and comes back a few seconds later carrying a black portfolio bag. She holds it out to me.

"Wow," I say. "Thank you."

I carefully pack the posters in the bag and lean it against my desk. It's not due for another month, but I'm ready to show it to Mr. Adrian.

I carry the big art portfolio bag on the bus and all the

way to school. At the end of history class, I lift it onto the table.

"Mr. Adrian," I say. "I've been working on my project. Can I show you what I have?"

"Please do!" he says eagerly.

I unzip the black leather bag and open it up on the table-top in front of him.

He looks carefully at each one. After he turns the last sheet over, he says, "This is really impressive work, Gibran. Incredibly thoughtful and so relevant. Well done."

"Thank you."

He flips back through the posters. "If you don't mind presenting this to the class sometime soon, I think it would be really meaningful."

I frown. "I don't know," I say. I'm not sure I want to face their questions while I'm still thinking over this myself.

"It's entirely up to you," he says. "Maybe we could also consider putting it up somewhere. With permission, of course..."

That sounds cool. "Maybe," I say.

I walk to lunch with James and David. They're amazed I've done a school project early.

I shrug. "It doesn't feel like work when it's stuff you actually want to know."

At lunch, I feel lighter than I have in weeks. We tell jokes and talk trash and mess with the girls. It's almost like a regular day. I almost think I can see June on the horizon. I can be in Lakeside but not of it, like W. E. B. Du Bois said about Harvard.

I've put my tray up and got my backpack on when my

advisor finds me heading toward the door.

"Uh, excuse me, Gibran?"

"Yeah?"

"Can I talk to you for a minute? I'll walk you outside if you're leaving."

"Okay," I say, confused. For a brief second, I imagine he's heard about my history project and wants to congratulate me or apologize for underestimating me before.

When we get outside though, he puts on a serious face. He steps to the side of the pathway and puts his hands in his pockets. "I have the unfortunate duty of telling you that you need to meet with Mr. Clarke after school."

"What?" I ask. "What for?"

"I am not at liberty to say. In fact, I don't have all the details. He'll be expecting you at four o'clock. That's the earliest your mother can make it."

"My mother?"

"Yes," he says. "She'll be attending as well."

This can't be good.

I'm sitting outside Mr. Clarke's office when Mom shows up, out of breath, with dark circles under her eyes.

"What's this about?" she whispers to me.

"I don't know. They wouldn't tell me."

She sits down next to me with a huff.

At four o'clock sharp, Mr. Clarke opens his office door. "Please come in," he says to us.

Mom and I sit in the cushioned chairs facing his desk. He closes the door, sits down opposite us, and folds his hands on the mahogany expanse.

He looks at me. "Do you know why you're here?"

"Here in your office? Here at Lakeside? Or here like my purpose in life?"

Mom glares at me. Mr. Clarke presses his lips together.

"I do not know why you've called us into your office today," I say with as much formality as I can muster. It's dripping with sarcasm, and I know they can tell, but he ignores it.

"You don't have any idea?" he persists.

Mom interjects. "He said he doesn't know. Can you please tell us?"

"Well. It has come to our attention that last week, you made a threat against another student."

I narrow my eyes. My mind races.

"A threat?" Mom repeats.

"Yes," Mr. Clarke says. "A senior named Nick Walsh filed a complaint."

Mom laughs out loud. "You have got to be kidding me," she says.

"I . . . no . . ." He clears his throat. "The official disciplinary action is for 'intimidation' . . . ".

"Intimidation," Mom repeats. She laughs as if he's told a joke that didn't land. "This is unbelievable."

Mom gets up and takes my head gently in her hands. She turns my head to the side. "Do you see this?" she asks Mr. Clarke. "Stitches. A head *injury*. This happened at *your* school. On *your* watch. My son had to go to the emergency room last week because of an incident in your dining hall, and there was not so much as an investigation." Her voice trembles with anger or hurt or both. "I did not receive one phone call checking up on him. And now we've forgotten all about that. And *he's* in trouble for—*intimidation!* Ha."

Mr. Clarke clears his throat again. "It gives me no pleasure to do this. However, I'm afraid we take these charges very seriously. I was informed that the incident in the dining hall was an accident."

Mom looks sideways at me as she sits back down in her chair.

"However, if you believe otherwise and you wish to pursue action against Malika, you can file a criminal case for assault—"

"Excuse me?" Mom says.

"No. No, no," I say.

Mom closes her eyes tight. "Wait a minute. You want us to get the *police* involved against a Black girl for an incident that took place at your school?" She squeezes her hands together like she's trying not to grab the crystal paperweight off his desk and throw it at his head. When she speaks again, her voice is soft. "Tell me one thing, please, Mr. Clarke. Do you care about my son?"

Mr. Clarke draws his head back. "I . . ."

She waits.

"Well, I . . . I don't know that I'd say I *care* about your son. . . . I would say I am concerned about him. . . ."

She nods. "I see. And now I see why so many Black boys have left this school without graduating."

Mr. Clarke's eyes dart everywhere. He is flustered, not sure whether to defend himself or deflect. When he speaks again, his voice sounds even more strained than usual. "I called you in here to let you know that the discipline committee will meet about this case on Friday, and next week, you'll be called to sit before the committee. As you know, due to your previous infractions, if you are found guilty of intimidation, your suspension will result in permanent expulsion."

Mom shakes her head. We are both thinking the same thing. That "if" is a lie. There's no way the committee won't believe that a white kid was "intimidated" by me.

"Yeah, I'm not gonna go in front of the committee," I say. They both look at me.

"I'm gonna withdraw from the school."

"Gibran, we need to discuss this," Mom says in her *I won't beat you in front of people, but I will when we get home* voice.

I turn to her. "It's the only way," I say.

She takes a breath to argue, but then she closes her mouth firmly. She knows I'm right.

"We all set here?" I ask Mr. Clarke.

"Well . . . if that's your decision, I will need a written statement for your file indicating your voluntary withdrawal."

Mom looks sick to her stomach. "This decision is not final," she says. I let her have that much. I know she doesn't like to rush into things.

"Understood," Mr. Clarke says. "If you can decide by Thursday whether you'll be sitting before the committee, and have your written statement to me by Friday, that will be fine."

"I'll do that," I say. I stand up and turn toward the door. Mom grabs her purse and follows behind me.

Once we're out of earshot of the office, she whisper-yells at me. "What are you thinking?! We can't let this happen! What about your scholarship?"

"That's exactly what I'm thinking about. They said I have to graduate. Maybe I don't have to graduate from *here*."

She is fuming. I don't know if she's more angry with me or with the school right now.

"You know I can't go in front of the committee," I tell her. "I didn't actually threaten anybody, but they're not gonna believe me. All I have to do is look at someone for them to feel intimidated. At this point, I can get expelled, or I can transfer. If we talk to Howard before Lakeside does, maybe I can transfer and keep my scholarship."

She grinds her teeth.

We get in the car, and she slams the door. Her hands are shaking.

"You want me to drive?" I ask.

Without a word, she climbs out and walks around the car to switch places with me.

That evening, the doorbell rings.

"Ay, whassup," I say to James and David, letting them in.

I don't have to wonder long whether they've heard the news.

"This is some bullshit," James says, just as my mom walks in. "Oh—I'm sorry, Ma." He stands up. "How you doing?"

She flops down on the couch opposite them. "I've been better. And you're right. This is some bullshit." She's wearing her robe and slippers, a sure sign she's done for the day, even though it's barely dusk.

"Do they even know what Nick said that started it?" David asks.

"Exactly," James says. "If you're in trouble, he should be too! If the school would deal with people like him, you wouldn't have to be the one always sticking your neck out."

"Yeah. It's messed up," I say. "But I can't be surprised at this point. These schools ain't for us. They're never gonna protect us."

Mom gazes at me. All the things she couldn't change for me seem to weigh her down. "I have to admit," she says, "I am pissed off at Mr. Clarke. I know he's in a tough position as a Black man in charge of that school. But I've had three kids go through there, and I've never seen the Black kids doing worse than they are right now."

"We want to fight it," David says. "We're ready to protest. We could take it to the press, make some noise about it. Nobody likes bad press. We could put some pressure on them to do this right."

Mom smiles sadly. "I appreciate that, boys. You are good friends to Gibran." She holds open her hands. "I just don't have the energy to fight anymore."

"Yeah," I agree. "I wouldn't mind embarrassing the school and Mr. Clarke. But honestly? I'm kinda glad to be getting outta there. And you know if it's not this, it's gonna be something else. This has gotta be the mildest thing I've done."

They try to persuade us. They want us to know that they're mad and that they care. I appreciate it, though I wish we could have used this energy before.

"Why don't you boys stay for dinner," Mom says. Then she turns to me. "Is there dinner?"

I laugh. "Yeah. I took out some chicken legs. I'll get started on it now."

We eat barbecue chicken, and they hang around late, hesitating to leave, still wanting to do something. I tell them I'm good. I can't totally relax until Howard confirms that they won't revoke my admission and scholarship. And I feel bad that Mom is so stressed. Other than that, knowing I'm leaving Lakeside feels like coming up from underwater to breathe.

"Yo," James says as I walk them to the door. "What about that history project you did?"

"Yeah, what about it?"

"Well . . . People should see it."

"Yeah," David says. "You wanted to take our protest further. Can't we use that? At least educate some fools?"

"I mean, I don't think I'm allowed on campus. . . ."

"Can you give it to us?" James asks. "We'll get it back to you in good shape, we promise."

"I don't know," I say, hesitant to part with it. "I'll think about it."

I used to fantasize about leaving Lakeside and going to a Boston public school. In fact, I daydreamed about it so much that I started keeping a list of the not-too-terrible schools in the district that might be options for me. I spend Tuesday calling those schools. I tell them the situation, making it sound hypothetical and mild, and collect information about transferring.

Mom's made inquiries too. We've talked to the people at Howard. On Wednesday night, after dinner, we move to the dining room table and sit down with our findings. After comparing everything, we agree on a small alternative school called Another Course to College.

"Well, that was hard," I say, "but not as hard as it could have been."

"You're right," she says. "Maybe it was about time you got out of there."

"Yeah." I lean back and rest my head on the back of my chair. For now, I put aside how weird it'll be starting a new school a month into senior year. I let the relief of never having to spend another day at Lakeside Academy wash over me.

Thursday afternoon, we drive downtown to meet with the principal of my new school. Mom makes me change out of my jeans into slacks. I don't see the point, but I don't argue.

We ring a buzzer to signal our arrival. A thin white woman with mouse-brown hair and red-framed glasses lets us inside and offers us a seat in the small lobby.

"Mrs. Callender will be with you soon," she tells us cheerfully as she sits back down at her desk.

Within three minutes, a small, brown-skinned woman wearing a tan business suit and low-heeled shoes emerges from the door behind the secretary.

"Gibran?" she asks, holding out her hand.

I take her hand. "That's me."

"I'm Mrs. Callender. Nice to meet you. Ms. Wilson?" She shakes Mom's hand too, and Mom's tight shoulders relax a little bit. "Please follow me." She holds an arm out, and we enter her office.

There are no windows, but there is plenty of light. I sit in an armchair and lean back. Mom sits on the edge of her chair and presses my foot with hers. She uses her eyes to tell me to sit up straight and close my legs. I do. Mrs. Callender smiles at us warmly.

"Welcome to Another Course to College," she says. "I've

read your file and your letters. I'd love for you to tell me, Gibran, what you think went wrong at Lakeside and what role you play in your future success."

"Well," I say, "like I wrote in my statement, that school was not a good fit for me. The private schools in general. Once I stopped trying to fit in, everything went downhill. They couldn't handle the real me. So I guess I have to find places where I can be authentically me."

"Hm." She clasps her hands and leans forward on her desk. "Are you expecting ACC to be a perfect match? To accept all of your . . . quirks?"

"I guess it sounded like this place is more open, so . . ."

She smiles. "We do accommodate different learning styles. And we have a diverse student body, though small. However, I encourage new students to consider how they can meet their environment halfway, wherever they find themselves. To speak plainly, a change in environment won't necessarily change the trajectory of your life."

I glance at Mom. I'm not sure if this is a warning or a pep talk or what.

"I'm on your side, Gibran," she assures me. "I want you to win. In order for that to happen, I want to see you stay focused on your future and act in your own best interests. Does that make sense?"

"I guess so."

"Good!" she says, like she's genuinely excited. "You're a smart young man."

I smile without meaning to. I can't remember the last time someone who's not my mom called me smart without making it sound like an insult.

She continues. "Your intellect might be threatening to some authority figures. On the whole, our society doesn't welcome Black men who think and question." She looks into my eyes, and I realize how rare that's become. "We want to prepare you for the world, Gibran. The real world. With all its flaws. I know you want to change the world. And I believe you can. It's important to know that, for all your talent and all your intelligence, you can also let the world pull you down. To be honest, I've seen boys just as smart as you come through these doors and not graduate. I've seen smarter boys than you do time behind bars. Every choice, big and small, matters for you. For your future."

Mom beams like this woman is reciting a script she wrote.

I don't have a problem with what she's saying, but I can't help pushing back a little.

"I hear you," I say. "I know I'm responsible for my actions. I also think it'll be easier to choose wisely when I'm not being tested all the time."

She nods once. "Fair enough."

She asks if we have questions, and then she takes us on a tour of the school. She introduces us to faculty and a few students. When she sees us out, I stop at the door.

"I do have one question for you," I say.

"Sure, what's that?" she asks.

"I know we talked about my start date being next week, but, um, there's this event I want to go to on Monday. It's an important, historic event that will really benefit me, so . . . I wanted to ask if I could start on Tuesday or Wednesday instead?"

"Hmm." She smiles. "Can I get you to do a presentation on that event for the entire school within a month?"

"Absolutely! I can do that."

She holds out her hand again. "You have yourself a deal."

She waves at us as we walk out the door.

"Take good notes!" she says.

I'm smiling as we get in the car. Mom shakes her head at me like she's both disbelieving and proud.

We pick up Thai food on our way home. It's not so much a celebration dinner as a relief dinner. Mom is relaxed for the first time in what seems like years, and I am too, so I take a chance and ask her about Uncle Kevin.

"You know that book *Black Power*?" I ask.

"Which one?" She scrapes up the last of her Thai fried rice.

"Stokely Carmichael and Charles Hamilton?"

"Oh," she says. "Right. Did you use it for your project?"

"Yeah," I say. "I used your copy. I found it in the attic."

"Mm." She swirls her iced tea and then uses the straw to stir up the sugar from the bottom of the cup. If she knows where this is going, she's not letting on.

"So, in your copy, there's this envelope."

Now she looks directly at me, sipping her tea.

"It looks like a letter? From Uncle Kevin."

Nothing.

"Did you ever read it?"

"Is it open?" she counters.

"No . . ."

She shrugs.

"Mom!"

"What?"

"Why wouldn't you read it? What if it's important?"

She purses her lips. "Hmph. I could guess what his letter would say. Nothing new, and nothing I needed to hear."

I cock my head.

"What?" she asks.

"You're really mad at him," I say.

"No, I'm not." She sips her tea. Glances at me. "Okay, maybe a little. I mean, I'm over it. But you know how they say, 'Once a person shows you who he is, believe him.' So I keep my distance. I don't hate him. I just . . . know I can't expect much from him." She looks down, and her voice softens. "That's how I keep from getting hurt."

I wait a bit before asking, "Well . . . what if the letter isn't what you thought?"

"Ha. Well, that ship has sailed now, hasn't it?"

"No, it hasn't. You could still read it."

"Why would I do that? Expect nothing, and you can't be disappointed." She recites this like a maxim and starts stacking the empty food containers together.

"Ma?"

"What."

"Could I open it? I want to read the letter he wrote you."

She stares at her empty plate and frowns. "Yeah. Sure."

I want to run upstairs and tear open the envelope, but I try to play it cool. I help clean up and wait til Mom's drawing her bath. I change my clothes, pull the envelope out of the book, and get in my bed. I pull carefully at the seal.

The paper is ripped from a legal pad, curled and dry from age. I unfold it carefully. The ink is faded but legible.

The writing gets tiny by the bottom of the page, like he was afraid he'd run out of paper. I lie on my back and hold the papers to my face. I read slowly, trying to make sense of what my uncle never got a chance to say. What my mom never wanted to hear.

# 22

Dear Dawn,

Congratulations! I heard about Umoja's success at BU.
That is remarkable. I am so proud of you. I always have
been. I should have said that more.

I don't want you to think that I'm gloating or something
because you've joined the struggle the way I want the
struggle to go. It's more than that. I don't know how to
explain it. There is so much to say. I'm finally putting the
pieces of my life—our lives—together in a way that I can
start to understand.

I didn't know what I was doing during those years
when I was fighting you. You weren't the enemy. Mom and
Dad weren't the enemy. I guess I didn't know where to go
with my new awareness, when my pain and shame were
converting to rage. I'm sure you thought I was judging you.
I guess I was. I'm so sorry, Dawn. I had no right. You are
one of the strongest, most remarkable people I know.

I've learned so much this week. We were both right all

along. I could only see the need for agitation, for righteous anger to fuel the fight. But you and Mom and Dad were right too. Agitation gets things going, but it's patience that keeps things moving. And strategy. Strategy keeps a steady flame alive. And strategy requires some level of unity.

Those are things I didn't see. I want to say I couldn't, but I don't know if I couldn't or if I refused. Maybe a little part of me somewhere inside enjoyed feeling Blacker-than-thou. God, I feel like such an ass—admitting this, but even more so for having lived it. I'm sorry, Dawn. Please forgive me. I will say I'm sorry as many times as it takes.

I didn't see the importance of unity. You counted on me, and I let you down. I forgot how to be a brother; I was so busy trying to convert you to my point of view. To show you what I saw, exactly how I saw it. It was urgent to me. I thought it was for your own good. But I think I pushed too hard, and I couldn't admit it.

I couldn't step back and see that family was more important. I definitely couldn't see that there was more than one way to resist. I wish that instead of trying to protect you by teaching you how to be a real revolutionary, I had kept supporting you. If you will let me back in, if you will trust me again, I promise I won't repeat that mistake.

I didn't even know what I wanted, and that was part of my frustration. The Black Muslims wanted land, but our family had land. The civil rights leaders wanted jobs for the people, but no one in our family lacked work. The Black Panthers wanted political power, but our parents were regular voters.

I suppose I wanted to have those things but to feel

like a person at the same time. I didn't want to have to be separate from our people in order to stay ahead. I didn't want to have to perform, to become a shell of myself, to say, in so many ways, *Don't mind my skin color; I'm really just like you.*

Most of all, Dawn, I didn't want that for you.

The first person I ever hated was the first person who made you feel like less than a star. The kids who dropped you as a friend. They took your voice. And the teachers. God, those teachers. The night of your costume party probably changed me as much as anything else. I can never forget your face that night. I wanted you to never be at their mercy again, to never let them hold the power to lift you up or crush you.

But I pushed too hard trying to get you to hate them as I did. I was the one to crush you next.

I remember the last time you asked for my support. When you still thought of me as someone you could count on. You were planning that big fundraiser, and you ended up doing it all by yourself.

Why did I act the way I did? I wanted to be right. I wanted to be listened to. But I also wanted to protect you. I didn't want you to be hurt again when the white people of our town didn't show up for you. I didn't want to stand there, watching, useless, again. When you went against my advice, I thought, you were on your own.

I was wrong, Dawn. You are never on your own. Not as long as I'm around. We fight for each other, even if we fight differently. We show up for each other. Please let me show up for you now.

I'm sorry, Dawn. I should have said it then, but I'm saying it now. I hope it's not too late.

We will keep fighting, sister. I am fighting for you, so you can shine bright and be recognized as the diamond you are.

I'm fighting for our future children. So they won't have to choose between having good opportunities in life and being their authentic Black selves.

If I fail, Dawn, please forgive me. If I die fighting, please forgive me. Forgive me now, Dawn, for misdirecting my fight at home.

Writing this down was painful. I don't know how to say these things. I am ashamed of any ounce of hurt I placed on you. Please write me back and tell me you forgive me. If you don't write me back, I won't bring it up again. If you can find it in your heart to forgive me, I swear I will make it up to you, even if it takes the rest of my life.

Dawn, if you ever have a son, and his fight is not easy, know that it is not you he is rebelling against. Know that he is fighting for his life. He may just not know how.

I love you always,
Kevin

PS—I am enclosing a book that I bought for myself and have finished reading. It's a clean copy because I only read it once. I'm trying to get out of my head and be a man of action. A good friend of mine says this will help me focus on doing the work. I hope she's right, and I hope you'll approve. And I hope you'll meet her someday. She is special, much like you.

BLACK & WHITE
DRAWINGS
TO COME

# 23

## GIBRAN
*Massachusetts | October 1995*

It's an apology.
  The letter is an apology.
  Mom was wrong.
  All this time, an apology, sitting in the attic in a box.
  Is it too late?
  It can't be. Mom has to read this. Now.

# 24

## DAWN
*Finchburg | 1956*

When I was little, back in Brooklyn, Kevin was my defender. He always let me keep up with him. He didn't leave me behind or complain about me tagging along like the other boys in the neighborhood did with their sisters. He made me feel like I was perfect just the way I was.

When we moved to Finchburg, Kevin was still my person. I started school ready to collect friends of my own, and in the beginning I did. I came home every day talking about my new friends. It was delicious, being the center of attention at school. It made up for the family we were missing because of the move.

It only took a month or two for things to fall apart.

"My parents said I'm not allowed to play with you."

That's how it usually started. A friend from school, awkward and shy, would tell me this at recess. Or after school.

Some were ashamed. Some were matter-of-fact. Either way, I was losing a friend. A door was shutting firmly in my face.

First Amy. Then Jane. Then Mary. Then Grace. My bribes of candy, jax, and embellished tales of New York City were not enough to keep them close. Their curiosity about the colored girl waned. Or their siblings tattled. One by one, sometimes in pairs, they announced the end of our friendship.

The only one left was Joanna.

I went to Kevin to find out what was wrong with me and what would happen next. He lay on his bed after dinner, reading, and I tiptoed in and sat next to him, unsure of how to ask. He knew something was wrong when I didn't speak.

He looked up from his Hardy Boys mystery. "Why the long face?"

I shrugged.

He waited.

I looked down. Played with my hands. Then I asked in a rush, my voice low as a whisper, "What's wrong with being colored?"

He put his book down. "Who said there's something wrong with being colored?" he asked.

I shrugged again.

The quiet surrounding my question seemed to disturb him more than the question itself.

"Well, someone must have said something," he pushed. "You never thought that before, did you?"

I took a big breath. "Mary said we can't be friends anymore because . . . her mom told her not to play with the colored girl. She said she'll get in trouble." It felt like a confession. As though I had done something wrong.

"Hmph," Kevin said. His face tightened with anger.

"And . . . not just her. Four other girls said the same thing." My eyes filled with glassy tears that I refused to let fall. "What if I lose all my friends?"

Kevin made a fist with his right hand and put his left hand, open and gentle, on my leg. "You're not going to lose all your friends," he said. "You're only going to lose the ones that aren't worth having. You're too good for them. Who cares about them anyway."

He cared. We both did. But what he meant, and what he showed, was that we had each other. That would have to be enough.

And it was. For years, it was. I thought it always would be. I thought he would always be my refuge.

## 1962

Kevin was becoming someone new, but for the moment, he was still mine.

I was changing too, just not as drastically as Kevin. Watching young people standing up—and sitting down— for our rights all over the country, trading in shame for pride, inspired me to stand tall.

I was in middle school now. That meant dances and dates. And dances and dates meant white parents getting even more nervous about their kids mixing with Black kids. God forbid anyone fall in love.

My first dance was a costume party. I decided I would make a statement. I would make my honey-colored skin an asset, not something to be overlooked, pitied, or feared.

"I need some African-print cloth," I announced at dinner

one night. I had finally decided on my costume.

"Ohh," Mom said, slicing her roasted vegetables and easing her curry goat off the bone. "What is it for?"

"The costume party at school. I'm going to be an Asante princess. They're giving out prizes for best costumes, and I'm going to win first place."

Mom called the family in Brooklyn and Queens to ask if they could find cloth for me. It took them a whole lot of asking around, but they made it happen.

While I waited for the cloth to arrive, I sewed a blouse. Mom helped me sew flared sleeves and a scalloped neckline. I slipped it on every night to make sure it was as elegant as I remembered.

When the material came for my skirt, I spent hours in front of the mirror, wrapping, tucking, tying, and pinning.

Mom found a book on African empires in Dad's bookshelves and showed me images. Queen Mother Yaa Asantewaa. Princess Pokou. Queen Hatshepsut. I ran to my room, hugging the book. I lay the book open on my bed, and finally, I cut the precious cloth. A large piece for the skirt, a small piece for a headwrap.

I completed the outfit one week before the party. To my perfectly wrapped skirt and headwrap I added gold earrings and sandals. I emerged from my bedroom wearing the ensemble and glided downstairs to show everyone. Mom, Dad, and Kevin gasped and gaped.

"Very nice!" Dad said, chuckling as I strutted.

"A true princess," Mom said.

"You'll *have* to win," Kevin said. "Look at you! They'll have no choice."

I squealed.

Two days before the party, I found out my best friend, Gail, wasn't going, and I panicked. She was my only Black friend in town, and her brother, John, was Kevin's only Black friend. She'd told me her parents didn't believe in Black folk going out after dark. I wanted Mom and Dad to talk sense into them. I wanted to get on my knees and beg them. How could I do this alone?

"I'll escort you," Kevin said. "And I'll come inside to see you get your prize."

He snuck back into the school gymnasium thirty minutes before the party ended, just like he promised. The judges were circulating, whispering to each other, and taking notes on clipboards. I stood with Joanna, drinking punch.

The band stopped playing, and Mr. Healy took the microphone. "Ladies and gentlemen, there are some truly splendid costumes here tonight, are there not?"

The crowd clapped. I scanned the room, my stomach flipping with excitement and nausea. When I saw my brother leaning against the wall by the door, my breath flowed easily again. He gave me a thumbs-up. I beamed, soaking him in, and turned back to the stage.

"And now," Mr. Healy said, "for the moment you've all been waiting for."

Kids adjusted their costume hats, collars, ears, and tails. I smoothed my skirt. My friend Joanna, my one friend besides Gail, grabbed my hand.

"We have three prizes tonight," Mr. Healy said. "Most original costume, best execution, and the grand prize, best costume. Here to present the prize for the most original costume is our very own Mrs. Lewin." He handed her the microphone.

"There are so many winners in this room!" she squealed. "We found it very difficult to choose. But without further ado, our prize for most original costume goes to . . . Michael Ross!"

Michael jogged to the stage amidst whistles and cheers, his white curled wig and blue-felt coattails flapping as he went.

"We have had an Eisenhower and a Benjamin Franklin, but this is our first George Washington. Splendid job, Michael!"

He shook their hands and accepted his ribbon.

"And now," Mr. Healy said, "the prize for best execution."

I took a shaky breath and looked back at Kevin for reassurance. He wiggled his eyebrows, making me giggle.

"Mary Smith, come on up!"

Mary squealed and gave several hugs before running up to the stage in her oxfords, buckets bobbing on either side of her body.

"We have seen some pioneers, we've seen some farmers, but in all our years we have not seen a milkmaid complete with over-the-shoulder milk-pail holder."

Mary smiled, showing full rows of straight white teeth. Mr. Healy handed her a ribbon. Mary curtsied and bounced off the stage.

Mr. Healy handed the microphone back to Mrs. Lewin. This was it. I squeezed Joanna's hand so tight she winced.

Mrs. Lewin's voice got more serious than bubbly. "Our last prize goes to someone whose costume will be remembered for years to come. This costume is unique, crafted with care and precision, and it fits the wearer perfectly, both in style and in concept. Please welcome to the stage our grand-prize winner for best costume: Dawn Wilson!"

I couldn't let go of Joanna's hand. All eyes found me, taking me in as they clapped. Kevin whistled from his post by the door. I soaked in the moment but forgot how to move.

Joanna extricated her hand from mine and gave me a soft push. I walked to the stage with my back straight. Mrs. Lewin put a hand on my shoulder. She consumed me from head to toe.

"Dawn's costume is original and well-executed and just so clever, isn't it? Dawn, you brought an authenticity to this costume that no one else could have. This school has never seen the likes of this. For your remarkable presentation as Aunt Jemima, here is your grand prize: two tickets to the cinema."

I hadn't heard correctly. That was my first thought. My mind was tingly from winning, and my ears were playing tricks on me. I looked out at the audience, and they were still smiling. I looked at Joanna, and her face was frozen, eyes wide and mouth open like she needed to say something, but she didn't know what. Then I knew that I had heard. Kevin was no longer leaning against the wall smiling. He was shifting from foot to foot, running his hand over his head, looking from the teachers to me and back to the teachers.

Mrs. Lewin thrust the prize at me. The coveted tickets to the cinema. The plans I had made for those tickets evaporated. There was no cinema, no prize, no celebration. There was only this moment, this horror.

Mr. Healy appeared at my other shoulder. "Take your prize, Dawn!" he said with forced cheer. "Congratulations!"

I don't remember lifting my hand. I don't remember leaving the stage. I remember the sound of clapping, and the chaperones concluding the party, and the other kids moving on to chatter as I walked straight to the door. I stopped at the trash can in the hallway, tore the envelope in four neat pieces, and threw the pieces in. I stared after them for a second, and then Kevin was beside me.

He didn't say anything. There was nothing to say. He held the door open for me, and I walked through. I shivered in the night air. He took his suit jacket off and placed it around my shoulders, then offered his arm to me. I placed my arm in his and we walked home together, letting the quiet of the night restore our sense of reality and peace. Walking home with my brother, I became a princess again.

## 1964

I didn't mind so much that Kevin was changing. I wanted to know who he was becoming, but as long as he remained my big brother, my best friend, my protector, I could handle the change.

It hurt me to see him being harsh with our parents though. I cringed when he poked at them with sarcasm and argumentation. I was happy to absorb his energy for the sake of keeping the peace at home, especially since it had been my idea to attend the March on Washington, and it was that trip that had sparked his change. Spending hours in his room, biting my cuticles, letting my behind go numb, growing quieter listening to his lectures and musings—those nights were a small price to pay for some measure of family harmony. As long as he remained my brother.

## 1965

I ran into Kevin's room, plopped onto his bed, and folded my legs underneath me. I had figured out a way to do more, to make a difference from our safe, protected cocoon.

"Okay," I said, not waiting for him to look up from his book. "A fundraiser. Like, a talent show, maybe . . . or a concert! In the school gym, or the hall at the Unitarian church."

"Sure," he said, still reading. "That could work."

We had participated in fundraisers since we were small. We sang. We marched. We picketed at the closest Woolworth's. Now Dad was planning a trip to a civil rights conference at his alma mater, Howard University, and I wanted to collect a major contribution to send him with. I had six months to plan.

"But Dawn," Kevin said, finally looking up from his book, "you don't have to send it to Howard just because Dad's going there."

"Well, I know. But why not?"

"They're partnering with the SCLC."

"I know," I said. "I know they're not radical enough for you."

He scoffed. "They're not radical at all. They don't want to change the system. They want to join it."

Like many other young Black people at the time, Kevin had lost patience with The Southern Christian Leadership

401

Conference's nonviolent platform and integrationist goals. Just this once, I wished Kevin's politics could take a back seat to my new idea. I wanted someone to be excited with me about doing *something*. Gail was down South visiting her extended family. I could have enlisted Joanna, but it wouldn't be the same. I bit my fingernail, then dropped my hands and left his room.

I found some sturdy paper and thick pens from Mom's art supplies and sat at the dining table. I used a pencil to make straight lines with a ruler, then shaped the curves and lines of oversized letters for a flyer. I was in the flow when Kevin's voice made me jump.

"Listen," he said. "If you really want to make change, why don't you fundraise for SNCC?"

There it was. He needed it to be his way. The Student Nonviolent Coordinating Committee was becoming controversial, just how Kevin liked it.

I picked up my paper and held it at arm's length. "Kevin," I said, with as much patience as I could muster, "you know how people are reacting to their talk about becoming an all-Black organization. We live in Finchburg. How many people do you think would actually support that?"

"See there? That's exactly the problem." He folded his arms. "We can only get ahead in the ways *they* want us to, at the pace *they* want us to—"

I turned on him. "Most Negroes aren't supporting them either!"

That energized him. "Because they're afraid! They're afraid of what will happen if we stop begging for scraps and really stand up for ourselves on our own terms."

I slammed my flyer facedown on the table and stared out the window.

He went on. "If you're going to put in all this effort, it should be for a worthy cause. The SCLC isn't hurting for money. They've got the whole Black bourgeoisie behind them. And the man too."

"They can still use more funding," I said. My eyes stung, but I refused to cry.

"I'm telling you, Dawn—"

He chuckled, and that's when I snapped.

"Just forget it!" I yelled. I threw my pens down on the floor. "I don't need your help! If it's not a *worthy cause* to you, I'll do it by myself!"

And that's what I did.

For months, I planned, I prepared, I recruited. I solicited donations, I advertised until every man, woman, and child in town had to know about the fundraiser. I was doing something, something big.

Mom and Dad were thrilled. The night of the event, the house smelled like Christmas. Mom made a feast to celebrate my hard work. We had dinner early, then I left on my own to set up the hall. Mom and Dad came an hour early to help.

As the program ran and the money poured in, I marveled at what I had done, creating this event from an idea, a goal. It was like making art, but this was getting real people to populate my tiny universe and do good. All the phone calls and visits to solicit donations and performances. Finding a restaurant to cater dinner for free. The food looked and smelled delicious, but I was glad I had eaten at home. My stomach fluttered all night.

When I took the stage to run the auction, I looked for Kevin first. He wouldn't be able to resist being proud of me now. He would be ready with a thumbs up or an encouraging smile.

Mom and Dad were at a table up front. The seat reserved for Kevin was empty. I looked over to Gail and John's table. He wasn't there either.

I fiddled with my notes and got on with the program, but it bothered me more and more. When the auction ended and the choir was performing, I whispered to Mom and Dad to ask if they'd seen Kevin.

They shook their heads.

His empty seat screamed at me. I scanned the room for the thousandth time, sure I'd missed him. I kept an eye on the door, expecting him to rush in or sneak in or come up from the bathroom. Maybe he had gotten sick and left early.

After they helped with some of the cleanup, I walked Mom and Dad to the car. I peeked in the back seat to see if Kevin was in there reading a book. I rushed through the rest of the cleanup, and I drove the five minutes home slowly, searching the dark streets for a sign of my brother.

When at last I entered the house, Mom and Dad were sitting in the dimly lit living room, talking quietly. Mom stood up. "Dawn," she said. I ran up the stairs and opened Kevin's bedroom door.

I stood in his doorway, holding the doorknob, breathing heavily, my coat still on. Kevin had been lying on his bed, reading; he placed the book down and sat up.

"Hey," he said.

I looked around his room.

"Where were you?" I whispered.

I kept looking around, as if answers would seep from the corners, from the furniture. I shook my head, blinking hard.

"You just..." I flapped my arms, unable to say it. I started to turn away, but then I faced him again. "I looked for you. The whole time. Even on the way home."

He bit his lip. Gave a half shrug. "How did it go?" he mumbled. "Did the good people of Finchburg support the integration they've been fighting against since we got here?"

The night was over. The magic of having done something vanished. I pulled off my heeled shoes and held them by the straps. Kevin stood and opened his mouth, but I backed away. I turned and stormed down the hall to my room, slamming the door behind me.

I shrugged off my coat, dropped everything on the floor, and collapsed onto my bed. I tried to focus on the money we had earned. The gift Dad would be bringing to the conference. This big, grown-up thing I had done. But instead, I just kept seeing the back of Kevin's head as I had opened the door to his room.

# 25

## GIBRAN
*Massachusetts / October 1995*

All this time lost, over that? Damn. It makes me wonder which of my stupid fights with my sisters could be the last straw. But I guess it wasn't just the fight. It's that she expected more from him. Once upon a time, he was all she had. So for him to abandon her, even once, felt like losing everything, and she couldn't go through that again.

After she explains it to me, I can see why Mom was so hurt. It sounds like Uncle Kevin was slow to realize how he let her down, and then too proud to say sorry right away. But once he saw how hard she took it, there was the letter left sealed in the unread book. He's spent years trying to be the good big brother again, even I can see that. But maybe it was too late. He'd lost her trust. They had both left home for college and never lived in the same house again. There was time to forgive, but no opportunity to get close again.

Maybe she needed to hear the words. To see that he knew what he'd done. Maybe that's why she's always been so strict about me and my sisters saying "I'm sorry" to each other after we fight.

"So," I say, after she's told me her stories. We're lying on opposite ends of the couch, facing the TV as if it's on. "What now?"

She bites her fingernails and stares at the TV. Then she drops her hand from her mouth and sits up. She pulls the drawing he made of her from the pocket of her robe, unfolds it, gazes at it, and sighs. Her voice cracks the tiniest bit as she says, "I have to call my brother."

On Saturday, I'm sitting on the porch with Supreme when a car that looks familiar but out of place pulls up in front of the house. There's a couple in the front seat, a man and a woman, and a teenager with braids in the back. She yawns and stretches, looking tired as hell.

The man in the driver's seat parks and jumps right out. He's tall and light-skinned, wearing jeans and a black sweatshirt that says, in bold red, green, and yellow letters, "READ."

"Whaaat?!" I say under my breath, standing up.

Supreme gets up too. "What's happening? We got a problem?"

"Nah, it's cool!" I jog down to the sidewalk, and Uncle Kevin runs right into me, grabs me in a big bear hug, and lifts me off the ground.

I laugh, embarrassed in front of Supreme, but after Uncle Kevin pats me on the back a hundredth time, laughing like he's found gold, he goes to Supreme next, looks him in the eye while shaking his hand, and says, "How you doing, young brother?"

"Good, sir, how are you?" Supreme says, sounding more formal than I've ever heard him before.

"You know," Uncle Kevin says, stroking his chin, "you look like a reader." He goes to the trunk of his car and pulls out a crate of new and used books. He puts it on the porch and tells Supreme to choose as many books as he can carry.

"Wow, thank you, sir," Supreme says.

I don't think they're more than ten years apart in age, but Supreme looks like a kid right now the way he's smiling.

Auntie Valerie and my cousin Laila step out of the car, stretch their arms, and shake their legs.

"Kevin," Auntie Valerie says, "we just arrived and you're already pushing books on people?" She kisses me on the cheek. "How've you been, baby?"

"Good, thank you. I can't believe y'all are here! Mom didn't tell me."

Uncle Kevin laughs. "It was a pretty last-minute decision. Where is she?"

"Upstairs," I say.

Leila gives me a side-hug while Uncle Kevin bounds up the stairs.

"Where's Amir?" I ask her.

"Stayed home. For the march."

"Cool."

I feel kind of bad that Uncle Kevin is up here and his son will go to the march without him. But I also feel loved.

Uncle Kevin rings the doorbell, and Mom opens the door.

Her smile is shy, but her eyes beam, filled with years of guarded love. He opens his arms. She buries her face in his chest, and they hold on to each other for an eternity.

The hardest thing about this visit is sharing Uncle Kevin with Mom. I know they have a ton of catching up to do, so I try not to be impatient for my turn.

We have a loud family dinner with Ashanta, Kareem, and the baby, and the house feels full in the best way. After Ashanta leaves, I play cards with Laila, and then we watch *The Last Dragon* while Mom and Uncle Kevin talk. Finally, Mom goes to bed, and Uncle Kevin joins us in the living room.

"I love this movie!" he says. "'You sure look like a master to me,'" he says in a high, flirty voice, imitating Vanity.

I laugh, and Leila punches him. "Dad! Please! We're trying to watch."

"I'm sorry, I'm sorry."

He whispers the rest of his corny commentary to me. My cheeks hurt from laughing.

When the credits start rolling, Leila yawns. "Where's Mom?" she asks.

"She's been asleep," Uncle Kevin says.

"I'm going to bed too," she says.

"Night, princess."

Alone with Uncle Kevin, I have so much I want to ask him, and I don't know where to start. He speaks before I do.

"I owe you, nephew," he says. "You're a good man."

"What'd I do?"

"Your mother." He shakes his head. "You know, as well as I knew her, it never occurred to me she'd not even read my letter? I mean, damn! I poured my heart out in that thing."

"I know."

He pulls a squeeze ball from a crack in the couch and tosses it from hand to hand. "I guess I deserved it."

"I don't know. Twenty-something years of the cold shoulder? That's a serious grudge."

He chuckles. "She was protecting herself. Like I taught her to—but I didn't mean from me."

"Right. You know, she gave me the newspaper clippings from your occupation at Columbia."

"Really? She still has those?"

"Yup. They're falling apart, but they're there."

"Huh. Yeah, that was, uh, that was an intense time." He catches the ball and squeezes it.

He seems far away, and I want to give him space, but I have to know. "What was it like? I mean, after? It must have felt amazing to stop the gym and everything. Didn't you want to keep that momentum going until this whole country was forced to change?"

He frowns. "We were . . . temporarily elated when the gym construction was canceled. We had some victories. But over time . . ." His face is serious, almost sad. "For one thing, the backlash was no joke. Violence, repression . . . there was an intentional, systematic dismantling of the movement." He shudders. "And then . . . You watch a movement and everything you're trying to do get co-opted by the 'powers that be'—institutions that don't want to make true change. They just want to stay in power. To change the reality, you'd have to upend the entire system. They can't have that. So they make symbolic change, compromise, to quiet people down and keep the system running smoothly, you know?"

"Damn," I say. "That's deep. I mean, I couldn't even get my old school to do that much."

"Well, they already had their symbolic change, right? A Black principal."

This hits me like a brick.

"You were supposed to keep your head down," he says. "No one can tell them they're not helping Black kids when they have one of us propped up at the head. But they can't prop up someone whose goal is to upend the whole power structure. They find the right people to improve their image without threatening the system." He throws the ball back and forth between his hands, then holds it in one hand while pointing a finger at me. "You know the best way to destroy racial solidarity? Give some Black folks some status. They'll become committed to the system too."

"Dang," I say. "That's messed up."

"It took me years to see this though," he says. "It's the same way they destroyed class solidarity, by creating the whole idea of 'race' to begin with."

"Man. You ever think about writing a book or something?"

He looks at me, as if to see if I'm serious.

"For real," I say. "You got mad knowledge. People don't talk about this, and then when shit goes down, they make us feel like we're the problem. Like it's our fault."

"Yeah." He nods. "I mean, I talk to anyone who'll listen. A lot of people like to think we're past this stuff."

"That's what I'm sayin."

He twists his lips, then shrugs. "I'll think about it. Maybe you and I could write something together."

I don't know what I'd have to add, but if that's what it takes to get him to write his story, I'm with it. "Cool," I say.

"Cool," he says. "Back then . . . I didn't have this perspective, but that year really changed me. I kind of saw how many jobs there are to do in the struggle. A lifetime isn't enough. But every day makes a difference. You feel me?"

"I guess." I say. "Moms says I gotta be patient or else I'ma burn out."

He nods. "We saw a lot of that."

"I know. I did this project on the freedom fighters and where they are now."

"Oh yeah? Can I see?"

"Okay."

I go up to my room and bring down the portfolio with my work in it. I open it up on the floor and spread out the pages.

Uncle Kevin's mouth forms a small O. "It's the half faces!"

"You remember those?"

"Do I remember? Man, your mom and I used to spend hours collecting photos for these. She'd grab the newspaper as soon as your grampa finished reading it. Any time there was a nice photo of a Black person, she'd cut it out and add it to her collection in this little shoebox. When it was time to draw, we'd fight over who got which picture. Sometimes she'd cut one in half and make me use one half while she used the other half. She wouldn't let me see hers until we were both done." He laughs. "So many memories."

He leans over my project and reads each profile one by one, nodding like he hears music playing. He mutters an occasional "Mm" or "Damn." When he's finished, he looks at me.

"You *are* a handful," he says. He smiles so proudly, I can't help but grin. "Did your mom ever tell you the motto of the Black studies movement?"

"Nah, I don't think so."

"'Academic excellence and social responsibility.'" He surveys my work again. "You're gonna fit right in at Howard. And you better come by my bookstore at least once a week."

"No doubt," I say.

I've never seen my uncle this way. He's always been fun and animated, but now he's really . . . happy. Like there's been this missing piece, and he finally found it, and all's good with the world. Maybe he was trying to prove himself, to make up for something. I'm so glad Moms is finally letting him back in.

Now I wonder. If this is what hearing each other could do for them . . . what if I could tell Mom the stuff I couldn't say? I'm not ready yet. And neither is she. But maybe someday. I could see it.

*What I would say*

See moms you been the only one to show me the path

Still sometimes the things I'm going through it feel like you ain't knowing the half

I know you don't want me to grow like my dad

And take heed to the responsibility in every moment I have

You know I last through the wrong still you teachin me right

Tell me to achieve my goals cause my dreamin ain't life

You know we been under attack it's a reason to fight

And when they all fade to black they'll be seein the light
You say we stronger when our people unite
Not everybody will listen
To stay aware you can't get lost in the vision
Can't survive without the love that my mama is givin
You always there my foundation cause my father is missin
You don't wanna see me caught in the system
So I'ma strive for a better life then I'ma give you honorable mention

People thought it wouldn't happen. The media predicted there was no way a million Black men would show up in Washington, DC. Even Black people were skeptical. If they did show up, could so many Black men get together without fights breaking out?

They were wrong. And it is beautiful. Faces in every shade of Black and brown, as far as you can see. Onstage are men and women, religious leaders, political leaders, music stars, and a child in a dashiki who recites a poem. Gang leaders calling truces, community activists and youth leaders and their charges.

I ache to be there. But I have the next best thing.

The Day of Absence event in Roxbury is packed. The community center has the gym doors open for easy-flowing foot traffic. A wall-sized screen displays the live event from a projector so people can see it from the gym floor, the second level, and the lobby. Tables of pastries, coffee, and fruit line the walls, and younger children play in the day care room.

Uncle Kevin is with me. James and David came too. They say they'll face the consequences at school with no regrets. I hope they won't get in too much trouble for me. When their faces light up at the sight of that sea of Black men on the big screen in real time, I know they're not just here for me.

Mom called out of work and came with Auntie Valerie and Laila. And then there's another surprise.

"Ay, yo," David says, "look who's here."

Malika, Tanya, and Lisa walk in, followed by Chris, Trey, and a handful of other Black kids from Lakeside.

"Oh, snap!" I say.

They come over and give me hugs.

Malika chastises me. "You left without saying anything."

"My bad," I say. "What is this, did they give y'all the day off?"

"No. We didn't ask." She smirks at me. "You're not the only rebel, you know. Some of us are just more slick about it."

"Wow. Okay."

"Besides," Tanya says. "It's not right how they did you. We walked out in protest and solidarity."

"For real?" I can't believe this.

"Yeah. And guess what we left in our place?" Lisa says.

"What?"

"Your profiles."

I look at James and David.

They nod.

Malika says, "Lining the street between South and North Campus."

415

"A little Day of Absence gift," James says. "We're not there, but the freedom fighters are."

"Wow. That's . . . that's whassup."

"Yeah, Iono about them, I'm just here for the food," Trey says, heading over to the tables.

Everyone laughs. We collect donuts and juice and crowd around the big screen.

"Be warned though," Lisa says, "if Mr. Farrakhan gets on his misogynistic high horse or any other funny business, we'll walk out of here in protest too."

I laugh. "Word. That's cool."

Maya Angelou takes the stage, and we hush as the speakers send her assured voice into the space.

She reads a poem that's an invitation, an invocation, telling us to come together, to clap hands, to invite joy.

*"The ancestors remind us, despite the history of pain,*
*We are a going-on people who will rise again."*

I feel light all over, weightless and tingling. Maya turns from the podium. And then she can't resist, on her way off the stage, throwing her classic line over her shoulder at the microphone:

*"And still we rise!"*

The audience roars, and we do too.

# List of Acronyms and Organizations

## CORE

Congress on Racial Equality: Founded by Black and white students in 1942, CORE used nonviolent protests to push for integration and voter registration. In 1964, three volunteers were murdered by the Ku Klux Klan. By 1968, the group abandoned its commitment to nonviolent protest, moved to a Black Power focus, and limited white involvement.

## IDA

Institute for Defense Analyses: Established in 1959, the IDA brought together leading research universities and government agencies that funded military research. The IDA did not disburse funds, but members of the IDA were given priority for funding.

## SAS

Society of Afro-American Students: Founded in 1966 at Columbia University to bring together Black undergraduate and graduate students.

## SDS

Students for a Democratic Society: a nationwide radical leftist organization that advocated for student power and free speech, and against war and injustice. Before the 1968 occupation at Columbia University, the group was divided between members interested in discussing political theory and recruiting, and members eager for direct action.

## SCLC

Southern Christian Leadership Conference: Established in 1957 and led by Dr. Martin Luther King, Jr., the SCLC aimed to coordinate nonviolent resistance throughout the South.

## SNCC (pronounced "Snick")

Student Nonviolent Coordinating Committee: Founded by students in 1960, SNCC members used direct action and community organizing for political participation, including voter registration, and became a leading civil rights group. In 1966, Stokely Carmichael was elected the chair of SNCC. When he stepped down in 1967, H. Rap Brown was elected.

## Nation of Islam (NOI)

A political and religious organization founded in the 1930s aiming to uplift the Black American community socially, economically, and spiritually. Some of the original teachings, such as race-based separation and the divinity of a human being, were incompatible with traditional Islam. Prominent leaders from the Nation of Islam who converted to traditional Islam include Malcolm X and W. D. Mohammed, the son of the Nation's founder, Elijah Mohammad. W. D. Mohammed successfully led the mass conversion of many members toward orthodoxy starting in the mid-1970s. In 1995, Minister Louis Farrakhan was the leader of the Nation of Islam.

# Author's Note

I began writing this story as a way to understand a trend I saw in my generation of Black youth in preparatory schools: while many of us continued along the path and lifestyle for which such schools groom students, several of us, particularly Black men, dramatically diverged from that path. The choice to leave the track to which we were led seemed to involve culture and identity. I felt a need to understand the choice, its roots in the individual, the family, society and history, and how the consequences of that choice affected people's lives.

Gibran's story and Kevin's story were both inspired by real people, families, events, and institutions. Readers often want to know which parts are true and which parts are invented. I love to study history and learn what people have lived through, so those questions interest me as well. However, when understanding what shapes people and cultures, I find that the meaning people make of their experiences is almost more important than what actually happened.

When I asked people who lived through these events to read my drafts and give me feedback, I didn't ask about the accuracy of the facts and details; I asked whether the story felt emotionally true. In some cases, changes I made to fictionalize the story helped clarify the plot, environments, and character evolution. In other cases, real details I uncovered in my research revealed deeper layers to the story that I then felt compelled to include. (For example, the fact that the security guards who stopped Black students at Columbia were often Black and Puerto Rican themselves.) In other cases still, true details shared with me were so incredible or complicated that I couldn't incorporate them without distracting from the focus of the story. As they say, truth is often stranger than fiction.

I was a teenager in the 1990s, and I grew up hearing my mother's stories about the Black students' occupation at her college in 1968. I didn't find out more about those sit-ins until I was writing this book. For Kevin's story, I relied heavily on research. In addition to history books, documentaries, and online archival records, I spent time in the archives at the New York Public Library's Schomburg Center for Research in Black Culture, where I examined primary documents such as clippings, videos, letters, pamphlets, magazines, and speeches. I followed the general timeline and facts of the Columbia occupation quite closely, from the point of view of a fictional character.

When writing historical fiction about real events, one must make decisions about using the names of people and places. For the Columbia events, I used the real names of administrators and the police inspector, but I changed the names of students and created composite characters to represent the leadership of the protests. I made this choice in part to honor the Black students' tactic of resisting the media's tendency to create a sensational story centered on an individual leader or hero. The media highlighted one student from the SDS leadership, and gave a (white) face to the story of the protest. They were unable to do so with the Black students, who deliberately sent multiple representatives to represent the demands, as a way of staying focused on the issues. For a long time, the role of the Black students in the protests was not recognized as the determining factor it was. For more about the events at Columbia, see *A Time to Stir* by Paul Cronin, and the associated website, http://www.thestickingplace.com/projects/projects/columbia/

## Note on the Malcolm X Speech

In the book, Kevin hears Malcolm X speak shortly after the March on Washington. The speech he hears is an amalgamation of the content of real speeches delivered in Harlem during earlier rallies and at other later appearances nationwide. I combined them for the sake of the story.

## Notes on the Columbia Protests

*What happened with the Columbia students' demands?*

Columbia's gym was eventually built *on Columbia's campus.* However, the university's expansion and the resulting displacement of community continues to be an issue.

Columbia cut formal ties with the Institute for Defense Analysis.

*What happened to the protestors?*

Seven hundred students were arrested and charged with trespassing. All charges were later dropped.

SDS called for a student strike on May 1, 1968. Almost the entire student body and faculty responded in solidarity. Hamilton Hall was again occupied by students three weeks later, and police were called to campus again.

Throughout the summer of 1968, students held "liberation classes" on campus.

The following year, students pushed to establish a Black Studies program at Columbia but were unsuccessful. Over time, courses in Black studies were added. In 1993 the Institute for Research in African American Studies was founded, and finally, in 2019, the Board of Trustees voted to create the African American and African Diaspora Studies Department.

*What happened to those responsible for the violence at Columbia University?*

President Kirk left Columbia later that year. The New York Police Department and the tactical police force suffered no consequences for their actions. In some of the interviews years later, some police officers who were present that night expressed no remorse for the outcome. In their opinion, they did what they were there to do and felt it was justified.

*Why did police behave that way?*

Many readers may be surprised to discover that hundreds of police officers would treat wealthy white students in this way. There were, of course, some police officers who did not participate in the violence. A handful of survivors report that one officer told their colleagues "I've got this one!" and then, once the other officers moved on, told the student to run. These stories are rare, and the fact that those well-meaning officers felt compelled to hide what they were doing from the other officers speaks volumes.

Analyses of the events list several factors in the brutality carried out that night. Among them are:

The class difference between the university students and the police force. Most police officers were (and are) working class, without college degrees, and saw university students as spoiled rich kids who didn't appreciate what they had and needed to be taught a lesson.

White students' lack of fear of the police. During the week of police presence on campus, some students taunted them and called them names; many more openly resented the police presence on campus. After nearly a week of standing around bored, restless, and being disrespected, many officers were eager to show the students who was boss.

The involvement of the tactical police force. The TPF is trained for riots and situations precinct officers are not equipped to handle. When they are called to a job, they expect to clear the place by any means necessary.

Many who lived through the events were radicalized by the police violence and profoundly altered by seeing the distortions and lies published about them in the *New York Times*.

In an interview fifty years later, one survivor asked: "What happened to my privilege?" I think the following statement, issued by the strike steering committee after the events of April 30, 1968, is an eloquent answer to that question.

"Students have been clubbed, beaten, and carted off in police vans by the hundreds. Faculty members have been carted out on stretchers. And with that, it is clear: University violence against students and faculty is an extension of the University's violence against Black people, against the community and seizure of park land, against third-world struggles and IDA weapons systems, against employees of Columbia and denial of unions and decent wages, and now, in a 3 a.m. police raid, violence is used against students and faculty. The nature of the University was clearly revealed. The trustees and administration respond only to their outside interests. Student and faculty demands are met with violence. But the struggle has not ended yet."